WHAT WE

NEED

TO SURVIVE

by

MICHELE PIRAINO

For Sharon,
Enjoy
— Michele Piraino

ISBN: 978-0692338360

Printed in the USA

Dedication:

To my daughters: Kimberly, Carolyn, and Monica
and in memory of my husband, John

Acknowledgements:

My friends and family, for their encouragement and support,
my coach and consultant, Mary K. Dougherty, Boot Strap
Publishing, Barb Anderson for cover design and formatting, Ilene
Thater, my editor, Monica Piraino, my daughter, Brand & Butter LLC
for website design, Denise Hartung, my sister, for author's photo

"Ebony and Ivory live together in perfect harmony,

Side by side on my piano keyboard, oh Lord, why don't we?

We all know that people are the same where ever we go.

There is good and bad in everyone.

We learn to live; we learn to give each other

What we need to survive, together alive."

lyrics by Sir Paul McCartney

"Faith is taking the first step even when

you don't see the whole staircase."

Reverend Martin Luther King, Jr.

Chapter 1

September
ERICA

OMG! I can't believe it's the first day of my junior year in high school! God, it's a beautiful day. I can't wait to see everyone. No one was around this summer, and all I did was work in Mom's shop and volunteer on the pediatric unit at the hospital. That was great though. I really love those kids.

"See you, Mom. I'll be late because cheerleading practice starts today after school. The first game is already this weekend."

"Have a good day, honey. I'll be busy with the summer clearance sale and getting out the rest of the new fall merchandise. You haven't seen all the new stuff. It's really pretty nice. I think you might even like it. Speaking of clothes, is that your best choice for the first day back?"

"Not the best impression for some of the teachers that don't know you yet. I think they've gone too far in distressing those jeans. They're more shabby than chic. They just looked ripped to me. I think you look prettier in brighter colors. Hair looks cute, though."

"You're always a critic, Mom." *I know she wishes it were a twin set and Capri pants.*

I've really got to stay focused this year. Junior year is important and will fly by quickly. I can't believe I'll be taking the SAT's in the spring. I don't even want to think about it! It stresses me out. Dad says it's really important to get high scores, to get into a good pre-med program. Maybe I'll get a math tutor. I'm not too worried about the reading and writing scores. I guess I got Mom's genes. I'm much better in subjects like English and foreign language. Why would you go to college and major in literature and minor in art history?

Where do you go with that? What does Mom really care about anyway? Yeah, her pretentious, little boutique... what about things that really matter? I know she logs a lot of hours into charity work. Is it because she really cares about the causes, or does she do it for appearances and to fill up her time? She's got to be Dr. Tom McIntyre's beautiful, capable wife. I remember when I asked Dad why he became attracted to Mom. He had no trouble answering. He said, "God, she was just so beautiful. She would walk into a room and everyone would look. She could play beautiful music on her violin and paint. I was very drawn to her watercolors. But your Mom is so confident in everything she does. And what a cook! On our second date she brought me those killer brownies. She can really work a room, and her golf swing is better than mine." So there you have it. Yeah, Mom is great at everything.

Erica spotted her friend, Christy, walking into the building. "Hey, Christy, can you believe we're juniors already? What do you have first period? I've got Chem. What a way to start the day. I see a few new faces this year. A lot of urban-suburban kids. But I like how that mixes things up. Are you ready for cheerleading? I'm so glad you're on the squad this year. I love fall, because fall means football!"

"We've hardly seen each other this summer. I know you did a lot of volunteer time at the hospital," Christy said. "I give you a lot of credit for doing that. I hate the smell of hospitals and I would never be able to handle seeing sick kids. Me, I just worked at Wegmans all summer. But I really got to know my produce. It's not such a bad place to work. I got addicted to their bakery cookies. We did spend a week a Grandma's beach house. I love Cape May. Hey, real cool jeans! See ya at lunch."

Mr. Novak. He's new. I did hear that Mr. Kaminsky retired. Mr. Novak is kind of cute. I've got to do well in this class. I liked bio, but Mrs. Jeffers wasn't such a great teacher.

"Good morning. I'm Mr. Novak. Keep an open mind about this class. You might even like it. We're going to start out by assigning lab partners. Your lab partner can also be your study buddy. I find that a random selection is the best way to go. Hope the chemistry is good with your partner, pardon the pun. If it's not working out with your partner by the end of the first marking period, let me know. We can consider a switch. I'll pass around the list so you can see who your partner will be."

Dwight Johnson. I don't know him. That tall, black guy is the only person in the class I don't know. I hope he is good in science and that he's also a nice guy.

"Okay, people. Find a seat next to your partner."

"Hi. I'm Erica McIntyre."

He extended his hand, "Dwight Washington, It's my first year at your school. You have probably guessed, I'm one of the urban-suburban students."

"Welcome. It's your school now."

"Thanks, it's nice to meet you." *He seems nice, but really kind of shy. He spoke so softly. I think he was nervous.*

Chapter 2

BEVERLY

I can't believe I just dripped coffee down my blouse. I've got to get going. I'll just have to change into something at the store. Pam's probably already there. I hope Tom's not too late at the hospital today. I really want us all to have dinner together on Erica's first day back. She's always more talkative when her dad's around. It is such a beautiful day. I think I'll put some salmon on the grill. I'm glad I made those brownies last night.

"Hi, Pam, you're here nice and early. Good, we've got a lot of merchandise to turn over and I want to get out of here on time, first day of school and all. Those mums next to the door could use some water. I'll water them and then I better change. I spilled coffee all down my blouse."

"Bev, I hear your phone. I'll bring it out to you."

"Beverly, this is Martha Graham."

"Martha, you sound so upset, what's going on?"

"It's Dr. McIntyre. He's had a heart attack. Oh, honey, I'm so sorry. I just can't believe that dear man is gone!"

"What do you mean gone? Talk to me Martha! Tell me what happened! Put one of the nurses on!"

"Mrs. McIntyre, this is Lisa. Martha's just not doing too well, so I'll try to fill you in. I'm just so sorry. We're all in shock. Dr. McIntyre was late for rounds. We tried to page him and then tried his cell… no answer. Then we tried to overhead page him and STAT page him. Security heard the paging and looked in the parking garage. Pete found Dr. McIntyre slumped over his steering wheel. They got him to ED in minutes, but it was too late. Attempts at resuscitation were all unsuccessful. Oh my God. This is such a tragedy. I'm just so sorry!"

"NO! OH GOD, NO!"

"Bev, what is it? Tell me!"

"It's Tom, he's dead. Heart attack! Can you believe my Tom had a heart attack? He's in such good shape, never smoked a day in his life. Oh my God! I've got to get Erica and get over to the hospital. Pam, take care of things here, okay?"

"Can you please find out what class Erica McIntyre is in right now? I need to talk to her. It's an emergency. I need to tell her that her father has died unexpectedly."

"Oh my God, Mrs. McIntyre, I'm so sorry. Please sit down. I'll find Erica and bring her to you. Let me get you some water. Here, you can sit in this office, and you'll have some privacy."

"Mom, what are you doing here? Is everything okay? No, I can tell something is very wrong. Tell me. God, Mom, tell me now!"

"Honey, there's no easy way to tell you this. Dad's gone. He had a heart attack in the parking garage of the hospital. They couldn't bring him back. It's just so hard to believe."

"No, Mom, you're wrong, you're wrong! Please, Mom, don't touch me! I just won't accept this. It's a mistake."

"No, honey it's really true. Come on. Let's go to the hospital and see your Dad."

"Can you bring us to where ever you are holding Tom McIntyre?"

"Right this way Mrs. McIntyre. We're all so sorry."

Beverly looked down at her husband. *He looks so quiet and peaceful, like he's just sleeping. But his color is grey. He feels just so cold.*

"Come on, Erica, we have to call Grandma Helen."

"Oh, Mom, poor Nana, I'll call her. I know how to talk to Nana."

"Okay, honey."

I better call Murray's Funeral Home to come and pick up the body...my Tom.

Oh God, how will I ever live without him? How will Erica every get over this? Tom was only 47. I can't believe I'm a widow at 44.

Everything is happening so fast. My world is spinning out of control. Word got out fast. People keep dropping by the house.... people from the hospital, friends, and lots of kids.

I'm glad the kids are here for Erica. She's not accepting much comfort from me. I'm glad Tom's mother took a sedative and went upstairs to rest. We don't have the warmest relationship, but we do respect each other. I know she'll help me get Erica through this. She was so good with her when Tom's father died.

Now, the next day, day two without Tom, I have to make arrangements. That is something I'm usually good at. I'll call Father McMahon at St. Joseph's. I hope they can do the funeral on Saturday. There is no school, and Erica's friends can come. More people from the hospital can come. Who should give the eulogy? I think Tom's partner, Peter Dwyer. Yes, and probably Tom's brother. Tom and I never talked about these things. I'm sure he would want to be buried at Mt. Hope cemetery. Johnny's in the children's section, but maybe John can be moved closer to his father. God, so many decisions!

I know Tom would want to have everyone party at the club after the service. His golf buddies are sure going to miss him.

Yellow roses, Tom's casket will have to be covered in yellow roses. Danny Boy. Someone will have to sing Danny Boy.

"Erica, are you okay? It's so nice that your friends have been around. I'm just so sorry you have to go through this. But we've got to go through it to get through it."

"Oh, Mom, the next few days will be so awful. Life will be so awful without Dad. Will I ever feel normal again? What's with all this food? Why do people think they have to bring all this stuff over? Enough is enough! Some of this food looks gross."

"Honey, I think it will be okay. It will take time. Just don't shut me out. I love you so much. We've got to be there for each other, and I'm worried about Nana. We've got to keep her close."

"Okay, Mom. I'm beat. I'm going to bed."

Day three without Tom, calling hours. The line for people to pay their respects is way out the door. I'm really touched that some of Tom's patients and their families came by.

"Your husband saved my son's life. When we learned our little boy had a brain tumor we were just devastated. Dr. McIntyre's surgical skill and patience with Danny were a gift sent down to us from God. This is Danny now." The cute little guy just looked up with a confused look on his face. "As you can see he's doing just fine, just a happy, healthy, little boy. Please accept our most sincere sympathy. We will never forget your husband."

Finally, it's Saturday, funeral day. Will we get through it? How am I going to face every day without Tom? How will I help get Erica through this, and then there's Helen. The rain today is so soft. It's comforting in an odd sort of way.

Chapter 3

ERICA

"Mom, I'm so nervous about going back to school. I know the kids will be all nervous and jerky around me. I'm not sure I'll be able to concentrate. Do you think I should take some time off?"

"I'm not sure just hanging around the house is really going to help. Wallowing in your sorrow is not going to change anything. I know you are emotionally exhausted, but maybe getting back into your routine and being with your friends will help. This is such an important year for you, honey. Don't you think that Dad would want you to get on with your life? Just one day at a time. Today's plan: the first day back to school."

"Okay, Mom. See you later. I'm going to stop by Nana's after practice to see how she's doing."

"Why don't you bring her home with you for dinner?"

The kids at school are really okay. Most of them I saw at calling hours or at the funeral anyways. When I get to chem, Mr. Novak is really sweet. His eyes are a little teary when he says welcome back. I take my seat next to Dwight.

"I saw you at my Dad's funeral. It was really nice of you to come. You barely know me."

"I just wanted you to know that I care. I know what it's like growing up without a father and I feel for you. My mom is a nursing assistant at the hospital. She said that your Dad was a really good man."

Dwight seems like such a nice guy, still so shy. He can barely make eye contact with me. I wonder what happened to his father.

"What do you have sixth period, Erica? I have study hall and if you want we could meet in the library and I could fill you in on what you missed in chem."

I was really planning on meeting Christy, but she isn't so good in anything science. I need to get used to studying with him anyway. "I've got that period free, too. I'll meet you in the library. Thanks."

"Dwight, how are you in science? I love it, and besides, I need good grades in math and science to get into a good pre-med program."

"Pre-med. That's awesome. I want to study bio-medical engineering, so I got to get the goods, too."

"Do you mind me asking what happened to your dad?"

"I'm ashamed to say, he's in prison. I barely know him. He won't be out for a very long time. Armed robbery ... He didn't do the shooting, but the owner of the business was severely wounded and now he's in a wheel-chair. My father is not a man to admire...not like your Dad. People said some really great things about him at the funeral."

"It sounds like your life isn't so great either. How is it for you coming to school here?"

"I'm grateful for the opportunity. Things are pretty busted in my neighborhood. City schools are awful. We have to go through metal detectors just to get in. The teachers are burned out just trying to maintain discipline. I guess when people are poor they just don't see things as getting any better and stop trying. A lot of my friends have quit school and just hang out all day. My Mom's pretty strict. She wouldn't let that happen. She works so hard. I just can't do anything to break her heart."

"Oh, no, there's the bell already. We didn't get much done. But I'm glad we're getting to know each other. See you tomorrow, Dwight."

He's pretty nice, not as shy as I thought. He has such a sweet smile.

It's good to see Nana working in the garden. "Hi, Nana, how's it going?"

"Erica, sweetheart, I'm okay, but how about you? You went to school today? That had to be kind of tough."

"It was better than I thought it would be. Mom said that it was time to go back. You know Mom. She's always the rock, nerves of steel, do the right thing. I hear her though, crying softly in her room at night. You see her during the day and nothing seems any different."

"Your father always admired your mother's strength and her ability to move on, and get things done. You might think that she was dependent on your father, but I see it that he was very dependent on her. She kept his life running smoothly."

"I guess not all that smooth. Dad must have had enough stress to have a heart attack."

"Don't, Erica. Your father's heart attack was nobody's fault. No one knows when the Lord will call us home. I just take comfort in knowing that your father is with your brother and grandfather now. Do you want to go bring these flowers over to cemetery with me?"

"Okay, Nana. Do you want to come home with me after, for dinner? Mom wanted me to ask you."

"That would be nice."

Chapter 4

DWIGHT

"Ma, I left my chemistry notebook on the kitchen table. Do you know where it's at? I really gotta have it. There's a big test tomorrow."

"I told one of your sisters to put it up in your room. Is chemistry going okay?"

"Yeah, the teacher's pretty cool, and I really got a great lab partner. Her name is Erica McIntyre. Do you know her father? He's a doctor. She's pretty nice and smart too. I feel real bad for her losing her Dad and everything. She seems pretty down."

"If she's anything like her father, I'm sure she's pretty special. Her father was just the nicest man. He took the time to talk to everybody... housekeeping people, transport workers, nursing assistants, everyone. His patients loved him."

"You know I'm taking chemistry this semester too. Maybe we'll be able to help each other. I can't wait to finish all these math and science courses and start the nursing classes."

"Mom, I can't believe you have the time for college, what with your job at hospital and taking care of me and the twins. They doing alright in fourth grade? Whew, that was a long time ago for me."

"I guess okay. They're not in the same class, though. Denise's teacher seems pretty good, but Danielle's teacher is pretty close to retirement and seems a little burned out. I'm just glad I didn't have school last night and was able to go to parent's night. School tonight, though. There's a pan of mac and cheese in the freezer for you and your sisters for dinner and some frozen broccoli, too. Can you make sure the girls get started on their homework after dinner? Danielle really needs help with her math."

"Okay, Ma, have a good day."

I'm glad that tomorrow's Friday and Mom can be home with the girls. I'd like to check out the football game. Erica says it's going to be a good game. Some of the players she introduced me do seem okay. I know some of them play basketball, too. I'm sure she looks pretty cute in her cheerleader outfit. *I'm kind of surprised she feels up to going to the game. It's a good sign. She had seemed so down. I guess she has her good days and bad. I hope Mom doesn't have a problem with me going. I can just hear her...*

"No drinking. No weed. Remember how lucky you are to be at that school. Don't mess it up!"

Oh shit, late for chemistry. "Hey Erica, how's it going? Did you start studying for the chemistry test yet?"

"A little, but I'm really going to hit the books tonight. Do you maybe want to meet at the library tonight and study together?"

"Wish I could. I've got to watch my sisters tonight. My mom's got school. She's going to college at night to get her nursing degree. It seems like it will take her forever, just taking a few courses a semester. She's very goal-oriented, always working hard to make things better for us. I have a job after school, but it doesn't really help much. At least she doesn't have to give me any spending money. She has her heart set on me getting a scholarship so I can go to college. So what's your mom like? How's she doing?"

"She owns a boutique in the village. She went to college, but as far as I know the only other job she had was working at an art gallery. She's all about perfection and achievement, though. She's always busy. Does a lot of work for charity... fundraising and stuff. She's trying not to let it show, but I think she is really having a hard time with my father's death. She does her crying alone at night in her room. I've also noticed she's drinking a lot more wine, but not drunk or anything. My mom and I butt heads a lot. My father and I have always been closer. I had a brother, too, John. He died when he was four. He had a problem with his heart. My mom got through that, but she had my dad to help her. My dad helped me, too, after Johnny died. I was in fourth grade and I just didn't get it."

"Try to give your mother a break, she's whatcha got now. She's got to be hurting as much as you."

"We better figure out how to get this Bunsen burner started, but I'd like you to tell me more about your brother sometime."

Chapter 5

RUBY

I am so exhausted and my feet are killing me! Could we be any busier today? Just not enough nurses scheduled today. Cranky doctors... I swear when I'm a nurse, no way am I going to let some doctor yell at me. I think pizza tonight, and I'll rent a movie for the girls. I think Dwight mentioned he wants to go to the football game at his new school tonight. It seems that he likes it there. That makes me so happy.

He talks a lot about Dr. McIntyre's daughter. What a nice man he was. God, if all the doctors behaved like him, the hospital would be a better place for everybody. I wonder about his wife. She has to be one lucky woman to be married to him.

Who's the only man I ever had? Mr. Jerome Taylor. Oh, he was cute and real charming. He had me with just his smile. Mama warned me about boys like him. I should have listened. I was just another black girl, pregnant and eighteen. And what's wrong with me, sleeping with that man again when he's out on parole? Just once, and twins this time! Lord, please don't let my girls make the same mistakes as me. I'm not as worried about Dwight, because I know he's disgusted with the man who's his baby-daddy. He wants better for himself, and he knows not to get some girl pregnant.

Maybe if I have some time this weekend I'll make an apple pie and Dwight can bring it to the McIntyre's. The twins love the public market. We'll go get some apples tomorrow.

I can barely keep my eyes open, but I better stay up until Dwight gets home.

"How was the game?"

"I had a really good time. We won thirty-five to ten. Some of the kids at that school are really okay."

"Dwight, I thought maybe I'd make a pie for your new friend, Erica, and her mother. We could bring it by after church."

"That sounds real nice, Mom. I think I know where they live."

"Reverend James was really long-winded today and was that church ever hot!"

"Where are we going, Mama?"

"Your brother is going to drop this pie off at a friend's house. He goes to school with her, and her daddy just died. He was a nice doctor from the hospital. Is this the house, Dwight? We'll just wait here."

Erica answered the door, looking very surprised to see Dwight.

"Hi. My mom made you and your family this apple pie. She feels awful about what happened to your dad."

"Oh, that was so sweet. Is that her in the car? Let me go down and thank her."

"Mom, this is Erica."

"Hello, honey, it's so nice to meet you. Your daddy was the kindest man. I knew him from the hospital. I'm so sorry for your loss. If there's anything we can do to help, just let Dwight and me know. We're praying for you."

"Oh, thank you, Ms. Washington. There's my mom. Please wait just a minute. I know she would want to thank you. Mom, this is Dwight Washington. He's my chemistry partner at school, and this is his mom. Ms. Washington made us this apple pie and it smells heavenly."

"I'm Ruby Washington, and these are my daughters Danielle and Denise. I work at the hospital. Your husband was a wonderful man. We all miss him. I'm just so sorry for your loss. You are in my prayers, Mrs. McIntyre."

"Please call me Beverly. Thank you so much for your kindness."

"Erica seems real nice, Dwight. I saw how you were looking at her. Forget about it. That girl's just not for you."

"Don't worry about it, Ma. We're just friends and we study together. She's going through a rough time. We like to talk. Don't forget I know what it's like not to have a father."

"I know you go to school in a rich white neighborhood, but don't forget who you are. There are plenty of nice girls your age at church. Nice black girls."

"Ma, I'm not looking for a girlfriend right now, okay? So don't worry about it."

24

Chapter 6

ERICA

"Mom, aren't you going to be late opening up the shop?"

"Pam is going to handle things this morning. I'm not going in until after lunch. I've got some of your father's affairs I need to handle this morning. I'm meeting with his attorney. I'm not looking forward to it. I've got kind of a headache."

"Maybe you should take it easy on the wine in the evening."

"Point taken, Erica, what is going on with your day?"

"Just the usual, I might be a little late for dinner. Dwight and I are meeting at the park to study. It's going to be such a nice day. The leaves are really beautiful. Not too many days like this left."

"Okay, have a good day, honey."

I'm kind of worried about Mom. She's not her usual self. She needs to get her shit together. Doesn't she know that I need her too? I can't handle it if Mom falls apart.

"Hi, Christy, what's up? I haven't seen too much of you lately, you're always with Ben. Are you and Ben still hot?"

"Oh yeah, we're doing just fine. What about you? You seem to be hanging around that new kid, Dwight."

"He's helping me a lot in chemistry and he's pretty good in math, too. He's really a nice guy and really easy to talk to. Not too many kids feel comfortable talking to me about my dad."

"Oh, Erica, I'm so sorry, I've been a really lousy friend. I'm one of those people who don't know what to say, so say nothing."

"I know you care, Christy. It's been tough, though."

"Are you starting to be interested in him, Dwight, I mean?"

"I don't know, maybe a little. I think he's cute. What would you think if I was falling for him?"

"That's your choice, Erica. Probably not one I'd make. Oh God! What would your Mom say, you going out with a black guy?"

"Don't know. But we're really not going out. Not yet. If you're not cool with it, how can I expect my Mom to be?"

"I'm okay with it. I just said that it wouldn't be my choice. Bobby Bauer told Ben he was thinking of asking you out. What do you think?"

"Bobby's really cute, but I think he's kind of dumb. I'm not really interested."

"See you at cheering."

"Hi, Dwight, I'm really glad we decided to study in the park. I just love this time of year. My dad loved the fall, too. We had all kinds of plans to go looking at colleges this fall. Who knows if my mom will be up to it? I was thinking of taking a drive to Syracuse this weekend and checking out SU. What do you think? "

"Are you kidding, SU? My dream is playing basketball at SU. I know it's a good school, too. "

"Do you want to go with me? We can take my car and maybe make a day of it. If the game's not sold out, we could maybe go to the game, too. Let's see if they're home and who they're playing. I'll check it out."

"Do you think you could go?"

"I'll have to touch base with my mother. I don't know what her work schedule is this weekend." Dwight made a quick call to his mother.

"Great, the twins are spending the day with my Aunt Sarah, going to a church picnic, and having a sleepover with her girls. She said that I'm good to go."

"Can I pick you up about ten o'clock?"

"How 'bout I just meet you here at ten? You really don't want to be driving around my neighborhood if you don't know it."

"Oh, are you sure? Okay. I'll check and see about tickets if they're playing at home."

"Cool, it's a date. We better get studying for this chem quiz."

Did Dwight say it's a "date"? I guess it is. I hope Mom's cool with it. I guess I'd better get home for dinner.

"Mom, I'm home. I'm starving. What's for dinner?"

"Helen gave me some tomatoes from her garden. I roasted them and I'll make a simple sauce for pasta."

"Is she coming over?"

"She is."

"Mom, before Nana comes over, can I ask you something?"

"What's up?"

"Is it okay with you if Dwight and I drive to Syracuse on Saturday and check out the campus? We thought we'd also go to the football game."

"Will it be just you and Dwight?"

"Yeah, so is it okay or not?"

"I guess so. But what's with you and Dwight. Are you interested in him?"

"Maybe, I don't know. He's just so nice and one of few people at school I can talk to about Dad. Would that not be okay with you if I were interested in him, like as a boyfriend?"

"REALLY, Erica, do you really need a complicated relationship in your life right now?"

"Complicated, because he's black?"

"Yes. That's not really what I want for you, especially right now."

"You mean not now and not ever."

"No, I didn't say that. I don't want to see you hurt in any way. I don't want to worry about you. God, Erica, life is stressful enough already!"

"Mom, please just try to keep an open mind."

Great, Syracuse is playing LSU. I don't care how much it costs, I'm buying two tickets.

Chapter 7

Beverly watched her daughter take off in her little red Mustang for the day. She couldn't help but remember the look on Erica's face when Tom gave her that car for her sixteenth birthday. *Tom always spoiled her, but she has been very responsible. I'm not so sure about this day she has planned with Dwight. As much as we think we're without any racial or ethnic prejudice, are we really? I'm not sure I'm ready to see my daughter on the arm of a black guy. Maybe I'm more worried about what other people will think.*

Beverly finished her second cup of coffee and headed off to her shop. She looked at herself in the rear view mirror. She didn't quite like what she saw. She looked tired, just really tired. Her roots could use a touch-up. She decided to change into something different when she got to the shop, something a little brighter.

"Hi, Pam, I need a little boost today. Help me pick out a cute outfit. I'm kind of a mess. I really don't want to scare off the customers."

"What's going on? " Pam asked. "You do look a little tired and stressed out today."

"Oh, Pam, right now it's just hard being me … Beverly without Tom. What's even harder is being a single mother of a teenage daughter. I just don't have the energy. Tom was so good with Erica. She listened to him and trusted his judgment. I never seem to say the right thing. I guess overall she's doing okay. She's doing well in school, still enjoying cheerleading, and looking ahead to college. But she seems to be hanging around with different friends."

"Bev, I remember when my father died. I was about Erica's age. Some kids got it and some not. I guess you've got to respect her feelings. What about you? There are probably not too many women you know who are widows at your age. Being divorced is just not the same thing. Have you thought about maybe a bereavement group for young widows?"

"Pam, you know me well enough to know that's not my thing. I've just got to try harder. I'm even sick of me. It's been over a month. I've just got to get on with it and stop feeling sorry for myself."

"Here, try this cute yellow sheath dress. It would look really cute with this little black cardigan. Come on, Bev, go get changed. Put on a little brighter lipstick, too."

Beverly didn't know what she'd do without Pam. They had been friends a long time, ever since her no-good cheating husband left her for his secretary who was ten years younger than she. Bev had given her a job and now couldn't image life without her friend.

Beverly heard the alert that she had a message. "Mom, we're here. The campus looks awesome."

Erica and Dwight circled the campus trying to find a good place to park. "Dwight, do think that this is an okay spot?"

"If I was lucky enough to have this car, I would treat it like a baby. It's a tight spot. I'm afraid somebody's going to put a ding in your door. Better keep looking. "

"I guess I am pretty lucky to have a car. I notice you taking the bus a lot."

"You do whatcha gotta do. My mom usually has her car and gas money is tight. Look up ahead. I think that looks like an okay spot."

Erica locked up her car and they walked around the campus. They stopped for coffee and sat on a bench in the quad.

"I really like it here," said Erica. "I can see myself being happy here, and Syracuse is just far enough from Rochester to be away, but close enough to go home as much as I want. I'm worried about Mom when I go away to school. Hey, but that's two years away. Hopefully, Mom will be back to herself my then. Hey, what about you? Will you be worried about how your mom will manage when you're away?"

"No, not really, my mom is the strongest lady I know. Always has been. Besides, I'll probably end up at Monroe Community or Brockport State. My only out is maybe getting a scholarship. I'm a pretty good basketball player. I've just got to keep the grades up."

"You're going out for basketball? I didn't know that! I love Friday night games in the winter. What position do you play?"

"Usually, center, because I'm so tall."

"How tall are you?"

30

"Last I was measured, six feet five. We had a pretty good team at my old school. It could have been better with a different coach. Coach wasn't paid much, so he didn't put much time into practices. I'm sure your coach has to be much better."

Erica grinned. "Do you even know who it is, Dwight?"

"Nope," he said.

"It's Mr. Novak this year. I'm sure he'll love it when he finds out your going out for the team."

"That's cool, Erica. We'd better get over to the Dome if we want to catch the kick-off."

They found their seats. "Yes! Erica cheered. Syracuse is going to score on their first drive. I can't believe we're here. This is so much fun!"

"I'm having a good time, too," said Dwight as he smiled and wrapped an arm around Erica.

OMG! Did he really just put his arm around me? You know, I like it. To be honest, I really do like him and not just as a friend.

Dwight looked over at Erica. He couldn't stop thinking about her. He could not believe he was sitting at a Syracuse football game with his arm around a pretty white chic. *And is she pretty! She's 'girl next door' kind of pretty, but not a girl that would live next door to me. Her hair is blonde and silky, and it smells really good, and those beautiful green eyes! But she's nice, too. No sassy attitude. She's just not like any other girl I've ever known. I just better remember who she is.*

Syracuse beat LSU twenty-seven to fourteen. "That was fun," beamed Erica. "Let's walk around campus a little more and then I guess we'd better start back."

It was almost seven o'clock when they got into Rochester. "Do you want to stop and grab some dinner? I'm starved!" said Erica. "I know this great little Italian place in East Rochester."

"That sounds good."

They got a table by the window. Dwight surprised Erica when he pulled out her chair. She was very touched. "Aren't you the gentleman?"

They talked easily as they ate their salads and pizza. The check came.

"My treat," Erica said, as she reached for the check.

"No, you don't," said Dwight. "I've got this." Erica couldn't help but wonder where he got the money.

"I work some shifts at Wegmans after school and on the weekends. It helps out a little. Plus Wegmans has that work-scholarship program. Right now they've got me working in the deli."

"Well, thanks for dinner. I enjoyed it. I enjoyed everything today."

"Erica, thank YOU. It was all your idea and I loved that you asked me. But all good things come to an end. We better get going. Why don't you just drop me off at the school, and I'll get the bus from there."

"Oh, come on," said Erica. "I'll just drive you home."

"Please, I just don't want you driving around in my neighborhood."

She dropped him off at the school. Before getting out he leaned over and kissed her softly on the lips.

"Thanks again. See you on Monday at school."

"Take care, Dwight."

Erica couldn't help smiling as she drove home. *This is the happiest I've felt since Daddy died. What is it about Dwight that I like so much? He just seems so honest and true. He doesn't try to show off. He's not cocky like a lot of the guys I know. And I love how he kissed me. It was just one soft, easy kiss, nothing more. It was nice for our first kiss.*

Erica walked in from the garage and saw her mother dozing in the recliner in front of the TV, glass of wine at her side.

"Mom, I'm back. We had such a good time."

"I thought you'd be home sooner."

"We stopped for dinner when we got back into Rochester. Didn't you get my message?"

"Guess not," she said, frowning. "But I'm glad you had a good time. How did Dwight get home? You didn't drive him home did you?"

"No, he wouldn't let me. He said that he doesn't think his neighborhood is very safe."

"Where does he live, anyway?"

"I don't know, somewhere in the city, just off Lake Ave., I think. I just dropped him off at school, and he took the bus home."

"Well, that's good anyway." Beverly said, adding, "Erica, just be careful."

"Goodnight, Mother." Erica said, clearly annoyed.

Dwight was watching college football on TV when his mother got home from work. "Hey, Mama, how was your night?"

"It's a full moon. Patients are always very agitated when there's a full moon. I've been running all night. But how about you, did you enjoy your day?"

"I had a great time. I loved the school. Wouldn't I just love to get a scholarship to Syracuse?"

"Keep working hard. And I don't just mean on the basketball court. They'll want a well-rounded student. Who all went today?"

"It was just Erica and me."

"It was just Erica and you?" Dwight could see a subtle look of disapproval on his mother's face.

"Look, Dwight, I'm not sure you know what you're doing. She's a white girl, and a rich white girl. What do think you're doing with her? Get some sense, boy."

"Don't worry about it, Ma. Good night. See ya in the morning."

"Okay, I'm expecting you'll be going to church with me and the girls."

Chapter 8

On Monday morning Erica met Dwight at his locker. They had some time before their first class. "I really had a great time Saturday," said Erica. "I really like spending time with you."

"Me too," said Dwight. "I don't know any girls like you. I guess I don't know any white girls. But it's not just that you're white. You're smart and just really sweet. You don't have an agenda. You do your own thing and don't seem to care what other kids think."

"Dwight, is that a problem, I mean that I'm white? I know that it's the twenty-first century, but for some people it's still a problem. I hope that you know that it's not a problem for me."

"No, you're being white really isn't the problem. The problem is that our worlds are so different. Do you know what I mean? My family doesn't have much. My neighborhood's poor. People struggle and many have given up trying. A lot of my friends have quit school. They hang out and drink or smoke weed. They get into trouble. Why would you want to hang out with me?"

"I guess I don't see any of that. You're just a nice guy that I like spending time with. Let's just forget about the rest of all that, Okay?"

"Right, we better get to chem."

Later Erica and Dwight met for lunch in the cafeteria. Erica could sense a few eyes on her when she sat across from Dwight. "Hey, Dwight, come over for dinner tonight. I could really use some help with my math."

"I can't, I've got to work. What about tomorrow? My mom's on the day shift this week, so I won't have to stay with the girls. Are you sure you're mother will be okay with it?"

"Okay, Tuesday it is. My mom will be fine."

Erica and Christy changed for cheerleading practice. "Hey, Erica, I saw you with Dwight at lunch. How's it going with him? Did the weekend go okay?"

"Saturday was great. I loved Syracuse. Dwight's a very easy guy to be with."

"What do you mean 'be with'?" Christy asked. "What happened?"

"Oh, calm down. We just had a really nice time. But he did kiss me."

"I knew it! You're really in to him. I think that it's okay, but I'm not so sure that's what everyone else thinks."

"Look," said Erica. "They'll just have to get used to it. Get this... I invited him over for dinner tomorrow."

Christy couldn't help but laugh. "OMG, what will your Mom do? It's like that sixties movie, Guess Who's Coming to Dinner." Erica and Christy were really into watching old movies.

"That's very amusing. Come on, Christy, I was hoping for you to be a friend with all this. Who else am I going to talk to?"

"Okay, Erica. It's hard to get used to, that's all."

Beverly was sorting through the mail when Erica walked in. "Hey, Mom, how was your day?"

"It was okay, honey, how about yours?"

"Not bad for a Monday," said Erica. I've been having some problems with math. My math teacher is awful! He's so mean and he shows so much favoritism to the boys. I invited Dwight to come over for dinner tomorrow night, and he's going to help me with my math after dinner. He's just really smart. I hope that's not a problem."

Beverly's jaw dropped. She was really caught off guard. "No, it's not a problem, honey. You know your friends are always welcome." Beverly headed for the refrigerator and poured a glass of chardonnay. I've got to be cool. "Do you have any requests for dinner?"

"How about making enchiladas, Mom? Maybe you could make brownies for dessert."

"That sounds good."

"Mom, I'm glad you're okay with me and Dwight."

Beverly took a sip of wine. She wondered, Am I okay with it, do I really have a choice?

Ruby was a little more vocal about it. She was not thrilled that her son was going to dinner at the McIntyre's.

"Dwight what are you doing, son? You are way out of your league with that girl. Now you're going to her house for dinner? What's up with that?"

"I'm just going to help her with math. We're friends, Ma. Can you just be cool with it?"

"Sure. But what about when you want to have your new friend over HERE for dinner?" Ruby asked. She was really feeling aggravated.

"Ma, you knew I was going to be meeting a lot of new kids when I changed schools. I know it's because she's white."

"I never thought my son would be one of those black men that ignored all the wonderful women of his own race and went for a white girl."

"It was not my plan. She's just a really nice girl, and I'm very attracted to her. She's very smart. We like a lot of the same things. Can't you just get beyond that she's white? You liked her father, and last I knew he was white."

"I wasn't attracted to her father. I just think he was an honorable man, that's all."

"Well, okay, Ma, maybe I'll just go over to Marcus' house and smoke weed tomorrow night."

"Now that was really uncalled for, Dwight."

I'm just going to have to be a little more open-minded, vowed Ruby. *Maybe it's okay. I wonder how her mother feels about all of this.*

Dwight caught the bus for home as soon as school let out on Tuesday. He decided to make a stop at Wegmans on the way home to pick up his paycheck. Then he decided to buy some flowers. He'd bring some to the McIntyre's and then he had a thought. *I'll buy some for Mama, too. Maybe it'll soften her up some.*

He saw the pink roses. Erica seemed like a pink rose kind of girl. For his mother, he got some purple mums. *Seventeen bucks,* he cringed, and then remembered the money he spent over the weekend on dinner. *Maybe I can pick up some extra hours next week,* he thought.

Dwight headed home and took a shower. He put on a clean pair of jeans and decided to wear a button down shirt instead of his usual tee shirt. His mother was pleased with the flowers.

"You have a nice night, Dwight. Remember your manners."

"Okay, Ma, see you later."

Dwight noticed that Erica changed clothes, too. She answered the door with a big smile on her face. "Flowers, how sweet, they're beautiful! You didn't have to do that. You're doing me a favor, coming over to help me with math."

Beverly wiped her hands and came out into the foyer. "Hello, Dwight. Did you bring those pretty roses? How nice. I'm glad you're here. Erica says you've been a good friend and a great study partner."

"It's really nice of you to have me for dinner, Mrs. McIntyre. Something smells really good."

"Enchiladas, Erica's favorite."

Dinner went well, thought Beverly as she did the dishes. She looked in on the kids as they studied at the dining room table. *He really is a handsome boy. I'm just so nervous about all of this.* She poured another glass of wine and sat down at the kitchen table to catch up on her email.

"Hey, it's after ten," said Dwight. I'd better get going. Are you feeling a little more confident about the math?"

"Much better, why don't you let my mom drive you home?"

"No, it's okay. I'll just walk into the village and take the bus. Let me say good night to your mom."

"Thanks for a great meal, Mrs. McIntyre. Goodnight."

"Oh, you're welcome Dwight. Say hello to your mother for me."

Erica walked Dwight to the door and closed the door behind her. They walked down the driveway.

Dwight held her and kissed her. "I'm so glad you came over tonight," Erica said. Dwight kissed her again, longer and slower this time.

"I like spending any time I can with you. See you tomorrow."

Beverly noticed the look on her daughter's face when she came back in the house. She decided to just let it go. *I'm glad somebody's happy*, she thought.

"Goodnight, honey. I'm going to turn in."

Erica kissed her mother. "Thanks for everything tonight."

Beverly hated bedtime. She had trouble falling asleep. *God how I hate this bed, it seems so big.* She went to the dresser and pulled out a pair of Tom's pajamas. She laid them out on his side of the bed. *Oh*

God, this is bad. I just miss him so much. What would Tom think about this new love of his daughter's? Would he be okay with it? Oh probably. Tom was much more liberal than me. Although I'm not sure anyone would be good enough for his Erica.

Maybe I should see a shrink. I'm really not myself. I'm just so tired. I can't sleep, can't concentrate, and just can't get it together. I always thought I was better than this, stronger. I managed to keep it together after John died. Everyone says loss of a child is the worse death to deal with. But I had Tom. We faced it together. They say that a lot of marriages fall apart after a couple loses a child. I think Tom and I became closer. What the hell am I going to do the rest of my life? Will I never have a man hold me again? Oh God, I'm so lonely.

Beverly tossed and turned most of the night. The last time she looked at her bedside clock it was 4:36.

Chapter 9

Erica went to Dwight's locker after last period on Friday afternoon. "Are you going to the game tonight? It's the last home game," she said.

"I can't. I've got to work."

"How late do you have to work? Joey Sanders is having a party. Maybe you can meet me later."

"I don't even get out until midnight. It's just not going to work this time."

"Don't worry about it," said Erica. "I'm not even that crazy about going. But why don't you call me sometime over the weekend? I'd really like to see you."

"Yeah, I'd like that too. Hey, lean over Babe. I just want to give you a quick little kiss. Be cool," he said.

Erica felt like the whole school saw them kiss. She could feel the heat in her face.

"Okay, call me," she said.

Erica decided to go to Joey's party. She caught up with Christy in the locker room after the game.

"Saw you and Dwight at his locker this afternoon." said Christy. "Looks like you're going public with your thing for Dwight."

"So what, I don't care. I really wish he could come to the party tonight. He's working."

"Oh, come on," said Christy pulling her arm. I can't believe tonight was the last home game. I know Joey's party will be a lot of fun."

The party was really getting going when they got there. Erica looked around. Just as she thought, there were no parents in sight. *This ought to be good.* Erica and Christy weren't into drinking, but watching their friends make complete A-holes out of themselves was always amusing.

Erica and Christy were chatting with some other girls when they saw Ben and Bobby Bauer walk in the door. Christy went over to Ben. Bobby came up to Erica. She could tell that he had already been drinking.

"Hi, Erica, what's up? I haven't seen you around much lately."

"You know, I really thought we could go out sometime. I'm sure I could show you a good time. You could probably use a little fun in your life right now, what with your father dying and everything."

"That's very sensitive of you Bobby, but I really don't think so."

"But why not, I think I'm just what you need." He really got into her face this time.

"Really, Bobby, no thanks, I'm just not interested."

"You know what that say, 'Once black, you never come back!'"

Erica turned her back and walked out of the party. She passed Christy and Ben on the way out.

"I'm out of here!" she said.

As soon as she got in her car, she could feel the tears coming. *What a complete jerk! I knew he was dumb, but a bigot too?* Erica couldn't stop crying. She really needed to talk to someone now, but whom? She didn't think her mom could handle this conversation. She checked the time... *eleven thirty; I know Nana's asleep by now. Maybe I'll go see her in the morning.* Erica blew her nose and started her car.

When she got home, she saw her mother had fallen asleep in front of the TV. Beverly always tried to wait up for her. Erica nudged her lightly.

"Mom, I'm home. Go up to bed."

Erica went up to her room. She dialed her father's cell. She knew her mother would keep the account going so she could hear her father's voice. *"Hello, you have reached Dr. Thomas McIntyre, please leave your name and number and I will get back to you as soon as possible, if this is a patient emergency, please call 911. Thank you."*

"Oh God, Daddy, I miss you. I really need you now." Erica was sobbing now.

She saw that she had missed a call from Christy.

Erica called her back. She told her what Bobby had said. "Are people really talking about us, saying stuff like that?" asked Erica.

"I heard just a few comments, but nothing as crude as Bobby's. If this makes you feel any better, Bobby threw up on himself as he was walking out the door. The party ended after that. Joey thought it was getting out of hand. He was afraid one of his neighbors would call the cops."

"That's why I like Dwight so much. He's just nice. He's not trying to prove anything. He's very genuine."

"I think it will be okay," said Christy. "The kids, everyone, will get over it. I just hate to see you so upset."

"Thanks. I'll be alright. I'll catch up with you later this weekend. Bye."

Erica finally fell asleep. It was after ten when she woke up. Her mother had already left for the shop. She decided to call her grandmother and ask her if she wanted to go to lunch.

"Hi, Nana, it's such a nice day. Do you think you want to go out to lunch?"

"Oh, that sounds nice, honey. Where do you want to go?"

"How about the Village Café, maybe we can get a table outside."

"Why don't you pick me up in about an hour?"

It was such a nice day for late October. It was sunny and about seventy-two degrees. Erica and Helen got a table and looked at their menus. "I'm starved," said Erica. "I'm getting a big fat cheeseburger and sweet potato fries."

"Oh, that sounds good, but I'm going to get a spinach salad. So tell me, honey, how's it going for you?"

"Can I ask you what you think about something, Nana?"

"Why, of course. What's on your mind?"

"Well, I really like this boy at school. His name is Dwight. It's kind of complicated, though, because he's black. He's one of the kids in the urban-suburban program. He used to go to a city school and got the opportunity to transfer to my school. Not everybody is cool with me liking a black guy. What do you think about it?"

"It probably wouldn't have been accepted when I was your age, but things have changed a lot. One of your father's best friends growing up was black. His name was Samuel, and he and your father were friends since second grade. Remember, your father grew up in Brooklyn. There were faces of all colors. It was very multi-ethnic. Sam spent a lot of time at our house and your dad at his. They played football together in high school and stayed friends in college, even though they went to different colleges. Do you remember seeing his picture in your parents' wedding album? Tom and Sam were in each other's weddings."

"Oh, Nana, I do remember that. I didn't know they grew up together. Where is he now?"

"Sam died in his early thirties. I believe it was testicular cancer. I think your father continued to keep in touch with his wife. She was at your father's funeral."

"Was she? There were so many people there. I didn't know a lot of them."

"Her name is Olivia. She's a white woman. I think her and Sam's marriage was difficult for their families to accept at first, then it seemed to work out. Tom said that they were one of the happiest couples he knew. So, Erica, I think you have to be true to yourself. If you like him and think he's a good person, then I think that's all that matters. Just remember, some people might not be okay with it and may be cruel. What does your mother think?"

"I guess that she's okay with it. She's afraid that I'll be hurt because of what people may say. She's nervous, too, because he lives in the city. You know Mom. She worries a lot about appearances."

"Let's walk a bit. I could use an ice cream cone," said Helen. They walked down Main Street in the village. "So tell me about your mom, how's she doing?"

"Not so great. I worry about her. She hasn't played any golf when her friends have called to ask her, and I know she's missed some of her committee meetings. She never plays her violin. Dad loved it when she played. She drinks a little more wine than usual. She seemed so strong in the first couple of weeks. Now I know she's struggling."

"It's got to be hard for her, honey. Right after someone dies, everyone is there for you. There's so much to do. Then when the dust clears, you realize you're on your own. The love of your life is never coming back. It was awful for me when Grandpa died, but I had a lot of support from women my own age who had gone through the same thing. There are not so many widows your mother's age around for her to lean on. It will take time. Healing is all about time. Try to be patient with her."

"I'm lucky that I have Dwight. He's been very understanding and supportive. A lot of the other kids just don't get it. They're really nervous around me."

"Well, I'm glad you have him, honey." They bought their ice cream and kept on walking. Let's drop into your mother's store and say hello."

Beverly had just finished waiting on a customer when she saw her daughter and Helen walk in.

"What have you two been up to?" she asked.

"Oh, Nana and I just went to lunch and out for ice cream. It's such a nice day."

"Everybody's been out and about today. The shop's been busy. Do you see anything you like? We got a lot of new merchandise in."

"Oh, I love these boots! Can I try them on?"

"Sure. The red leather is really beautiful," said Beverly. "Do you want them?"

"Oh, yes! Thanks."

"Well, I'd better get back to work. I'll see you later at home. Bye, Helen. You take care."

Erica drove her grandmother home. "Thanks, Nana, for lunch. I love you."

"I love you, too, honey. I think things will work out. It will just take time."

Erica always felt better after spending time with her grandmother. She was a pretty cool lady for 76.

She felt her phone vibrate in her pocket. It was Dwight.

"Hi, Dwight, Are you already finished with work?"

"I'm just getting out. How was the party last night?"

"Not great. I went home early."

"Maybe tonight can be better," he said. "I thought maybe we could meet up and catch a movie. My mother and the twins have plans tonight, so I'm free."

"Oh, I'd love to go to the movies. Let me check it out with my mom when she gets home, and I'll let you know."

"Okay then, give me a call. Bye."

"Mom, hi, would you mind if I went to the movies with Dwight tonight?"

"Actually, that would be fine. Pam asked if I wanted to go to dinner with a few of her friends. So that will work out for both of us."

"That's great, Mom." Erica called Dwight and they made plans to meet at the theater. She wanted to look really good tonight. She took a shower and washed her hair. She decided to wear her favorite jeans, a black v-necked sweater, and her new red boots. She looked in the mirror and was pleased with how she looked.

"Bye, Mom. Have fun tonight."

"You're not picking Dwight up, are you?"

"No, we're meeting at the theater. Don't worry I'll be home by midnight."

"Okay, have fun, honey."

When she drove in to the parking lot of the mall, she could see Dwight waiting for her in front of theater. She could feel her heart beating a little faster.

Dwight gave her a big smile. "I'm really happy we could go out tonight." They walked up to get their tickets. Erica pushed a twenty though the window to buy the tickets.

"Oh, you don't have to buy the tickets," said Dwight.

"It's no problem," she said. "That popcorn smells SO good. I'm going to get us some popcorn." They got their popcorn and sodas and found their seats. The movie started soon after they sat down.

Midway through the movie, Dwight reached over to hold Erica's hand. She looked over at him and smiled. *I feel almost normal tonight*, she thought.

"That was a great movie," said Dwight. They started to make their way out of the theater. Erica saw one of her mother's friends up ahead. Oh, she so didn't want to have to speak to her. No such luck.

"Hi, Erica, how are you honey?"

46

"Hello, Mrs. Goldstein. I'm fine, thank you. This is my friend Dwight." Dwight gave her a polite "Hello."

"How is your mother doing? I've been trying to get together with her."

"Oh, Mom is doing okay. She just has a lot going on right now. I'll tell her you asked about her."

"Okay. Nice to see you honey."

Rebecca Goldstein reminded Erica of Mrs. Olsen on "Little House on the Prairie," a real busy-body. She could just hear her saying, "Do you know who I saw at the movies? I saw Erica McIntyre, and she was with some black guy. Poor Beverly, doesn't she have enough to handle?"

"Do you want to get something to eat? We could maybe go to that Asian place in the mall. I know they serve pretty late."

"Let's do it then," said Dwight. He took her hand and they walked over to the restaurant.

After they ordered, they started talking. Erica told him about what happened at the party. A very dark look came across his face. "If he bothers you again, let me know. I'll take care of it."

"He's just a really dumb jock. He was really drunk. I don't think he'll be a problem."

"It's too bad about him. Most of the guys I've met so far have been pretty cool. I'm looking forward to basketball. Does Bauer play basketball?"

"No, I don't think so. What else are you doing his weekend?" asked Erica. Dwight wiped a little duck sauce off her lip.

"I've got to work again, how about you?"

"I'm not looking forward to tomorrow. It is my little brother's birthday. He would have been twelve. It's always a hard day, and now my dad won't be around to help us get through it."

"Why don't you tell me about him?"

"His name is John, after my grandfather. We called him Johnny. He was really a neat kid. He was really into airplanes. He always wanted to go to the airport and watch the planes come in. He had airplanes all over his room. He said that he was going to be a pilot when he grew up. He loved baseball, too."

"How did he die?"

"He was born with this terrible heart defect called Tetralogy of Fallot." There are lots of problems. There is a hole between the ventricles of the heart, and there's a problem with a valve in the pulmonary artery bringing blood up to the lungs. The aorta is not in the right position, and the walls of the right ventricle are very thick. It's easier to understand when you look at a diagram of the heart." Dwight listened intently but looked really perplexed.

"Whoa, that's heavy."

"I know. It's really complicated. My dad helped me to understand it when I got older. Bottom line is that kids with this don't get enough oxygen into their blood and turn blue really easily. He had surgery when he was about two months old. He really did great, too."

"Then what went wrong?"

"When he was four and started growing really fast, he began having some problems again with his oxygen. He had to go to the hospital to have a special test called a cardiac cath. Something went very wrong during the procedure and his heart stopped. They couldn't bring him back. It was so awful. I didn't understand. I was only in fourth grade. He was only supposed to be gone overnight. I was staying with my grandmother. My parents got home and told me Johnny wasn't ever coming home, because he died and went to heaven. The house was very quiet and very sad for a long time."

"Oh, Babe, that's all so horrible. I'm sorry." Erica could see that his eyes were all glassy.

"So, that's Johnny's story. Thanks for letting me tell it. That's why it's so important for me to become a doctor. I want to help kids with heart problems."

"I'm sure you will. It looks like they're getting ready to close. We'd better get going." They paid their check and Dwight walked Erica to her car.

"Dwight, will you get in the car a minute? I hate saying goodnight out here." He got in and took Erica in his arms. "I had such a nice time tonight," she said. "I'm really glad we could get together."

He took her in his arms and kissed her, slowly at first, and then with a little more urgency. "You better get going, Cinderella, it's almost midnight."

"Okay, Dwight, take care. I'll see you Monday."

Erica was surprised when she got home that her mother wasn't back yet. *I hope Mom had a good time*, she thought, *she could really use some fun.*

Beverly's night was not at all fun. Pam's friends were a little hard to take. Two of the women were divorced, and the woman who was married was kind of bitter. All she did was complain about her husband. There was some serious male-bashing going on.

One of the women, Diane, actually said, "You know, Bev, it's not so bad that your husband is dead. Men are no good. Eventually they all let you down. You're probably better off. At least now you won't have to go through the hassle of a divorce, and you'll end up with more money."

"Diane, what the hell is the matter with you? I can't believe you just said that!" exclaimed Pam.

"Oh, I'm so sorry. That was so insensitive of me. Please excuse me." She threw some money down on the table and left.

"She needs some serious help," another woman said. "Diane has turned into such a bitch."

The mood then got a little lighter at the table. After the other women left, Pam and Beverly went to the bar for a drink. "Oh, Bev, I'm sorry. They were really rough tonight. Sometimes they can be a lot of fun. Diane's divorce was particularly ugly and she has been dating some not so nice men."

"So, Bev, how are you really doing?"

"Oh, I guess I'm okay. My biggest worry is Erica. She has this new boyfriend, Dwight. He's one of the urban-suburban students. He's a black kid from the city. He seems like a nice kid, but I don't know if she's ready for that relationship."

"What do you mean?" asked Pam. "Having a serious boyfriend, or is it that he's black?"

"I guess it's both. It's not just that he's black. It's not like he's a black kid from the suburbs. He's an inner-city kid. His world is so different from hers. I'm not sure I want her exposed to those harsh realities."

"What do you suppose Tom would have thought about it?" Pam asked.

"You know Tom was very liberal. Erica was very special to him, so I'm not sure how he would have felt. I'm also worried about sex. I don't think she's sexually active, but I see the way she looks at him."

Pam took a big sip of her wine. "Oh, come on, Bev, you know a lot of teenagers are sexually active. That would be an issue whether he was black or white."

"Oh, you're right. But I'm also worried about what people will say. People can be so cruel. I just don't want her to get hurt. I just see this relationship as so problematic. She seems happy, though. In some way Dwight is helping her cope with her father's death."

"What about you, Bev? What are you doing to help yourself heal?"

"Oh, I don't know. I'm just so damned lonely. I just take it one day at a time. How do you ever get over losing the love of your life? Tom and I were really tight."

"If a support group isn't your thing, would you consider seeing a therapist? After my divorce, and then Kyle telling me he is gay, I knew I needed someone to help me sort everything out."

"I didn't know you went to a therapist, Pam." said Bev.

"I don't see her anymore, but at the time she really helped me to navigate the storm. Let me see if I still have her card." Pam dug through her purse. "Here she is. Her name is Dr. Elizabeth Meadows. Maybe you should set up an appointment. If she doesn't seem like a good fit, you don't have to go back. She really helped me to sort out by feelings and find my inner strength."

"That's not a bad idea, Pam, thanks. I think I'm particularly down this week, though, because Johnny's birthday is tomorrow. He would have been twelve. I can't believe he's been gone eight years already."

"Oh, Bev, you have had to cope with so much. Please consider calling Dr. Meadows. It's okay to accept help sometimes."

"We better get going. Erica is out with Dwight, and I told her to be home by midnight. Here it is twelve thirty, and I'm still out."

Pam could see Bev was crying the whole drive home. Pam pulled into the McIntyre's driveway and hugged her friend. "Call me if you need me, ANYTIME. Think about making that appointment. I love you, Bev. Bye, you take care."

Beverly quietly opened the door to her daughter's room. She was relieved to see that she was home and asleep.

Beverly got up early Sunday morning. She was determined to make the best of the day. She got the newspaper and poured herself some coffee. She read an article about poverty in Rochester's inner city. She knew it was bad, but she didn't realize that Rochester had one of the highest rates of teen pregnancy and HIV in the entire country... higher even than in New York City. *Oh God*, she thought, *even more reason to worry. I've got to keep the lines of communication open with Erica.*

She got out the waffle iron and started frying up bacon. She knew the smell of bacon was sure to get her daughter up.

"Mom, it smells so good down there! What are you making?" Erica came down the stairs and gave her mother a kiss on the cheek.

"I was really in the mood for waffles. Waffles always remind me of Johnny," Beverly said. Remember how when he was only two, he used to try to get the waffle iron out of the cabinet by himself? 'Waffies', he would say."

"Oh, Mom, I know. Today is his birthday."

"Let's try to make the most of the day, honey. Maybe after breakfast we could go for a walk and then go over to the cemetery."

"That sounds good, Mom. How was your evening with Pam?"

"It's always good talking to Pam, but I really didn't care for her friends... bitter, divorced women. Even the woman who was lucky enough to still have her husband had nothing good to say about him. It just made me miss your father more."

"Oh, Mom, you don't need to hang around women like that. I have a few friends whose parents are divorced. They talk about how it has changed their parents, especially their mothers."

"Mom, there is this one girl I cheer with, you know Ashley, her mother was so disgusted with men that she became a lesbian. Can you believe it? I feel so bad for her."

"Oh, that IS awful. What about Dwight's mother? She's a single mother. What does Dwight say about her?"

"I guess she's really strong and hard-working. Dwight's dad is in prison, but Dwight says that she is determined to make life better for herself and her kids. She works full time at the hospital and goes to school at night so she can get her nursing degree. Dwight says she's really strict."

"I'd like to get to know Ms. Washington better," Beverly said.

"I'd like to get to know her, too," Erica said. "I only met her that one time she brought over the pie. Maybe we could invite their family over sometime."

"That's a good idea. Do you want to walk in about an hour, honey?"

Beverly and Erica walked along the canal for almost an hour. Beverly was hoping to get her daughter to open up a little more about her relationship with Dwight, but that wasn't happening. They walked back home to get their car and stopped to buy flowers before heading to the cemetery. They bought white mums and a pumpkin for Johnny's grave. For Tom's grave, Beverly insisted on yellow roses.

They walked through the cemetery and first went to Johnny's grave. "Do you think that we should have your brother's grave moved closer to your father's?"

"Mom, the thought of that is so disturbing! I think Johnny belongs here in the children's section. Besides, I love that he is here by this maple tree. It turns such beautiful colors right around his birthday. You should do a watercolor of this tree sometime. Dad always said that he loved your paintings."

"I haven't painted in such a long time. I just never seem to find the time." They started walking towards the section of the cemetery

52

where Tom was buried. His headstone was still not placed. Beverly and her daughter knelt down to pray.

"Oh, Mom, do you think our life will ever be normal again?"

"Erica, I'm not sure what normal is anymore. I guess we're doing our best. You go to school and I go to the shop, but I know it seems like a grey cloud looms over our heads. You seem to be happy with your new friend, Dwight."

"I am, Mom. I guess you could call him my boyfriend. He's just the sweetest guy. I really like him. Do you think you would ever get married again, Mom, or date?"

"Oh, I'm so not ready for that. Yes, I'm very lonely for your father. He was the love of my life. I'm not sure I could ever be with another man."

"But, Mom, you're so young."

"Honey, right now it's hard for me to look to the future. I just try to get through each day."

They made sandwiches for lunch went they got home. Erica told her mother she needed to study and went to her room.

Beverly went out and sat on the deck. She had so much on her mind. No wonder she was exhausted all the time. She decided to take Pam up on her suggestion of making an appointment with a therapist. She also pondered maybe giving Pam more of a managerial role at the shop. She knew Pam could use the money. *Maybe it would free me up a little*, she thought.

Chapter 10

Beverly woke up Monday morning feeling a little better. She had actually gotten a good night's sleep. She got to the shop and opened for business. Mondays weren't usually very busy. She thought that maybe she would talk to Pam about taking on more responsibility at the shop.

Pam walked in. "Good morning, Bev. I was thinking about you yesterday. It was probably a difficult day. How did it go?"

"Better than I thought. Erica and I talked a little. She wasn't at all antagonistic, like she can sometimes be."

"Did she say much about her new boyfriend?"

"No, not much really, only that she really likes him."

Later in the morning Beverly went into the back room at the shop and got out the business card for the therapist that Pam recommended. She took a deep breath and punched in the number. "Hello, I'd like to make an appointment with Dr. Meadows. I would be a new patient."

"I'm sorry, Dr. Meadows isn't accepting new patients right now, but I could give you an appointment with one of her associates, Dr. Martino. Are you okay seeing a male therapist?"

I have no idea, Beverly thought. Oh, I got up the courage to make this call; I'll just make the appointment. "Oh, I guess that would be alright."

"I have an opening Thursday at four o'clock, will that work for you?"

"Thank you. That will be fine. Good-bye."

When Beverly went back behind the counter she saw that Pam was waiting on a casual friend of hers, Rebecca Goldstein. The only reason they were friendly was because their kids went to school together. She and Rebecca were both booster club parents. "Hi, Bev, how are you? How are things going for you? Are they getting any better?"

"I'm just taking it one day at a time. I guess I'm doing okay, but thanks for asking. I'm sorry I've been so poor at returning calls."

"Did Erica tell you I bumped into her?" Rebecca asked. "I saw her at the movies."

Beverly could feel her heart skip a beat. That meant that she had seen her with Dwight. Beverly was sure that Rebecca came in the shop today to sniff out the situation. *I'm going to be cool about this*, she thought.

"Oh, she didn't mention seeing you."

"Who was that she was with, a new boyfriend, maybe?" Rebecca asked.

"I'm sure she was with Dwight Washington. He's a new student and her chemistry lab partner. He seems like a really nice kid. So anyway, what is it you're shopping for today?"

"Oh, I'm just checking out your new clothes for the fall. Could we maybe go to lunch in the next couple of weeks?"

The phone rang. "Will you excuse me?" Beverly asked. "I'll be in touch." Beverly escaped to the back again when she got off the phone. *Oh, God*, she thought. *Why Rebecca of all people, should Erica and Dwight bump into her? She has such a big mouth. Why do I care what she thinks anyway?*

When she heard Rebecca leaving, she came back out. "You handled that just fine," said Pam. She seems like the kind of woman that could really get under your skin."

"She's not really my favorite person. I guess I'd better get used to comments like that."

"I can relate to that. After Kyle came out, a lot of people made some not so subtle comments about the situation. What's wrong with some people anyway?"

"I made the appointment," Beverly said. "But Dr. Meadows was not taking new patients, so I booked with a Dr. Martino."

"Good for you. I've heard he's also very good. Good luck with that."

Erica's Monday at school wasn't going so well. She had hoped that the incident with Bobby would have blown over, but some of the kids were still talking about it. She couldn't believe it, Bobby actually caught up with her when she went to her locker.

"What do you want Bobby?" she asked. "Why don't you just leave me alone?"

He looked contrite. "I guess I was kind of a jerk, and I'm sorry, but I would still like to take you out."

"Are you kidding me?" Erica laughed. "No way... look Bobby, I'm just not interested. I'm sure you'll have no problem finding someone else to go out with, you're such a fascinating guy... big football player and everything."

"I said that I was sorry," he said.

"And I said that I'm just not interested."

She could see Dwight coming down the hall. He gave Bobby a not so subtle bump against his shoulder as he walked up. "Hey, Dude, what's going on?" he said.

"Just talking to Erica, is that okay?"

"Sure, just be polite." Dwight gave Bobby a cold stare.

"Erica, we're going to be late for math." Erica and Dwight took off and left Bobby standing alone with a dumb look on his face.

"He better not bother you again," Dwight said.

"Don't worry, I can handle Bobby. I've known him since fourth grade."

Later that day, Erica was in the locker room changing for cheerleading practice when she heard some of her fellow cheerleaders talking about the party and the incident with Bobby.

She turned around and looked at the girls and said, "Okay, can it be over already? Our football team is actually in the playoffs and we've got a lot of practicing to do."

When Erica got home, she could tell her mother was not in such a good mood. "What's up, Mom?"

"Why didn't you tell me you ran into Mrs. Goldstein? She came into the shop today, and you know how nosy she is. She wanted to know about you and Dwight."

"Come on, Mom, who really cares what she thinks?"

"Are kids saying anything to you about Dwight?"

"Just a few are Mom, but I can handle it. Besides, I really don't care. They'll get used to it. They will be talking about somebody else soon."

When Dwight got home, he walked over to his old high school to see if anyone was around playing basketball. Maybe if he shot a few hoops, it would help him calm him down. He didn't like to see Erica getting hassled. He saw some of his friends playing ball.

"What's up, D? How you liking your new school?" his friend Willis asked.

"It's cool, but I miss you guys."

"I heard you got yourself a new girlfriend, a nice, rich, white girl. Pretty, too."

"Who told you that, man?"

"Your sister, Denise, told my sister, Tanya," said Willis.

"She is pretty," said Dwight as he took a long shot at the basket and made it.

"You doin' her?" another guy, Andre, asked.

"You shut the fuck up about her," Dwight said and grabbed the ball for a lay-up.

"Okay, take it easy man, no need to be so touchy, just asking."

"Hey, I've got a little weed," Andre said. "You guys want to get high?"

"No, not for me," Dwight said. "I've got to get going. See you around."

Playing basketball didn't do much to improve Dwight's mood. When he got home, his mother jumped on him, too

"Where have you been? You were supposed to pick up your sisters at Aunt Sarah's and get them started on their homework." Ruby was very aggravated with her son. "It seems like you've got no time for your family anymore."

"I'm sorry, Ma. I ran into a couple of guys and we were just shooting a few hoops. It seems like I never see those guys anymore. My new school is tough and you know I've been working a lot."

"I know, son, but I think your new friend, Erica, takes up a lot of your time. You know, if you really like this girl, I would like to get to know her a little better. Why don't you bring her over here sometime?"

"Okay, Ma, I'll do that real soon. I've really got to hit the books right now."

Ruby thought about her son and his new girlfriend as she started cooking supper. She decided that she was going to give Erica's mother a call and ask to meet her for coffee. Maybe that would be a good start. The more she thought about it, the more she liked the idea. *Why put this phone call off*, she thought. *I'm working evenings this weekend, maybe she can go Saturday morning.* She got out the phone book to see if the McIntyre's number was listed. There was a listing for Thomas and Beverly McIntyre. She dialed.

"Hello, is this Beverly?"

"It is."

"Well, hello again, this is Ruby Washington. I hope you are doing well. I wanted to know if maybe you would meet me for coffee. It seems Dwight and Erica have become very fond of each other, and I thought we should also get to know each other."

Beverly was not prepared for this call, but this woman was trying so hard to be nice. "I would like that Ruby. I have a shop in the village, a few blocks from the high school. It opens at ten o'clock on Saturdays, but I could meet you about eight-thirty and we could have breakfast. Do you know the Village Café on Main St? It's right down from my shop. We could meet there."

"That sounds fine. Thank you."

"Well, thank you for asking me Ruby."

Erica walked in as Beverly was hanging up the phone. "Who was that Mom?"

"It was Dwight's mother. She asked me to meet her for coffee."

"Did she really? That's nice. Dwight has a lot of good things to say about his mother. He says she's kind of strict. She probably just wants to get to know you better because Dwight and I are friends. It was probably hard for her to make that call, Mom."

"Oh, I'm sure it was. I'm glad she called. I'd like to get to know her better too."

"How long is it before dinner?"

"About twenty minutes."

"Alright, call me when it's ready." Erica went upstairs and called Dwight. "Hi. Did you know that your mother called mine, and that they're meeting for coffee?"

"Oh, that sounds like my mother. She's very direct. Maybe it's a good idea. I guess it's starting to show, how we feel about each other."

"I think it's a good idea too," Erica said. "What are you doing?"

"I'm working on my history paper, which really isn't my thing. But I'm hoping I can get at least a B+. Maybe you can read it tomorrow and let me know what you think."

"Okay, I'll see you tomorrow then."

"Bye for now, Babe"

"So, Ma, I hear you're meeting Mrs. McIntyre for coffee. What's that all about?"

"Is it okay if I'm interested in knowing more about your new girlfriend's family? Yes, I did say girlfriend, because that is apparently what she is."

"I think she's really pretty," said his sister, Denise.

"And why are you shooting off your mouth about stuff you don't know about? I heard you were telling Tanya that she is my girlfriend."

"Well she is, isn't she? I hear you talking to her on the phone."

"I told you that you better shut up about it," said her twin, Danielle.

"Now that's enough, all of you!" said Ruby. "You girls should just mind your own business. Go get your homework started."

"Ma, I wish you would just give Erica a chance. She really is a very fine girl. I like her, okay?"

"Alright, son, just don't let your schoolwork slip. You respect that girl. Think before you do anything that could ruin your future."

"Ma, I get the message."

On Thursday, Beverly had her first appointment with Dr. Martino. *Oh my God,* she thought when he walked into the room and shook her hand. *He is so good-looking.* He looked to be in his early to mid-fifties. He was in good shape and had just the right about of salt in his salt and pepper hair. *Will I really be able to confide in this man?*

"Well, Mrs. McIntyre, or is it alright to call you Beverly? What brings you here?"

"Beverly is fine. I'm a recent widow and I'm having a very hard time adjusting. My husband's death was unexpected and I have a teenage daughter. I'm just not myself. I wake up and it's just so hard to face the day."

"Well, Beverly, how long ago did your husband die?"

"It's been almost two months now. His name is Tom."

"Two months isn't a very long time. Why don't you tell me about Tom? Tell me about your marriage."

Beverly found it very easy to talk to this man. He didn't say much, but he seemed to listen very intently, passing the Kleenex just when she needed it. The hour went by very quickly.

"I think we've made a good beginning. I hope you'll come back next week."

"Yes, I will. It's good to talk to a neutral person, someone who doesn't already know me or Tom."

"Well, next Thursday, then. Go easy on yourself." He smiled and shook her hand.

I can't believe I told him all I did about Tom and me. I guess that's what therapy is all about. I really don't think I could speak like that to a group. I don't think I would be comfortable in a bereavement group. Her heart skipped a beat. *Is it possible that he might know Tom? No, he seems very ethical. He would have advised another therapist.*

Beverly had another thought. *Maybe I'll call Sam's wife, Olivia. She became a widow in her thirties. Olivia is white. She could probably give me some perspective on Erica's relationship with Dwight. I know it was a little rocky for her and Sam navigating an inter-racial relationship. I haven't talked to her in a long time, but we did speak very briefly at Tom's funeral.*

As she drove home, Beverly felt calmer than she had in a long time. *Hopefully by Thanksgiving, things will seem better,* she thought

Chapter 11

This will be a busy weekend, thought Beverly as she was getting dressed Saturday morning. First she would have breakfast with Ruby Washington, then all day working at the shop, and the football game that night. Beverly wanted to watch Erica cheer at the high school play-offs. She knew that her daughter was very excited.

Beverly walked over to the diner from the shop. She immediately spotted Ruby sitting in a booth waiting for her. *Ruby looks young*, she thought. *She is probably in her mid thirties.* She could see where Dwight got his good looks.

"Hi, Beverly, I thank you for meeting me."

"Oh, I think this is a good idea. It seems that Dwight and Erica are very fond of each other. I wanted to get to know you, too," said Beverly.

They ordered. Ruby ordered oatmeal and Beverly got her usual egg white omelet.

Ruby took the lead. "Beverly, I don't know what you think, but I think that this could be a very complicated relationship for your daughter and my son. As if teenagers aren't complicated enough. I'm just so pleased that Dwight got the opportunity to go to Lyndon B. Johnson High School. I want him to do well so that he can maybe get a scholarship for college. I'm worried that his mind his more on your daughter than on his school work."

"I don't know, Ruby. The kids do seem to be studying a lot. Isn't studying what got them together in the first place?"

"Yes, that's so," replied Ruby. "But I do see the look on my son's face whenever Erica's name is brought up."

"I know that Dwight helped to ease some of Erica's sadness after her father died," said Beverly. "I'm grateful for that, but yes, I'm concerned about their relationship. Please don't misunderstand me. From what I can tell, Ruby, you have raised a really nice boy."

"Thank you. Let's just tell it like it is," said Ruby. "My son is black and from a poor city neighborhood. Beverly, you were married to a doctor, a really fine man. Your daughter is white and has been raised in an affluent suburb. How is all of this going to work out?"

"Ruby, I appreciate that you are so candid about your feelings. Please believe me. I've been thinking the same things. I think their feelings are genuine, so I guess we can't change that. We just have to keep the lines of communication open."

"Beverly, tell me. Are you alright with your daughter seeing someone of a different race?"

"I admit, I was a little taken aback at first, but I think I'm alright with it. One of my husband's best friends was black and he married a white woman. I say 'was,' because his friend died, also. They had a beautiful relationship. How about you? Would you have preferred that Dwight not be interested in a white girl?"

"Yes. It always bothers me a little bit when black men ignore the wonderful women of their own race and seek out white women. I guess we can't choose who our children decide to love. I think Erica is my son's first love. From what he tells me, your daughter is very special. You've had the chance to get to know my son a little, but I haven't had the opportunity to spend time with Erica."

"Well, I guess we'll have to change that," Beverly said. "Ruby, why don't you tell me a little about yourself?"

"You already know I work as a nursing assistant at the hospital. I work on a surgical floor. That's how I knew your husband. He was so friendly and courteous to everyone. He always asked me how my classes were going. I go to school part time at the community college. I'm working on my nursing degree. Most of my classes are in the evening. It's kind of a struggle... work, school, and three kids, but I manage. I just know I can make life better for my kids if I increase my earning power. I'd like to get a house in a better neighborhood."

"Oh, Ruby, you do have a lot on your plate. You sound very determined."

"Enough about me, how are you doing after losing your husband?"

"I'm overwhelmed. I know I'm very fortunate that I don't have financial worries, like some women do after losing their husbands. I have a very good person who works for me at my shop, so that's going well. But I have to say, I'm really lonely and always worried about Erica. She's all I have now."

"I guess I'm too busy to be lonely," said Ruby. It would be nice to have a good man in my life, but I just haven't found him yet."

Beverly wasn't sure what she should say. She remembered Erica telling her that Dwight's father was in prison. She looked at her watch. "Ruby, I really have to get to the shop now. I'm so glad we got together this morning. Thank you for thinking of it. Please, let's keep in touch." Beverly shook Ruby's hand and picked up the check.

"You take care now, Beverly. I'll keep you and Erica in my prayers."

Beverly thought that breakfast went pretty well. She wasn't sure how to read Ruby, though. *Was she alright with Dwight seeing Erica or not? She probably has mixed feelings just like me.*

Pam had things under control at the shop. "Hey, Bev, how did it go?" Bev had called to tell her about breakfast with Ruby.

"I guess it went well. She's a very proud black woman. She's very direct, but nice. I think she's very smart. She's beautiful and she's young. I'd say she's probably no more than 35."

"So, do you feel better about Dwight and Erica then?"

"A little, I guess. I had my appointment with Dr. Martino."

"Was it good to talk to him?"

"It was. I like getting a man's perspective on things. Tom wasn't just my husband, he was by best friend. I miss talking to a man."

"What's he like?" asked Pam.

"He's very attractive."

Pam was a little worried about her friend seeing a male therapist, but she would keep that to herself.

After she closed up the shop, Beverly went home to change for the football game. She knew Erica was very excited about the team being in the play-offs for the state championship.

It was a nice night for football, but it had gotten very chilly. *I can't believe that it's November already,* she thought. Beverly found a seat near some of the other cheerleader moms. Erica looked radiant. She was very proud of her daughter. At half-time, she spotted Dwight walking around with some other kids. Beverly recognized most of the kids he was with. It looked like he was getting along okay, socially, at his new school. *I wonder what's up after the game*, she thought.

They won by a field goal in the last thirty seconds. It was a great game. Erica saw Beverly and ran up to her for hug. "Oh, Mom, wasn't that a great game? If we win the next one, we're state champs! Dwight and I are going to get something to eat. Is that okay?"

"Midnight, okay? Have fun." She saw her take off with Dwight.

At home, Beverly opened up a bottle of merlot and decided to watch a little TV.

Erica and Dwight went to the drive thru at McDonald's. They got hot chocolate and fries and found a place to park for a while. They didn't do much eating or talking. Dwight couldn't keep his hands off her.

"You looked so pretty out there tonight. I couldn't wait until the game was over so that I could just hold you and kiss you. I hope I make the basketball team, because then we'll be together at every game."

"Oh, I think you'll make the team," Erica said smiling. "Do you think we can meet at the library tomorrow to study?"

"I'm not sure if my mother's working. Call you tomorrow?" asked Dwight.

Erica dropped Dwight off at his bus stop. He kissed her again and said "Goodnight, Babe, sweet dreams."

As Erica drove home she couldn't help thinking how warm and happy she felt. She then had a dark moment and became a little teary. *Oh, Dad would have loved to be at the game tonight,* she thought. He tried to get to as many football and basketball games as he could. She and her dad talked about the games the next morning. Then she wondered, *how would Dad feel about me and Dwight?*

Beverly was still up when she got home. They talked for a while. Erica asked her mother about breakfast with Ms. Washington.

"I think it went well, honey. She's really very nice, but I can see that she is very protective of her children. She has a lot of dreams for Dwight. She mentioned that she wants to get to know you better."

"Me, too, I only met her that one time she dropped the pie off. Mom, do you think Dad would be okay with me seeing Dwight?"

"Oh, honey, that's a really hard question. He loved you so much. I'm not sure he would be completely okay with any boyfriend you had. But he was fair, and a good judge of character. I think he would have liked Dwight."

Then the tears came and Erica couldn't stop crying. "Mom, I miss Dad so much. He would have loved being at the game tonight. I want him to meet Dwight."

Beverly held her daughter. "I know, honey. I miss your Dad, too. I hate that he's missing out on everything. I have to believe that Dad can see us and he knows we are doing okay. I'm sure he is very proud of you. I think it's time we start going to mass again. I'm ashamed we haven't been to church since the funeral."

"I know, Mom, but I was just so angry that God took him away from us. Why us? First he took Johnny, and now Dad?"

"I've asked myself the same questions, honey. There are no answers. Dwight's mother told me she is praying for us. Maybe we should have more faith in the power of prayer. Let's call Nana first thing in the morning and tell her we will pick her up for church."

"Okay, Mom. She'll like that."

Beverly had not been raised Catholic. Her family was Lutheran. She converted to Catholicism before marrying Tom. It was important to him that they be married in the Catholic Church, and he wanted to send his kids to Catholic grammar school.

After Erica went up to bed, Beverly thought about her conversation with Erica about faith, and God, and losing Tom. It was the first really intimate moment she shared with her daughter since Tom died. She slept pretty well that night.

They all went to mass the next morning. As they were walking out, Father McMahon approached and told them how happy he was to see them. "Don't underestimate the healing power of God's love," he said. "He is there for you. He listens."

After they got home, Erica got a call from Dwight. "Babe, I can't meet you at the library. My mother is working the three to eleven shift and wants me home with the twins."

"I wish you could come over and study here," said Dwight.

"Hey, let me ask my mom. She doesn't want me driving over to your house, but maybe she would bring me over. All ask her and call you back."

"Good luck."

Erica was surprised that her mother agreed to take her over to Dwight's. She called him back and asked for directions.

Beverly wasn't completely thrilled about the plan, but agreed. She was curious to see where the Washington's lived. She realized that some concessions had to be made.

Their street wasn't so bad, but Beverly could tell that just a few blocks down Lake Avenue, the neighborhood got rough. You could tell that Ruby took pride in her home. The bushes were neatly trimmed, the front porch was in good repair, and there was a pot of mums next to the door. Beverly dropped Erica off and told her to call when she was ready to come home. *This is a milestone. Now I actually know where Dwight lives, and I have given Erica permission to go to his house.* Her heart sank a little. She didn't think to ask if his mother would be home. *I guess I just have to trust her.*

Ruby had not yet left for work when Erica got there. This is good, Ruby thought. *I can get to know Erica a little better.* Erica had the same thought. She didn't know why, but Ms. Washington made her a little nervous.

"Can I get you two a snack before I get dressed for work?"

"Oh, no thanks, Ms. Washington, I just had lunch."

"Dwight tells me you are a cheerleader. Do you think my son will make the basketball team?"

"Oh, I think so," Erica said. "Our team is really lacking height. Besides, our chemistry teacher, Mr. Novak, is going to coach this year. I know he really likes Dwight. He knows Dwight is a really hard worker and is very committed."

She seems very sweet. She had better not break my son's heart, though. She could have any boy at her school that she wants.

"Well, if you'll excuse me, I better start getting ready. Dwight, keep an eye on your sisters. They are both working on a project for school up in their room."

"Got it covered, Ma."

As Ruby drove to work, she couldn't help but wonder if it was a good idea to leave those two alone. She knew Danielle and Denise wouldn't miss a thing and would tell her if anything happened.

As it turned out, Dwight and Erica did study. Dwight so wanted to take Erica up to his room and lock the door, but he was too smart for that. A. He respected her too much; and B. His sisters were sure to nark on him to his mother. Besides, he knew it had been a big step for her to have been allowed to come over to his house.

At about four o'clock Dwight made some popcorn and got them some soda. Of course, the twins smelled the popcorn and came down. They wouldn't leave Erica alone. They asked her questions about everything, the last question being, "So, are you Dwight's girlfriend?"

Erica blushed. "Well, I guess so. Are you guys alright with that?"

"Oh yeah, we are," they laughed. "Dwight's last girlfriend, Yvette, was not so great. We didn't like her. She was nasty."

"Hey, you two," said Dwight. "She wasn't my girlfriend. She just thought she was, and besides it's none of your business. Now you guys can get some popcorn and go in the other room and watch TV, if you're done with whatever you were doing for school."

"Your sisters are really cute," said Erica.

"And so are you," he said and tipped up her chin for a quick kiss. "Let's get back to math, and then maybe you can look at the essay I wrote for English."

Erica called her mom at about five o'clock. She knew her mother would want to pick her up before it got too dark. When they saw Beverly's car pull up, Dwight kissed Erica and walked her out to the car. "Thanks, Mrs. McIntyre, for bringing Erica over. We got a lot done. See you tomorrow, Erica."

When they got home, Erica could see that her mother had her violin out. *Mom must be feeling better*, she thought.

On Monday, at school, everyone was so excited that the football team had only one more game to win to be state champs. Erica passed Bobby Bauer in the hall. "Hi, Bobby, great game, you threw some awesome passes."

He looked very surprised that she spoke to him. He smiled and said, "Thanks, Erica. So are we okay now? You're not mad at me anymore?"

"No, Bobby, I'm not."

"So, now maybe you'll go out with me?"

"No, that hasn't changed. Good luck next week."

Christy caught up with Erica. "Is Bobby still bothering you?"

"No, he was okay today."

"So, how's it going with Dwight?"

"Good. My mom actually let me go over to his house yesterday to study."

"So, what is his house like? Is his neighborhood really bad? Were you nervous there?"

"No, his street isn't too bad, but you can see that a little way down the road, you get further into the city and it isn't so great. I got to talk to his mom a little. She's nice, but she makes me a little nervous."

"Christy, I really like him. Do you hear much talk about us anymore?"

"Not so much. I think everybody is getting used to it. I see the guys being much friendlier to him."

"He's going out for basketball."

"Oh, that's cool," Christy said. "I'll catch up with you later."

When Erica got to chemistry, she could see Dwight talking to Mr. Novak. She could hear they were talking about basketball.

Beverly stopped on the way to the shop to pick up coffee and scones for herself and Pam. "Hi, Pam, did you have a good weekend?"

"It was an interesting weekend." Pam said. Kyle and his new boyfriend invited me out for dinner. Kyle is only thirty-two. I think this guy, Mark, is probably close to fifty."

"Oh, that's got to be hard to take. What does your ex have to say about Kyle?"

"Kyle came out four years ago, and Mac still refuses to acknowledge it. He has totally shut down about anything having to do with Kyle. I'm not sure Kyle has talked to his father since."

"Oh God, life is so challenging!" Beverly said.

"How was your weekend?"

70

"It was good. Big step, I let Erica go over to Dwight's house. I saw where he lives. It really wasn't so bad. I think Erica and I are doing a little better. We're talking more."

"Pam, I've been thinking about cutting down on the amount of time I spend here in the shop. Would you be interested in taking on more of a managerial role? Of course it would mean I would pay you more. I think I'll hire another person to help work the floor."

"Oh, that would be great. I could really use the money," said Pam.

"Let me think about it some more, and we'll iron out the details later in the week."

Chapter 12

I can't believe it's less than two weeks before Thanksgiving, Beverly thought as she was driving home from work. *Maybe giving Pam more responsibility will help the holidays go a little smoother. December is always so busy at the shop. Basketball season will be starting and Erica will be all involved in that. I wonder if Dwight will go out for the team? These will be the first holidays since Tom died. I am so nervous about getting through the holidays.*

Dwight was in the gym for basketball try-outs every day after school. Erica wondered how he would swing basketball with all his other responsibilities. His mom depended on him to help with his sisters, and he had his job at Wegmans. She talked to him about it at lunch.

"Well, Babe, I'm not sure. I don't even know if I'll make the team. I think my mom knows basketball may be my ticket to college. I think she'll try to help me make it work. My Aunt Sarah, my mom's sister, is good about letting the girls come over, and she lives pretty close by."

"What does your family usually do for Thanksgiving?" asked Erica.

"My family and Aunt Sarah's family usually get together. My grandparents come up from Atlanta and spend a few days up here. My grandfather is a minister. My mother's brother, Uncle Theo, sometimes comes too. How about you, what are you doing?"

"Our gathering is pretty small. My grandmother will come over. My mother is an only child. My grandparents on her side don't like to travel and they'll want to stay in Connecticut. My Dad's brothers and sisters all live in different states. I guess I'm really dreading the holidays this year."

Dwight reached across the table and put his hand over hers.

"What are you doing this weekend?" asked Erica.

"I've got to work. I wish I could go to Buffalo and watch the state championship game. I bet you're pretty excited about going."

"Oh, I am. I don't think our school has ever played in the championship. I've got to tell you, I'm more excited about basketball season, because I know you will be playing. Do you like the guys going out for the team?"

"I do," said Dwight. "I'm glad Bauer doesn't play, even though I can see he's a good athlete. I'm getting to know your friend Christy's boyfriend, Ben, a little better. He's a good guy."

"He was captain of the JV team," said Erica. He and Bobby aren't as good of friends as they used to be. Bobby's gotten so full of himself."

"Yeah, he had better stay away from you."

Bobby showed up out of nowhere and walked by their table, as he was leaving the cafeteria.

"Hey, Bauer," Dwight said. "Good luck on Saturday."

Bobby turned around. "Thanks, man." He just kept walking.

"I don't want trouble with anybody at this school," Dwight said to Erica.

"I've got to ace this math test to bring up my average," fretted Erica.

"You will, Babe. We should get to class."

It was Thursday, and Beverly had her second session with Dr. Martino. *God, he's so good-looking,* she thought again as he walked into the room. They talked some more about her marriage.

"It was such a good partnership. We rarely fought about anything. Maybe sometimes we disagreed about things pertaining to our daughter, Erica."

"Is Erica your only child?"

"We had a son, John, who died when he was four."

"You have suffered the loss of a husband and a child. That's so difficult."

They spent the rest of the session talking about Johnny. Beverly knew she would look forward to Thursdays and seeing Dr. Martino.

Erica was in a really good mood when she got home. "I really think I did well in that math test," she said. Thank God that Dwight is so good in math. He's really been helping me. Did I tell you he's going out for basketball? It will be so great. I'm sure he'll make the team."

"He certainly has the height," Beverly said.

"Honey, we have to start thinking about Thanksgiving. Maybe we should go out of town this year and do something different. Uncle David invited us to Tampa and said that we could bring Nana."

"Mom, you know how I feel about Aunt Vicki. I know Dad didn't like her, either. When they were up for the funeral, Aunt Vicki was so obnoxious. I heard her criticizing Uncle David about the eulogy he gave for Dad. I thought his words were very sweet."

"We could go out."

"Like to a restaurant?"

"Mom, I think that would be so awful. I don't care if it's just you, me, and Nana."

"Okay, I'll talk to her about it."

On Friday, there was a big pep rally at school to get the football team psyched for Saturday's game. Erica and Dwight went together. They later met up with Christy and Ben.

"Hey, my parents went to their friends for euchre club. They never get home before midnight. Do you want to get pizza and come over?" asked Christy.

They all agreed and headed over to Christy's. Nobody even brought up alcohol. Ben had the game tomorrow, and Erica and Christy weren't really drinkers. Erica knew Dwight wouldn't ask.

They hung out and enjoyed the pizza. Christy brought the plates back into the kitchen and Ben followed her. They disappeared. Probably to Christy's bedroom, Erica thought. Erica and Dwight did some serious making-out on the couch in the family room. At about eleven o'clock, Ben and Christy emerged.

"Hey, Dwight, can I give you a ride home?" asked Ben.

"Thanks, man." The boys left.

"I'm so glad Ben offered to take Dwight home," Erica said. "It's always so awkward, because my mom won't let me drive in his neighborhood, not at night anyway."

"Ben's cool with it. He likes Dwight."

"So, what was going on with you two?" Erica asked with a silly smirk on her face.

"Okay, we've done it, a couple of times now. I have been going out with Ben since eighth grade."

"So, what's it like?" Erica asked. She couldn't believe she was having this conversation.

"Not so great the first time, but now I'm really enjoying it."

"Are you worried about getting pregnant?"

"No. I think my mother knew Ben and I were getting hot, so we talked, and she took me to her doctor and I'm on the pill."

"You never told me!"

"Take it easy. I just went a few weeks ago."

"I don't think my mom would be as cool about it as your mother is."

"Trust me, she was reluctant. She said that no way was she going to be a grandmother at forty. She's an OB/GYN nurse. I guess she's more realistic and open-minded about teens having sex. It's part of her job. It was hard to work up the nerve to talk to her, but she was pretty cool."

Erica hugged her friend. "I knew you looked different. I'd better get going. See you tomorrow at the bus. I'm so excited about the game."

"It was a close game. They won by a touchdown in overtime."

Dwight got a call from Erica as he was leaving work. She told him all about the game. When he got home, he could see that his mother was not in a good mood.

"What's wrong, Ma?"

"Our schedule came out at work yesterday. I've got to do a twelve hour shift Thanksgiving Day. I have to work 7AM to 7PM."

"That's okay. You can meet up with me and the twins at Aunt Sarah's after work. I'm sure there will be lots leftover."

"Aunt Sarah and her family are going to Atlanta. Granddad hasn't been feeling well. He got a real nasty cold that turned into bronchitis. He and Grandma don't want to make the trip this year, so Sarah's wants to go there."

"Ma, I'll keep the girls busy during the day. Maybe I'll take them to a movie or something. You can buy an entire Thanksgiving dinner for

76

four at Wegmans, and I think it's only thirty-five dollars. We can eat it when you get home."

"That's not the Thanksgiving I had in mind for my family."

"What if I cook the turkey? I can check it out online. How hard can it be?"

"Dwight, you are a sweet boy. Let me think about it."

Dwight felt bad about the situation. His mother tried so hard. It seems like she never caught a break.

Erica and Dwight talked for a long time on the phone on Sunday. "Hey, Babe, have you ever cooked a turkey?"

Erica couldn't stop laughing. "No, why are you asking?" Dwight told Erica about how their Thanksgiving plans fell through, and how upset his mother was.

Erica knew her mother was in a pretty good mood, because she had her violin out again that afternoon. She had a plan. She told her mother about Dwight's Thanksgiving.

"Mom, maybe we should really do something different this year. Do you think we could have Dwight and his sisters over here for Thanksgiving? Mrs. Washington could come after work for leftovers and dessert? What do you think? I'm sure Nana wouldn't mind. Isn't Thanksgiving all about sharing?"

Wow! This really takes me by surprise, thought Beverly. She looked at the sweet and eager look on her daughter's face, and found it hard to say no. *Maybe it would help them get through the day. This is something Tom would have really liked. He was so hospitable to everyone.*

"I think it's a good idea. I'll call Ruby and talk to her about it."

Ruby couldn't have been more surprised when she got Beverly's call later that night.

"Oh, that's so kind," Ruby said. "But won't we be imposing?"

"No, we would love to have you. My family is small and Erica and I really wanted to do something different this year... it being the first Thanksgiving without my husband."

"Well, I'm honored that you asked. Can I send over a few dishes? These are dishes that I can make ahead of time. I like to make glazed sweet potatoes with pecans, and we always have macaroni and cheese."

"That would be nice Ruby. You will come after work, won't you?"

"Oh, I'll look forward to it."

Beverly felt good about her call to Ruby. *Do people really eat macaroni and cheese on Thanksgiving? There's a lot I need to learn about African-American culture.*

Erica and Dwight were thrilled.

On Monday, Beverly filled Pam in on their plans. "How about you, Pam, what are you doing this year?"

"Colleen is boycotting Thanksgiving with her brother this year. She does not approve of Kyle's new partner because he is so much older. She said that he's 'creepy'. Colleen's going to my ex's. My plans are still up in the air."

What the hell, thought Beverly. *I might as well really mix it up.* "Pam, why don't you, Kyle, and his friend join us?"

"Are you sure?"

"I think it would be fun."

"Kyle's new boyfriend, Mark, is older, but he's really nice. He has a great sense of humor. Colleen hasn't completely accepted that her brother is gay. Mark works as a baker. He owns his own bakery. I've seen some of his wedding cakes. He's very talented. He could bring dessert."

"Sounds like a plan."

Beverly told Dr. Martino about her Thanksgiving plans at their session later that week. "I can't believe my WASPY self is having Thanksgiving with an African-American family and a gay couple," she laughed.

"You're evolving, Beverly." *He has a very sexy smile,* thought Beverly. *I wonder if he's married.*

Erica came home from school in such a good mood. Dwight did make the basketball team. She was thrilled. Beverly told her about her invitation to Pam, her son, and his date. Erica said that she was 'cool' with it.

As Beverly was preparing dinner she got a call from Tom's partner, Peter Dwyer. "Bev, how are you doing, honey? I'm so sorry I haven't kept in touch with you since Tom died. It's all been so hard for me to deal with, but that's no excuse."

"That's okay, Peter. I know how busy you have probably been. I should really have called you to tell you how much I appreciated your touching words at Tom's funeral."

"You know, Bev, I've been a coward and a little nervous about facing you."

"Why have you called, Peter?"

"Susan and I are having a dinner party next Saturday night for a few doctors and their spouses in the department. We hired a new guy and we wanted him to get to know everyone. We thought that you would round out the party nicely. The new guy, Brad Williams, is single."

"Peter, is this like a blind date or something?"

"No, it's not that. Bev, everyone wants to see you. People are concerned about you. Think about him as just your dinner partner."

"I don't know Peter. I'll have to think about it. Can I call Susan on Monday and let her know?

"Good enough, but I really hope you'll come, Bev."

"Okay, Peter, bye for now."

"Mom, what did Dr. Dwyer want?"

"Oh, first he did a lot of stumbling around about why he hasn't called since Dad's funeral. Then he invited me to a dinner party next Saturday that he and Susan are having for a new doctor they hired in the department."

"Are you going?"

"I don't know. He said that I'll be this guy's 'dinner partner.'" Beverly held up two fingers on each hand in quotation marks.

"Mom, it sounds like a set-up to me. Are you really ready for that?"

"No, but I do think that I have to get out a little more and face some of the people I haven't seen since Dad's death."

"I think people act weird at first, because that just don't know what to say. At least that's how it was for me at school. Then it got better. Just go, Mom. You over think everything!"

Beverly decided to go. She told Pam she was taking Friday afternoon off to go to the salon. She really needed her hair cut and colored. She decided to get a manicure, too.

God, who should be there when she got to the salon for her appointment, but Rebecca Goldstein?

"Hello, Bev, how are you, honey?"

Beverly could see that she wasn't going to be able to avoid Rebecca and would be forced to make small talk with her.

"I'm fine, thanks." Beverly knew her tone sounded clipped.

"Rachael tells me that your Erica and Dwight Washington are quite an item. How do you feel about that?"

"He's a very nice kid, Rebecca. Erica's thrilled because he's made the basketball team. It's just good to see my daughter happy."

What a bitch she is! Thank God Amy came over to bring me to the sink for my shampoo. Maybe she should pay more attention to what's going on with her own daughter. Erica told me she was very concerned that Rachael had an eating disorder. Poor Rachael, I'm sure she could never please her mother.

Beverly agonized over what to wear to the Dwyer's. *Black... when in doubt, just wear something black.* Erica came in as she was getting dressed.

"Mom, what's with the widow's weeds?"

"I don't know. It seems like a safe choice."

Erica pulled out another dress for her mother. It was a simple silk sheath, kiwi-colored. "Mom, I love this dress on you. It looks so good with your hair." Beverly's hair was auburn. "Just wear this dress and those big pearls that Daddy gave you for your birthday. Come on, Mom, you own a very fashionable boutique. I know you can do better that that black dress. Let me step up your makeup a little," said Erica.

"I can handle my own makeup, thanks."

Beverly decided to wear the kiwi. She finished her makeup and checked herself out in the full-length mirror. She thought she looked pretty good. The glass of chardonnay she drank as she was getting ready helped to ease her nerves a little.

"What are you doing tonight?" asked Beverly.

"Ben, Christy, Dwight and I are going to the movies."

"Midnight, Erica."

"Got it, Mom, relax."

Susan Dwyer always hosted really nice parties. She tried really hard to put Beverly at ease. Peter got her a glass of wine and introduced her to Brad Williams. He was pretty average looking, *maybe a bit nerdy*, she thought. They were seated next to each other at dinner.

"Beverly, I know your husband recently died. I am sorry for your loss. I never met him personally, but I do know of his excellent work. I heard him speak at a neurosurgery conference in Boston last year."

"Your words are really kind, Brad, thank you. What made you take this job at the University of Rochester?"

"My last position was at Columbia Presbyterian. I really wanted to relocate and get away from the city. I really think that I'll like Rochester."

Beverly helped Susan clear the table and stayed to chat with her in the kitchen. "So, what's Brad's story?" Beverly asked.

"Peter told me that his ex-wife is a nurse at Columbia Pres. He found out she was having an affair with another doctor at the hospital. He was very humiliated. I think it was a nasty divorce. I don't think they have any children."

"Bev, are you interested in him?"

"Oh God, no, I'm so not ready for that. I'm not sure that I'll ever be ready."

"I'm really glad you came tonight. It's got to be so hard to be a widow at your age. I know how tight you and Tom were. You two always seemed to have such a great marriage. You must miss him so much."

"I do. It's not only being a widow that's difficult. It's hard being the single parent of a teenager. I hate that Erica doesn't have a father. She thought her father walked on water."

"Bev, if there is anything Peter and I can do to help, please let us know. I know we have boys, but they are teenagers."

Beverly was glad the Dwyer boys didn't go to the same school as Erica. She didn't want to hear any commentary about Erica and Dwight.

Beverly said goodnight to everyone after dessert and coffee. Brad came into the foyer and helped her with her coat. "Can I call you for coffee or a drink sometime?" he asked.

This was exactly the awkward moment she didn't want to deal with. "This is still a difficult time for me Brad, maybe just not now. Goodnight. It was nice meeting you."

Widow or not, thought Bev. *I just would not go out with him. He is so not my type.*

Erica was already home. How'd it go, Mom?" Beverly told her daughter about her evening including the offer at the door. "Honey, he's kind of nerdy. No way! Your father was the love of my life." They both laughed.

"Mom, you really have to be more open-mined."

That night, Erica had trouble falling asleep. Her mind just kept wandering. First, she thought about her little brother. She could still see his sweet little face. *What would he look like now? Mom and Dad had such an active social life. It was really hard seeing Mom going out by herself. Will she ever remarry? Mom's softened a bit since Dad died. I think we're getting along a lot better. She's not so critical. I know she's struggling. Mom used to be so confident about everything, not so much anymore.*

She's been pretty cool about Dwight. I really can't imagine talking about sex with Mom. Her expectation is probably that I just won't have sex, not for a long time, anyway. I can't believe Christy's mother actually got the pill for her. I like Dwight so much. I think I love him. I'm not really ready to go all the way with him, but I know that's not so far away. He's very patient. He never pressures me in any way. I can tell he really wants me. I always imagined that the first time I would have sex would probably be in college. I'm only seventeen. I can't help how I feel about him, but I know our relationship is still pretty new.

Back on the other side of town, Dwight lay in bed thinking about Erica. *I've got to be cool. If I really want sex, I know other girls that are all too willing to oblige. Yvette is still always flaunting her stuff for me. That girl is nothing but trouble. I don't want to be with anyone else. I can't even imagine disrespecting Erica in any way. I've just got to be patient.* He thought about what his friend Marcus always says, "You can't think with the little head, you've got to think with the big head." Dwight always laughed when he said it, but he knew it was good advice.

Chapter 13

Ruby's heart skipped a beat when she saw the letter with the return address "Attica Correctional Facility." She was glad she got to this letter before Dwight saw it.

Ruby ripped open the letter. Jerome was going up before the parole board. He said that he had no place to go if he was granted parole. He wanted another chance at being a family. Ruby ripped up the letter. *There is no way!* The last time Ruby let Jerome back into her life, she got pregnant with the twins. As much as she loved her girls, she was still angry at herself for letting it happen. *He's nothing but trouble. I can't believe he's changed much. I'm sure he'll get back into his nasty cocaine habit and get himself back into trouble. I've finally turned things around a little for me and the kids. I've got to keep him out of my life...forever!*

I think maybe I'll talk to Reverend James about this. He's always got some good advice.

She called her sister, Sarah. Ruby told her about their plans for Thanksgiving.

"Get out of town!" Sarah said. "I can't believe you're going to some white family's house for Thanksgiving. I feel bad we won't be together this year, but I think I really need to see how Daddy's doing. So, Dwight is really serious about this girl?"

"Her name is Erica, and yes, he is quite taken with her. She seems like a very sweet girl. Her mother, Beverly, is okay too. I think it was pretty nice of her to invite my family. Listen to this: I got a letter from Jerome today. He's up for parole. He says that he wants to be a family again."

"What are you going to do? It would kill Daddy if he found out you took up with Jerome again."

"No chance of that. I gave him his last chance when I let him back into my life, and he got me pregnant with the twins. It didn't take him long to get back in trouble again. My kids don't need him for a father and I don't need him in my bed. Do you know that guy, Michael Harvey, at church? He's Michelle Martin's brother. He just moved to

Rochester. I think he's pretty cute. He's a teacher. I won't mind going out with a man like him. But it's not like I have time for a man in my life right now, what with my job and school."

"Girl, you work way too hard. You should think about yourself sometimes. It would be nice to see you with a nice man in your life. You are really looking great, too. It shows you lost those ten pounds."

"Well anyway, Sarah, have a happy Thanksgiving. Give my love to Mama and Daddy. Call me and tell me how he's doing."

"Well, honey, make the most of your Thanksgiving, too. I'm sure you'll have lots to tell me about when I get home. You take care."

Ruby made sure her kids wore their best for Thanksgiving at the McIntyre's. She laid the girls' outfits out before she went to work. She made her dishes for Dwight to bring the night before. She wrote out instructions about reheating.

Beverly and Erica went to pick up Dwight and his sisters at noon. Dwight got into the car and presented Erica with a bouquet of pink roses. He kissed her on the cheek. His sisters giggled.

"Dwight, you shouldn't be spending your money on flowers for me, but I love them." She knew her mother had plenty of fresh flowers in the house for Thanksgiving, so she would put them up in her room.

"You made this day happen. That really means a lot to me."

Helen was already there. Erica introduced Dwight and the girls. You could tell Dwight's sisters were so excited. Beverly got some DVDs for them so they wouldn't get too bored, but Helen got them interested in playing cards.

"Your grandmother is cool," said Dwight. "She's being so nice to Danielle and Denise."

Pam arrived with her son and his friend, Mark. Introductions were made. You could tell that Kyle and Mark felt a little awkward at first, but the party warmed up pretty quickly. Mark had a great sense of humor and kept everyone entertained. The guys got interested in a football game. Erica helped her mother and Pam in the kitchen. *Mom's turkey smells delicious. Even if this day turns out to be a disaster, the food will be good,* thought Erica.

84

"Erica, Dwight seems like such a nice guy, and his sisters are really adorable," Pam said.

"Thank you for saying that, Pam" said Erica.

"No, honey, I mean it. I can see why you like him so much. How's he adjusting to your school?"

"I think he's doing great there. He made the basketball team. I'm so psyched!"

"Bev, we've got to make a point of going to the games. I love basketball," Pam said.

Dwight walked into the kitchen. "My sisters are having so much fun." You could hear the laughter from the living room. He put an arm around Erica. "Do you want to take a short walk before dinner?"

"Mom is that okay? Do you need my help right now with anything else?"

"No, you two go ahead. Right now there's not too much to do. I think Pam and I are going to have a glass of wine and join everyone in the living room. I think we'll probably sit down around four o'clock."

Dwight and Erica got on their coats and walked around the village. They held hands. The Erie Canal ran through the village. The walkway was lined with benches. They sat down for awhile and watched the ducks. It was a very cool day, but the sun was out. With the sun shining down on her and Dwight's arm around her, Erica felt very warm, like she was glowing.

"Babe, this is so nice. I just love that we could spend today together. That's quite a dynamic going on back there. It's like a scene from a movie or something. Wait until my mother gets here. She'll shake it up a little more. She can come off like a hard ass sometimes, but she can really cut loose."

Erica laughed. "For sure, it's not your typical Thanksgiving, but I think it's going well."

"That guy, Mark, is so funny!" she said. "He's so flamboyant, but I think he's nice."

"The dude actually said he thought one of the football players for the Bears was cute... a real cupcake!" Dwight was laughing now.

"I think he probably thinks about cupcakes a lot," Erica giggled. "He's a pastry chef."

Then the mood got a little more serious. "Are you doing okay, it being the first holiday without your father and all?"

"I can't deny that I haven't been thinking about him. I wish he was here to meet you."

"I wish I could meet him too." Dwight took Erica in his arms and really kissed her. "We'd better get back. I could sit here all afternoon with you in my arms, but I think we'd be missed."

When they got back it seemed a though everyone was still having a good time. Beverly gave the twins a job in the kitchen. Kyle and Mark were opening more wine. It was just about time to eat.

Beverly took Erica aside. "Do you think we should say grace, honey?"

"Why would this year be any different?" I don't think I could get through saying it though," Erica said.

"I don't think I can either. I think that maybe we could skip it this year."

Leave it to Helen, she had it handled. She had already talked to the girls. Danielle and Denise had a special grace that they both agreed to say.

Beverly lit the candles and Mark poured the wine. They all sat down. *Mom's table is beautiful, as always,* thought Erica.

Denise started her part of the grace. "Thank you dear Lord, for this wonderful meal and our new friends we now have because of Erica, my brother's girlfriend. We are so happy they invited us."

Then Danielle added, "And God bless the people in our families that aren't here with us today, especially Erica's father and her little brother. We pray our granddaddy in Georgia is getting better. Amen."

Beverly wiped away a tear. "Oh, thank you, girls. Your grace was so sweet and just right for today."

The twins really know how to ham it up, thought Dwight. *What they said was really kind of nice. Mama would have been very proud.*

Everyone seemed to be enjoying their meal. "Dwight, I've got to get your mother's sweet potato recipe. They're delicious!" Mark said. "You really know how to roast a turkey, Beverly."

"I'm really digging the mac and cheese," Kyle added. "Mom, I'm glad you brought my favorite... the roasted Brussels sprouts."

"We are going to have a lot of leftovers," Beverly said. "Everyone's going home with goodie bags."

Dwight and Erica announced that they were doing the dishes. Kyle and Mark insisted on helping. Beverly, Pam, and Helen went in the living room to finish their wine. The twins watched TV.

Ruby got there a little after seven. Beverly introduced her to everyone. "You must be starving. Let's go in the kitchen and fix you a plate. You can bring it out here and join us. Can I get you a glass of wine?"

"Oh, no thank you, I don't drink. Just water, please."

Ruby had taken the time to change into black jeans and a pretty sweater. She looked really nice. It showed that she was a little nervous. Ruby saw the picture of Tom on the end table. She talked about Dr. McIntyre and how kind he was, and how he was so popular with the staff. Helen was very touched by her comments.

Beverly told Ruby about the very special grace her daughters gave. She asked Ruby about her family. It kind of shows that she's the daughter of a minister, Beverly thought.

Beverly made coffee and everyone gathered back at the table for dessert. Mark managed to keep the mood light and had everybody laughing. He had made a red velvet cake, decorated in autumn colors for dessert. Helen had made a pumpkin pie.

"I can't believe that you made red velvet cake!" exclaimed Ruby. "I'm a girl from the South. I love red velvet cake, and it's so beautifully decorated. Beverly, did you make this? It one of the best I've ever tasted."

"Oh no, that was Mark. He is a pastry chef and owns a bake shop in the city."

"Here's right back at you Ruby, with a compliment on the sweet potatoes. Kyle is all about your mac and cheese."

"Well, I'm a pumpkin pie guy," said Dwight. "This is delicious, Mrs. McIntyre."

"You just call me Helen, Dwight."

It was after ten before the Washington's left. Ruby gave Beverly a hug. "I can't thank you enough for hosting my family for Thanksgiving."

"Oh, you're very welcome, Ruby. It was my pleasure."

Kyle and Mark left. Erica sat with Helen in the living room while Helen had another cup of coffee.

Pam and Beverly had another glass of wine in the kitchen.

"I was so nervous about today," sighed Beverly. "I think it went really well. Dwight's family is really nice. I'm still not convinced that Ruby is really okay with Dwight and Erica's relationship."

"I was a little nervous about today, too. Mark is not so subtle about being gay, and I wasn't sure how everyone would be with that. Kyle hasn't been out that long. I guess I'd feel a little better if Kyle was with someone more his own age."

"Mark was really pretty charming," said Beverly. "I think he lightened things up a little. I understand your concerns, though. What did you think about Ruby?"

"Oh, I think she was a little nervous. She seemed to relax a little after a while. She's really very pretty. We've probably got ten years on her, me even more."

"Well, I got through the first Thanksgiving without Tom. For that, I am grateful."

Ruby had lots of questions for her kids on the drive home. Danielle and Denise told her how much fun they had, but that they did miss their usual Thanksgiving at Aunt Sarah's.

"I was with Erica, so it was a real good day for me," said Dwight.

Ruby frowned. "I knew it! You have really fallen for that girl. Please be careful son. Don't get me wrong, because I really like this girl, but I have so many dreams for your future. I just don't want anything to get in the way."

"Ma, would you be saying the same things if she was a girl from the neighborhood?"

"I don't know how to answer that," Ruby sighed.

"Well, I like her!" said Denise. "Me, too," said Danielle. "We saw Dwight holding her hand under the table."

"Girls, you just leave your brother alone."

"Ma, our first basketball game is the first Friday night in December. Do you know your work schedule yet? I would love it if you came. Erica's a cheerleader, you know."

"If I'm not working, you bet I'll be there. Is Wegmans going to give you a hard time about your schedule with basketball?"

"I don't think so. There are so many kids working part time. I'll probably get stuck working a lot of Saturdays and Sundays, though."

Dwight went right up to his room when he got home. He couldn't wait to call Erica. "Hey, Babe, I'm just here all by myself thinking about you. I just wanted you to know how much you mean to me."

"I'm thinking about you, too. Will I see you this weekend?"

"I've got to stay with the girls tomorrow, because my mother's working. I've got to work in the evening."

"I'm going to give my mom some help at the shop tomorrow. You know, Black Friday, and everything, the shop will be busy."

Dwight laughed, "Your 'Black Friday' should be about me."

Now Erica was laughing. "Pretty soon every Friday will be 'Black Friday', because we'll be together for basketball games. I can't wait. Do you know what number you'll be wearing?"

"I'll be number 4. Mr. Novak is going to be a great coach. He's got a lot of energy."

"Our last coach was really good, too. He took a job coaching college ball. Everyone was worried that they wouldn't find a good replacement for him. I guess we got lucky. We got a good chemistry teacher AND a good basketball coach. I've got to admit I have a little crush on him."

"Alright, Babe, don't you be talking like that."

"Maybe Saturday then," Erica said. "Can we see each other Saturday?

"I've got practice in the morning until noon, after that, I'm free. Maybe we can go out Saturday night."

"Okay. Maybe we can catch a movie or something. I know my mom has this big fund-raising event she has to go to because she sits on the board at the cancer center. Let's go to a late afternoon movie and then maybe get some dinner after."

"That sounds good, Babe. Check out the movies and let me know."

It was very busy at the shop on Friday. Erica knew that her mother really appreciated her coming to help out. She ended up staying until the shop closed. Neither one of them was interested in leftovers, so they picked up a pizza on the way home.

Beverly poured herself a glass of wine, and she and Erica sat on the couch to eat their pizza. Beverly thought it was nice to spend this quiet time with her daughter.

"I kind of dread going to this event tomorrow night by myself," she said. "It was always easy going to these things for the hospital on your father's arm."

"But, Mom, Dad always said that it was you that knew how to work a room."

"I guess we were just a good team."

Erica looked at her mother and saw the deep sadness in her eyes. *Oh, Mom, please don't start crying*, she silently pleaded. She and her mother sometimes had their problems getting along, but lately her mother had been so great. She had really softened. *Mom has seemed to accept me and Dwight and that means so much to me.*

"Mom, what don't you call that nerdy doctor you met at the party? I bet he'd be glad to be your date."

"Oh, honey, he's so not my type. Besides, I can't just call him up tomorrow morning and ask him to go."

"Sure you can, Mom. He would probably be elated that you even thought to call him. You should give him a chance."

Then Beverly thought about it. *It seems just so pathetic to go by myself. I really should go, though. What the hell, maybe I'll call Brad and ask him. I wish I would have thought about this before.*

On Saturday morning Beverly called Susan Dwyer to see if she could get Brad's number.

Susan was thrilled that she was going to call him. She and Peter were going too.

"Hi, Brad, this is Beverly McIntyre. I'm so embarrassed for the short notice, but I wonder if you would like to go with me to this fund-raising event for the cancer center tonight. It's black tie. Maybe you would get a chance to meet some more people connected to the medical center. You'd be doing me a real favor, because I just don't want to go to this thing solo."

"I'm so flattered you called. It just so happens I have a tux that I can whistle out of my closet. Just give me your address and let me know what time to pick you up."

When Beverly got off the phone, she had some regrets. *Oh God, I hope I'm not leading him on. He sounded so excited.* She told Erica when she came down.

"Oh, Mom, it's just one evening. Just see how it goes. I'm really glad you called him. Let's go plan your outfit."

They decided on a floor length black satin skirt with a silver brocade jacket. The jacket nipped in at the waist and really showed off Beverly's small waist. She would pin up her hair and wear dangling earrings. Beverly had to admit that she always enjoyed dressing up.

Erica didn't get a chance to see her mother dressed before she left. Dwight borrowed his mother's car and he picked her up for a three thirty movie.

Beverly had a glass of wine to mellow out before Brad came to pick her up. She was a little nervous. When she saw him, she had to admit he looked more handsome in a tux. She noticed he had gotten new glasses which were more fashionable, and he didn't look quite so nerdy.

He kissed her on the cheek and helped her with her coat. Brad drove a really nice car. It was a black Jaguar, not what she expected. He had a very dry sense of humor which she didn't pick up on the first time she met him. They chatted easily on the way to the event.

Beverly noticed a lot of surprised faces when she walked in with Brad. It was probably better than those sad, wrinkled brow looks, and those "How are you these days, Beverly?" She couldn't stand those looks or the comforting hand on the shoulder.

They mingled for the cocktail hour and Beverly introduced Brad to several people she knew. Wouldn't you know it? Rebecca Goldstein and her husband were there. Rebecca's husband, Jake, was an oncologist, and actually a very nice guy. They were headed straight for her and Brad. Beverly could feel herself tense up. She thought that Brad could sense her uneasiness.

"Well, hello, Bev" chirped Rebecca, "I'm surprised to see you here, and with such a handsome date, no less."

"Beverly was kind enough to invite me so that I could get to know some more people at the medical center. I just took a position in the Neurosurgery Department. I'm Brad Williams."

Brad shook hands with Rebecca and Jake. Fortunately another couple stepped up to say hello, so Beverly didn't have to make small talk with Rebecca.

They found their table and sat down. They were seated at a large table for twelve, with some of the other board members. Beverly was happy to see that the Dwyers were at their table.

Brad was a good date. He kept Beverly's wine glass full and was very much a gentleman. Beverly was finally starting to relax and was almost enjoying the evening. When Tom died, his obituary had stated that in lieu of flowers, donations to the cancer center to fund research for pediatric brain tumors would be appreciated. The request netted a fairly large sum. After dinner there were a few speakers. Beverly was asked to stand, and an announcement was made about her gift. This took her by surprise. No one had told her she would be acknowledged tonight. *Thank God I don't have to speak.* She thought as she stood up and smiled with a nod.

She was also very surprised when Brad asked her to dance. He was actually a very good dancer. She didn't feel quite right in his arms. Would she ever feel right in the arms of any man again?

Erica wasn't having any problems in the arms of Dwight that night. After the movies Erica and Dwight went back to the McIntyres'. There was still so much food left over from Thanksgiving. Erica heated up some leftovers for them to eat. After cleaning up they went into the den to watch TV. The movie, "Jerry Maguire" was on.

"I love this movie!" Erica said.

"Oh, I like it too. Let's watch it." They really didn't pay much attention to the movie, because they couldn't stop making out. They kept the action from the waist up, but Erica had her sweater off and her shirt unbuttoned. Soon Dwight had her bra unhooked and was caressing her breasts. Minutes later her shirt and bra were totally off and he was kissing her all over. Erica couldn't believe how good she felt, but she was also a little nervous. She wasn't really ready to go any farther, and she was afraid her mother might get home soon.

"Dwight, I'm not sure when my mom is getting home. I don't want her to walk in on us."

"I guess I got a little carried away, Babe. You are just so hard to resist. You're so beautiful. You better get buttoned up again."

He put his arm around her and they finished watching the movie. It was after eleven when the movie ended. "Babe, I better get going." He gave her one last long, tender, kiss and took off.

I can't believe Mom isn't home yet. She must be having a good time. Erica set the sleep timer on her TV and got settled into bed. She found it hard to pay attention to anything on TV because her mind was on Dwight. She could still smell his cologne. She finally drifted off.

Brad dropped Beverly off at about twelve thirty. She was relieved when he just kissed her cheek. "I'm going to ask you again, can I call you to go out sometime?"

"Well, of course. You were so sweet to go with me at the last minute tonight."

"The pleasure was mine, pretty lady. Thanks again for inviting me."

Beverly closed her door and smiled. *I think I underestimated him.*

Chapter 14

As Erica drove to school on Monday, she couldn't help but think how well things were going. Her mom seemed to be doing a little better, Dwight made the basketball team, and their relationship was going really well. The kids at school seemed to accept that they were together. *I almost feel guilty. Life seems so good right now but still no Dad. Would Dad like Dwight? Would he accept that he's my boyfriend?* After she pulled into the parking lot at school, she did something she hadn't done in a long time. She called her father's cell phone. Then she thought about basketball. *Dad always came to the games, not only to watch me cheer, but he really liked basketball.* She would really miss not seeing her dad in the stands. The tears came and they wouldn't stop. *What is the matter with me? Maybe it's PMS.* She totally missed homeroom and was late for chem.

"It's really nice of you to join us this morning, Miss McIntyre." Dwight gave her a very concerned look. Dwight's eyes were a soft, warm brown. *I could melt looking into his eyes,* Erica thought. *He could show you how much he cared by just looking at you.* Mr. Novak asked to speak to her after class.

"Erica, is everything alright? It's not like you to be late for class, and you look very troubled today. I could see that Dwight was doing most of the work during lab."

"I guess I'm having a bad day because I'm missing my dad. I was thinking about him on the way to school. I just got to thinking that he won't be coming to the basketball games this year. He'll never get to see Dwight play."

"Dwight's a good guy," Mr. Novak said. "I've noticed you two are pretty tight. He's going to be a big asset to the team."

"I didn't have the privilege of meeting your father, but I can tell he raised a very fine daughter. Keep your father with you in spirit. Your high school years will fly by, try to enjoy them. I'm sure that's how your father would want it. I lost my father when I was in high school, too. I remember that just when I thought I was doing okay, something would really set me off, and I would get all sad again. I felt like I was on some kind of rollercoaster. It was a very tough time."

"I guess I was going down that rollercoaster this morning," Erica said. She felt the tears coming again. Mr. Novak was being so nice. He passed a box of tissues.

"If ever I can help you in any way, please let me know. I'm here for you. You better get on to your next class. I can see Dwight is waiting for you outside the door."

"Thanks, Mr. Novak. I'll be okay. Like I said, I'm just having a bad day."

"Erica, what's going on with you today? It kills me to see you so down," Dwight said as they walked down the hall.

"It's just one of those days that I can't stop thinking about my dad."

"Let's not eat lunch in the cafeteria today. Let's take a walk at lunchtime." Dwight suggested.

Juniors and seniors were allowed to leave school at lunch time. They had an hour and it was a quick walk to the village. Dwight and Erica bought a slice and a soda at the pizza shop and sat down on a bench. It was still pretty warm for the last week in November.

"Babe, is there anything I can do to help? Was Mr. Novak giving you a hard time? I didn't like how he called you out when you were only five minutes late for class."

"No. He was really being so nice. He was telling me about how his father died when he was in high school, too. He also said that he noticed we were 'tight', whatever that's supposed to mean. I guess teachers notice a lot." Dwight held her face in his hands and kissed her. He had big hands with long, slender fingers. "I guess it shows how I feel about you, Babe."

"Dwight, you always know just what to do for me. I don't know how I'd be getting through this semester without you."

"We better start walking back. I can't just be sitting here on a bench in the village kissing a pretty white girl in the middle of the day. What will people say?"

They both started laughing and it really lightened up the mood.

They both had practice after school. Erica went to the girls' locker room to change. One of the girls on the squad, Paige, could sometimes

96

be kind of a bitch. "So, I bet you're happy that your big hero is on the team." Her tone was very haughty.

"Just what is that supposed to mean?"

"What do you see in him? What's the matter with all the guys you've known and gone to school with since kindergarten?"

"You know, Paige, I really don't think I need to explain my feelings for Dwight to you or anybody else."

Erica had really bad cramps and she was now getting a headache. She took some Motrin before heading into the gym.

She gave Christy a ride home from practice. She told her about Paige's snarky comments.

"Oh, come on, Erica. You're not going to let her bother you, are you? She's just probably jealous and really pissed that Mike isn't first string. You know how she is."

"I've always liked Mike," Erica said. "I really don't know what he sees in Paige. Dwight told me that besides Ben, Mike was one of the first guys to really welcome him on the team."

"Forget about Paige. She's always been a little jealous of you."

Beverly was in the kitchen preparing dinner when Erica got home. "Erica, I got a call from the attendance office asking if you were ill. I told them that as far as I knew you were in school. I called your phone, but it was off. Didn't you get my message? So did you go to school?"

"Of course I did! I was running late and just missed homeroom. I checked in at the attendance office after Chem."

"Well, I was wondering, because Pam mentioned she saw you and Dwight in the village at noon. I'm really not that crazy about you and Dwight hanging out in the village at lunchtime. Did Dwight have anything to do with you missing homeroom?"

Erica was really irritated. She was not in the mood for a confrontation with her mother. "No, I didn't even see Dwight until Chem. Lots of kids like to walk to the village for lunch. Why is it a problem? So, what's Pam, a spy now?"

"Look, Pam just mentioned that she saw you. She said that it was nice that kids were allowed off-campus at lunchtime, especially on such a nice day. She wasn't spying on you. That's so unfair. I really don't appreciate your attitude tonight."

"I've had a really lousy day and I have some pretty bad cramps, okay? Let's just drop it!"

Erica stormed off. She turned around and said, "I'm really not hungry, Mom. I'm just going to take some Motrin and start my homework."

Beverly poured another class of Merlot and finished making the pasta. *I'll make a plate for Erica. Maybe she'll want it later. I haven't seen this Erica in a while. I wonder what's going on with her. We had been getting along so well. Maybe it is just her period.*

Erica never did come down for the pasta. She acted kind of cool and distant the next couple of days.

Dwight wasn't relating well to his mother, either. She was really edgy. He tried to talk to her about it.

"Mom, what's wrong lately? You seem like you've got a lot on your mind."

"Oh, it's a lot of things. They're giving me a hard time about my work schedule. It's really hard arranging the time off for my classes right now, because we're short-staffed. I'm a little worried about Granddad, and then there's something else that I just can't discuss with you right now."

"Well, take it easy on yourself, Ma, it will all work out." Dwight gave his mother a hug.

Ruby was really worried about Jerome's parole hearing. What was she going to do if he got released? *What if he really has changed? Didn't the kids have a right to have some kind of relationship with their father? I just don't trust Jerome. I can't let him back in my life. The twins have never even met him. The last time he saw Dwight, his son was just a little boy. I need to talk to Reverend James.* She decided to call his office and make a counseling appointment. She met with him after work the next day.

"Ruby, what brings you here today?" Reverend James was in his mid-fifties. Ruby always thought that his sermons were very inspirational. He seemed very down to earth, and he had a good perspective on the challenges of life in Rochester's black community. She told him the Ruby and Jerome story.

"Unfortunately, Ruby, this is a story I've heard too many times. Do you love this man?"

"No, Reverend, I don't think so… not anymore. I don't think I ever really did love him. I was a young girl when I first met him, and I was very flattered by his attention. He was a little older than me. I let myself get pregnant. He never cared to be much of father to Dwight. He was always getting into trouble. He has some kind of charm that could always catch me off guard. I think the attraction was physical rather than emotional. I'll never forgive myself for getting pregnant again by him. My twins have never even met him. He got back into using drugs, and stealing for drugs, and ended up back in prison. He says he's a changed man, and he wants forgiveness."

"Ruby, the Lord teaches us the importance of forgiveness. You can forgive him, but that doesn't mean you have to let him back in your life, especially if you don't love him. You don't owe this man anything."

"But, Reverend, is it right to deny by children the chance of having a relationship with their father? That's what I struggle with."

"Ruby, you said that your girls never even met him. What have you told them?"

"Jerome ended up back in prison before I even gave birth to the girls. That's how fast he can get into trouble. I told my girls that he left before they were born. I didn't say where he went. I just said that he wasn't ready to be a father. That's no lie. He knew I was pregnant and he knew we already had a son. If he really wanted to be a father to his children, he would have stayed out of trouble."

"He sounds like a very weak man, Ruby. What about your son? Do you ever talk about Jerome with your son?"

"Dwight was only eight when Jerome violated parole and ended up back in prison. He was never around much even before that. He would visit, but we never lived together. Dwight and I have talked a lot. I think he's curious about his father, but he is also is also very hurt that he was abandoned by him. He's angry, too, for all the pain he has he has caused in my life. My sister's husband has stepped in and been more of a father to him than Jerome could ever be."

"Your son is almost a man now, seventeen? Do you think that you should have another discussion with him about his father and the possibility of his parole?"

"That's what I struggle with, Reverend. Dwight is such a good boy. He works very hard in school and has a part time job. He's always helping out with the girls. His hard work has paid off. He was chosen to be an urban-suburban student. He goes to a real good high school. I don't want anything complicating his life. I'm hoping he'll get a scholarship for college. He's a great basketball player. Oh Lord, there's something else. He has a girlfriend there. She's a white girl from a very good family… an affluent family."

"Ruby, YOU have a good family. Just because you made a few bad choices, doesn't mean that you are a bad mother. You have worked very hard to make a good life for your children. What's really bothering you? Is it that this girl is white, or is it that she has money?"

"Reverend, I've never liked it when black men seek out white women, when there are plenty of fine black women for them to choose. I have to say, I can see why my son likes this girl. She is very sweet and genuine. I knew her father, who was a doctor at the hospital where I work. He recently passed."

"It sounds to me that your son and this girl can see something beyond color, and beyond material worth. A relationship like theirs can be difficult, but many make it work. It sounds to me like Dwight has a very good head on his shoulders and a very good heart. Why don't you just tell him the news about his father and listen to what he has to say. Just remember, he is almost a man now."

"Well, thank you, Reverend, that sounds like good advice."

"Ruby, tell me, are you seeing anyone?"

Ruby's heart skipped a beat. She knew that Reverend James was a married man.

"No, Reverend. I really don't have the time just now."

"I had coffee with Michelle Martin's brother, said Reverend. He just moved to Rochester. He asked about you. I think he wants to meet you. He seems like a real nice guy. He teaches history. Why don't you stay for coffee hour after services on Sunday and I'll introduce you."

"Okay, Reverend, I'll do that. Thank you for all your good advice."

100

I have to have that talk with Dwight, thought Ruby.

On Thursday, Beverly had her own counseling session. She had a lot to talk about with Dr. Martino this week. She told him about her Thanksgiving with its eclectic guest list. He asked her how she felt about Erica dating someone of another race. Beverly thought she could be honest without being judged.

"It's not what I wanted for her first relationship. To be honest it's not what I want for her, period. Does that make me a racist? I guess I never really thought of myself as a racist. I have to admit I really like this boy. He's bright and ambitious and so well-mannered. He makes Erica happy. He's been able to connect with her in a way no one else has since her father died."

"Just because you prefer that your daughter date someone of her own race doesn't make you a racist. You aren't forbidding her to see him, and it sounds like you have been very welcoming to him."

He got up and brought over his lap top. "Let's look up the definition of 'racist' in the dictionary. Racist is defined as 'a person who believes in racism, the doctrine that a certain race is superior to any or all others.' And 'racism' is defined as 'abusive or aggressive behavior towards members of another race on the basis of such a belief.' I don't think these words apply to you."

"His name is Dwight. His mother and I have talked. She kind of feels the same way as I do, in that she would prefer to see her son with a girl that's black. I am more concerned about their socio-economic differences. Dwight lives in the inner city."

"It does sound complicated. I think you are handling it well. You are respecting your daughter's choices and are trying to be supportive of her. She needs that from you right now."

Beverly also told him about inviting Brad Williams to be her date at the event. She saw him raise his eyebrows.

"That surprises me, Beverly, that you would be ready to do that."

"I only did it because I didn't want to go alone. It's not because I was attracted to him." She could feel the heat in her face. "I almost felt safe asking him, because I knew he wasn't someone I would ever be interested in. I thought of him merely as an escort."

"Well, you could have not gone to this event, period. I think it shows a lot of personal strength that you did go. Good for you. How did it go?"

"I actually had a better time than I thought I would. It turns out this man is really very nice. I found that I liked him much more than the first time I met him. It was good to have some male companionship. I really miss that." Then Beverly couldn't help but wonder if Dr. Martino was single.

"Do you think you might see him again?"

"I don't know, maybe. He asked if he could call me to go out again. I said that it would be alright. But now I wish that I didn't. It just seems too early. I probably should never have called him in the first place. I don't want to lead him on in any way. I guess I really don't know what I want."

"Beverly, it's difficult for anyone your age to jump back in the dating world again. Being a recent widow probably makes it more difficult. Maybe you can begin by just being friends."

"I'll try to keep an open mind about it. Thank you, I'll meet with you next week."

Beverly thought she felt a little better about things after leaving Dr. Martino's office. She hoped that Erica would be in a better mood tonight than she had been earlier this week. Maybe she would take Erica to her favorite Thai restaurant for dinner. It would give them a chance to talk. She was already home from school when Beverly got there.

"Hi, honey, how was your day?"

"It was okay. I'm sorry I was such a bitch this week. I was feeling a little depressed and missing Dad so much. It was probably hormones, too. You know how it is when the monthly bill comes."

"Missing your father is just something that's always there. You can be fine, and then boom, something hits you. What was it, honey?"

"I just want Dad to meet Dwight. I'll miss him at the games. It's just not the same at home without him. Nothing seems as much fun anymore."

"I'll try to get to as many games as I can. I'm really looking forward to watching Dwight play. I'm sure Helen will come with me and maybe sometimes Ruby, too."

"Oh, Mom, you'd really ask her to come and sit with you?"

"Why of course!" The first game is next Friday, right?"

"It is. Dwight will be wearing number 4."

"Honey, I thought it would be fun to go Thai tonight. Are you up for it?"

"Sure let's go. I'm just going to quick get changed."

While Erica was upstairs, Beverly got a call on her cell from Brad Williams. He wanted to take her to dinner on Saturday night. She said that she'd go.

Beverly told her daughter about her date Saturday night.

"So, I guess he's not as nerdy as you originally thought. So DO tell, Mom."

"Well I think he was a little more relaxed the other night. He has a really good sense of humor. He was just really easy to talk to. He polished up really nicely in his tux."

"He's handsome then?"

"He's okay looking."

"Well, on a one to ten scale, where would you put him?"

"Oh, Erica, you're such a brat!" But Beverly was laughing.

"Well, on this scale, who would be a ten?"

"Let's just say, George Clooney," Erica said.

"Okay, I guess he's a six or seven, then. He's very tall, dark brown hair, and brown eyes."

"I guess he's a 6.5 then. Well where would Dad be on this scale?"

"Oh, that is so unfair! Your father was always a ten, at least to me."

"If you're going out with Dr. 6.5 on Saturday, is it okay if I go out with Dwight?"

"Sure, I'll just need to know the details." That night Beverly had a very erotic dream. She was on the couch in Dr. Martino's office, but she was with George Clooney. Tom walked in and said, "Bev, it's time to go. Is Erica's game at six or is it at seven?"

Chapter 15

Erica was very excited about Saturday night. It was Dwight's birthday this weekend. He had practice Saturday morning, and he had to work Saturday afternoon until six. Erica wanted to take him out to dinner after he got out of work. She asked him at school on Friday. Their plans were all set.

She was taking him to her favorite Italian restaurant. Dwight loved Italian food. She already bought him a gift. The basketball players always had to wear a shirt and tie to school on game days. Erica bought him a light blue Ralph Lauren button down shirt and a maroon tie. She thought it looked really sharp. Dwight was turning eighteen. His mom was having a family dinner for him on Sunday. Dwight already asked her to come. Erica was so excited. She would be with Dwight most of the weekend.

Beverly was getting ready for her date with Brad after she got home from the shop. Erica wandered into her room. "Mom, do we have any wrapping paper?"

"There's some in the cabinet in the mud room, top shelf. What did you buy Dwight?"

Erica showed her mother the gift for Dwight. Beverly agreed that it was a really nice shirt and a beautiful tie. She thought he would like it. "Tell him happy birthday for me. You're going to Portofino for dinner, right?"

"Yeah, he loves Italian. I love their lasagna there. Where are you and Dr. 6.5 going?"

"Erica, are you always going to refer to Brad as Dr. 6.5?" Beverly couldn't help but laugh. "I think we're going to the new restaurant that they opened in the art gallery."

"Well, you look nice Mom." The door bell rang and Erica ran down to get the door.

Brad introduced himself to Erica and took a seat in the living room.

Erica went back upstairs. "Mom, for a guy his age, I think you could maybe give him a solid seven. He does seem a little nerdy...very conservative, but still pretty nice."

"Whatever. You and Dwight have a nice time. Please be home by curfew, midnight, okay?"

Beverly and Brad talked easily during dinner. She told him a lot about her life with Tom when he was alive, and how difficult it was making the transition to being single again. She told him how she was struggling with being the only parent to a teenage daughter. She didn't talk about Erica's relationship with Dwight. She wasn't ready to go there yet.

"Beverly, your daughter is beautiful, and really quite charming. I could see that she was really sizing me up. Unfortunately, my ex and I never had any children. She never really wanted children, and I didn't push the issue. As it turns out, she only cared about what SHE wanted, and in the end she didn't want me. I think she just wanted to be married to a doctor, and then she got bored with me. But I don't want to bore you."

"I guess we all have our baggage, Brad." She told him that she had another child that died. She told him all about Johnny.

"Beverly, you have certainly had a lot to deal with. I'm glad that you are sharing this with me and letting me get to know you."

They went to the bar for a night cap. Brad had a scotch and Beverly had an Irish coffee. She and Tom always had a fondness for Irish coffee. She hadn't had one in a very long time. It made her feel very warm inside.

Brad took her home and kissed her lightly on the lips when he brought her to the door. "I really enjoyed your company tonight, Beverly." He kissed her again. "Goodnight."

"Thank you, Brad, I had a lovely evening. Take care."

I really did have a nice time, Beverly thought. Erica wasn't home yet, it was a little before midnight. Beverly kicked off her shoes and turned on the television. She'd wait up for Erica.

Dwight had borrowed his mother's car that night. Erica told him about a good place they could park for awhile. It was getting harder for her to resist Dwight, because she liked him so much and was so turned on. They were still taking it kind of slow. He knew she wasn't quite ready to go any further, but it was killing him.

106

Dwight dropped Erica off in time for her to make curfew. "My mom said to come over at about four tomorrow, see you then, Babe."

Erica sat with her mom for awhile before she went up to bed. Beverly thought it was a good opportunity to talk to her about her relationship with Dwight. "So, tell me honey, what's going on with you and Dwight?"

"Mom, what do you mean?"

"Erica, I think we need to talk about your physical relationship with Dwight."

Erica cringed. This was a conversation she didn't want to have with her mother. It was so awkward. She would almost be more comfortable talking to Nana about this.

"Mom, we aren't having sex, if that's what you mean."

"Honey, I don't think that someone your age is really ready to have sex, but I hope you know I would listen and we could talk about it. It's a very big step."

"Relax, we aren't there yet." She headed up to bed.

Oh God, thought Beverly. *I can't believe I just opened that door with Erica. I hope she will be able to let down her guard and talk to me.* Then she thought about her own sex life. *I'm so not ready, either. Will I ever be able to be with someone after Tom? If I continue to see Brad, I'm sure it will become an issue. Tom, why did you leave us?* Beverly was crying now. She knew she would have a very restless night. There was always too much on her mind.

Dwight found his mother downstairs in the kitchen when he got up. She was busy cooking.

"Happy birthday, baby, I can't believe my son is eighteen years old today! I'm so proud of you, Dwight, you are such a good son."

Dwight kissed is mother. "Thank you, Mom. Whatever you are cooking smells so good."

"It's the pulled pork, slow-cooking. You had better get yourself something to eat and get showered for church."

Dwight poured himself a bowl of cereal and flipped through the paper to the sports section.

Ruby thought it was a good opportunity to talk to him for a few minutes about his father. She didn't want him to find out about the parole hearing from someone else or read about it in the paper. "Dwight, I need to tell you something. I got a letter from your father. He is up for parole. He says if he gets out, he wants to come back and try to make us a family again. How do you feel about that, son?"

"Ma, I can't let him hurt you or mess with your feelings. That's just not fair. He's never been any kind of father to me, and the girls don't even know him. Things are going good for us now. My vote is no. Do you still love him, Mom?"

"No. I just don't want to deprive you of having a relationship with your father... if that's want you want."

"Like I said, he's not much of a father. Ma, let's just let it be. I really don't want to see him."

"Okay, baby. That's alright."

Dwight kissed his mother again on the cheek. "I love you, Mom. I'm going to get into the shower now."

Ruby felt relieved. *He is such a good boy,* she thought.

Ruby and her kids sat in their usual pew for church services. She decided to take Reverend James' advice and go to coffee hour. She saw Michelle there with her bother. They were talking to Reverend James and his wife. Reverend James saw Ruby and winked. He said, "Michael, there's someone I want you to meet." He brought him over to where Ruby was standing and made the introductions.

Ruby thought he was very good-looking. He told her how he was new to Rochester and was just starting to get to know some people. Right now, he really just knew people he worked with at school. They chatted easily for a while. *He is very easy-going,* thought Ruby. *He's not at all cocky. I wouldn't mind going out with this man, but Lord, would it just complicate my life?* Dwight was talking to one of his friends and the girls were with Sarah's kids.

"Ruby, would you mind if I called you to go out sometime?"

"She smiled. You know, Michael, I'm really busy trying to juggle work, school, and my kids right now, but I'd really like that. Give me a call, and I'll try to make it work." Michael got out his phone and put in Ruby's number. "Well alright, then, I'll be calling you."

He's pretty hot, thought Ruby as he walked away. *I'll just have to make the time to go out with him if he calls.*

Beverly insisted on dropping Erica off at Dwight's for his party. It would be dark when it was time for her to leave. Dwight would drive her home. Beverly was still very nervous about her daughter being in that neighborhood, especially after dark.

There was a houseful at the Washington's when Erica arrived. Besides Ms. Washington and the twins, there was Dwight's aunt and uncle and their four kids. One of Dwight's friends, Marcus, was also there. Dwight introduced Erica to everyone. His Aunt Sarah and Uncle Henry were really nice. His uncle was a fireman. His aunt ran an in-home children's day care. Marcus seemed a little rough around the edges, but he was nice. Dwight's mom really put on a nice spread. Everything was delicious. She made pulled pork, mac and cheese, collard greens, and cornbread.

Erica brought her plate into the kitchen. "Ms. Washington, you are a great cook. I've never had collard greens before, they were great. Is there anything I can help you with?"

"My sister, Sarah, made the cake. Dwight likes this chocolate cake she makes. If you like chocolate, and who doesn't, you will love this cake, too. It's crazy good. You can help me with the candles. I'll get the ice cream. That shirt and tie you got him are really so nice. He loved your gift. He told me how he has to wear a shirt and tie on game days, and he will wear them Friday for the first game."

"Will you be able to come on Friday?" Erica asked.

"Oh, I wouldn't miss it, honey. I'm hoping to get to as many games as I can." Erica thought Dwight's mother was starting to warm up to her a little bit.

After cake, Dwight opened up presents. The party was starting to break up. Marcus took off, and Sarah and Henry started to round up their kids. Dwight's oldest cousin was about fifteen. Her name was Tamika. The other kids were younger and were playing with the twins. They were really cute. The younger kids were all pretty wound up and were running all over the house. Tamika was not at all friendly. She looked at Erica in a way that made her feel like she didn't belong there. Everyone else was so nice and welcoming. *I guess I can't expect everyone to like me, or approve of me and Dwight together,* thought Erica.

Dwight got his mom's car keys to take her home. "Thank you so much, Ms. Washington, for inviting me. I'll see you Friday."

They went to their parking spot along the canal and made out a little in the car before Dwight brought her home.

"Erica, I can't tell you how much you mean to me. I was so proud of you tonight. I can't believe that I'm lucky enough to have you for a girlfriend." Erica saw the tender look in his eyes. She thought his eyes looked a little watery.

"Dwight, you've made my life worth living since my father died, so I feel the same way." Now she had a lump in her throat.

He gave her one last very tender kiss and started the car. Once they got to her house, he walked her to the door. "See you tomorrow, Babe."

When Erica walked in she could see that her mother had been playing her violin. That usually helped her relax. She told Beverly all about Dwight's party.

"Did you feel out of place at all?" Beverly was very curious, as she thought that Erica was probably the only guest there that was white.

"No, not really, but he has a girl cousin a little younger than me who wasn't at all friendly. Everyone else couldn't have been nicer." Beverly was also curious about the menu. Erica told her that everything was delicious, but she thought it was probably "soul food". She told her about the collard greens.

Beverly laughed. "I'm glad you had a good time, honey. Is Ruby going to the game on Friday?"

"She's planning on it. Maybe you can sit together."

"That will be fine. I think Helen is coming, also. I hope Ruby brings the twins. Helen got such a kick out of the girls at Thanksgiving." Erica was so excited about the beginning of basketball season.

Beverly thought that her life was finally starting to even out a little.

Pam was doing a really great job with managing the shop. Beverly felt much less stressed. She had hired a few new part time workers, so sometimes Beverly only went in for part of the day. She got to the shop a little after eleven on Monday morning. "There was a special delivery for you this morning," said Pam.

"What was that?"

"These beautiful roses, here is the card." The roses were a really pretty salmon color. They were from Brad. The card said, "Thank you for having dinner with me. I enjoyed your company, Brad."

"I guess you have an admirer, Bev. Tell me about him."

Beverly told Pam about her date with Brad. Pam knew about her asking Brad to the event for the cancer center. She never really said much about that night, so Pam didn't want to pry.

"I don't know, Pam. The more I get to know him, the better I like him. He's such a gentleman and so unassuming. I know it's just too early to start a relationship right now. I don't need any complications in my life."

"Does it have to be complicated?" asked Pam. "Does he have any kids?"

"No, he's divorced, but never had kids. I just haven't dated in so long. I just don't know if I'm ready."

"Just take it slow," Pam said. "You're going to find that there just aren't many single men in their forties or fifties without an agenda. Most of them are looking for younger women. If he's nice why not give him a chance?"

"I will, for now. Erica seems okay with it. She actually encouraged me to go out with him. Dwight has been very good for her. She's softened up a lot lately."

On Thursday, Beverly had her appointment with Dr. Martino. He asked if Brad had called. Beverly told him about her date and the flowers he had sent.

"He must be very interested in you. Men don't send flowers to women if they don't think the relationship will go anywhere."

"What are you saying?" Beverly knew what he was implying, and she couldn't believe they were going to talk about this.

"Well, if you continue to see him, I'm sure your relationship will become more intimate. Are you ready for that?"

"I don't know. Tom was the love of my life. It feels disloyal to want another man. But I do know that I miss being with a man. It's really still so soon though. Brad is very considerate. I don't think he'll pressure me in any way."

"Beverly, you're still young. Your Tom is never coming back. You can fall in love again. People do it all the time. I think you'll know when it's right. Now tell me about you daughter and how things are going with her."

Beverly and Dr. Martino had a discussion about teenage sexuality. He said that it was good that she was able to have a discussion about sex with her daughter. For a lot of parents, it is out of their comfort zone.

"Beverly, I know you don't think so, but you are really doing well navigating the rough waters. I think we had a very good session this week."

On Friday, Dwight met Erica at her locker to walk her to first period Chem. Erica thought he looked really hot in the shirt and tie that she bought him. They walked in together. She could feel a lot of eyes on them. She still was not confident that everyone was accepting of her relationship with Dwight. She was determined that thoughts like these wouldn't dampen her spirits today. She couldn't wait to watch Dwight play tonight. She tried to concentrate on Mr. Novak's pop quiz.

The gym was really crowed for the first game of the season. Beverly and Helen got there early. They saved some seats for Ruby and the girls. Beverly saw Ruby and the twins walk in. Ruby scanned the crowd. She spotted Beverly and Beverly motioned her to come over. "Hi, Ruby. Hi, girls. Are you all excited about the game tonight?"

"I know I am," said Ruby. I know Dwight's a little nervous. I hope he plays well."

The cheerleaders did their opening cheer and the starting players for the game were introduced. Beverly could see the proud look on Ruby's face when her son was announced. Beverly couldn't help but feel proud for her. They stood for the national anthem. Dwight stood next to his opponent for the jump ball and the game began. Dwight scored his first basket in the first thirty seconds of the game. He was now being heavily guarded. The opposing team quickly realized he was a threat. Ruby was very vocal during the game. She was really enjoying it. By the end of the first half, Dwight had already racked up eleven points, three at the foul line.

"This is so much fun!" Helen said. "Ruby, you must be so proud of your son. He is really a fine athlete."

"My boy has always loved basketball. I'm hoping it will be his ticket to college."

You could tell the girls were thrilled to be there. Their eyes lit up when the cheerleaders did some of their more gymnastic cheers. All that throwing of girls up in the air made Beverly a little nervous. It was a wonder that there weren't more injuries. Erica loved it. She waved to them all after her last cheer.

It was very fast moving game and it seemed like it was over in no time. They won 58 to 51. Dwight had 18 points. Erica was ecstatic. Beverly and Ruby gave each other a hug. "That was awesome!" exclaimed Ruby. "They just don't have the money to put so much into sports programs in the city schools," she said. "I'm so glad Dwight has the opportunity to play here."

"Well, he certainly has talent," said Beverly. Ruby said that she really needed to get going, as she had to work the next day. They all said their goodbyes. Beverly knew Erica and Dwight were going out after the game.

She found Erica outside the gym and gave her a big hug. "Oh, honey, you must be so proud of Dwight tonight! Your squad looked great too. The cheers were perfect. Your back flips were awesome."

"Thanks, Mom. I'll be home by curfew."

Mr. Novak was out and about talking to some of the parents and students, and receiving lots of congratulatory praise. He saw Erica. "Wow, Dwight is good! We are so lucky to have him."

Dwight finally emerged from the locker room. He spotted Erica immediately and hugged her. She could smell his soap. Everyone was high-fiving and congratulating him. He looked very proud, but was also very modest in accepting all the praise.

They went out with Christy and Ben for pizza. Erica really wanted to be alone with Dwight, but that wasn't going to work out tonight. Ben was going to give him a ride home.

Erica got call from Dwight just as she was getting into bed. "I just wanted to say goodnight. I love you, Babe."

"I love you, too. Goodnight." Erica couldn't believe she had just said it.

Chapter 16

Erica got up the next morning feeling so happy. She had the best boyfriend in the world. Then she thought about Christmas. It would be here in three weeks. They managed to get through Thanksgiving, but what about Christmas? Her dad was all about Christmas. He liked to go all out for the holidays. So did Mom. This was the weekend they usually got their tree and it was always huge! *I can't believe how my mood just turned upside down,* she thought. Her mom had already left for the shop. She knew Dwight had to work. She thought that maybe she and Dwight could do something when he got out of work. She called him and left a message. He called her back on his break. He was getting out at one o'clock, and would be free then. He wanted to take her ice skating. Erica loved the idea. Erica would pick him up at Wegmans, have lunch there at the café, and then head out to the skating rink. It was an outdoor rink right in downtown Rochester. Her dad sometimes took her there, but she hadn't been there in a long time.

She took a shower and decided to stop over to her grandmother's for coffee. Erica stopped at a bakery in the village and picked up some cinnamon rolls. They were Nana's favorite.

Helen was very happy to see her granddaughter at her door. They talked about the game and how Dwight was such a great athlete. "He's an amazing boyfriend, Nana."

"I'm so glad it's working out for you, honey. Are your friends more accepting of your relationship? I think your mother is."

"Most of the kids at school are pretty cool with it. Mom's been okay, too. Did you know she's seeing someone?"

"No, really, I'm surprised she's ready for that. Your mother is still young. I'm sure your father would want her to get on with her life. But still, she always said that Tom was the love of her life. The sun rose and set on your father, as far as she was concerned. Have you met him?"

"I have. He seems okay, but not at all like Dad. Oh, Nana, our lives have changed so much since September, and so fast. Can you believe that it's almost Christmas?"

"I know, honey. I guess we will just have to lower our expectations a little this year. It will probably be a little difficult. But look, we got through Thanksgiving just fine."

Erica and Dwight met up at the café in Wegmans and bought their lunch. Erica loved the market salad at Wegmans. Dwight loved their meatball subs. It seemed like Dwight had a lot of friends at work.

When they were leaving the store, walking out to the parking lot, they saw a very ugly incident occur. There was a guy with Down's syndrome that worked at Wegmans. His name was Gary. His job was to help people put their groceries in their car, and also to round up and return the grocery carts. Some kids took a cart and slammed into Gary hard enough to knock him down. They yelled, "Hey retard, you forgot a cart!" They ran to their car and took off. Gary was very upset. His glasses fell off and were broken. He was crying.

Dwight ran over and helped him up. "Hey, Gary," he said, "it's okay. Those guys are a bunch of ignorant jerks. Some people are mean for no reason. Are you okay?"

"I guess so. I just don't know why they did that. My glasses are broken now. How can I work? Will the manager be mad at me?"

Dwight took Erica aside. "Would it be okay if we gave him a ride home?" She said that it was fine. She was appalled by what happened.

"Come on, Gary," Dwight said. He gave Gary a hug. "I'll go and talk to Mr. Smith with you." They went back into the store and found the manager in the office. Dwight explained to him what happened. Gary was still very upset. Mr. Smith told Gary he could take the rest of his shift off and he would still pay him.

Dwight introduced Erica to his boss. "We'll take Gary home and I'll tell his mother what happened to upset him so much."

"Is that okay, Gary?" asked Mr. Smith.

"Oh, yes, I know Dwight is my friend."

"Thanks for helping out with this situation, Dwight."

"It's okay. No problem."

Erica watched Dwight walk Gary up to his house. He had a protective arm about his shoulders. She saw him talking to Gary's mother at the door. *That's why I love him so much*, Erica thought. *He is the kindest, most gentle guy I've ever known.* She kissed him when he got back in the car. "Oh Dwight, you were so good with Gary. Not everyone would have taken the time to do what you did. I just love you for that."

Erica and Dwight had a great afternoon skating. It was a beautiful afternoon... sunny and just the right temperature. Dwight had to stay at home with the twins that night. His mom had a date. Erica was planning on starting her Christmas shopping. She and Christie were going to the mall. Erica felt kind of guilty that she hadn't been spending much time with her best friend since she met Dwight. Her mother was going somewhere with Dr. Williams.

"Does your mom date a lot?" asked Erica.

"No, never," said Dwight. "I'm glad she is tonight, though. She never has time to do anything for herself. He's some dude she met at church. He seems okay." Dwight told Erica about the conversation he had with his mother about his father maybe being paroled.

"I just don't want to see my mother hurt. We are doing just fine without him. I kind of hope his parole is denied. My Uncle Henry has been more of a father to me and the girls then he ever was. Do you think that's cold of me, Babe, hoping he doesn't get out?"

"I think you have a right to your feelings and I think you, and your mom, and the girls deserve better."

I can't even imagine would it would be like having a father in prison, thought Erica.

Beverly and Brad were going to dinner with Peter and Susan Dwyer.

When Beverly and Susan were in the ladies room, Susan asked her how it was going with Brad.

"The more I get to know him, the more I like him. He's nothing like Tom of course, but he's really very nice."

"Well, I can tell he's very smitten with you, Bev."

"Bev, we have that committee meeting for the cancer center on Wednesday. Rebecca Goldstein wants the three of us to go to lunch after. Would you consider it?"

"Oh, Susan, you know she's not my favorite person. She's such a busy-body. I have kind of been avoiding her since Tom died. She left me messages that I've never returned. I guess if I bite the bullet and go to lunch with her, maybe she'll leave me alone. I'm only doing it because you'll be there."

"It will be okay," said Susan.

After dinner, Brad invited them all over to his house for a night cap. "Your house is really very nice. Whoever decorated it has really nice taste." Beverly told him.

"Oh, that would be my sister. She came in from New York and took pity on her brother. We went shopping."

"Well, I love it," said Beverly. "I think that you must have helped, because it seems like your place really reflects your style, too."

The Dwyer's left, so Beverly and Brad were now alone.

They sat together on the couch and Brad reached for her and held her in his arms. His kisses were much more passionate than ever before. They ended up in Brad's bedroom. Beverly hadn't made love to a man other than Tom since she was twenty-four years old, but it was okay. It was more than okay. It was really good.

"Are you okay with all of this, Beverly?"

"I think so, Brad, but it was really a big step for me."

"I'm so happy that I was the lucky guy." They got dressed and he drove her home.

"Beverly, I've got to speak at a neurosurgery conference in New York City next Friday. Would you consider going with me next weekend? I love New York at Christmastime. We could maybe go to a show and do some shopping."

Beverly was really caught off guard. *Oh my God,* she thought, *that's really a big deal, but I can't believe I just slept with him! It does sound nice, though.*

"Can I let you know tomorrow or Monday?"

"Sure. No pressure. I just thought it would be fun."

Should I be feeling guilty about sleeping with Brad, she wondered. *Oh God, if Erica found out. If I do go to New York, and I kind of want to go, what will I tell Erica? There are some designers I was planning on meeting to order some merchandise for the shop. Maybe I could do that when Brad's speaking at the conference. I'll miss the basketball game on Friday. That's not such a big deal, because I think it's an away game.* She and Erica were planning on getting their Christmas tree tomorrow. She would talk to her about New York. She wasn't going to tell her she was going with Brad, though.

Erica was in a pretty good mood when she came down for breakfast. Beverly made Erica her favorite ham and cheddar cheese omelet. "Honey, I am thinking about going to New York City on Friday to meet with some new designers and do some buying for the shop. I haven't done it in a very long time. I'd come back on Sunday. Would that be okay with you?

"That's fine, Mom, I've got the game on Friday and I'll probably do something with Dwight on Saturday. I'm sure Nana would love it if I stayed with her. She mentioned she was going to bake some Christmas cookies next weekend. I love baking with Nana. Just go."

They got their tree that afternoon. It was not as big as usual, but it was still a nice tree. They ordered Chinese food and decorated the tree that night. They put on some Christmas music. Neither one of them felt much like talking.

Finally, Erica said, "Mom, how are we going to have Christmas without Dad?"

"I'm sure it will be very different. We've come a long way. We'll just have to get through it. Look, we put the tree up and I think it looks beautiful!"

Erica kissed her mother and told her she was going up to her room to do a little studying before she went to bed. Beverly poured herself a glass of Merlot and gave Brad a call. He was thrilled that she was going. He told her that he would get tickets for the first flight out Friday morning. He was scheduled to speak at eleven.

"Beverly, are you okay with sharing a hotel room?"

Her heart skipped a beat. "Sure, Brad, that will be fine. I told Erica this was a buying trip and that's really partly true. That's what I'll be doing when you're at the conference. I'll meet you at the airport Friday morning. I'm not telling her that we will be together this weekend. I'm not sure she would be ready to hear that."

"I understand. That's fine. I'll email you the flight information. I'm so happy you're going with me."

Pam was doing a great job managing the shop. She did all the holiday decorating. It looked great. She was very surprised when Beverly told her about her plans for the weekend.

"Good for you. I know it's a big step, but you deserve a little fun. He sounds like a really nice guy. We'll be fine here."

As promised, Beverly had lunch with Susan Dwyer and Rebecca Goldstein after their committee meeting on Wednesday. She was so not looking forward to it.

"So," said Rebecca, "I hear you've been seeing a lot of Brad Williams."

"Well, yes, we've been out a few times, but I wouldn't say I been seeing him a lot."

"Whatever, Beverly, it seems like you and your daughter are doing just fine in the romance department."

"Oh come on, Rebecca, I know Rachael has a boyfriend. Do you have a problem with Erica seeing Dwight or me seeing Brad?"

"No, I'm just surprised, that's all." Beverly was starting to feel really annoyed now.

Susan wasn't sure what this conversation was really about, but she felt the tension between the two women.

"Look, Rebecca, if you have something to say, just say it."

"Well, your family isn't so perfect, is it Bev? You're letting your daughter date some inner-city black kid, and your husband has been dead for only three months and you're already with someone else."

"Why does that bother you?" asked Susan.

"Susan, do you think Beverly knows that her perfect husband was screwing one of the pediatric residents?"

"Rebecca, I've never heard that!" Susan said. "What's wrong with you? Just shut up!"

"I'm sorry to ruin your lunch, Beverly. I just thought you should know the truth." She got up and left.

120

"Susan, is that really true what she said about Tom?"

"Oh, honey, I doubt it. Peter would have said something to me. Rebecca is just a bitch. I guess I just never realized it until today."

"So, what's going on with Erica?"

"She does have a new boyfriend, and he is black. He's one of the urban-suburban students. He's really a nice kid. He's her study partner in chemistry and he's also on the basketball team. It took a while to get used to, but now I really like him. He makes Erica very happy."

"Well, this lunch was a disaster, Bev. I'm so sorry about everything that Rebecca said."

"I'm going to try and forget it.

Beverly was glad she had her appointment with Dr. Martino the next day. She would need a lot of help recovering from the beating she just got. She couldn't sleep that night. *Could it be true what Rebecca said?* Beverly felt like her life was spinning out of control. Yesterday she had felt so confident. She and Erica got through putting the tree up without Tom, and she was happy that she had just started a relationship with a really nice man. She was accepting the reality that Tom was gone and she and her daughter were making a new life. *Why would Rebecca say something like that? What did she know?*

Dr. Martino could see how upset his patient was today. "So tell me everything," he said. The tears started and Beverly couldn't stop crying. She was trembling. First she told him about what Rebecca said.

"This woman sounds very vindictive. Why would she want to say something so hurtful do you think?"

"I'm not sure. She has a daughter who is the same age as Erica. Rebecca has always been into comparing the two girls. Her daughter has some serious problems... an eating disorder. Erica is just more easy going and more well-rounded. I guess that bothers her. I've always had the sense that her marriage isn't that great, either. I don't think her husband pays much attention to her. He is a very dedicated oncologist. He's a very nice guy, but he spends all his time at the hospital with his patients. Rebecca always seemed a little envious of what Tom and I had. She doesn't work or have a career. She has a lot of time on her hands. I don't know. I guess she's just not very happy. I've never liked her and maybe it shows."

"Hey, we don't have to like everyone. That's no excuse for her to be so mean. Anyone with any sensitivity would know that you are very fragile right now. True or not, this isn't the time to bring it to your attention. I think the problem is you're wondering if it could be true. Am I right?"

"Of course it is. No one wants to hear that their spouse is cheating. I'm not naïve. I know things like that go on all the time at the hospital. I also know that rumors are always floating around. I just can't believe it could be true. Tom and I were very tight. I think I'd sense it. Tom was very principled. But why would she bring that up out of the blue?"

"Maybe she heard a rumor. That doesn't mean it was true. If it was true, does it change how you feel about Tom? Would you have forgiven him?"

"Oh, I think I would have. I don't think I could ever stop loving him."

"Let it go then. So, let's move on to the new man in your life. What's going on there?"

She told Dr. Martino about her plans for New York.

"Good for you, Beverly. You're forty-four years old. There's time for new love in your live. I have to say, I'm glad you took this next step in your relationship with Brad before that women accused Tom of his affair. I wouldn't have wanted you to take that step feeling hurt or as a payback for some supposed infidelity of Tom's. Tom's gone, Beverly, and it sounds like he loved you very much. He would want you to be happy. You have a wonderful time in New York."

She was planning on doing just that.

Dwight continued to excel on the court. He racked up eighteen points in Friday's game. Erica couldn't be more proud of him or more in love with him. He was working on Saturday, but they had plans to go out Saturday night. She was going to bake Christmas cookies with Nana during the day. Her grandmother said that she had lasagna in the freezer and Dwight could come over for dinner before the movies. Her lasagna was awesome. Erica was really looking forward to her day.

122

Dwight brought Helen a poinsettia when he came over that night. He always knew just the right thing to do. He couldn't stop raving about the lasagna, and he ate three pieces. Nana just laughed. "I miss feeding growing boys," she said.

After the movie, Erica said, "Dwight, we can go over to my house for a little while. Remember, my mom's in New York?" They didn't get the chance to be really alone that often.

When they got to the McIntyres' house, Erica turned on the Christmas tree lights and flicked on the flame in the gas fireplace. "We usually have lights up outside, but it probably won't happen this year. I guess I have to accept that Christmas will be different." Erica loved classic rock and roll. She and her Dad listened to music from the sixties and seventies all the time. She put on her favorite James Taylor album. Her Dad played the classics on a turntable. He had a pretty extensive vinyl collection. Dwight was intrigued. The music and soft lights really set a mood. They started making out, of course. Things were getting pretty heavy. Erica had such strong feelings for Dwight. She really wanted him. She thought she was ready.

"Babe, we're going kind of far here. Is this what you want?"

"Dwight, come on, let's go up to my room. I think I want you to make love to me."

"Erica, you know how I feel about you. I would never do anything to hurt you. Are you sure?"

He knew it was probably her first time. He tried to take it slow.

Afterward, Dwight just held her in his arms. He was so tender. Erica felt so peaceful and so complete. He kissed her and just kept stroking her hair. Dwight loved her hair. It smelled sweet, and was soft, and silky... just like her.

"Babe, as much as I wanted you, we've got to be more careful than we were tonight. I pulled out, but next time we'd better use a condom. I just wasn't prepared tonight."

"Oh my God," Erica gasped, "I got so carried away I didn't even think of that! We'll be more responsible next time." Erica remembered hearing that you couldn't get pregnant the first time you did it. She hoped it was true, but she really knew better.

They laid there in each other's arms. She didn't want the night to end. At midnight they got dressed, turned off the lights and the fireplace, and locked the door. Erica drove Dwight to his bus stop.

"You know I love you, Babe," he said. "Tonight was very special to me."

"I love you, too." She drove back to her grandmother's house. Nana was already in bed. She was so happy that she made love with Dwight, but she was a little nervous too. *I better wash those sheets before Mom gets home tomorrow.* She grabbed a handful of cookies and went up to bed. Once she did fall asleep, she slept very soundly.

Her mother slept very soundly, too, in the arms of Brad Williams.

The next morning, Erica got a call from Dwight. "Babe, get out those Christmas lights, I'll be over about one o'clock to put them up." He pulled up with his sisters and they got the outside of the house decorated. It looked awesome. When Beverly's cab pulled up, it was already dark. She noticed the lights right away.

"Erica, I'm home! Who did the lights?"

"Mom, Dwight came over and did it. Wasn't that just so nice?"

"Oh, sweetheart, it really was."

On Monday, another flower delivery came to the shop. This time it was red roses. The note just said, "Merry Christmas, it was a wonderful weekend, Brad."

Beverly smiled. *Maybe Christmas won't be so bad after all.*

Chapter 17

Back on the other side of town, things were going well for Ruby, too. At the end of December she would be done with all her pre-requisite courses, and in January could start the real nursing classes. She knew they would be easier than the science and math courses because she had already been taking care of patients for five years. She knew her way around the hospital. Her new nurse manager was much more supportive of her going to school, and was accommodating with Ruby's schedule. She already knew she had Christmas off this year, because she had worked Christmas last year and she worked Thanksgiving this year. She was taking the kids to visit her parents in Atlanta. Her father surprised her with airline tickets. Christmas was on a Saturday this year. It was less expensive to fly right on the holiday. They had tickets for the first flight out Christmas morning and would be in Atlanta in time for the eleven o'clock services at Daddy's church. They were coming home on Tuesday.

Ruby got another letter from Jerome. He said he was sorry, but his parole was denied. She wondered what he did. He probably got into some kind of trouble in prison. She wouldn't be surprised if he got into a fight. He has some real anger management issues. She was actually kind of relieved. She really didn't want him complicating her life, and Dwight was adamant about not wanting to see him. Ruby was so proud of her son. His grades were great and he was becoming a very popular student in his new school, thanks to basketball. She thought it was more than that, though, Dwight was just a really nice kid. Ruby got a letter from his boss at Wegmans telling her about the incident with Gary, a boy with Down's syndrome, and how Dwight had stepped in to help. She was so touched. Reading about it brought tears to her eyes. Dwight never said a thing. The letter also said that Dwight would be employee of the month.

And then there was Michael. Their first date was great. She was hoping that he would ask her out again. She thought that he would. Finding the time to go out was the real problem. She had finals coming up. She still had to get a Christmas tree and do a little shopping. She hated thinking about the shopping part, because money was so tight.

Every Christmas everyone who worked on her unit at the hospital got a hundred dollar bonus. She had a little money saved from all the overtime hours she had worked when staffing was short. All that didn't amount to much. Still, she would have gifts for her family.

Ruby talked to her son when he got home from basketball practice. She told him about the letter she got from his boss and how proud she was of him. Dwight didn't know about "employee of the month" yet, but he was thrilled. Employee of the month always got a $25 Visa gift card. He wanted to get a nice Christmas present for Erica. That would help. Mr. Smith didn't waste any time in getting that letter out. The incident with Gary had only happened Saturday.

Ruby told Dwight about going to Atlanta. He was disappointed that he wouldn't get to see Erica on Christmas Day. Maybe he could at least see her on Christmas Eve.

"Ma, I can take the girls out after dinner and pick up a Christmas tree. I checked out the trees the boy scouts are selling. They don't cost much. I've got some money. I'll buy it."

"Oh, Dwight, that would be a big help. I have news about your father. His parole was denied." A dark look came over her son's face.

"I really don't care," he said. "Like I told you before, he's not much of a father."

Life was too good for Dwight right now. His father was nothing but trouble. Dwight didn't want him messing up his life. He knew his father would be stoked to watch him play ball. He didn't have that many memories of his father, but he did remember going to the park with him when was probably about the same age as the twins. His father tried to teach him how to dribble and shoot baskets. *I wouldn't want him showing up at my school for a game,* Dwight thought. *Prison is a good place for him. I think Mama feels the same way. I'd love to have Uncle Henry watch me play. I'm going to get him a ticket for the next home game.*

Dwight knew he had to stay focused. Finals were coming up and he had a big game on Friday. He had so much going on, but had only Erica on his mind. He couldn't believe he had made love to her for the first time. It was sweet. He just wondered when they'd get the opportunity to be alone again. He couldn't wait to make it with her again. *I'm so in love with that girl. I better remember to get those condoms.*

He called her later that night. He wanted to talk to her about his father and also about his family's plans for Christmas.

"It sounds like you're kind of relieved about your father. I know you were kind of worried about seeing him if he got out. So, you won't be here Christmas Day?" Erica asked.

"No, but we'll just have to find a way to see each other on Christmas Eve."

"Oh God, I hope so. My mom and I haven't talked too much about what we're doing on Christmas. Are your nervous about the game on Friday? Baldwin's undefeated and they killed us last year."

"That's what Coach said. I'm not nervous though, basketball usually isn't something that gets me nervous. I'm more worried about that history test on Friday. I know my mom's got to work Friday night, so she won't get to the game. I think I'm going to get a ticket for my Uncle Henry."

"I think my mom's planning on going. Don't worry about the history test. Do you want to meet at the library tomorrow night and we can study together?"

"That's probably okay. I'll let you know tomorrow. Bye for now. Love you, Babe."

Dwight got a call from his friend, Marcus. He sounded pretty worked up.

"What's up, Dude?"

"Dee, you're not going to believe this, but Whitney's pregnant!"

"Are you serious, and you're the father?"

"So she says, and I believe her. I really don't think she's been with anybody else. You know I like her, but for sure, I don't want to be a daddy."

"So, what's she going to do?"

"She's talking about having an abortion. She said that she saw what happened to her sister when she had her first baby in high school and she doesn't want that. Her sister is only twenty-one and already has three kids."

"You okay with her having the abortion? It's your kid."

127

"Yeah, like I said, I don't want to be a daddy, but it's hard to think about her killing my baby. Dee, nobody else knows. Don't say anything, okay?"

"No, I won't tell anybody. Marcus, I'm here for you, man."

Dwight got off the phone, and his heart sank. He had been friends with Marcus since kindergarten. He felt bad that he didn't get to see him too much since he changed schools. Marcus wasn't a bad guy. He was still in school, and he stayed out of trouble. He smoked a little weed, but that was all. He felt bad that his friend got himself in this situation. Dwight sensed that his friend was confused and hurting. Marcus always tried to act tough, but he knew his friend was very sensitive. Whitney could be very mean. He never understood what Marcus saw in her. Dwight really didn't like her. He bet that she was putting a lot of pressure on Marcus. She only cared about herself.

Oh, sweet Jesus, he thought. *I can't let that happen to Erica and me.*

That night, Dwight had a very disturbing dream. He was shooting hoops at the playground where his father took him as a little boy. Whitney came by with a baby in a stroller. The baby looked just like Marcus and wouldn't stop crying. Whitney smacked him and gave him a bottle. "Where's Marcus at?" Dwight asked.

"You didn't hear? He's in prison for attempted murder. He says your daddy said to say 'hi'."

The next night at the library, Dwight still had trouble concentrating. He had so much on his mind.

"Dwight, what's wrong? You're not yourself tonight?"

"It's something I just can't share with you, but I'm okay. I'm just a little distracted, that's all. Let's go outside and get some air, maybe it will help."

Erica and Dwight walked around the block. The village looked so pretty, all decorated with tiny white lights. It was so clean and peaceful. He took Erica in his arms and kissed her. "I'm alright, Babe, I just needed to hold you a minute."

They stopped in the coffee shop and got hot chocolate to go and headed back to the library. *She's the most beautiful thing in my life,* he thought.

Beverly brought Brad to the game on Friday night. "Number 4 is an exceptional player," Brad said. "I love watching him play." Beverly hadn't told Brad about her daughter and her boyfriend from the inner city. It was probably about time she filled him in.

"Brad, that's Dwight Washington, my daughter's boyfriend. It's a relationship that was a little hard for me to get used to, but he's really a great kid."

Behind them there was a black man cheering loudly every time Dwight scored. "Yeah, that's my nephew, way to go boy!"

Beverly turned around. "Hi, I'm Beverly McIntyre. I think you've met my daughter, Erica."

"Yes ma'am. I'm Henry Barnes, Dwight's uncle. It's very nice to meet you. This is Vince Brown, a friend of mine from the fire department. Wow! I didn't know Dwight was this good."

Beverly introduced Brad, and they all got back to watching the game.

Erica was a little surprised to see her mother and Dr. Williams in the stands. She wasn't sure how she felt about it. *It should be my dad*, she thought. *I guess they're getting pretty tight.* She wasn't sure what Dwight's plans were after the game. She knew his uncle was at the game.

It was a real close game, but Ben scored a 3- pointer at the buzzer and they won. Christie was ecstatic. Dwight called her from the locker room after the game. He said that he was going to catch up with his uncle to thank him for coming to his game, and then he told her that he was going out with some of the other players. It was Coach Novak's birthday. They were all taking him out to some restaurant to celebrate. Erica was disappointed. She was hoping to spend time with him tonight. Her mom and Dr. Williams wanted to take her to get something to eat. It wasn't what she really wanted to do, but she was kind of curious about what was going on with her mother and Dr. Williams.

They decided on Chinese. They started out with spring rolls and pork dumplings. Erica ordered her favorite house lo mien. Dr. Williams was very reserved, but really very nice. Her mom seemed very relaxed. Erica noticed how she smiled at him from time to time. Maybe her mother was really starting to have feelings for this man. It seemed okay when Mom was just dating him, but if this was a real relationship, Erica wasn't sure how she felt about it. It was hard for her to wrap her head around it. Thinking about her mother being intimate with a man was just too much.

"Your school's team is really very good," Dr. Williams said. "I really enjoyed the game." Erica decided she'd drop a little bomb. "You know, Dr. Williams, number 4, Dwight Washington, is my boyfriend. Isn't he an awesome player?"

"Please call me Brad. What did he have, 15 points tonight? He is very good. The other team's defense really had a challenge with a player like Dwight tonight. Do you know how tall he is?"

Erica liked that he was taking an interest in Dwight, and he didn't register any shock that he was her boyfriend. Maybe Mom told him. "He's six foot five. His big dream is to get a basketball scholarship to a good college, maybe Syracuse."

"I definitely think that would be possible. I've got to say, as a neurosurgeon, I was a little uneasy watching you cheerleaders. I hope your coach puts safety before the show. "

"My dad would get a little uneasy, too. I don't know about anyone at my school having been injured."

Her mom wasn't saying too much. Erica had her own car. "Well, thanks," she said. "I'm really tired. I think I'm going to go home. Mom, do you need any help in the shop tomorrow?"

"That would be nice, honey, if you can spare the time. I'll see you at home."

Beverly and Brad went back to his place. Beverly told him about her ambivalent feelings regarding her daughter's relationship. Brad listened patiently, but he didn't really have much to say about it. He was more interested in what was going on between the two of them. Beverly wished she could stay at Brad's for the night. She really hated sleeping alone. Erica heard her mother come in. It was well after 1 AM. It confirmed her suspicions about her mother's relationship with Dr. Williams.

As promised, Erica helped her mother out at the shop. She was glad that she offered, because one of the women scheduled to work had called in sick. The shop was always busy at Christmas time.

Rachael Goldstein came in with her mother. "Hi, Rachael," Erica said, "There are some really cool jeans that just came in. Do you want to try anything on?" Rachael found some jeans and a few sweaters she wanted to try on and went to the fitting room. Mrs. Goldstein went over to talk to her mother. Erica tried to pick up on their conversation. Mrs. Goldstein was apologizing for something. Her mother looked very angry. "Really, Rebecca, I can't believe you came here to the shop to talk about this. I really don't want to discuss this with you today, or ever."

Rachael came out, Mrs. Goldstein paid for the jeans, and they took off.

Erica went over to her mother. "You look so upset. What was that all about?"

"She was just trying to apologize for some really rude comments she made when we were having lunch the other day."

"What did she say?"

"Honey, it's something you don't need to hear. It's probably just a lie anyways." Then her mom went to wait on a customer.

Dwight had to stay in with his sisters that night. Beverly and her daughter were going over to Helen's for dinner.

Beverly was happy to accept the invitation. She was tired after being up late last night with Brad and working all day at the shop. She could still feel some tension over her encounter with Rebecca. She wouldn't have to worry about dinner, and Erica would be happy to go. Helen had a way of bringing Erica around if she was troubled or in a bad mood.

Helen roasted a chicken. They had a lovely dinner. Helen broached the conversation about plans for the Christmas holidays. It was the elephant in the room. Beverly poured herself another glass of wine.

"You know I spoke to David this morning. He and Vicki and the kids are planning on coming up here for the Christmas holidays. I couldn't be happier. I miss my grandkids, and I haven't seen them all since Tom's funeral."

Oh Lord, thought Beverly, I hope they are planning on staying at Helen's. She adored her brother-in-law, but like Erica, she couldn't stand Vicki. David was four years younger than Tom. They had a daughter, ten, and a son, twelve. Beverly didn't have a problem with the kids. She always got a little lump in her throat around their son, Sean, because he and Johnny were the same age. They loved playing together. Their daughter, Holly, was very sweet, but that Vicki! She had something to say about everything. She kept David on a very short leash.

"Don't you worry Bev, they can all stay here."

"Oh, Nana," Erica whined. "How will we endure Aunt Vicki?"

Leave it to Erica to tell it like it is, thought Beverly, but she was smiling on the inside.

"Oh, honey, you've got to be used to Aunt Vicki after all these years," said Helen. "She doesn't mean half of what she says. She just doesn't have a very good filter."

"Well, I think she's a nasty bitch!" said Erica a little too loudly.

"ERICA! Now it's you that doesn't have a very good filter," Beverly said. "We don't have to like everybody, but she is family... Uncle David's wife, so we just have to try to accept her and do our best to get along with her."

Helen put her hand over Erica's. "Honey, you can choose your friends, but not your family. It will be a difficult Christmas for all of us. I'm sure Aunt Vicki realizes that, and she'll be fine. Now tell me, what are Dwight's plans for the holidays?"

"He's going to his grandparents in Atlanta. He will be here on Christmas Eve, though, because he's not flying out until Christmas morning."

"I can have sort of an open house on Christmas Eve," Beverly said. "Maybe Dwight can come over for a little while, anyway."

Maybe if I call it an "open house," I can get away with asking Brad too. I might even ask Pam to stop over. I'll make it work. I used to plan great parties. I can do it again.

"We can spend Christmas Day over here," Helen said. "I'll have to get a tree. Erica, will you help me with that? I'll have the tree delivered from the farm market, and maybe you can come over sometime next week and help me decorate it."

"Sure, Nana, I'd like that."

Chapter 18

Erica couldn't believe that it was only a week before Christmas. She still hadn't gotten Dwight's present. She didn't want to go overboard, because she knew he wouldn't be able to afford much for her. Erica saw a really handsome cashmere scarf at a men's store in the mall. She was thinking of getting it for him. It was so soft. It reminded her of his gentleness. She was also going to get him the James Taylor CD with the song that was playing before they made love for the first time. She wondered when they would be able to make love again. It was hard to find time to be alone, and she just wasn't going to make it with him in the back seat of a car. Then there was the birth control issue.

I probably should talk to Mom about this, but I'm really not ready to share this part of my life yet, even with Mom. I can't believe I haven't even told Christy. I guess condoms will be okay, because I'm sure we won't be able to do it much. It feels so special to be with him. I've got to find a way for us to be alone together before Christmas.

They had an away game that Friday night. She didn't think her Mom was going, and she knew Ms. Washington wasn't going, either. Erica hoped she and Dwight could go out after the game. Her mom was already at the house when she got home from school. She was letting Pam take charge of so much more at the shop. Normally, she would not have left until the shop closed.

"How was your day, honey?"

"It was okay, I guess. You know our game is away tonight, don't you?"

"I remember. I've already got something started for dinner so that you can get back to school for the bus. Brad has concert tickets and asked me to join him. We'll probably go out for a drink after."

"Mom, you and Brad seem pretty tight. What's going on with you two?"

"We're friends, Erica. It's nice to have male companionship. I'm with women all day at the shop. I miss your Dad so much. Without Brad, I would be really lonely."

Yeah, friends with benefits, Erica thought. Then she pushed the thought out of her head. She couldn't even think about her mother having sex with someone.

"Well, I'm happy for you, Mom."

"Erica, your father was the love of my life. I'll never stop loving him. You are alright with me seeing Brad, aren't you?"

"Mom, it's okay. It's just a little hard for me to get used to. It just seems so soon, that's all."

"Like I said, Erica, it's just a friendship."

Does Mom really think I'm that naïve? Whatever... I guess Mom has a right to her own life.

"Did I tell you that Dwight's mother met someone? He's a teacher. Dwight said that she's going to a Christmas party with him tonight. He said that his mom never dates, but he's happy for her."

"Ruby is still a young woman. I'm happy she met someone nice. I guess I'll see you later tonight then. What are your plans for tomorrow?"

"I can help you in the shop tomorrow if you need me, but Dwight and I are planning on studying for finals when he gets out of work at about two o'clock. Are you okay with that?"

"That's fine, honey. Good luck tonight, I've got to get changed."

As she was getting dressed for her evening with Brad, Beverly started feeling a little guilty. *Are things moving a little too quickly and a little too soon for Brad and me?* She had a sense that Erica knew they were sleeping together. *Oh God,* she thought. *How can I expect my daughter to keep sex out of the equation, if I can't?* She worried about Erica having sex with Dwight. *Would she come to her and talk about it? No, probably not.*

Beverly suddenly became very overwhelmed. Just when she thought she was doing okay and surviving life without Tom, she'd get hit by a wave. She was crying now. *God, I wish it was a normal Christmas! I wish it was Tom that I was going to a concert with. We would come home and make love in my own bedroom, and we could talk about our daughter's relationship with her new boyfriend.*

Her crying made a mess of her makeup. She did some quick repairs. She heard Brad pull in.

"Beverly, you look beautiful tonight, but I can tell you've been crying. Tell me about it," he said. He held her.

Beverly just couldn't talk about it with him. "I'm okay," she said. "I was just having a moment."

"It kills me to see you so unhappy."

"I don't think unhappy is the right word. Sometimes I just get overwhelmed by all the changes in my life, and it IS Christmas. Nothing seems right this year."

"Come on. We'll relax and listen to some good music. Later, I'm hoping I can take your mind off your troubles."

She did enjoy the concert. She knew some of the violin players. Beverly told Brad that she was a fairly accomplished violinist.

"You never cease to amaze me. Will you play for me some time?"

"I will."

"Can you come back to my place for a little while?" he asked.

Beverly checked her watch. It was only ten o'clock. She didn't want to stay out too late, because she wasn't sure what Erica and Dwight were up to. She also didn't want Erica to be suspicious about what she and Brad were doing. *God*, she thought. *This is getting complicated.*

Brad opened a very nice bottle of champagne. He had also bought fresh strawberries and chocolates.

After their second glass of champagne they ended up in bed.

"I wasn't sure if I'd get to see you over Christmas, and I just wanted tonight to be a little special."

"What are your plans?" she asked.

"I'll be here in Rochester. I offered to take call."

"I'm having an open house on Christmas Eve. Do you think maybe you can stop over?"

"If I can, I'd love to." He reached over to open the drawer in his night stand, and he pulled out a small wrapped package.

"Merry Christmas, Beverly, open your present."

She couldn't believe he got her a present. He was just too nice. Beverly thought he was really pushing their relationship forward, maybe a little too

135

quickly. He bought her a pair of beautiful gold earrings that he had seen her admire in New York. He had called the store and had them mailed to him.

"Oh, thank you, Brad. You know I love them, but you shouldn't have."

"Just enjoy them. It's so nice having a beautiful woman I can buy a gift for."

She kissed him. "I so wish I could stay longer, Brad, but I have to get home. I'm not sure what Erica is up to tonight, and I want to make sure she makes curfew. You know I'd stay if I could."

He laughed and kissed her again. "I'll take whatever I can get." He got dressed and drove her home.

Erica was in the kitchen eating popcorn when she came in. They talked about the game, and Beverly told her about the concert. For sure, she didn't want to show her daughter the earrings.

"Mom, is it okay if Dwight and I study here tomorrow afternoon? Sometimes the library is really noisy on Saturdays. There are always a lot of little kids there on Saturday. Maybe he can stay and have dinner with us. Is that okay?"

"I don't see why not. I've had a really long day. I'm going to turn in. Goodnight, honey."

The shop was really busy on Saturday... it being one week before Christmas. Erica felt kind of guilty when she took off about one-thirty. Her mother didn't seem to mind. She called Dwight to let him know that they could study at her house.

They studied all of about twenty minutes before they started making out.

If we're going to make love, it is better sooner than later, Erica thought. *Who knows when Mom might come home?*

"Come on, Dwight. Let's go up to my room."

He smiled. "He reached into his pocket and held up a foil packet. Babe, this time I came prepared."

They made love and he held her for a while. They talked a little about Christmas.

"Dwight, do you think you can come over for a little while on Christmas Eve? Mom's having an open house."

136

"Maybe I can for a little while. We always go to Aunt Sarah's and Uncle Henry's on Christmas Eve. My mom will expect me to be there."

"We'd better go back downstairs and study. I'm not sure when my Mom is leaving the shop." They got dressed, and Dwight helped her make the bed.

Erica knew her mother would be beat when she got home. She was also feeling a little guilty about having sex in her bedroom when her mom was working so hard at the shop. She saw there was ground beef defrosted in the refrigerator, and there would be stuff she needed to make chili in the pantry. She and Dwight started dinner. Dwight said that he had watched his mother make corn bread a million times, and he knew how to make it. Erica made a salad while the chili was simmering.

Beverly was very pleased when she walked in and smelled dinner cooking. It didn't even occur to her that maybe Erica and Dwight were having sex instead of studying chemistry. They had a very pleasant dinner. The kids continued studying after dinner, and Beverly offered to take Dwight home later in the evening. He insisted on just a ride to the bus stop.

Dwight thought that his mother was in a really good mood that weekend. She must have had a good time with that guy, Michael, at his Christmas party. It was nice to see his mother happy.

"Ma, do you think you could help me pick out a Christmas present for Erica?" Ruby was flattered her son asked for her help. "Sure, I was planning on finishing up some shopping today. After church we can come home and have some lunch, and then we can head out to the mall."

Dwight wished he had more money to spend on Erica's gift. Ruby said, "Girls always like jewelry. It doesn't have to be expensive to be nice. Erica looks like a girl with simple taste. Let's look at the bracelets." There was a sterling silver charm bracelet with a single heart-shaped charm. Dwight asked to look at it. He thought it would be perfect, not only because a heart is the symbol of love, but also because Erica wanted to be a doctor that helped kids with heart problems. His mother had some sort of coupon which made it more affordable.

"Oh, I think she'll love that bracelet, Dwight. Make sure they gift wrap it for you."

"Ma, will it be okay if I stop over to the McIntyre's on Christmas Eve, just an hour or so before heading over to Aunt Sarah's? I just want to be able to see Erica before we leave."

"That should be okay, but just not too long."

The week passed by very quickly. They had a home game on Tuesday night. Dwight had his highest scoring game ever… nineteen points. Erica was thrilled for him. On Wednesday, Mr. Novak passed back their chemistry tests. "Congratulations, you two, you got the highest grades on the final." The rest of the day passed quickly. It was the last day before Christmas vacation. There was no basketball or cheerleading practice after school. Dwight and Erica were planning on walking into the village for hot fudge sundaes after school.

It was going to be a white Christmas. It was snowing lightly when they walked to the village. Erica and Dwight liked so many of the same things. They both loved hot fudge sundaes. They talked about finals and how relieved they were that they were over. Dwight was most worried about history, and he got a B+. Erica was ecstatic because she aced her math final. It never would have happened without Dwight's help.

Dwight looked deeply into Erica's eyes. "I hope you know how much you mean to me, Babe. I am so in love with you."

"Oh, Dwight, I love you too. I'm going to miss you so much when you're in Atlanta. How did this happen? How did we fall in love so fast?"

"I don't know, Babe, but it feels so right. I'll be back before you know it. I know this is going to be a rough Christmas for you without your dad around. I wish I could be here for the whole weekend."

Erica had tears in her eyes. "Don't cry now, Babe. It will be okay."

They finished their ice cream and Erica said, "I'm going to drive you home today."

"Erica, you know how I feel about you driving alone in my neighborhood. I'll just take the bus."

"Dwight, it will be fine. It won't be dark yet. You have to work tomorrow, don't you?"

"Yeah, I do, and my mom's working. I'll have to pick up the girls at Aunt Sarah's and stay with them after I get out of work. So, I guess I'll see you on Christmas Eve then. Call me and let me know what time. Now you keep your chin up, Babe. Remember how much I love you. He gave her a very soft, sensual kiss and got out of the car.

She felt so warm inside as she watched him walk up the driveway. Then her mood flipped. *How can I be so happy and so sad and the same time? My mind is moving in so many directions. Maybe it's PMS. I wish I would just get my period. I'm kind of nervous about it. It's hard to even think about. I wish that Dwight wasn't going to Atlanta. I need him. I can't imagine Christmas without Dad. It's going to be so sad, and I really don't want to deal with Aunt Vicki. I'm sure Mom's new man will be around. I'm not sure how I feel about that. I wish it was just me and Mom and Nana.* Erica really wasn't concentrating on her driving. She saw the flashing red lights in her rearview mirror and pulled over.

Her heart skipped a beat when she saw the policeman walk over to her car. She put down her window. "I'm sorry, officer, did I do something wrong?"

"Yes, miss, you missed the stop sign at the last block. Could you please show me your license and registration?" He went back to his car and ran her license. *Oh God*, she thought, *Mom's going to kill me if I get a ticket.*

He came back to her car. "What are you doing in this neighborhood?"

"I was just giving my boyfriend a ride home. He lives not far from here, just a few streets away.

The officer raised his eyebrows. "How did you miss the stop sign?" Erica saw him peering in her car, probably looking to see if she had her phone out. He was leaning in a little, too, probably to see if he could smell anything on her breath.

"I guess my mind was wandering a little. My dad just died this year, and I was thinking how rotten Christmas was going to be without him. I know that's not really an excuse. I'm usually a very cautious driver."

"Well, Erica, I'm very sorry about your father, but I'm afraid I'm going to have to give you a ticket. I see you have your senior license, and that your driving record is clean. If you come to traffic court and bring your mother, I'll be present and can speak to the judge. I can maybe convince him to be lenient, considering the circumstances."

"Thank you. I'm really sorry officer." He handed her the ticket. "Now you concentrate on your driving, young lady. Your dad would want you to drive safely. It will be okay. Don't let it ruin your Christmas."

Oh God! Mom will be so mad! I don't know what she will be more angry about… that I was driving alone in Dwight's neighborhood, or that I got a ticket. Erica called Dwight after she pulled into the garage.

"Oh, Babe, I should have never let you drive me home."

"It could have happened driving back from the bus stop. It was my fault. I just wasn't concentrating on my driving. Do you think I should wait until after Christmas to tell my mom?"

"Erica, just tell her the truth. I think you should tell her right away. It might make her angrier if you wait. Look, everybody makes mistakes. Your mom is reasonable. It will be okay."

Her mother walked in a few minutes after she got off the phone with Dwight. "Hi, Mom, I've got to tell you something. It's probably going to make you really mad. I'm really sorry about it. Dwight and I went out for ice cream after school, and I drove him home. It was barely dark yet."

"Is that it?"

"No. I got a ticket for going through a stop sign. I just missed it. I swear I wasn't on my phone. My mind was on something else, and I wasn't concentrating on my driving. I know that's bad. I'm really sorry. I know I broke the rules about driving alone in Dwight's neighborhood, and I'm sorry about that, too. But Mom, it could have happened anywhere."

"Erica, you're so right. I AM angry about you driving alone in Dwight's neighborhood, especially at night. I'm surprised he went along with that. I thought we had an understanding about that and I trusted you. I've always thought of you as a pretty good driver. I can't believe you weren't more careful, considering you were driving somewhere that we've agreed is off limits. Maybe this is a good lesson for you. You must always be cautious and concentrate when you're

140

driving. You're not a very experienced driver yet. We'll deal with the ticket in traffic court, but I'm not sure what the consequences should be for breaking the rules about driving in Dwight's neighborhood."

"Okay, Mom, like I said, I'm sorry." Her sorry had a bit of an edge to it. She took off for her room.

Beverly sighed and got a bottle of Chardonnay out of the refrigerator. *Oh Christ,* she said to herself, *it's just another issue I have to deal with. Merry Christmas, Beverly.*

She sipped her wine while she got dinner started. *Maybe I'm being a little hard on her,* Beverly thought. *My mind has been very distracted too. I just keep thinking about Christmas and getting through the holidays without Tom. I'm sure she's thinking about Christmas without her dad, and she's probably upset that Dwight will be gone for most of the weekend.* Beverly mellowed a little by the time she poured her second glass. She went upstairs and knocked on Erica's door.

"What is it Mom? Can you possibly make me feel worse than I already feel?"

"Honey, can we talk?" Erica let her in. Beverly tried to speak calmly, and in a more gentle tone. "I don't want this to ruin our holidays. It's a ticket. No, I'm not happy about it. I'm just relieved you're okay and didn't get into an accident. Everyone gets a ticket sooner or later. I know you probably just wanted to be with Dwight as much as you can before he leaves. So, let's just put this incident aside for now. Will you come down and have dinner with me?"

"Okay, Mom. Thanks for understanding."

Neither one of them had much to say during dinner, both afraid to break the truce.

"Did I tell you I picked up some gifts for Ruby and the twins?"

"Oh, Mom, that is so nice. What did you get them?"

"There's a pair of earrings at the shop I'm sure that Ruby would love. I got the twins each these really cute long sleeve tees with a sparkly design. For Dwight, I bought a movie gift card. They're really not extravagant gifts, but I just wanted to do something. Do you think that they could come to the open house?"

"I don't know, but I'll ask Dwight."

"I'm just keeping the shop open until noon on Christmas Eve. I think Pam and Jackie can handle it. I've got a lot of cooking to do. Can you help me tomorrow night and Friday morning? I've told people to stop over anytime after four o'clock."

"Sure, Mom, we'll get it handled."

Beverly had a busy Thursday. The shop was non-stop busy and she had her regular appointment with Dr. Martino. She told Pam how much she looked forward to her weekly sessions with Dr. Martino. "I honestly don't know what I'd do without him to talk to. He is so good at helping me put everything into perspective. He thinks in much the same way as Tom did. He handles me like Tom did." Pam was a little worried that her friend was developing feelings for her therapist.

"Hello, Beverly. How was your week?"

"There's always some sort of challenge," she said. She told him about Erica's ticket. She also told him about the guilt she was feeling about her relationship with Brad. She felt like she was sneaking around to hide her relationship from Erica.

"Beverly, you're a grown woman, and a single woman. You are allowed to have an intimate relationship. Your daughter probably suspects that. She sounds like she's old enough and mature enough to understand that. There's a difference between sneaking around and being discrete. It appears to me that you are just being discrete. She probably has an intimate relationship of her own. I know you are mother and daughter, but on some levels, you are on the same playing field. I think you just need to respect each other's privacy."

"You don't think I'm setting a bad example?"

"No, I don't. Beverly, as hard as it is to accept, adolescents are having sex. That doesn't really have anything to do with your relationship with Brad, or whether her father is alive or not. Erica is just discovering her own sexuality. You've already opened the door for her to discuss her relationship with Dwight. Just keep that door open. Hopefully she will come to you when she's ready. The schools do a pretty good job at counseling teens about sex."

"As for the ticket, it is really hard for us as parents to turn over those car keys. It was a pretty minor offense. I think the bigger issue is

142

that she violated your trust about driving in Dwight's neighborhood. Maybe you need to speak to them both, together, about that issue. Adolescents manage to get themselves into a lot of scrapes along the way. Don't always blame yourself and assume it is because of bad parenting. I know it's difficult for you, because you don't have Tom to share the parenting burden. She would probably get into these scrapes whether Tom was alive or not."

"This was a good session, Beverly. I hope Christmas will bring you some peace and joy. Be kind to yourself, happy holidays." He shook her hand, putting his other hand over the top. She cried all the way home.

Even though she was tired, Beverly was glad she had a lot to keep her busy on Thursday night. She really didn't mind cooking. It was something she was good at, and it was something she could control. She almost found that it relieved her stress. Erica put on an apron and was eager to help. Ruby called.

"Beverly, I'm so pleased that you invited us, but the girls and I really won't be able to come over tomorrow. We always have a family gathering at my sister's house, and I have so much to do to get packed and ready for an early flight on Christmas morning. Dwight wouldn't miss his last chance to see Erica and say Merry Christmas, but we just can't join him. I hope you understand."

"Oh, Ruby, I do. It's wonderful that you have the opportunity to visit your parents. Have a wonderful holiday."

"Thank you, Beverly, you have a blessed Christmas."

Beverly and Erica chatted a little while they were working. Beverly thought it might be a good opportunity to open up that door about a discussion of Erica's relationship with Dwight.

"So tell me, honey, how is going with you and Dwight?"

"Everything's great Mom, things couldn't be better. You know how I feel about him."

"Tell me about it."

She wasn't taking the bait, and Beverly couldn't just come out and ask her daughter if she was having sex, or if she needed help with birth control.

"Mom if this is about sex, don't worry about it." The door closed.

Chapter 19

Erica woke up Christmas Eve morning with that familiar feeling. She had cramps. *Oh thank you, God, I'm getting my period.* Her mom was already busy in the kitchen. Erica kissed her. "Merry Christmas, Mom."

Beverly took a break and sat down to have breakfast with her daughter. "So who is coming?" Erica asked.

"Well, Uncle David, Aunt Vicki, the kids, of course, and Nana. Pam, Kyle, and his boyfriend, Mark, are stopping over for a drink. I think that Peter and Susan Dwyer and their boys are coming. I invited Dad's secretary, Martha Graham. He was always so found of her, and I know she doesn't have family in town. I know Dwight's coming for a little while, and Brad's going to try and come. He's on call, but he'll come if he can. The Barrett's said that they would come. Melissa is in town and she wants to see you."

"Oh, I'd love to see Melissa. She was the best babysitter ever. I can't believe she's a resident at NYU. I'd like Dwight to meet her."

"I think people will just be coming in and out. I think we have enough food. Maybe you and I can go to midnight mass after everyone leaves."

"That would be nice, Mom."

Helen, David, and Vicki, along with their kids were the first to arrive. Erica hugged her Uncle David. Of all her father's brothers, he was her favorite. *What does he see in Aunt Vicki?* Her cousin Sean looked taller every time she saw him. Erica wondered what Johnny would look like if he were alive. Molly was cute. It was obvious that she idolized Erica. They hugged. Molly was a chatterbox.

Erica saw Dwight walking up to the door. She went out and shut the door behind her. He kissed her and kissed her again. She laughed, "Are you sure you're ready for this?"

She escorted Dwight in and made the introductions. Beverly was in the kitchen. He went in to say hello and gave her a package. "My mom made this for you. It's pound cake...my Grandma's recipe. She only makes it at holiday time. She is really sorry she couldn't come by." The package was beautifully wrapped. Beverly gave Dwight a large gift bag for his family. She gave him a hug. "Merry Christmas, Dwight, I'm so glad you were able to come."

Erica brought Dwight into the den so that they could be alone for a few minutes. They exchanged gifts. "Oh, Dwight, I just love this bracelet. I know why you chose a heart. A heart means love, but for me, it is also a symbol of what I want to do with my future. It's about my Dad and my little brother. You are just so sweet." When she kissed him she had tears in her eyes. She put the cashmere scarf around his neck.

"Oh, Babe, this is so soft. When I have it around my neck, it will remind me of you, and I'll think of your arms around my neck. I haven't forgotten the James Taylor music that was playing that first night we made love. Your gifts are so special."

They went back into the other room for a little while and made the rounds talking to the other guests. It was time for Dwight to go. Erica walked him to the door. She slipped on her coat and walked him to the car. "Hurry back, Dwight. Merry Christmas, I love you."

"I love you, too, Babe. You'll be on my mind. I'll call you."

Everybody seemed to be having a good time. Mom put out quite a spread. She heard Kyle's boyfriend, Mark, telling some story, and there was hysterical laughter. It was nice to see Melissa. She told her about life as a surgical resident. "Your boyfriend seems really nice. He's very handsome. Why don't you tell me about him?" They talked for a long time. Erica thought of Melissa as kind of a big sister.

"Melissa, do you think it's an issue that Dwight's black?"

"No, not at all, it's only an issue if it is a problem for you or for Dwight. You are just used to living in a community of predominantly affluent white people. I think you will realize how really diverse the world is when you go off to college. Your color and economic status won't be what identifies you. It's a really mixed bag in college. Good for you, going for what you want."

Erica really liked Dr. Dwyer and his wife, Susan. She spent a lot of time talking to them. Dr. Dwyer made it a point of telling Erica that he thought Dwight was a very impressive young man. "The boys and I could have talked basketball all night with him," said Dr. Dwyer.

Beverly, Susan, and Helen chatted with Dad's secretary. She was very emotional. "The hospital just isn't the same without Dr. McIntyre. We all miss him so much. His patients talk about him all the time."

Dr. Williams was the last to arrive. Erica still had trouble calling him Brad. Susan Dwyer took Erica aside. "Do you like Brad? It was Peter and I who introduced them. He's really a nice man. I can understand that it's probably a little strange seeing your mom with another man. I hope you are okay with it."

"Yes, it is hard to get used to. He seems okay. I just want my mom to not be so sad anymore. If going out with him makes her a little happier, I'm good with that. She seems to be getting back into some of things that used to interest her. She's even playing her violin a little."

"Oh, honey, I'm so glad to hear that. I hope you're doing alright, too."

"Oh, I think I'm as good as I can be right now. School's going really well, and you've met Dwight. Things are okay."

Erica bought a platter back into the kitchen. Pam was talking to her Mom. "Bev, you've been really holding out on me. He's really quite a catch. I've been divorced four years now, and I've never been lucky enough to meet someone like Brad."

"Pam, I'm really not trying to catch anybody. We're friends. You know that Tom was the love of my life. Brad's just very good for me right now."

Pam laughed, "Okay, but for a guy his age, he's really pretty hot."

OMG, Erica thought. *Are Pam and my mother really talking about men that are hot!* She couldn't resist getting into this conversation.

"Pam, what do you think? On a scale of one to ten with George Clooney being a ten, where would you rate Dr. Williams?" Pam started laughing so hard she almost choked on the meatball she was eating.

"Oh, I'd give him a solid 8."

"Mom and I gave him a 6.5, but I think Mom's probably moved him up a little."

"Erica, he was painfully shy when I first met him, almost nerdy. He's not anymore."

"Maybe he has a friend for you, Pam," Erica said. They all laughed, and then Brad walked in and kissed her mother on the back of the neck. She had worn her hair up with a really pretty pair of gold earrings that Erica hadn't seen before. Her mother really blushed.

"You throw a great party, Beverly. I didn't know what a fantastic cook you are. These brownies are insanely delicious!"

Erica felt like throwing a little dart. "Oh, they're Mom's specialty... my Dad's absolute favorite. She made them for Dad when they were dating. He said that it was one the things that won his heart."

Her mother gave her a look. "Whatever, it's a good recipe," Beverly said.

Everybody left but Nana, Uncle David, Aunt Vicki and the kids. They all sat around talking. The kids were in the other room watching a movie. Leave it to Aunt Vicki to get the ball rolling.

"So, Erica, you have a boyfriend. He's not somebody I'd expect to see you with."

"What's that supposed to mean, Aunt Vicki?"

"Well, the obvious. How did you meet him?"

Beverly was feeling her blood start to boil. "He's a classmate of Erica's. He's her lab partner in chemistry and a great basketball player. You know, Erica is a cheerleader."

"We've all grown very fond of Dwight," added Helen.

"If you like him, Erica, I'm sure I'd like him, too," Uncle David said. "I didn't get much of a chance to talk to him." Uncle David was always doing damage control.

"Bev, it didn't take long for you to put yourself back on the market." Another shot from Aunt Vicki.

"I'm not 'on the market.' He's just a friend." Her response was clipped.

"Oh, really, I got the sense that he is more than just a friend."

Uncle David jumped in. "Vicki, let's round up the kids and get back to Mom's."

He followed Beverly into the kitchen while Vicki went to get the kids.

David hugged Beverly. "This was such a lovely party, thank you." He had tears in his eyes and a big lump in his throat. "It seems like Erica is doing okay. She seems happy. I did like her boyfriend. Forget what Vicki said. So what if you're seeing someone? You're young and beautiful. You deserve to be happy. Tom would want that for you. I want that for you. Back when you two were dating in college, I had a little crush on you. If you are interested in Brad, I think he's a lucky man."

"Oh, David, you are so sweet." Beverly was crying now. "Life is so overwhelming. I can't tell you how sad and lonely it is to be a widow at my age. Missing Tom is so painful. He was the love of my life. Erica misses him. She wants her father. You know how close they were. Being the single parent of a teenager is a big challenge. Dwight has been able to connect with Erica in a way no one else can. He's a good kid."

He hugged her again. "You're a strong woman. I admire how you're keeping it together. I'll see you at my mother's tomorrow. Sleep well."

Beverly and Erica went to midnight mass. "Well, Mom, we made it through Christmas Eve."

"We did, honey, Merry Christmas."

Erica went up to bed. While she was changing, she heard that her mother had gotten out her violin and was playing "Oh Holy Night." She went downstairs. "Oh, Mom, that was beautiful. Please play it again. It really didn't seem like Christmas Eve without you playing your violin. You know how much Dad loved it."

"I'm glad you enjoyed it, honey."

The next morning, Erica surprised her mother by making them breakfast. When Beverly walked into the kitchen, she could smell bacon and fresh hazelnut coffee. Erica was working on the French toast. "This is lovely, Erica. Everything smells heavenly."

They ate breakfast and talked about the party. "Mom, can't we just put a contract out on Aunt Vicki?"

"Oh, that's an idea. She was pretty obnoxious. Do you know who she reminds me of?"

Erica thought of it immediately. "Rebecca Goldstein?"

"Yes! Can you believe it?"

Erica and Beverly exchanged their gifts and got ready for Christmas Day at Helen's. At least this seemed normal. It was their tradition to spend Christmas Day at Helen's.

Erica decided that her Uncle David must have had a talk with her Aunt Vicki, because she didn't really have anything offensive to say all day. Erica spent most of the day playing board games with Sean and Molly or helping Helen in the kitchen. Dwight called later in the day.

Today wasn't as bad as I thought it would be, Erica thought as she got ready for bed. She had a message on her phone from Dwight. "Just calling to say I love you and Merry Christmas. I miss you," he said.

Beverly got her own call. Brad called her to see how her holiday was. He said that he had been in the OR all day. He had been doing surgery on a little boy injured in a car accident. The little boy had serious head trauma. Brad said that it had been a very difficult day. He sounded very tired.

"I just couldn't go to bed without telling you how happy that I am that you're the lady in my life."

"I'm sorry you had such a tough day, Brad. I'm glad you called. My day wasn't too bad. I'm just so glad Christmas is over for this year. I'm looking forward to a new year. Don't make any plans for New Year's Eve. I've got something planned for us."

"I'll look forward to it. Goodnight, Beverly."

"Thanks again for calling, Brad."

I'm not sure why I got Brad pumped up for New Years Eve, Beverly thought. *I hope Erica has plans so maybe Brad and I can spend the whole night together. I hope I'm not leading him on. To be honest, I think I am developing stronger feelings for him. I hope it's not because I'm just so damned lonely. Probably what David said is true. Tom would want me to get on with my life. I loved Tom. When he was alive, I never wanted any other man. It's nice to have Brad. I need to be careful. Brad was wounded badly in his marriage. I would never want to hurt him in any way. He's seems a little vulnerable.*

The day after Christmas was a Sunday this year. Beverly decided to keep the shop closed. She needed the rest. She was planning on going to a late afternoon movie with Pam. Erica spent the day with Christy. They hit the mall for the after Christmas sales.

That night Erica talked to her mother about her New Years Eve plans. "Christy's having a party. I'm just so hoping that Dwight will be able to go with me."

"So tell me about the party," Beverly said.

"It's just a bunch of kids from school. Relax Mom, her parents are planning on being there all night. They are having another couple over to help them chaperone. Christy's mom is making all the food. She's really excited about it. If it's okay, I'm planning on sleeping over."

"That sounds like fun. I hope Dwight can go, too. It's fine if you sleep over. Tell Christy's mom I'd be glad to make something to send over."

Erica told Dwight about the party. He thought he would be good to go.

Dwight finally got home on Tuesday night. Erica was counting on seeing him Wednesday. She met him for lunch, and later they went over to the McIntyre's. Beverly was at the shop. They went up to Erica's room as soon as they walked in the door. Dwight said that he couldn't wait to make love to her.

I'm really getting to like sex, Erica thought, but what I like most is how I feel afterward lying in Dwight's arms. I feel so complete, so satisfied and happy. But I feel a little guilty about keeping it from Mom, and even though we use condoms, I'm still a little nervous about getting pregnant.

Dwight told Erica that he had to work on Thursday and Friday, but he would be home in time for the party. They made love again then got dressed and went downstairs in case Beverly came home early.

Ruby and girls stopped in at the shop. The twins were very excited to be there, looking around and taking everything in. Ruby thanked Beverly for the gifts that she sent over. She was wearing the earrings. Danielle and Denise gave Beverly hugs and thanked her.

"They are such a nice family," said Pam.

"They are. Ruby is such a strong woman. She works so hard at everything... her job, school, raising her kids. I wish there was something I could do to make her life easier. I really admire her."

Beverly told Pam she was making plans for New Years Eve. Beverly told Pam that she was developing stronger feelings for Brad and how tricky it was because of Erica.

"Oh, Bev, you deserve happiness. Erica seems to have found happiness in her own relationship with Dwight. Just let things unfold with Brad. He seems like a great guy."

Beverly was planning on a romantic evening with Brad. She would make him a great dinner, open some good bottles of wine, and they would just relax. Since Erica was staying at Christy's, she was planning on letting Brad stay the night.

Brad looked so handsome when he showed up at her door. He was clearly looking forward to the evening. Like Dwight, Brad was very impressed with Tom's vinyl music collection.

They put on Carole King's "Tapestry" album. Brad brought a very nice bottle of champagne. They drank champagne, and Beverly served her crab cakes in the living room in front of the fire.

She set a beautiful candlelit table for them in the dining room. She made beef tenderloin, a potato gratin, and fresh asparagus. She had Brad open up her favorite merlot and pour.

He held up his glass. "Here's to you, pretty lady."

"And to you," she said.

"Beverly, this is quite a meal. You really went to a lot of trouble here."

"It was my pleasure. I enjoy cooking. It's actually helps relieve my stress."

They finished dinner and went back out into the living room by the fire.

"Beverly, would you do something for me?

"What's that?"

"You told me that you play the violin. Would you play something for me?"

She got out her violin and played her favorite sonata by Bach.

"Oh, Beverly, that was beautiful. You are really quite a woman." She put her violin down and he held her and kissed her.

"Flattery will get you everywhere. Put on some more music. I'll be right back."

Beverly put her chocolate soufflé in the oven and went back out to Brad. He had put on some soft music and asked her to dance with him.

He's really quite a romantic guy, she thought. He kissed her neck while they were dancing. *That makes me feel a little crazy.* She couldn't help but think how different Brad was than her Tom.

Tom was animated and charismatic. His personality filled up the room. He had a great sense of humor. I miss how easily he made me laugh. He was the man every woman wanted to be with. He was a big flirt. I felt like a lucky woman, because he chose me. Brad is not like that at all. He's the quiet, reserved guy in the room. Brad lets a woman feel like HE's the lucky one. Before Tom, I would never have been attracted to a man like Brad, because he is just too easy. I guess I've changed.

She heard the oven timer go off and bought out her chocolate soufflé. "What a way to a man's heart," he said.

At midnight they toasted to a new year and new beginnings.

Brad was thrilled that Beverly had asked him to stay the night. He admired one of the watercolor paintings she had in her bedroom. Tom loved that painting too. She painted it on their honeymoon in Martha's Vineyard. She wasn't about to tell Brad that. Having Brad in her bed was bittersweet. She had done nothing to change her room since Tom died. It almost seemed like the three of them were in the room. Soon it was clear there was only one man in her bed and that was Brad.

She made them breakfast the next morning and Brad took off. He knew that it probably wouldn't be good if he was there when Erica came home.

Erica had a lot of fun at Christy's party. Any time with Dwight was a good time. It was hard to be alone with him. *OMG,* she thought, *I can't believe we made love in the backseat of my car.* Erica just said that she and Dwight were going to Wegmans to get more pita chips for the dip she brought. They went to their favorite parking spot. *I didn't think I'd ever do anything like that. I just needed to be with him.*

Erica and Christy stayed up talking after everybody left. Erica finally confided in her friend about her relationship.

"I suspected that you two were having sex," Christy said. "So, you talked with your Mom about birth control?"

"Nope, I didn't. I'm just not ready to talk to her about it. It's such a private thing. It was hard to even tell you. We're being careful... using condoms."

"Are you kidding me, condoms?"

"I looked it up on the CDC website," Erica said. "It said that used properly, condoms only had an eighteen percent failure rate. I think that's okay for now."

"Oh, Erica, you be careful."

Chapter 20

Christmas vacation was over, and school was back in session. Erica was glad that the holidays were over. She was anxious to get back to classes and cheering basketball games. Dwight was having an awesome season. Mr. Novak said that if he continued to do well and kept his grades up, he had a really good chance of getting a basketball scholarship. *I'm glad I don't have to worry about getting a scholarship,* Erica thought. *I know Mom and Dad have enough money to send me to any college I want. I just have to have the grades, extra-curricular activities, and teacher recommendations to get in.*

She and Dwight were planning on getting some study guides to start preparing for the SAT exams. They were planning on taking them in the spring. If they were unhappy with their scores, they could take them again in the fall.

Erica had a court date for her ticket. Beverly had let the ticket issue go during the holidays, but she hadn't forgotten it. Traffic court was in the evening. The cop who had given her the ticket was in court. He seemed like a nice man. Erica and Beverly talked to him before court started. Erica noticed that Officer Malloy seemed quite taken with her mother.

"I understand that Erica just lost her father. That has to be so difficult at such a young age."

"Yes, it's been difficult for both of us." Beverly said. "This was so unlike Erica. She's always such a careful driver. She has really never been in any kind of trouble. She's a good student. I know she really regrets that this happened."

"Yes, Ma'am. May I speak to you privately a minute?"

"Mrs. McIntyre, my sympathies are with you. I'm sure it is very difficult being a single parent to a teenager. I'm sorry I had to ticket your daughter. I really don't want to add to your burden at this time. To her credit, she wasn't drinking or using her phone when I stopped her. I know she has her senior license and has taken Driver's Ed. My bigger concern here is her driving in that neighborhood alone after dark. This city has a horrific crime problem. It's appalling what happens on the streets of the inner city. I certainly wouldn't want my daughter driving there alone at night."

Beverly could feel her eyes brimming with tears. "Yes, officer, we had talked about that, and she clearly broke the rules. I had thought we had an understanding."

"Teenagers are a challenge, Mrs. McIntyre. I know this particular judge can be rather hard on teens, but I will try to speak on your daughter's behalf."

"Thank you," said Beverly. She wasn't sure what she thought about Officer Malloy. It was something about the way he looked at her. In the end he came through for them.

The judge was a stern woman, probably in her late fifties.

"Miss McIntyre, you must realize that running a stop sign is a serious offense. You could have caused serious injury or death. You could have been hit by another vehicle, or you could have hit someone else. After listening to Officer Malloy's remarks, I must say that I don't give any extra credit because you weren't drinking or using your cell phone. That is the expectation. You do, however, have a clean driving record. I am compassionate about the fact that you recently lost your father, and I am sorry about that. You will get three points on your license for a moving violation and a $200 fine. I hope I won't see you in my court again."

After they got out of court, Officer Malloy came over to them. He put a hand on Beverly's forearm. "I'm sorry, as I said before, that judge is very tough. Here is my card. Please let me know if I can ever be of assistance to you. Please take care. Drive safely, Erica."

"God, Mom, that judge was so mean. Officer Malloy was nice, though. I think he had a little thing for you."

"He told me he was very concerned about you driving in Dwight's neighborhood. You can't break that rule again, Erica, EVER. Just so you remember that in the future, I am taking your car keys for two weeks, starting tomorrow. You will have to work off the fine at the store on Saturdays. I'll have Pam track your hours at the rate I pay any of the part time workers, until the $200 is paid off."

"Mom, are you serious? I can't drive for two weeks, not even to school?"

"No, Erica, you were driving after school when you got the ticket. I had no idea that you drove to Dwight's after school. What else are you doing that I don't know about?"

"Mom, it was the first time I ever did that. Can't you give me a break, just this once?"

"No. You violated my trust. I really worry about you sometimes, Erica. I feel that I set reasonable limits. You have to respect them."

"But Dad..."

"Erica, don't try to manipulate me. Unfortunately Dad isn't here to help me sort out this situation. I think what I've decided is fair. Please, let's just drop it."

Erica was really not happy about this. She was sure she could get Christy to pick her up for school, but it was really going to cut into her time with Dwight.

She called Dwight when she got home. "I knew I shouldn't have let you drive me home that afternoon," he said. "Your mother is going to be so disappointed in me."

"She'll get over it."

"Maybe you should just accept your punishment. Two weeks isn't that long. You said that you and your mom have been getting along really well lately. It's not worth shaking things up."

Erica knew he was right.

That Saturday she put her time in at the shop. It was so slow. January wasn't a busy month. She was really bored. At least she knew that Dwight was working too. Beverly told her that she and Brad were going out with the Dwyer's that night. They were going to dinner and a movie. Maybe Mom will be cool and let Dwight come over. She called Dwight to see if he was free. He had to stay with his sisters because his mother was working.

"Come over here?" he asked.

She really didn't see how that would work. She talked to her mom.

"Well, I guess Brad and I could drop you off and pick you up on our way home. Just make sure Ruby is okay with it."

Ruby was fine with it.

Erica was really warming up to Brad. He really was a very nice man. His Jaguar really looked out of place in Dwight's neighborhood. He walked her to the door and shook hands with Dwight. "You two have a nice evening," Brad said.

Ruby had left them a pan of macaroni and cheese for dinner. The twins were so excited that Erica was there. She and Dwight watched a movie with them, and the girls finally went up to bed. The plans for studying for the SATs fell through when she and Dwight started making out. Dwight got up and went upstairs to see if his sisters were really asleep.

Soon Erica had her jeans off, and she and Dwight were making love on his living room couch.

OMG, Erica thought, *this is so risky!* But she couldn't stop herself.

"Babe, it's cool. My mom never gets home until midnight when she works the evening shift."

Erica felt a little guilty, but not that guilty. Before she had much time to think about it they were making love again.

She heard her phone vibrate on the coffee table. She was unable to reach it in time. It was her mother. She took a minute to catch her breath and called her back.

"Sorry, Mom, my phone was in my purse in the other room."

"Brad and I will be over to pick you up in about twenty minutes."

She and Dwight tried to wind things down a bit. Soon, Brad was at the door.

When they got back to the McIntyre's Erica went right up to bed. Brad stayed to have a drink with her mother.

"Brad, do you really think Erica and Dwight spent the evening studying for the SAT's?"

He smiled, "Probably not." Brad liked Beverly's daughter, but she was always a factor in the Brad plus Beverly equation. He would really have liked to spend the night with Beverly. It clearly wasn't going to happen tonight.

The month of January proved to be very snowy and also very busy. Erica was very wrapped up in the new school semester, basketball, studying for SATs, and of course seeing Dwight as much as possible.

Beverly was busy ordering the new spring merchandise for the shop. She did a lot of charity work. After the holidays, committee meetings started up again with renewed energy. She wished she had more time to spend with Brad. He had a very calming influence on her. It was hard to find time to be alone together. Beverly felt like she hadn't spoken to Ruby in a while. She thought she should reach out to her. They needed to be on the same page when it came to Erica and Dwight.

They met for breakfast. Ruby told Beverly about school. She was excited because she was finally starting her real nursing courses. She was finally seeing light at the end of the tunnel. Hopefully next May she would graduate and be a registered nurse. Ruby also said that she was dating a man she met at church.

"Good for you, Ruby. Michael sounds like a good guy." They talked about how tricky it was to date and have any kind of an adult relationship when you had kids.

They were both thinking about Dwight and Erica's relationship, but it was a hard conversation to initiate. They just didn't go there. Even though they never got around to talking about Dwight and Erica, Beverly was glad she had asked Ruby to breakfast. She really liked her. She really understood what it was like being a single parent. Beverly admired Ruby. She was a strong, confident woman who seemed comfortable in her own skin. Besides Pam, Beverly didn't really know any other single parents that she felt comfortable talking to.

Dwight seemed to be good at everything, at least Erica thought so. The teachers seemed to like him too. He wrote a paper on Martin Luther King Jr. for Black History Month. Mr. Miller read it to the class. Erica was surprised. Dwight always said that he wasn't very good in English and history. He had been asking for her help. This paper he wrote himself. She was very proud of him.

"Did you show your Mom that paper?" asked Erica.

"No, Babe, I didn't. I really didn't think it was that great."

"Well, that's not what everybody else thinks. Will you print me a copy? I want to show it to your mom. She would love it. You should keep it for college applications."

Erica woke up on Tuesday and looked at the date on her phone. She couldn't believe it was already February 1st. Her heart skipped a beat. She realized that her period was over a week late. She had been too busy to really think about it. *Maybe I'm panicking for no reason,* she thought. *My periods are a little irregular sometimes.* She really didn't want to think about it.

By the next week, it was the only thing she could think about. She didn't want to talk about it with anybody, not even Dwight or Christy. Just to reassure herself, she went to the Internet. Web MD said that it was normal for teens to have irregular periods. That reassured her a little bit. *When I do get my period,* she thought, *I think I'll go to Planned Parenthood and maybe get a prescription for birth control pills.*

For now she was going to concentrate on school. She had a lot going on. She had an English paper due. They had to choose a classic novel that was on the assigned reading list, and do a character analysis of one of the characters. Erica chose Mattie in Edith Wharton's, "Ethan Frome". It was such a sad love story. She remembered how hard she cried after the part where Ethan and Mattie are in the tragic sledding accident. Dwight was doing Atticus Finch from Harper Lee's, "To Kill a Mockingbird".

The cheerleading squad was learning some new cheers for the second half of the season. She also had student council. Studying for SATs was always looming over her head.

Valentine's Day was on a Monday this year. There was a home game Friday night, and on Saturday there was a Valentine's dance at school. There really were not that many school dances. This was a dance sponsored by student council. It was actually Erica's idea. The money from ticket sales were being donated to the cardiology unit at the medical center. They always needed funds for patient amenities.

Beverly was very proud of her daughter. Erica told her that she had the idea for the dance, because of the connection of Valentine's Day to hearts. Dwight was relieved that he was able to go. When he told Ruby about the dance, she made arrangements for the twins to go to Sarah and Henry's for a sleepover. She had to work, and she didn't want to make Dwight stay home to babysit.

Beverly thought her daughter looked beautiful for the dance that night. She wore a red silk halter- style dress. The dance was semi-formal. She and Dwight made a handsome young couple. Beverly took their picture when he came to the house. Ben and Christy were going to pick them up.

Beverly had her own plans. Brad said that he had something special planned. He picked her up and brought her over to his house. As they walked in, Beverly heard soft music playing, a beautiful table was set, and she could smell something delicious cooking. Brad had hired a personal chef. He was such a romantic.

At about ten o'clock, Beverly got a call from her daughter asking permission to stay over at Christy's that night. She was having such a nice evening with Brad and really wanted to spend the night, so she told her that it was okay. Then she had second thoughts. She should have made a call to Karen Logan, Christy's mother, to make sure she was aware of the plan and would be home. After Erica got that ticket, Beverly was having trouble completely trusting her daughter. Beverly knew it would be hard to relax, unless she made that call. She felt comfortable calling Karen. They weren't close friends, but often communicated about activities involving the girls. Karen reassured her that she and Bill were home, and it was fine if Erica stayed over.

Beverly had a wonderful evening with Brad. She always slept soundly in his arms.

The dance was a big success. Erica was thrilled with all the money they were able to raise. She and Christy talked about the dance. She was having such a great night that she didn't even think about not getting her period yet, until now. She wanted to confide in her best friend. She told Christy her period was three weeks late.

"Oh, Erica, I can't believe it! You have got to be so freaked out! Did you take a home pregnancy test yet?"

"No, because at first I thought I was just a little late, but I would get it soon. I was so busy with everything, and I just stopped thinking about it. Maybe I was in denial. Now I'm a little scared. Do you really think I could be pregnant? We have been using condoms. I thought we were being careful."

"Of course you could be. Condoms aren't such great protection. You've really got to take a test. We'll go to the drug store and buy one tomorrow." Christy hugged her friend. "I'll be with you when you take it. You've got to know, I'm here for you whatever happens. Have you said anything to Dwight?"

Erica was crying now. "No, like I said, I've tried not to think about it."

"We will know soon enough tomorrow. Let's try to get some sleep," Christy said. Erica didn't sleep at all that night.

Christy finally woke up about nine. Erica could hear the rest of her family was up downstairs.

"Hey, I'll just tell my parents we are going out to breakfast. We'll go buy the test."

Erica wasn't very hungry, but she knew Christy was. Christy was always hungry. They went to the drug store and bought the test. Their plan was to go the Village Café for breakfast, and Erica would take the test in the bathroom there. She didn't want to take the test at her house or at Christy's house either.

"Let's eat first. I'm starving." Erica ordered French toast which she hardly touched. Christy wolfed down a large stack of blueberry pancakes and bacon. She ordered more coffee for them while Erica went to the bathroom.

The pregnancy test they bought was the brand that you could just pee on the stick. She forced herself to look at the stick. It was clearly positive. *This is a huge problem,* she thought. *What am I going to do?* She stuffed everything back in the bag. She didn't want the next person who came in to see what she had been up to. Christy took one look at her friend and didn't even have to ask her what the test showed.

"Okay," she said, "we are just going to keep calm and talk about this." Erica was trying to hold back the tears.

162

"I've just ruined my life AND Dwight's life. My mother will be furious. She's already been through so much, and now I'm going to lay this problem on her. Dwight's mother will be furious too. She has so many dreams for him."

"Erica, YOU didn't ruin Dwight's life, he loves you. I'm sure he was a willing participant. You will have to figure this out together. He's a good guy. He'll stand by you, no matter what. You're not the first girl to get pregnant in high school."

"God, Christy, I won't even be eighteen until July. I'm not ready to be a mother."

"Well, there are options, of course," Christy said.

"I know, but it's going to be so hard to figure out what option is right for me, and what's right for Dwight."

"Erica, you're the one who has the baby growing inside of you. It's got to be YOUR choice."

"I can't believe this! My dad has been gone for only five months, and now this happens. I never thought I would have been someone who would have had sex in high school, but I had such strong feelings for Dwight. I love him. I wanted our love to be complete. I should have been smarter about this. You talked to your mom and got on the pill. That was smart. That's what I should have done. My mother gave me plenty of opportunities to confide in her. I just kept telling her it wasn't an issue. She was cool with me dating a black guy, and I guess I just didn't want to push it. I didn't want her to think less of Dwight or less of me, because we were having sex."

"You will just have to tell her. She probably suspects you're having sex. Sometimes I don't think you give your mom enough credit. She for sure loves you. She'll help you figure it out. She'll probably need time to accept this news. You've got to tell Dwight first, and soon. You've got to see a doctor. Do you feel any different, physically, I mean?"

"No, I'm fine. I'm just so scared. I feel a little ashamed. God, what would my dad think if he was alive? He would be so disappointed in me."

"Oh, don't go there, Erica. Let's get out of here."

Christy paid the check and drove them back to her house. Erica got her things and Christy drove her home. She gave Erica another hug. "Keep me in the loop, okay?"

Beverly was already home. "How was the dance, honey?"

"Oh, it was great, Mom. We raised a lot of money. I've got a lot of school work to do. I'm going up to my room to study."

Beverly sensed something wasn't quite right. Whenever something was bothering Erica, she always sought immediate refuge in her room.

Erica called Dwight. "Dwight, do you think you could meet me in the park by the canal this afternoon, I really need to talk to you."

"It should be fine, Babe. Is three o'clock okay? Is something wrong?"

"Let's just talk then," she said. I'll see you at about three."

Chapter 21

Erica lay on her bed and sobbed into her pillow.

Oh God, Erica thought. *I have no idea what I'm going to do. How can I not love that I have Dwight's baby growing inside of me? But this is so not the right time. We have another year of high school and we both want to go to college. What a mess now. I can't believe that I let this happen.*

"Mom, I left something at Christy's. I'll be back before dinner."

She saw Dwight walking into the park and she immediately ran to his arms. "It will be okay, Babe. Let's take a walk and talk about it. For February, it was a pretty nice day. The sun was out, and there were a couple of inches of new snow on the ground.

"Dwight, I'm pregnant."

"Are you sure, you took a test?" Erica could see the panic in his soft brown eyes.

"I took it this morning. I knew I was late, but tried not to think about it."

"You didn't say anything last night. You seemed happy, not worried or anything."

"Well, now I'm really worried. What am I going to do?"

"Erica, you know I love you. We're in this together."

"I so dread telling my mother. I can't even believe how hurt and angry she is going to be."

"Oh God, my mother will be angry too. She talked to be about it so many times. It would go something like this:

"Dwight, don't you be getting some girl pregnant. You have a future ahead of you. I have dreams for you. Be smart. I was foolish enough to get pregnant at eighteen and it's been a struggle since." She would always add, "But I love you so much. I'll never regret having you."

"Babe, this has to be your decision. I'll support you in whatever you decide to do."

"Dwight, this is our baby, which we made out of our love... whether we planned to or not. I just don't think I could kill our baby. I've always thought abortion was wrong."

"You know, Babe, I don't think guys feel as strongly about abortion. I'm sure it's because they aren't the ones carrying the baby."

They sat down on a bench, and Dwight held her. "Are you feeling okay?"

"I can't tell I'm pregnant, if that's what you mean. I just feel a little numb."

"When are you going to tell your mother? Should we tell her together?"

"I had better talk to her myself."

"In my old high school, there were always girls who were pregnant. They continued to go to class. I guess that doesn't happen here so much."

"No, it doesn't. If it happens, their parents probably make some kind of arrangements for them. People here have the resources to do that."

"When do you think the baby would be due?"

"I'm thinking probably late September, maybe October. So I guess most of the hardest part of the pregnancy would be this summer."

"Erica, maybe with our mothers' help, we could make this work. It doesn't have to ruin our plans or our futures. We just might have to modify our plans a little."

"Dwight, don't you feel a little ashamed?"

"Ashamed? No, I could never feel ashamed about making love to you. Come on, I'm going to buy us some hot chocolate."

They sat on a bench and drank their hot chocolate. Dwight had his arm around her. Erica finally stopped trembling. "Dwight, I can't even tell you how scared I am. I can't stop feeling ashamed."

"You're ashamed we made love?"

"No, I'm ashamed I just wasn't smarter about it. I should have got the pill or something better than condoms."

"So when do you think you'll tell your mother?"

"I think that I'm going to tell my grandmother first. She has a way of helping me put things into perspective. She always has some really good advice."

166

"I won't say anything to my mother, until you're sure what you're going to do," Dwight said.

"I'm going to have our baby."

"Okay. I love you. We're in this together." He kissed her and walked her to her car.

Dwight caught his bus home. *Oh God, how could I have let this happen, what now?*

His mind was moving in a million directions. Everything was going so well in his life. He was doing so well in school and on the court. He was on the way to achieving his dream of getting a scholarship to college. He wondered if he would have to go back to his old school. His mother would be so hurt and disappointed. He loved Erica. He hated that he put her in this situation. He thought of his friend Marcus. Whitney ended up getting an abortion. Marcus said that he felt a little guilty whenever he saw a baby. He wasn't the same Marcus. Whitney was already with somebody else. He knew it wasn't the same for him and Erica. He couldn't see Erica having an abortion.

Maybe I should talk to Uncle Henry first. He might have some advice or let me how I should tell Mom about this. Dwight felt a pounding headache coming on.

Ruby was studying at the kitchen table when he walked in. She took one look at her son and she knew something was troubling him. Dwight went to the sink for a glass of water. "Ma, do we have any Tylenol or Motrin or something for a headache?"

"Is something bothering you, son?"

"I just have a bad headache."

"Why don't you go upstairs a take a nap before dinner?" *I hope it's nothing more than a headache*, she thought. *He doesn't look so good.*

Ruby knew her son loved pork chops. He barely touched his dinner. He excused himself and went up to his room. He never came back down. She wondered if it has something to do with Erica. *Maybe they had a fight or something.*

Ruby saw her son's light was still on when she went up to bed. She knocked on his door, and he said that it was okay to come in. She looked around his room. Dwight didn't have the usual messy room of a teenage boy. It was almost always neat. There were posters on the walls, mostly of basketball players. He also had a poster of Beyonce, like most boys his age. There was a quote he had pinned up by Martin Luther King, Jr. "Faith is taking the first step even when you don't see the whole staircase." He had lots of books.

She sat on the edge of her son's bed. "I know something's wrong. Will you talk to me about it?"

He started to cry. Ruby couldn't even remember the last time she saw her son cry.

"Ma, you're going to be so disappointed in me, but I've got to tell you. I've got to tell someone. Erica's pregnant."

She held her son. "I'm glad you trusted me enough to tell me."

"You know I love Erica. We just got in deeper and deeper. We were being responsible. We were using protection."

Ruby wanted to keep her cool and say the right things. After all, how hard could she come down on her son when she made the same mistake at eighteen?

"Well, we'll just have to figure this out. It doesn't have to ruin your future. I won't let it. Do you know what Erica plans to do?"

"She wants to have the baby, Ma. She's Catholic, and I don't think she believes in abortion."

"Has she told her mother? Lord, that woman has had enough trouble in her life."

"I don't think she's told her yet. She just took the test today."

"So, she probably hasn't been to a doctor yet."

"No, I'm sure she hasn't."

"Alright, Dwight, you had better get some sleep." Ruby kissed her son and went to her own room.

Oh Lord, I'm only 36 years old and I'm going to be a grandmother. I didn't see this coming. I knew he loved her, but Erica seemed so innocent. I didn't think she was a girl that would be having sex in high school. I'll bet he was her first time. Oh, I hate even thinking about this. I'm not going to let this ruin his life. Lord, you've given me a lot of challenges before. Please help me with this one. Please help my boy.

It was February break. There was no school all week. That was good for Erica, because she got almost no sleep. After finally getting to sleep about five AM she finally woke up about ten. She called Helen and asked if it was okay for her to come over.

"Sure, honey, are you okay? You don't sound like yourself."

"I'm okay, Nana, but I just need to talk to you about something."

"Well, I'm making your favorite Italian wedding soup. Why don't you come over, and we'll have lunch."

"Okay, Nana. I'm just going to take a shower, and I'll stop at Wegmans and pick up some fresh bread."

"That would be nice, honey. See you soon."

She knew Dwight was working today. He had asked for some extra hours over break. It was Monday morning. The deli was really busy. Dwight had a line of customers to wait on. He spotted her. Erica saw him raise his eyebrows and smile. She knew he wouldn't be able to talk. She felt a little better just seeing him this morning. Erica bought her bread and headed over to Helen's.

She felt calmer just walking into her grandmother's house. Nana had a cute little dog, a red mini dachshund, named Frankie. Frankie ran up to greet her, always looking for affection.

"So what is it, honey, what's troubling you?"

Erica started crying immediately. "Oh, Nana, everyone is going to be so disappointed in me. I'm pregnant." Helen reached out and held her granddaughter.

"Well, at least I know how much you love Dwight, that's important. Have you told him?"

"Yes, he knows, but I haven't told Mom yet. Dwight said that he will support me in any way he can."

"Nana, I want to have this baby. I could never have an abortion. I could never kill our baby. Nana, do you believe in abortion."

"No, honey, I'm Catholic. I don't"

"I know it will be difficult, but you two love each other. If Ruby, and your mother and I help you, I think it will be alright...not easy, but alright. Just think, Erica, you will give me my first great-grandchild."

"But, Nana, I want to finish high school, and go to college, and medical school. Dwight has dreams of going to college."

"Honey, you can still do those things. The road will just be a little bumpy along the way. You are certainly not the first girl to get pregnant in high school, and you won't be the last."

"How am I ever going to tell Mom? She is going to be so angry. I know I should have talked to her and asked her to help me with birth control."

"Sometimes being so much in love can cloud your judgment. What's done is done. Oh, I'm sure she'll be a little angry at first. It's not what she wants for you. Losing your father at such a young age is hard enough. Now you're going to have a baby. That's a lot for a seventeen year old to handle. It will be another shock for her. I think after she gets over the shock and the anger, she'll realize that she will have a new grandchild in her life. She'll have a new baby to love."

"How do I tell her? I still haven't seen a doctor. I should probably tell her soon."

"We can tell her together."

"That's okay, Nana, I'd better tell her myself."

Helen patted Erica's hand. "It's going to be okay."

Erica sat at Helen's table and cried a few minutes more.

"Go into the bathroom and wash your face with some cold water, then come in and we'll have our lunch."

Erica looked in the mirror. She looked tired, but she really didn't feel any different. She hoped Helen was right about how her mother would react. *Maybe I'll tell Mom tonight,* she thought. *I can't stand this hanging over my head, and I want to go to a doctor. I want to make sure my baby is okay.*

She and Helen had lunch. Helen gave her a jar of soup to take home. Helen hugged her granddaughter and said, "I love you, Erica, and I'm here for you, no matter what."

Erica checked her phone after she pulled into the garage. She had a message from Dwight asking her to call.

"Hey, Babe, are you okay? I'm sorry I couldn't talk to you when you were in the store today. I've got to tell you, I told my mother. She took it way better than I thought she would."

"REALLY, she did? I talked to Nana and she was very understanding too. She didn't act really shocked or mad or anything. She said that she would help us because she knew we loved each other."

"I do love you, Babe."

"I'm going to tell my mom tonight."

"Okay, Babe, call me and tell me how it goes. Good luck."

She heard Beverly pull in. Beverly walked into the kitchen and put the mail down on the table.

"Hi, honey. I'm just going to change and you can help me get dinner started. You look kind of tired, are you okay?"

"Yeah, Mom, I am tired, but I'm okay."

Beverly came down and poured herself a glass of Merlot. *God,* Erica thought, *for sure she'll need the whole bottle tonight.* "What can I do to help Mom?"

"You can start peeling potatoes. I had a meat loaf in the freezer that I took out to defrost this morning. I'll start washing the lettuce for salad."

"Mom, I've got to tell you something, and you're going to go ballistic."

Another ticket, Beverly thought, *or maybe she was failing something in school?* Beverly's heart skipped a beat.

"I'm just going to say it... I'm pregnant."

Beverly slammed the cupboard door so hard it knocked a small vase off the window sill. The vase smashed on the kitchen counter.

"Erica, how could you let this happen?"

"Mom, I think you know how I feel about Dwight. I love him. We were being careful. We were using condoms."

"Was Dwight pressuring you into having sex?"

"Mom, NO! I can't believe you think Dwight would do that. It's something we both wanted."

"Erica, I gave you many opportunities to talk to me about this. You assured me that your relationship hadn't gotten that far. I could have helped you with more reliable birth control. I feel like you've deceived me."

"Mom, it's a very private thing, just like your relationship with Dr. Williams. I haven't asked you about that."

"Erica, that's enough! I'm an adult woman, and you are seventeen years old! Have you decided what you are going to do about this?"

Erica glared at her mother. "What do you mean? It's not what I planned, but I'm going to have my baby."

Beverly took a big sip of her wine and put the meat loaf in the oven. "Let's both just take a break and cool off a little. We'll talk some more after dinner."

Beverly was furious. *This is so not what I want for my daughter*, she fumed. *This isn't a complication I want in my life, either. I was just feeling like I was starting to heal and that I was in control again. I had hope for the future, now this. God, Tom, where are you when I need you?*

Beverly didn't eat much dinner, but she poured herself another glass of wine. Erica ate everything and went for seconds on the mashed potatoes. Lately she just felt better if she had food in her stomach. She discovered when she was hungry she started to feel really nauseous. Beverly cleaned up the dishes and sat back down at the table with her daughter.

"Erica, this is a bit of a shock for me. First we have to get you to a doctor and make sure you really are pregnant."

"Mom, trust me, I'm pregnant. I haven't had my period since Christmas Eve. I feel tired and hungry all the time, sometimes nauseous. My boobs are killing me. I took a test. It was clearly positive."

"Well, we still have to get you to a doctor."

"Mom, it doesn't have to ruin my life. I'm really sorry, but maybe if you can stop being mad at me, you can help me make this work."

Beverly took a breath. "Erica, you have options. You're seventeen years old. You aren't ready to be a mother. You could terminate the pregnancy or maybe consider adoption. There are many infertile couples out there that would welcome a baby from a beautiful and smart girl like you."

"Mom, I didn't choose motherhood. Motherhood chose me. I could never give away my baby."

"YOU have the right to choose."

"Are you serious, Mom? Are you going to go all Roe v. Wade on me?"

"It's what I believe. You made a mistake, meaning you weren't smarter about birth control. You don't have to pay for that mistake for the rest of your life. I think terminating the pregnancy is a reasonable choice."

"Mom, you can't even say the ugly word, ABORTION! We're Catholic, we don't do abortion."

"Erica, you know I converted to Catholicism after I met your father. There are some things the church teaches that I don't agree with."

"So, Mom, if you got pregnant with me or Johnny at an inconvenient time, you would just have had an abortion?"

Beverly vowed to remain calm.

"Erica, you know that isn't fair. These circumstances are different. I'm going to tell you something that I haven't shared with too many people, and yes, I told your father."

"When I was a freshman in college, I went to a mixer at a fraternity house. I had way too much to drink. I had been flirting with this one guy all night. He brought me up to his room…"

"Mom stop, I don't want to hear this!"

"That's too bad, because I'm going to tell you anyway. He seemed like a really nice guy. I can't really say he forced himself on me, but he was very persistent. I had sex with him. The next morning I had a wicked hangover and didn't remember a whole lot about the night before. When I saw him after that on campus, he barely acknowledged me. A month later I found out I was pregnant. I was so upset. I hated myself. My roommate took me to Planned Parenthood, and a compassionate counselor there told me I had to needed to forgive myself. I didn't have to ruin my life because I made a mistake. I terminated the pregnancy. I don't regret it. I was only eighteen, and I wasn't ready to have a baby."

"Mom, you've got to know my situation is way different. Dwight and I love each other. I could never hurt our baby. I couldn't kill any baby." Erica was crying now. Beverly now wished she never told her that story. *My God,* she thought, *what she must now think about her mother. The truth is that I have always felt a little ashamed about having that abortion.* Then Beverly remembered that Ruby had Dwight when she was eighteen. *I'm really not handling this well. Oh God, Tom, where are you when I need you?*

Since you're determined to have this baby, maybe the four us... you, me, Dwight and Ruby, should get together and discuss how we can make this work.

"Oh, Mom, that's what I was hoping for." Beverly got up and hugged her daughter. They were both crying now.

Erica went up to her room. She wanted to be alone, and she wanted to call Dwight. She told him about her conversation with her mother. She told him that her mother suggested she get an abortion, but she left the part out about her mother's own story.

"Babe, are you thinking about having the abortion now?"

"How could you even ask me that? No, I could never kill our baby."

"Erica, I really think it's going to be okay."

"Do you? Oh, I hope so." After she finished her call to Dwight, Erica did something she hadn't done in a long time. She called her father's cell phone. Then she cried herself to sleep.

Chapter 22

Beverly called Pam the next morning to tell her she wasn't coming in. She needed to come up with a plan. She needed to take control of this situation. The first thing she did was call her OB/GYN doctor to make an appointment for Erica. The doctor Beverly saw was male. She thought Erica would be more comfortable seeing a female. There was a younger new doctor in the practice that was female. She made an appointment for Erica later in the week. She knew she should probably meet with Erica's guidance counselor. She really didn't know how they managed pregnant students at her high school. Beverly decided she would make that appointment after talking to the doctor. She wondered if Ruby would be home. She knew her work schedule always varied. She took a chance and called her on her cell. She got her voice mail. Beverly left a message. "Hi, Ruby, this is Beverly. By now I'm sure you know about Erica's pregnancy. I want to set up a time for the four of us to sit down and talk. Maybe you and Dwight can plan to come here for dinner this weekend. Please call me when you get a chance."

Then she panicked. *Oh God, maybe Dwight hasn't told his mother yet. I hope I didn't mess things up more than they're messed up already.*

Ruby returned the call on her lunch break. *What a relief! Ruby already knew.* She explained how upset Dwight was when he told her. "I feel bad for the kids, I really do. Dwight said they were using protection. I know he loves Erica. I'm just so sorry this happened. I really couldn't come down on him too hard, because I was unmarried and pregnant at eighteen."

"Oh, Ruby, do you think we can help them work this out?"

"That's what I'm praying for. I think it's a good idea for all of us to get together to talk."

"Will Saturday work for you? You can come here."

"That should be fine. I'm off this weekend."

"Let's say six o'clock, is that okay?"

"Fine, we'll see you then. Thank you so much for calling."

Erica's appointment was on Thursday morning. Beverly had her usual appointment with Dr. Martino on Thursday afternoon. She was looking forward to it. They would have a lot to talk about.

Erica was very quiet all week. She spent a lot of time moping around the house. Beverly saw her with her SAT study guide. *Good for her. She is determined to pursue her plans for college and hopefully medical school.*

Dwight had signed on for extra hours at work. He, too, was very quiet. Ruby felt empathy for her son. She knew how disappointed he probably was with himself. Teen pregnancy wasn't an uncommon situation in his former high school, but she knew it probably didn't happen that often in his new school. She hoped it wouldn't ruin any future opportunities for him. She was worried about what the twins would think.

When Beverly got home from work on Wednesday, she noticed that Erica had gone to church to get ashes. She had probably gone with Helen. Beverly frowned. *I completely forgot that today is Ash Wednesday, but I haven't been very good about going to church.* She hoped that her daughter wasn't plagued by a lot of Catholic guilt about pre-marital sex. She knew that Erica probably felt punished enough already. Erica and Dwight met at the library Wednesday night. They thought they might review for the SATs to get their minds off everything, but of course the pregnancy was all they could think about.

"Do you want me to go with you to your doctor's appointment tomorrow?" Erica looked at Dwight. He had a sad, puppy dog kind of look on his face when he asked.

"I don't know," sighed Erica. "It's probably best that I just go with my Mom. But I'll call you as soon as it's over."

"Okay, Babe, whatever is best for you." He reached out to hold her hand.

Before this happened, they would probably had been thinking about where they could be alone to make love. Now Erica wasn't much in the mood.

"That dinner on Saturday is going to be pretty heavy," Dwight said.

"Oh God, I know. I don't know how I'm going to face your mother." Erica said, tears spilling out of her eyes.

"She'll understand. She's been there."

Erica drove Dwight to his bus stop. He held her and kissed her. "Erica, just remember that I love you. Good luck tomorrow."

Beverly and Erica sat in the waiting room. Beverly flipped through a magazine. Erica just looked around the room. She jiggled her leg up and down. It was something Erica did when she was nervous.

They were escorted back to an exam room. A nurse took Erica to obtain a urine sample, and then took her height, weight, and blood pressure. She came back to the room and the doctor came in shortly after. Dr. Carrie Anderson was young, probably in her early thirties. She was a petite brunette with bright blue eyes. She had a very friendly, casual manner. She introduced herself and shook both of their hands. "Erica, do you want your mom with you when we talk and do your exam?"

"I want my mom to stay."

"Well, let's start out with the ultrasound first to see just how far along you are." They had told Erica when she checked in that they would probably do an ultrasound. They made her drink four large glasses of water in the waiting room. She felt like her bladder was about to burst.

"There we are. I would date your pregnancy at seven weeks and five days. Look, this is the fetal heart beating." Erica and her mother looked at the ultrasound screen in awe.

"Let's talk some before I have you get undressed and do a physical exam. I want to know how you feel about this pregnancy, and make sure that you are aware of your options."

Erica told the doctor that her pregnancy was unplanned and that she had been using condoms. She told her that she was "upset" about the pregnancy, but she loved the baby's father and wanted to have the baby. Then Erica said, a little more loudly, "I don't believe in abortion, so I really don't want to talk about that."

"Okay. It sounds like you know what your options are, and I'm thinking you want to keep your baby, am I right?"

"I do. My mom, my grandmother, and my boyfriend's mom will help us."

I am setting your due date as October 2nd.

Beverly was a little taken aback. She wasn't aware that Helen knew Erica was pregnant, but then she knew that Erica told Helen everything.

Beverly didn't say much until Dr. Anderson asked her questions about Erica's medical history or the family's medical and genetic history. She made sure that it was noted that Erica's brother was born with Tetralogy of Fallot.

Beverly stepped out to the waiting room to give Erica privacy for her internal exam.

Erica was a little unnerved by the pelvic exam. She was glad her mother made the appointment with a female doctor.

"So, Erica, now that we are alone, tell me a little more about your relationship with your boyfriend."

"He's eighteen. His name is Dwight. We go to school together. I met him this past September when he was new to my school. He was very supportive to me after my dad died, when a lot of the other kids didn't know what to do. You're going to find out anyway. My boyfriend's African-American."

"Thanks for sharing that with me. Was he your first sexual partner?"

"He was. I fell in love with him, and it seemed right for us. We were using condoms."

"Sometimes you don't get them on soon enough, or they tear." The doctor continued, "This is a lot to handle, first your father's death, and now this unplanned pregnancy."

"Oh God, I know. I'm so overwhelmed."

"Your mother didn't say much."

"She's coming around a little, but she was pretty mad at first. She thought I should get an abortion."

"Well, it sounds like that wasn't right for you."

Erica really liked Dr. Anderson. She was really easy to talk to.

They left her office with a lot of information about pregnancy and a prescription for prenatal vitamins. They then went to the lab. She had to have several vials of blood drawn. *Oh God*, Erica cringed. *I hate needles! I can't believe I have to have an HIV test.*

When they got back to the car, she called Dwight. She didn't want to talk too much in front of her mother. He told her he got out of work at one o'clock. She said that she would meet him at Wegmans for lunch.

She wanted to show Dwight the ultrasound picture and tell him about the appointment.

"I changed my mind," Erica said. "Let's go to the Village Café. I'm so hungry for a burger."

They sat in a booth, way in the back. Erica showed Dwight the ultrasound picture, and he smiled. He leaned over and kissed her. "I guess we've got good chemistry, and not just in the classroom."

"You are so goofy! That's very funny."

Dwight watched Erica wolf down her burger and fries, happy that she wasn't feeling sick. He gave her his pickles. "Aren't you supposed to like these when you're pregnant?"

She was relieved that Dwight was keeping the mood light. "I just can't eat enough these days."

"So, you know your Mom called mine, right?"

"Oh, right, you and your mom are coming over for dinner Saturday night. That should be interesting."

"Babe, they want to help us."

"I know. My mom doesn't seem as angry anymore."

"It's going to be hard to face your mother," Dwight said with such a contrite look in his soft brown eyes.

"I feel the same way about seeing your mom."

She told Dwight about the rest of the appointment. She said that it went pretty well. Erica told him that the doctor put some restrictions on her cheerleading activities. She couldn't do any of the cheers that involved gymnastics. "I don't want to tell anyone at school about this until I have to. Christy knows, but I can trust her to keep it to herself. I'm not sure what I'm going to do. We have at least four games left."

"Why don't you just put an ace wrap on and say you screwed up your knee. At least you can put your uniform on and cheer on the sidelines."

"Dwight, that's such a good Idea. I hate lying, but in this case it's really not going to hurt anybody."

"I think a little white lie this time is okay," he said.

"Why don't I swing by the house and get my SAT study guide, and we can go to the library for a while," Erica said. "I need to do something to get my mind off of this for awhile."

"That's a good idea."

Beverly went to the shop after Erica's appointment. She was tempted to confide in Pam, but she just wasn't ready. She was for sure going to talk to Dr. Martino about it later that day.

He remarked about how stressed she looked as soon as she walked into his office. "Tell me, what's happened to make you look so sad and anxious? Sit down, let's get started."

"My daughter's pregnant." She reached for the box of tissues, because she could feel the tears coming. "I don't want this for Erica. She's determined to have the baby. I'm going to be honest with you. I'm pro-choice. I tried to convince her that it would be okay if she decided to have an abortion."

"I assume that's not what she wants."

"No. She really loves this boy, and she says she can't just kill their baby. Yes, she uses the word 'kill'. When I was trying to talk to her I made the mistake of telling her that I had an abortion in college." Beverly went on to tell Dr. Martino about own story.

"Beverly, it took a lot of courage and honesty to tell your daughter, and me for that matter, that you had an unintended pregnancy that you decided to terminate."

"But I don't think she respects me for that. She knows that the circumstances were different, but she just thinks abortion is wrong, period."

"It truly is for some women."

"It really brought back a lot of guilt feelings that took many years for me to get past. If you could only have seen the way she looked at me."

"You wish your daughter wasn't going to have this baby, but have you thought about the guilt she would suffer if she aborted a baby conceived with someone she truly loves?"

"You are probably right. I just wish Tom were here to help me handle this latest crisis. I don't know what he would have said. Erica was the light of his life. He was more invested in the Catholic faith then I am. I don't think he would have encouraged her to terminate the pregnancy, but I just don't know."

"Did you ever share with him your experience?"

"I did, after we were engaged. I didn't want there to be any big secrets between us. He only said that he was sorry, and that it had to have been awful for me. Tom never mentioned it again, ever."

"Beverly, you've told me you're an artist. Paint a new picture of this situation."

"How do you mean?"

"You've suffered the loss of your own little boy and your husband. This is new life, a brand new baby, a child to love and nurture. I know you are young, but this is your first grandchild. This child was conceived in a loving relationship."

"Erica wants to go to college and on to medical school. Dwight has dreams of college. How will these teenagers raise a baby and make all that happen?"

"Beverly, teenagers have had unintended pregnancies since the beginning of time. I know you didn't believe this could happen to your own daughter, but it has. You are a strong and kind woman. I know how much you love Erica. I know you will find the courage to help her make this work."

She told him that she had taken Erica to her first doctor's appointment and that she had set up a dinner with Dwight and his mother this weekend.

"Beverly, you have already accepted this and taken the first steps."

She felt better after leaving Dr. Martino's office. It felt good just talking to someone she trusted about this. What she really dreaded was telling other people. What would they think, and what would they say? Normally there wouldn't have been a basketball game during February break, but one of the scheduled games in January was called off due to weather, so there was a makeup game on Friday night. Beverly planned on going to the game with Brad and having dinner with him afterwards. She planned on sharing her news with Brad then.

Beverly told Pam at work on Friday. Pam hugged her friend. "I know this isn't what you want. It's got to be so stressful... stressful for all of you. I'll help in any way I can. Don't worry about anything here at the shop. I've got it covered." Beverly didn't know what she would do without Pam. Her loyalty was unconditional.

That night she and Brad sat in the stands and watched the game. Fatherhood didn't seem to affect Dwight's performance on the court. He was awesome. Erica had told her that there would be some scouts from Syracuse University at the game to watch him play. Beverly saw the men talking to Coach Novak. They had to have been impressed. She was happy for Dwight, but it also felt bittersweet. Would he still eventually go to Syracuse to play, even now? Brad asked Beverly what was up with Erica's knee. She had it wrapped. Had she been injured? Beverly explained that she would tell him about it later.

There was a little bistro downtown that served till late. After the game, Beverly and Brad went to say hello to Erica before heading out. Erica said that she was really tired. She said that she was planning on going home right after the game. Beverly remembered how fatigued you could be in the first trimester of pregnancy. She kissed her daughter goodnight.

Brad ordered a bottle of her favorite Merlot as soon as they sat down. "What is it, Beverly, is something wrong?"

"Oh, Brad, this is hard for me to tell you, but Erica's pregnant. Her knee is fine. She's just faking an injury so she won't have to do the cheers involving gymnastics."

"Beverly, I really don't know what to say. I know it doesn't change the way I feel about you, nor her, for that matter. You can tell how hard she's

182

fallen for Dwight. I'm not surprised they were having sex. I'm sorry she got pregnant, though. So how is she handling it? He looked deeply into her eyes. How are you handling it?" He took her hand and brought it up to his mouth and kissed it. His sweet, simple gesture made her cry. "Beverly, it's okay. It will all work out."

Brad was such a good listener. That was one of the things that Beverly loved most about him. He wasn't one to cast judgment. He was so calm and seemed to think carefully before he spoke. Tom was much more spontaneous and animated. They were two very different men.

"Let me order for you," he said. He ordered for her a plate of penne pasta with a luscious, vodka and tomato cream sauce. It had a slight smoky flavor with pieces of rendered bacon.

"Oh God, this is good," she said. For the first time all week, she actually felt like eating.

He ordered an Irish coffee for her after the meal. He finished up with a Scotch.

"Beverly, come home with me tonight." She took a minute before answering. Erica pretty much said that she knew that she and Brad were sleeping together. Everything was pretty much out in the open now. She needed Brad tonight. *I'll still be discrete,* she thought, *but I'm going to live my life, too.* She called Erica. It went right to voice mail. She let her know she was staying at Brad's for the night. She didn't want to be dishonest, and she didn't want her daughter to worry. Beverly loved sleeping at Brad's. She loved sleeping with Brad. He was a wonderful lover. He made her forget. He made her feel so secure.

That night she had a dream. She had her easel set up, and she was sitting on a bench painting in the park. Tom was pushing Erica on a swing. She was just a very little girl. She was laughing. Her blond hair blew in the breeze. He was talking to another man who was also pushing a child on the swings. The child had very dark brown curls. The other man turned to smile at her. It was Brad. She dropped her brush. When she stood up to bend over and pick it up, she saw that there was bright red blood trickling down between her legs. Beverly startled and the dream woke her up. Her heart was pounding. Brad reached out for her and held her.

Brad was already up and showered when she woke up the next morning. He kissed her and brought her in a cup of coffee. He had to get to the hospital for rounds. Beverly had already told Pam that she wasn't planning on coming in today. Pam knew about her dinner with Ruby and Dwight. When she got home, Erica was still in bed. After her shower, Beverly put a pot of coffee on. She started mixing the ingredients for her brownies when Erica came down.

"Oh, Mom, I can't deal with the smell of that coffee." She poured herself a glass of orange juice and went into the den. A few minutes later, she ran to the bathroom and got sick.

"Honey, the juice might be too much acid on an empty stomach. I'll make you some toast. I put the coffee maker in the pantry."

"That's really the first time I've gotten sick. I'm okay now." She sat on the counter and ate her toast. Beverly made her some herbal tea.

"Would it be okay if Nana came for dinner, too?"

"I don't see why not. We'll probably need her help to get you through this pregnancy and also to help with the new baby."

"She said that she's excited to be a great-grandmother." Beverly knew that was Helen's way of placating Erica.

Beverly was planning on making an easy dinner. She was making a roasted chicken, wild rice, and green beans, and of course the brownies for dessert. She was more than a little nervous about the dinner.

On Saturday morning, Dwight's Uncle Henry was in the kitchen having coffee with his mother when he came down. "Good morning," he said, "Why don't you get yourself a bowl of cereal and we'll sit down and talk." Dwight knew his mother had probably told his uncle the news.

"So, I guess you know, then," Dwight said contritely. "You've got to understand how I feel about Erica. I love her. We were using protection, but it happened anyway. I'm really sorry and know how disappointed everyone will be with me."

"You've got to make this right," Henry said. Your mom, and Aunt Sarah and I will stand by you. We will help you in any way we can, but you've got to be a man about this. You've got to be supportive to Erica. Show her you love her. She needs you. She can't do this alone. You're somebody's daddy now. That's a big responsibility. The welfare of your child will always have to come first."

"Uncle, I know this. Don't you think I know what it's like not having a father?"

"Just remember, son, you can be a father and still have your dreams, too. You just might have to work a little harder." Henry hugged his nephew and said that he had to get to the firehouse. He had a box of donuts with him. He put a big glazed donut on a napkin and put it down next to Dwight. He knew they were his nephew's favorite. "Bye for now. Have a good day."

"Ma, how will I explain this to the twins?"

"I'll figure out a way to tell them, son." But Ruby had no idea what she would say. They had their brother placed up on a pedestal.

Dwight and Ruby arrived at the McIntyre's promptly at six. Ruby walked in and held out her arms to Erica. She hugged her and just said, "It will be okay, honey." She hugged Beverly and then Helen before they all sat down in the living room. Erica and Dwight sat on the couch. They held hands. Beverly offered everyone a beverage. Everyone asked for water. *How am I going to get through this?* Beverly asked herself as she opened a bottle of chardonnay in the kitchen. Ruby seemed so calm. Well, the stakes weren't exactly even. She had the teenage daughter who would soon be obviously pregnant for the whole world to see. Then she chastised herself. *I've got to be fair. Erica was a willing participant.*

When she walked back into the living room, it occurred to her that she never even greeted Dwight. She handed him his glass of water. She placed her hand on his cheek. "Dwight, I'm so sorry, I didn't even say hello to you."

"That's okay, Mrs. McIntyre, you're probably really angry and disappointed."

"Yes, at first I was, but I'm starting to accept all this, and I want to help."

"Thank you, ma'am, I'm sorry I let you down."

"Dwight, I know Erica loves you. I'm sure you are not entirely to blame for this. Anyway, this isn't about blame. We want to figure out how to make the best of this situation. We want to do what's best for this baby and what's best for both you and Erica." The conversation was awkward at first, but got a little easier. Beverly and Ruby decided they would make an appointment at the school guidance office and discuss everything with them together. Helen just listened. She only said that she was looking forward to her first great grandchild. She was eager to babysit.

They sat down to eat dinner. The tension eased up a bit. It was agreed that they would just have to take this "one step at a time." Figuring out the school part was the first step. After the Washingtons left, Erica kissed her mother and Helen, then announced that she was she was exhausted and just wanted to go to bed. *God, I am so tired,* she thought, *and it's only nine.* She stretched out on her bed and put her hands low on her belly. *I'm too tired to even get undressed.* She fell asleep in her clothes.

Helen helped Beverly clean up. Beverly couldn't wait for her mother-in-law to go home. She just needed to be alone. After she left, Beverly poured herself another glass of wine and sat in her favorite chair. She got out an old family photo album. *If only I could have my old life back,* she thought. She looked at pictures of Tom and Erica and Johnny. The strength she felt earlier in the day was draining away. The tears were back.

Her cell phone vibrated. She had a call from Brad. She picked up the call. "Beverly, I can't get you off my mind. How did things go tonight?" She told him all about it. "I can tell you've been crying. I'm worried about the stress you've been under. Let me take you to a movie tomorrow afternoon. I'm free after rounds. Maybe it would be good to get your mind off things for a while. I'll pick you up at noon. We'll have lunch first." Beverly was relieved that Brad called. His concern was so genuine and sweet. She knew that if he hadn't called she would have gone upstairs and taken an Ambien. That definitely wasn't a good idea after the chardonnay. Instead, she went up to her room and watched an old movie until she fell asleep.

Chapter 23

Beverly had a wonderful afternoon with Brad. There was just something about him that made her feel so secure. *Maybe that's how Erica fell in love with Dwight,* she thought. *There was such a void in our lives after Tom died. The hurt was so deep.* Brad helped to seal off that hole in my heart, Beverly reasoned Dwight was that person for Erica.

With Brad, I just felt friendship for him at first. The physical attraction came later. I have to admit, I am beginning to have very strong feelings for him. It's happening to me, so how can I condemn Erica? I'm sure now that the sex was a natural progression of their feelings.

Am I falling in love with Brad too soon? Is Tom somewhere looking down on us thinking, "I've been dead less than six months and my wife is already sleeping with someone else, and my little girl is pregnant?" God, can my life get any more complicated? She was deep in thought when Erica and Christy walked through the door. They were laughing about something. It was good to see her daughter laughing. Beverly asked Christy if she wanted to stay awhile and have dinner. They could order a pizza.

"Mrs. McIntyre, it's okay, I know." That broke the ice. The three of them were able to talk freely. They talked about school and what the other kids would say. "I'm going to wait as long as I can before I tell them," Erica said, "Maybe I won't show for another couple of months."

"You know, Mrs. McIntyre, I'm going to be this baby's godmother. I hope it's a girl!"

It had been a heavy weekend, but Beverly thought that it had ended well.

On Monday, Erica was back to school. Vacation was over. Beverly filled Pam in on her weekend and told her she needed to call the school to make an appointment with the guidance counselor. Ruby gave Beverly her work schedule for the next few weeks. They wanted to meet with them together. She stepped away to the back of the shop to make the appointment.

They would meet the following Monday at four o'clock. As it turned out, Dwight's guidance counselor was the same as Erica's. They would all meet together. Erica and Dwight would also be present at the meeting. Mrs. Keaton, the guidance counselor, was very understanding when Beverly informed her of the reason for the meeting. She said that she was happy that the appointment was made early in Erica's pregnancy, and that it was good that they were all meeting together.

As the week progressed, things seemed almost back to normal. *I would love to get away*, Beverly thought. *Maybe if I could get away for awhile, I could wrap my head around all of this. My birthday is in March, maybe then*, she thought.

By the weekend, Beverly could tell that Erica was beat. She knew how lousy you could feel in the first trimester. She felt a little sorry for her. Ruby was working and Dwight was either working or watching his sisters. Erica didn't see much of him. She knew that Erica was feeling down because of that. *Oh well, this isn't going to be easy.*

Beverly and Brad went out to dinner with the Dwyers. She wasn't ready to tell them that Erica was pregnant. Susan followed Beverly to the ladies room. "You have been seeing a lot of Brad, haven't you?"

"I have, and I have to admit, I have feelings for him. He's not Tom, but he's really a good guy." As soon as she had said the "he's not Tom" part, she regretted it.

"Of course he's not Tom. But that doesn't mean you can't love him for the man he is."

"Oh, it's a little early to be using the word love."

"I'm just glad to see you with another man in your life. I can see the way he looks at you. He really cares for you. I hope it works out for you, Bev."

"Thanks, Susan, it would be nice if something worked out or something good happened in my life."

Susan sensed that there was something else, something Bev didn't want to share with her.

The rest of the weekend dragged on. Beverly took a long walk on Sunday and played her violin for a while. She was trying to get her stress down to a manageable level.

When Erica walked into the kitchen on Monday morning, Bev knew she was feeling a little rough. "I'll make you the tea and toast. Here, I bought the vitamin B6 that Dr. Anderson suggested. Why don't you take it? She say's it can really take the edge off the nausea."

"I'm just so nervous, Mom. This meeting at school will be so intense."

"I know, but I'll be there, and Dwight will be there. We've just got to do it."

Erica took the vitamin and grabbed the toast to go. She kissed her mother on the cheek.

"See you after school, Mom."

Beverly went to the shop. The spring merchandise was starting to come in, so that kept her busy for a little while. Brad called and asked if she wanted to meet him in the hospital cafeteria for lunch. His Monday was unusually light. She did.

When Beverly saw Brad a wave of attraction came over her. She always thought Tom looked sexy in his scrubs. That was ditto for Brad. She wasn't sure it was such a good idea to meet him in the cafeteria. She caught some stares. People knew she was Tom McIntyre's wife. She ran into Martha Graham. Martha always seemed to know everything that was happening in the department. She probably already heard that her former boss's wife was seeing Dr. Williams. She hugged Beverly and was very cordial. Beverly also saw Jake Goldstein. He came over to their table to say hello. She was sure Rebecca would find out that she was having lunch with Brad here at the hospital. Rebecca would have something to say about it. Beverly cringed. *Oh God*, she thought, *wait until she finds out that Erica's pregnant! It's people like her that I dread facing when the news is out.*

Brad knew she had the meeting at school later in the day. He was trying to calm her. "Let's talk about something else," he said. "I did some detective work, and I know you have a birthday coming up in March. Let's get away for a few days."

"Oh, I would love that!"

"Maybe we could string four days together. Leave on Thursday night and come home on Monday. I'll have my secretary look at my schedule and see what she can come up with. Do you think Helen would be able to keep an eye on Erica?"

"Oh, I think so."

"I've got to run, Beverly, let me know how your meeting goes." He was smart enough not to kiss her before he left. There was still staring.

Beverly ran a few errands after lunch and headed over to the school. She saw Ruby pull in the parking lot. She waited for her and they walked in together.

Donna Keaton was an attractive woman, very polished, probably in her early fifties. Beverly had met her once before, when Erica was a freshman. She wanted to talk privately with Beverly and Ruby before the kids came in.

"I'm so impressed to see the two of you in here together," she began. "I take it you two have met before?"

"We've gotten to know each other since my son and Erica started dating," Ruby said. Beverly admired Ruby. She was so poised. She didn't appear unnerved. "I want you to know, that Dwight really cares for Erica. He plans to be supportive to her in this pregnancy. These two kids have a very strong and loving relationship."

"I've seen them together," said Mrs. Keaton. "I agree. They are both great kids. We are proud to have Dwight here. He is an excellent student, and he has had an impressive season on the basketball court. And your Erica," she said, "has always been an asset to our school. We were in awe of her chairing the committee for the Valentine's dance. I can't believe how much money it raised for the hospital's cardiology unit. It has to have been tough for her losing her father at such a young age."

"We just want to help the kids get through this," Beverly began. "Erica wants to continue with the pregnancy. Unintended pregnancies are difficult to accept, and I know teen pregnancies are especially so. She has seen an obstetrician. Her due date is October 2nd. Will she be allowed to continue going to class or is there some policy against it?"

"I can assure you that this situation has happened at this school before. Teens are sexually active. It's helpful that you are both involved and supportive. That's not always the case. In answer to your question, yes, Erica can continue to come to school and attend classes and school activities, unless the doctor places specific restrictions on her. If she needs to stay out, the district will provide a tutor for her. Most of her third trimester will be during the summer. That will make it a little easier. After the summer, she might want to stay out until after the baby is born and she's ready to come back. We'll just have to see how it goes for her."

"Mrs. Keaton, will my son have to give up his spot in the urban-suburban program? I know that students in the program have to show good character and not have any disciplinary problems. I'm worried that you will make him leave."

Beverly's heart went out to Ruby. She looked so contrite.

"No, Mrs. Washington, Dwight won't be asked to leave. He's really adjusted well to our school, and he has never had a disciplinary problem. His teachers speak very highly of him. He is eighteen, and I wouldn't say having sex shows bad character, as long as it was consensual, which I assume it was. I'll speak with the principal, but I highly doubt he would want to see Dwight leave."

Ruby looked relieved, and Beverly had to admit that she, too, was relieved. She knew how upset Erica would be if Dwight had to leave the school.

"I both want you to understand that this will be hard, socially, for Erica and Dwight. High school kids can be very cruel. Erica, especially, will need a lot of support and maybe some mental health counseling. Let's have the kids come in, and we'll talk some more."

Erica and Dwight looked scared to death. "Relax, you two," Mrs. Keaton said. "Mistakes happen to the best of us. It's how you deal with the mistake that's important. Erica, as I explained to your mother, you can continue to come to school, as long as your doctor allows it. If you have to stay out, we can get you a tutor. Dwight, you can continue to come to school here the rest of this semester and again in the fall, as long as you stay out of trouble and keep your grades up."

"Yes, ma'am, I understand," he replied.

"I'll let you decide when you want to tell your other teachers and any students about the pregnancy. If you're uncomfortable telling your teachers, I can do so for you. I'll speak to the principal."

"If any situations with the kids come up that you can't handle, let me know. You two are both such good students. I hope you will continue to work hard at your studies. This doesn't have to be lost time. You still have bright futures ahead of you, which will include a brand new baby. I want you to know I will do anything I can to help you through this. My door is always open to you."

Dwight and Erica walked out of the office holding hands. Ruby and Beverly walked together to the parking lot. They hugged. "Thank you, sweet Jesus," Ruby said. "That went better than I thought."

Dwight was missing basketball practice for the meeting. He knew he would have to tell Coach Novak, at some point, about his situation. Today he just told him that he had an appointment he couldn't miss. Coach didn't question him any further. Dwight hated letting him down. *I feel like I've let everyone down,* he thought.

Erica and Dwight said that they were going to the library to study. They would take a break and get something to eat later. Beverly and Ruby understood that they probably had a lot to talk about, and both agreed that it was okay.

They got a table in the library in one of the more secluded areas. As soon as they sat down Erica started to cry. *Oh God,* Dwight thought, *it must be the pregnancy. She has been crying so much lately.* "Babe, I thought that all went pretty well."

"Did it, do you think so?"

"I thought Mrs. Keaton was pretty cool about it. I thought I was going to get kicked out of your school. There were always a few pregnant girls walking around my old school, but I'm sure that doesn't happen so much here."

"I can't remember anybody else."

"Babe, most of the time that you'll be real pregnant will be in the summer. You won't even be in school."

"Dwight, I'm 'REAL' pregnant now. I just don't feel like myself. Look at me... I'm a mess! I look like shit. I feel like shit. I just can't even imagine what the other kids or our teachers will say when they find out."

Dwight took her hand and tried to soothe her. "You don't look like shit. You look beautiful to me. The kids and our teachers accepted us, as a

192

couple, I think they'll be okay. It hurts me to see you so down. I only meant that it will be the summer when you will LOOK really pregnant. We can be together more, so I can be there for you. I'm going to treat you like a princess."

That made Erica smile. "Let's just wait until the pregnancy starts to show to tell anyone at school. As for our teachers, let's let Mrs. Keaton tell them, but not for awhile. I'm only eight weeks pregnant. What if I lost the baby, and we had told them, and then there was no pregnancy?"

Erica saw the hurt on Dwight's face.

"Is that what you want?"

"No, I'm sorry. I can't believe I said that. I know it happens, though. People announce really early on that they're pregnant, and then there's a miscarriage. That would be a lousy thing to happen, but it would sure make life easier, for us anyway."

"Well, you said that you wanted to have this baby, so that's what I want too. We'll just have to accept whatever happens. Babe, I want to tell Coach myself. He's been a mentor to me at this school. I think I owe it to him to tell him myself."

"Okay, but wait a little, alright?"

"Sure. When I do tell him, I know he'll have some good advice for me." Aside from his Uncle Henry, Erica knew that Dwight didn't have many males in his life he could look up to.

"Okay, Mommy, we've got to write up this chem lab."

Erica punched him playfully. "What did you just call me?"

They studied awhile and then went for burritos. "God, those were good," Erica said. Later on back at the library, she was complaining of wicked heartburn. "My stomach just can't figure out what it wants."

The rest of February was pretty uneventful. Basketball season was over. They lost their division title in the semi-finals. Dwight was disappointed, but he knew that now he would have more time for Erica.

Chapter 24

Beverly's birthday was on March 20th. Brad had made some great plans for them. They were going to Amelia Island. They would fly into Jacksonville, Florida Thursday night, rent a car, and drive to the island. He made reservations at the Ritz Carlton. They could play golf, go to the beach, and just relax. They weren't flying back out until Monday afternoon. Beverly was so excited. She loved the beach, and she had never been to Amelia Island. *God*, she thought, *I just can't get away from here fast enough.*

Helen said that she was happy to have Erica stay with her. Helen seemed okay with her seeing Brad and going away with him for the weekend. Beverly realized that she didn't really always give her mother-in-law enough credit. She really was a good person and had been very supportive. The SAT's were that weekend. Dwight and Erica had been doing some serious review work to prepare. Beverly thought that Erica was starting to feel a little better.

Erica had another doctor's appointment the day before Beverly was planning on going away for the weekend. Beverly felt a little less guilty about going, if first she knew everything was okay with Erica and the baby. Dwight came to the appointment too. Dr. Anderson introduced herself to Dwight. He shook her hand. Beverly never realized how shy he could be sometimes.

Erica had a first trimester screen ultrasound to check the baby for Down's syndrome. The only thing Dwight could think about was his friend Gary at Wegmans, the guy with Down's syndrome. He was relieved when Dr. Anderson said that everything looked normal, but Erica would also have to have a blood test to confirm the final results. Beverly was fascinated. The image on the screen actually looked like a baby this time.

Erica told the doctor that she was actually feeling better, not so sick and exhausted all the time. "That's because in another week you'll be beginning your second trimester. That's the easiest one, when you feel the best. All your blood tests from your last appointment look good, but you are a little anemic. I'm going to put you on an iron supplement to take along with your prenatal vitamins."

They went back to the McIntyre's after the appointment. Dwight stayed for dinner, and later he and Erica went up to her room to study for the SAT's. *I have never allowed them to go to Erica's room before,* Beverly thought, *well, I guess the game has changed.*

Beverly saw Dr. Martino for her usual Thursday appointment before leaving with Brad that night. She had a lot to share with him. "Beverly, it's really admirable how you're handling your daughter's pregnancy. I hope you know that."

"What I'm really worried about is when other people start finding out, which will probably be pretty soon."

"Try and come up with some sort of automatic response, so they can't catch you off guard. Maybe something like, 'life is full of surprises and challenges, I'm going to do my best to be supportive to my daughter'. Probably the less you say, the better. Some people will for sure make rude or unwelcomed comments. Vow to not let them get under your skin. So what else is going on in your life?" She told him about the weekend get-away with Brad.

"I need him. He's very supportive to me. I'm really developing some strong feelings for him, but I just feel kind of guilty. I feel like my time should be devoted to Erica, and it's just too soon. I feel like I'm being untrue to Tom, but at the same time I'm angry that Tom left me with this big, hot mess to deal with."

"Beverly, as I've told you before. Tom's gone. He's never coming back. You can't cheat on someone who is dead. It sounds to me that you have completely devoted yourself to helping your daughter. You deserve time to mend your own life. You deserve happiness. If you're falling in love with Brad, let it happen."

Beverly felt like she got a pass to enjoy the weekend. Erica and the baby were okay. Dr. Martino helped her to validate her feelings for Brad. She needed this weekend, and she planned to enjoy it.

Brad booked the tickets in first class. He ordered them a cocktail as soon as they took their seats. After the first few sips, Beverly could feel her stress start to dissipate.

Their room was awesome. It was dark when they arrived at the hotel, but she knew that their room had an ocean view. Beverly could hear the waves crashing on the beach when she stepped out on the terrace. She could smell the salt air. It was only minutes before Brad had her undressed and was making love to her. Beverly felt so good. This was just what she needed. Brad was such a romantic, and he was such a good lover. She felt very serene as she drifted off to sleep in his arms. She slept soundly and awoke to his kiss in the morning.

He made love to her again and put a call into room service for breakfast. Beverly pulled off a piece of her chocolate croissant and fed it to Brad. Then she kissed him, licking the chocolate off his lips. "Oh God, these are so good. You are so good...just what I needed this weekend."

"I'm thrilled to have you all to myself," he said. "You better not get me going, or we will never make our tee time." Beverly followed him into the shower.

Brad was really impressed with Beverly's golfing abilities. She had a bittersweet moment when she remembered the last time she played golf. She and Tom had played with the Dwyer's on Labor Day just before Tom died. Brad could see that she was suddenly lost in the moment. He said nothing. He just walked over to her and wrapped her in his arms.

After golf, they took a long walk on the beach. "Beverly, I'm in love with you. I know it's probably too soon for you to have the same feelings for me, but I couldn't let another day go by without telling you." Beverly didn't know what to say. She just held his face in her hands and kissed him.

Saturday was Beverly's birthday. She awoke to her cell phone ringing. "Hi, Mom, I wanted to be the first to wish you a happy birthday. I love you. Are you having a nice time with Dr. Williams?"

"Oh, honey, I am. Amelia Island is beautiful. We are staying at a beautiful hotel. Are you okay? Are you feeling alright?"

"Oh, I'm okay, Mom. Nana is taking good care of me, but I'm so nervous about today and the SAT's. It's making me nauseous again!"

"Have Nana make you the ginger tea and toast. Bring a snack in your bag. You'll be okay. Good luck, sweetie. Call me when you get out, okay? I love you, and thanks for calling. Bye."

Brad was smiling. "You're amazing, do you know that?"

Today they were planning on going horseback riding on the beach. Beverly was so excited. She knew she would love it. That night, Brad was planning on taking her to a restaurant in Fernandina Beach, a charming old seaport not far from Amelia Island.

She did enjoy the horseback riding. The only other time that she ever rode was when she and Tom were in Colorado on a summer vacation when Erica was away at camp. They rode with a guide out into the Rocky Mountains. She would never forget it. It was so beautiful up in the mountains. The air was so fresh and clean, and there were wild flowers everywhere. Riding on the beach was also incredible. It was beautiful in other ways.

She and Brad had a wonderful seafood dinner. It was a quaint, romantic little restaurant on the water. They sat outside and ate by candlelight. A strolling musician came by and played by their table. The waiter presented her with a slice of key lime pie, complete with birthday candle. Brad gave her his gift as they finished their second bottle of wine. It was a beautiful choker necklace with large pink pearls. He got up to put the necklace around her and fasten the clasp. He kissed the back of her neck. He looked at her and smiled.

"The color is beautiful with your skin. Those pearls make your face glow."

"Thank you, Brad, I love them. It's probably all that exquisite wine and being with you, that's really making me glow. This has been a wonderful day. I feel so relaxed."

However, her sleep wasn't very peaceful that night. She had another disturbing dream. She was on vacation with Tom and Erica. They were having dinner outside on the patio of some beautiful estate. Erica was so excited. "Mommy, blow out the candles on your cake." The cake was covered in pale pink roses. After dinner she went up to bed. She pulled back the covers and there was the head of a dead horse in the bed. Tom wasn't there when she called out for him.

Beverly bolted up in bed and was trembling. Brad held her, and she told him about the dream. "The 'Godfather' was one of Tom's favorite movies," Beverly told him.

Brad knew that he had to be patient, but it was hard competing with a dead man, because he was always there. He knew that Beverly was still very much in love with her husband, and she was probably feeling a little guilt about being in another relationship.

Back at home, Dwight and Erica walked out of the school cafeteria, the testing site for the SATs.

"Those were brutal, Dwight said. I guess your best is all you can do."

"I'm most worried about the math part," Erica said. They decided to pick up food at Wegmans for lunch. "Let's bring it back to my house, so we can be alone for awhile. When they were waiting in the checkout line, Dwight saw the guy that his mom had been dating. He was with another lady, and they looked pretty chummy. He was pushing the cart for her. She was kind of all over him, which he was clearly enjoying. Erica looked at Dwight and saw they he was suddenly very disturbed about something. She asked him what was wrong.

"See that dude over there? His name is Michael Harvey. He goes to my church. He's also dating my mother. They have been seeing a lot of each other. I think she's really into him. She says that he's a really good guy. He's a history teacher at one of the city schools. So, what's that all about teach?"

"So, what are you going to do? Are you going to tell her?" Erica knew he was upset, he hardly ever got angry.

"I don't know, Babe, but I couldn't stand to see my mother hurt. She deserves better than that. I've got to think about it."

She could tell Dwight was still bothered by it as they ate their lunch at the McIntyre's kitchen table. "Dwight, we haven't been really alone in a very long time." They went upstairs to her room. They made love for the first time since Erica found out she was pregnant. She thought that sex was actually better, and they didn't have to bother with the condoms. That was definitely a bonus.

"Erica, I've really missed being with you. You're body is changing in some beautiful ways. Are you sure it's okay to have sex when you're pregnant?"

"Dr. Anderson gave me a book about pregnancy. It's definitely okay. You just can't if you're having problems with bleeding or premature labor. It even says that it can feel better, which it definitely does."

Dwight smiled. "Well, let's do it again, then."

Erica felt happier than she had in a long time. Dwight gently put his hands on her belly. "Will this be my son or my daughter? What do you think?"

"I don't know, but when we have our next ultrasound at the end of April or early in May we can find out. Dwight, if it's a boy, can we call him Thomas after by father?"

"Sure, Babe, if that's what you want. But if it's a girl, how about Martina?"

Erica looked puzzled. "Why Martina?" she asked.

"Well, you got dibs on the boy's name, and I do like the idea of naming him after your father. But you know how I feel about Martin Luther King. Martina for a girl's name would be kind of pretty and different. You've seen that quote I have up on my wall. 'Faith is taking the first step even when you don't see the whole staircase.' Those words have gotten me though some tough times. His words are helping me now."

"Oh, that's beautiful. I love the name Martina, if it's a girl."

They got dressed and Erica drove him back to Wegmans. He had to work at four. Erica couldn't believe they were talking about what they were going to name their baby.

Dwight was still really bothered about seeing that guy his mother was dating at Wegmans. He thought maybe he would say something to his uncle about it. Ruby was working that night. Dwight had to pick his sisters up at his aunt and uncle's house when he got out of work at eight o'clock.

When he got there his aunt and uncle were sitting at the kitchen table working on their taxes. The kids were in the living room watching

TV. Aunt Sarah stood up and gave him a hug. "I made pulled pork for dinner. Can I make you a sandwich, Dwight?"

"That sounds great. I can't turn that down."

Sarah made him a sandwich and set it down on the table with a glass of milk. "It's okay, I know about you and Erica and the baby. You know I'll help in any way I can. I can't believe I'm going to be a great auntie." She smiled so sweetly. Dwight loved his aunt almost as much as he loved his mother.

"Aunt Sarah, this is so good, do mind if I have another?"

She made him another sandwich. "I've got tell you two something," he began. "I need some advice."

His uncle looked up from all the paperwork scattered across the table and peered at him over his glasses. "What is it, son? Is this about Erica?"

"No, Uncle, it's about my mother. I saw that guy she's been dating shopping at Wegman's, pretty cozy with some other lady. I know Mama really likes him, and it's been nice to see her happy, but there's something about that guy I've never liked. He's a little too smooth. He'd better not be stringing her on."

"Yeah, I kind of have that feeling about him too." Henry said.

"Do you think I should say something to her?" Dwight asked.

"Your mama's a big girl. She can handle herself," Sarah said.

Henry looked at his wife and just uttered "Uh-huh." Dwight knew his uncle would keep an eye on him.

Aunt Sarah served him a piece of pineapple upside down cake. After he finished his cake, he kissed his aunt and collected his sisters to go home. His aunt and uncle only lived two blocks away, but his mother never let his sisters walk it alone.

Erica loved staying at her grandmother's house. The guest room had a white, antique, wrought iron bed. The bed was so comfy. It was made up with a featherbed, soft white linen sheets, and a beautiful flowered quilt that Helen had bought when she was in Ireland. Erica went upstairs to take a nap. Taking the SATs had really tired her out. Frankie jumped up on the bed and snuggled up against her. She heard somewhere that dogs could sense when a woman was pregnant. She had a dream about a little boy that looked just like Johnny except his hair was dark, not blond like Johnny's. She was listening to his heart with a stethoscope. The little boy said, "Mommy, do I have a good heart?" The dream woke her up. I wonder if this means that I'll have a boy. I can't wait until my next ultrasound when I'll find out if everything is okay with the baby. Erica smelled something heavenly cooking downstairs. She went down to the kitchen.

"Nana, is that what I think it is... chicken pot pie?"

"It is, honey. I thought it would be easy on your stomach. Is that getting any better?"

"Much better, but I still get so tired."

"You're a busy girl, honey, and it's probably stress, too."

She told her grandmother about her dream. "All pregnant women worry about their babies, that they will be perfect and strong. I've been praying for you and your baby every day. At least, now, there are all sorts of tests they can do before the baby is born to see if everything is alright. When I had my children, I never even had an ultrasound. You just hold on to positive thoughts, honey. Take good care of yourself. The rest is in the good Lord's hands. Tomorrow you and I will go to mass."

"Okay, Nana, I haven't been in a long time, and I feel bad about it, because I know it is Lent."

"Well, we'll go tomorrow. We'll light a candle. I don't know why, but when I say a prayer after lighting a candle, it always makes me feel better. Now I'm going to get us some ice cream for dessert. The calcium will be good for the baby." Erica knew her grandmother loved ice cream. She gave her a generous dish of strawberry with hot fudge sauce.

"Oh, Nana, this meal was so good."

"Honey, I saw in the paper that one of my all time favorite movies, 'Gone with the Wind', is on tonight. Shall we watch it together?"

Erica loved old movies. This one was really good. It really helped to take her mind off everything. *I can't believe how relaxed I am*, Erica thought. *I hope Mom's having a good time. I can't wait to give her my present.* She found a great picture of her parents and had it enlarged to an eight by ten size. She found a unique sterling silver frame in a boutique store. She thought it framed the picture perfectly. Her mother and her father looked so happy. It was taken probably about ten years ago. They looked so young. *Mom is so pretty,* Erica thought, *and Dad was smiling in a way that made his eyes twinkle.* She also bought Beverly the latest novel by her favorite author, Jodi Picoult.

On Sunday, Erica and Helen went to mass and later went out to breakfast. "Nana, Mom's been really pretty good about accepting me being pregnant. I want to make her a birthday cake. I know her birthday was Saturday, but we can have it when she gets home tomorrow. I know she loves coconut cake. Will you help me make one?"

"Sure, honey. That's not a cake I've ever made, but I'm sure we could find a recipe."

Dwight also went to his church with his mother and sisters. They stayed for coffee hour. Dwight saw Michael Harvey heading over to her. He was with his sister, Michelle, who was a friend of his mother's. Dwight couldn't stand it. He walked over to stand by his mother. "Hi, Mr. Harvey," he said, "How's it going?" Michael Harvey gave Dwight his smooth smile and shook his hand.

"Hi, Dwight, it's good to see you. Your mother said that you had SATs yesterday? What did you think?"

"They were brutal, but actually not as bad as I thought. By the way, I saw you at Wegmans while I was working yesterday afternoon." Dwight turned a little so that he could look at him directly. He narrowed his eyes and said, "I'm sorry I wasn't able to come over and say hello."

Mission accomplished. Dwight could tell the dude got his message. However, the entire conversation went right over his mother's head. He walked over to his uncle and told him about it. His uncle smiled, then just said, "You be careful, son."

Erica called him later that morning. She told him about her plans to bake with Helen that afternoon. "Hey, Babe, my mom makes a great coconut cake. Do you want me to ask her for the recipe?"

"Oh, would you? Maybe you could bring it over and hang out when we make it."

"I can until four, and then I have to work again."

Ruby was thrilled to give out the recipe. "Dwight, are you alright with me seeing Mr. Harvey? I get the feeling you don't like him that much."

"I guess he's okay, Ma, you're the one who has to like him."

Ruby wondered what was on her son's mind. Dwight had pretty good instincts about people.

Dwight brought the recipe over to Helen's, as promised. Helen was growing very fond of Dwight. He hugged her when he walked in. "It's always nice to see you, ma'am." He sat next to Helen on a stool at the counter as Erica started measuring ingredients for the cake.

"My granddad loves this cake. My mom makes it for him whenever he comes to town." Helen asked Dwight to tell her more about the rest of his family. Dwight reminded Helen of Tom's friend, Samuel, not because they were both black, but because they had the same gentle manner.

The three of them chatted easily while Erica worked on the cake. She scraped the last of the batter into the pans. She gave Dwight the spoon to lick. "I think you did it. So far it tastes just like my mother's."

"Well it's still got to bake, and I have to make the frosting."

"I'm sure it will be great. I've really got to get going."

"Hang on a second. I just want to show you what I got for my mother's present. It's not wrapped yet." She went to get the picture.

"So, that's your father when he was a little younger. That's really a good picture. Your mother will love it. They both look so happy. You look a lot like your father, Babe."

"Nana, I'm going to drive Dwight to work. Can you put the cake in the oven and set the timer for twenty-five minutes? I'll be right back."

"Don't worry, honey, I'll take good care of your cake. Nice to see you, Dwight, please say hello to your mother for me."

Helen picked up the picture of her son and his wife. She had never seen the picture. Tom looked so young and handsome. She clutched the picture to her chest, and it brought tears to her eyes. *I can't believe he won't be around to see his first grandchild.* She studied the picture. *I can't picture Erica's baby. I guess I just never imagined having a bi-racial great-grandchild, but I'm sure the baby will be beautiful.*

204

Chapter 25

Beverly was home on Monday when Erica came in from school. She had made a pot of one of Erica's favorite soups... tomato basil. She was slicing bread for grilled ham and cheese sandwiches when her daughter walked in.

"Hi, Mom, I'm glad your home. I can't believe you had time to make that soup. You look great. I can tell you got a little sun. Tell me about your trip."

Beverly filled her daughter in on the details of her trip... the details she could share, anyway.

"So, what did he get you for a present?" Erica asked. She was dying to know.

Beverly went upstairs and brought down the pearls.

"Oh, Mom, they're gorgeous!" Erica tried on the necklace and went to look at herself in the hall mirror. "Mom, he must really care for you."

Beverly didn't know what to say. "Can I give you my present before dinner?"

Beverly stopped what she was doing at sat down at the kitchen table. She opened up the package that her daughter had so carefully wrapped.

"Oh, honey, I love this picture." She hugged her daughter. Seeing the picture only reinforced her conflicted feelings about her new relationship. A wave of sadness came over her, and she did her best to fight back the tears.

"Oh, Mom, I didn't mean to upset you. I found the picture, and I thought it was such a great picture of you and Dad. You guys look like movie stars. Open this one, this present won't make you cry."

Beverly thanked her daughter for the book. "These are such thoughtful gifts."

Beverly finished grilling the sandwiches and ladled up the soup. They continued to chat through dinner. Erica told her mother that she had gone to mass with Helen. "Mom do you realize that Easter is only less than two weeks away?"

Beverly sighed, "I guess I haven't thought much about it. It's kind of early this year. What do you want to do?"

"I don't know, Mom. Don't forget, no school the entire week after."

"Do you want to go somewhere?"

"No, not really, I just want to stay here and spend some time with Dwight. I think Christy is going on a cruise with her parents."

"Well, honey, like Thanksgiving and Christmas, we'll just have to make the best of it."

Erica got up and cleared the table. "Mom, go in the den. I've got a surprise for you."

Beverly picked up her wine glass and went to sit on the couch. She wasn't sure what Erica was up to. She brought the picture with her and looked at it again. She remembered a conversation she had with Dr. Martino. She had told him that Tom was still so present in the house. There was his record collection, his medical books, and awards... they were still all there. Beverly also told him that when she was particularly lonely, she would lay Tom's pajamas out next to her on the bed. Dr. Martino encouraged her to pack up his things. He had asked her if there were a lot of pictures of him around the house. She had told him, yes, there were pictures of him all over the house.

"Maybe you should work on putting those away, too, a little at a time. You can keep them in a drawer, and bring them out to look at whenever you want."

"But what about Erica, shouldn't she have the comfort of seeing pictures of her father throughout the house?"

"A few," he said, "but let her have all the pictures she wants in her room. If you make the changes gradually she probably won't notice."

Beverly held the picture in her hands and looked at it again. *Oh God, where will I put this?* The picture just made her feel more conflicted about her relationship with Brad. Then she wondered if it was Erica's subtle way of reminding her mother that she belonged to her father. *Maybe she wasn't as accepting of me going away with Brad as she appeared to be. I won't hurt her feelings. I'm going to find just the right spot for the picture.*

Erica walked in with the cake. "It's your fave, Mom, coconut cake. You're not going to believe this, but I made it myself. Ms. Washington gave me her recipe." She went back into the kitchen to get the plates and forks. She brought out a glass of milk for herself and a cup of coffee for her mother.

"Oh, Erica, this is really yummy. You've gone to a lot of trouble here."

"Nana coached me, but I made it. I've got to bring a slice over to her tomorrow, so she can try it. I'm going to bring a piece to school tomorrow for Dwight. He's got to tell me how it compares to his mother's."

"You're going to make me fat."

"Don't worry about it. I think you've lost a little weight since Daddy died. Speaking of weight, do you think I look any different? Can you tell I'm pregnant?"

"Your breasts look a little bigger, honey, but you really don't look all that different."

"I've put on five pounds already! Can you believe it?" Erica's petite, five foot four inch frame did look a bit fuller.

"It's only the beginning. Remember, Dr. Anderson said that the normal weight gain is 25 to 35 pounds. In less than a month, I think you'll probably start to show. Have you thought about what you will say when people ask you if you're pregnant?"

"I'll think of something when the time comes."

"Honey, hang on, I brought you something." Beverly went upstairs and came down with a bag. She pulled out something adorable for the baby. It was a yellow hooded baby sweater. "Kissed by the sun" was embroidered on it I with orange thread.

"Oh, Mom, I love it! It's so soft." She put the sweater up to her cheek. She also bought a little stuffed turtle that made a musical sound when you shook it. It came with a little book, "Tommy Turtle's Day at the Beach."

"I've got some homework to get to, Mom. Thanks for the baby presents. I'm glad you liked the cake." She went up to her room. Beverly put the cake under a dome and cleaned up the kitchen. The cake really was delicious. Erica was really sweet to go to this trouble. She cut another sliver and ate it with her fingers.

I feel like we can talk about the baby without the underlying tension. I wonder if the kids are starting to suspect that Erica is pregnant. She's probably going to have to start to tell people when she goes back to school after Easter break. Oh God, I dread all that drama.

Beverly opened her lap top and started looking at her email. The phone rang. It was Ruby. "Happy birthday, Beverly, did you enjoy your cake?"

"Oh, Ruby, I adore coconut cake, and the one that Erica made me is one of the best I've ever tasted."

"My father loves that cake too." Ruby said. "Dwight tells me that Erica is feeling better. I'm glad. When I was pregnant with the twins, I couldn't keep a thing down for four entire months. I made several trips to the emergency room to get IV fluids.

"Actually, Ruby, she really hasn't been all that sick. She is really tired, though."

"Beverly, I wanted to ask you about your Easter plans. Easter is less than two weeks away. Can you believe it? I was hoping that you and Erica and Helen could join us for Easter dinner. My work schedule just came out and I'm off."

"Oh, that would be really nice, Ruby. Erica and I were just talking about what we might do. The holidays are still a challenge for us. She will be thrilled."

"What can I bring?"

"Not a thing. Please just let me do something nice for your family."

"Ruby, I'm looking forward to it. Thank you."

"Okay, why don't you plan on coming at about two o'clock? Easter morning services at my church are pretty lengthy. I'm so happy you're coming, Beverly. Bye for now."

Actually, Beverly thought the invitation was kind of appealing. *I won't have to cook or worry about what we'll do. Erica will be happy, but then again she might feel very self-conscious around Dwight's family. I'll bet his aunt and uncle will be there. Erica's just going to have to get used to it. But there's Brad, I wonder what he'll be doing? Maybe I could ask*

Ruby if he could come, too. Oh God, no way, that would send all kinds of messages. My complicated life goes on. It was wonderful being with Brad, away from it all. I felt like a different woman.

Beverly had an email from Olivia Driscoll. Olivia used to be Olivia Carpenter. She was Sam Carpenter's wife. Olivia remarried after Sam died. Beverly forgot that she gave Olivia her email address at Tom's funeral. Beverly tried to think back to when Sam died. *God she was a young widow. I think Olivia was only thirty-two when Sam died.* Olivia wrote that she and her daughter, Robyn, were going to look at colleges in the Rochester area. She wanted to maybe get together for lunch or dinner. Robyn was the only child Olivia had with Sam. *I think Robyn was only three when Sam died. Actually this is good. Maybe talking to Olivia about interracial relationships and bi-racial children will help me get some perspective. I feel kind of guilty that I've lost touch with her, but it will be good to reconnect.* Beverly replied to her email, saying she would be happy to get together, and that her schedule was pretty flexible the week following Easter.

Beverly called Brad before going to bed. "Brad, I want to thank you again for a fabulous weekend. It was exactly what I needed, and your gift to me was lovely. I might not have ever said so, but I'm very happy that you're the man in my life now."

"Beverly, I love having you in my arms. I love having you in my bed. Oh, the things I'll do the next night we're together, 'Oh, The Places You'll Go!'"

Beverly laughed. "Okay, Dr. Seuss. You're not the shy reserved man I met not so long ago."

"You're not so reserved yourself. Goodnight Beverly, I'm so glad you called."

After she hung up, Beverly's feelings of guilt and confusion started to fester again. *Oh God, I feel like I need to say ten "Our Fathers" and ten "Hail Marys". He's so good to me. I've got to give a little back. Is it just the sex, male companionship, and the security I love, or is it Brad? I've got to be careful. He's such a kind and decent man. I don't want to hurt him. I'm not sure I'll ever be able to tell him I love him.*

Ruby had told her son about her plans to invite Erica and her family for Easter. Dwight was pleased, but he knew Erica would be nervous. He thought he had better call her.

"Babe, did you know that you and your family were invited here on Easter? My mom told me your mother said 'yes.'"

"Dwight, I'm so freaked out! I'm sure by then everyone will have found out. I'll feel so weird."

"Babe, it's okay. I'll be there. It will be cool."

"Do your sisters know yet?"

"Don't worry. My mom will talk to them, besides they love you. I think they'll be excited."

"Okay, I'll try to calm down about it."

"Erica, do you think it would be okay if I told Coach Novak before break? I just think he'd be a little hurt if he heard it before I got a chance to tell him."

"I guess that's okay, people are going to figure it out pretty soon anyway. I feel more pregnant by the second."

"Okay, Babe, see you tomorrow. I love you. If there's any of that coconut cake left, bring your baby daddy a slice."

Erica started laughing hysterically. "You just made me laugh so hard I started to pee!" She ran to the bathroom. "Bye, Dwight. I love you."

I wonder if Mom will invite Dr. Williams to come along. I hope not. Mom's probably told him I'm pregnant. She probably tells him everything. Erica put on her nightgown and got into bed. She put her hands on the little mound which was now her belly. *God, help me to get through this,* she prayed. She took out the book her mother had bought for the baby. "Okay, baby, I'm going to read you a story." When she finally fell asleep, she tossed and turned all night.

Chapter 25

Christy and Erica were in the girl's bathroom fixing their makeup. Christy looked her best friend over as she leaned against the bathroom counter. "Erica, OMG! I think you're starting to show! I can't believe how big your boobs have gotten."

"I know. I had to go up a cup size. I couldn't even zip up my jeans all the way this morning. Has anybody said anything to you about me?"

"No, but if I noticed, probably other people will too. Maybe you should start to tell a few people."

"I just don't know what to say. If they ask, I'll tell."

Dwight and Erica met up for lunch. Erica gave him his slice of coconut cake. "Babe, you nailed this. You didn't bring a piece for yourself?"

"Oh God, I couldn't. Can't you see how fat I'm getting?"

"Babe, you're beautiful. I like the rounded look of you."

Dwight went to talk to Mr. Novak after lunch, before afternoon classes started. "Coach, do you have a minute?"

"Sure, Dwight, what's on your mind?"

"I don't know how to tell you this, but I just wanted you to be one of the first to know. Erica's pregnant, and as you can probably guess, I'm the father."

"Oh, that's a lot for you two to handle. What are your plans?"

"We're going to keep the baby. Our parents know, and we all met with Mrs. Keaton. I know you must be very disappointed in me, Coach." Dwight's eyes were burning. He didn't want to cry.

"Sometimes we drop the ball. It will be how you recover and make the rebound which makes the difference." His coach smiled. "Sorry for the lame basketball analogy."

"I get your message, Coach. Erica and I are in this together. We plan on staying in school and going to college. Our parents are going to help us. I know what it's like to grow up without a father, and I don't want that for my child."

Dwight's sincerity really got to his coach. "I don't mean to pry, but do you want to tell me about your father?"

"He's in prison. I don't remember very much about him. I just have a few memories of him taking me to the park to shoot hoops when I was a very little boy. My mother has more than made up for having such a lousy father, and I have an uncle who has kind of been a father to me. He's a fireman. He's been coming to some of my games."

"Thanks for sharing all that with me, Dwight. I'm here to help you and Erica in any way I can. I still think you have a very good shot at a scholarship, if not to Syracuse, some other college."

Coach gave him a fist bump. "I'm wishing you and Erica all the best. Remember, I'm here for you."

"Thanks, Coach." Dwight felt hopeful after talking to his coach. *Maybe it will be okay.*

Erica was waiting for Spanish class to start. She could sense that Rachael Goldstein was looking her over. *God,* Erica thought, *Rachael is so thin.* Erica knew how much Rachael stressed over her weight and suspected that she had an eating disorder. She liked Rachael. She was nothing like her mother, so her comments took Erica by surprise. Her tone was gentle. "Erica, I don't know if I should say this to you, but I can't help but notice that you are putting on some weight. I know that can happen when you're depressed. Are you doing okay since your father died? It has to have been so hard for you. I know we're not close, but remember I'm a friend. I'm here for you if you ever need me."

"You're so sweet to care Rachael. I guess maybe I have put on a few pounds. Once cheerleading is over, I'm just not as active. Yes, it's been really hard since my dad died, but I think I'm doing okay. Rachael, what about you? I'm more worried about you. You keep getting thinner. Do you think maybe you need some help?"

Fortunately, for both of them, the teacher walked in and class began. Erica wasn't ready to tell Rachael yet. Rachael probably just noticed because of her obsession with weight. Erica needed more time, maybe after Easter break.

It was kind of a slow day at the shop. Pam asked Beverly how things were going with Erica's pregnancy. "I know the timing isn't right, but just think, Bev, your first grandchild. Soon you'll have a brand new baby to love and spoil." There were tears in Pam's eyes.

"Oh, Bev, I wonder if I'll ever have any grandchildren. Colleen puts her career before everything else." Pam's daughter was an ADA in the Manhattan District Attorney's office. "I have a better chance of grandchildren from Kyle. He and Mark are talking about moving to Connecticut to get married. They are even talking about adopting a baby or having a baby with a surrogate. Mark has always wanted kids. Kyle finally told me how old Mark is. He's forty-eight. Can you believe it?"

Pam and Bev looked at each other and laughed. "At least our lives aren't dull. We're kind of living a soap opera." Beverly said.

"We were invited to the Washington's for Easter. Erica is kind of nervous about facing everyone. She starting to round out and show a little bit. Do we have anything you think she might be comfortable wearing?"

Pam pulled out a light brown jersey knit dress. It had a v-neck and flared out at the bodice.

"Oh, I think she might like that," Bev said. "I'll bring it home to see what she thinks."

Erica was pleased with the dress. She tried it on. "Mom, do you like the dress with the flats or my boots?"

"I think I like the flats better. It has a more spring look. That necklace is perfect with it."

Erica told her mother about what Christy and Rachael said.

"Honey, I think you are starting to look pregnant. Maybe when you get back after break you won't be able to keep your pregnancy a secret any longer. You should be prepared with a response if anyone makes a comment."

"First I've got to get through Easter, then there's a week before I have to get back to school. Mom, is Dr. Williams coming with us to the Washington's?"

"No, I didn't ask him. He knows you're pregnant, though, if that's what you're worried about."

"So, what did he say?"

"He just wants to help in any way he can. Erica, you have to give him a chance. He's really a very nice man. I have to admit, I'm starting to have some strong feelings for him."

"That's okay, Mom. I just hope you're not going to rush into anything with him, that's all."

"Don't worry about it."

Beverly met Brad for dinner on Friday night. She asked him about his plans for the weekend.

"I don't have any plans," he said.

"Now I feel really bad about telling you this. Erica and I are going to spend the afternoon on Easter Sunday with Dwight's family."

"Don't feel bad, it's okay. I have a lot of work I need to catch up on. I have to present at a conference in Chicago in a few weeks. I need to start preparing for that."

"Brad, I think everything is pretty much out in the open now. Come home with me tonight?"

"And Erica, it's okay if she's there?"

Beverly took his hand. "Well I'm sure she knows we didn't have separate rooms in Amelia Island. She's a big girl now, all grown up and pregnant. I think that it's okay."

Brad smiled. "Alright then."

They had another drink at the bar before going to Beverly's. She was hoping Erica would be in bed before they got there. No such luck, she was still watching TV when they walked in.

"Hi, Erica, it's nice to see you."

"Hi, Dr. Williams, it's nice to see you too." Brad couldn't tell by her expression if it was all that true.

"Please call me Brad. Are you feeling as well as you look?" Erica's pregnancy was the elephant in the room.

"Oh, I'm fine, thanks. But I am really tired, so I'll say goodnight." She went up to bed.

Brad looked at Beverly and shrugged his shoulders. "I didn't know what to say."

"She's just going to have to get used to it." Beverly went to the kitchen to grab a few bottles of water. They watched the news and headed up to her room.

Brad noticed the picture that she had of her husband was no longer in the room. He was glad, maybe he wasn't competing with the dead guy anymore.

"Okay, we've just got to be a little quiet," Beverly said.

"Let me get you relaxed a little," he said.

"You've got to be great at preparing your patients for surgery," she said. Brad was a man that enjoyed foreplay, and he was very good at it. Maybe it was because he was a surgeon, but he had great hands.

The sex was quiet, but very satisfying. Brad rolled onto his side and looked at Beverly. "You are just what I needed tonight. I love you, Beverly."

Beverly smiled and stroked his cheek. "I'm happy you're here." She wasn't ready to use the word love in the context of their relationship. She thought that he probably knew that.

Brad told her that he had gotten a call from one of his friends back in New York. His ex was pregnant. "Maureen is ten years younger than me. We talked about having children, and she knew how much I wanted them. It wasn't until after we got married that she told me she didn't want to have a baby... ever. She was adamant about it. Being the oldest of six kids, she said that she raised enough kids already. I can't believe she's pregnant now, and she's going to marry the guy."

"Brad, do you still have feelings for her?"

"No, I definitely do not, but I can't deny that I felt a little hurt when I heard the news. Not hurt that she was remarrying, but hurt that she was pregnant."

"I can understand that," Beverly said. She kissed him. "Now it's my turn to make you forget."

Their marathon sex continued until well after two in the morning.

Beverly got up at seven and got into the shower. Erica was still sleeping. She went downstairs and started the coffee. She decided that she was going to make Brad a really nice breakfast. She started frying the bacon when Brad came down. He sat down at the counter and

Beverly came up behind him and wrapped her arms around him. "You will stay for breakfast, won't you?"

"You're a hard woman to say 'no' to." Beverly poured him some coffee. She was going to make him French toast stuffed with bananas and strawberries.

Erica walked down just as they finished eating. Beverly took a deep breath. *God, this is awkward.* Erica seemed to be taking everything in. She frowned. "Wow, Mom, you never make stuffed French toast." Erica looked at Brad. "Stuffed French toast was my dad's favorite."

Beverly looked over at Brad with a sympathetic look. She knew her daughter could be a little snot sometimes. Brad was cool. "I can see why," he said.

"I guess you forgot 'good morning,' Erica." She gave her daughter a dirty look. "Can I make you some?"

"No, not for me, I've got to have something that's healthy. Can you make me some poached eggs, please?"

"Okay, in a minute. It was clear that Erica was going to be difficult. "Would you like more coffee Brad?"

"No, thanks, Beverly, I want to get to the hospital to check on a patient. Breakfast was great." He kissed her on the cheek. "You ladies have a great day."

"Erica, what is with your attitude this morning?"

"I guess I wasn't prepared to see Dr. Williams so at home eating breakfast in our kitchen."

Beverly slammed the cupboard door when she took a plate out for Erica's eggs. Door slamming was one of Beverly's bad habits which surfaced when she was angry or frustrated. "That's not fair! I'm entitled to my relationship with Brad. I'm a grown woman. Look at you! You're pregnant! I guess you know about sex. I feel like I've been supportive to you in your relationship with Dwight, and I would appreciate if you could be respectful of MY relationship."

"Whatever, Mom, I guess I'll just have to get used to it."

Beverly was very hurt. She felt very overwhelmed all of a sudden and began to cry. "Look, don't you know how much I miss your father.

216

He was the love of my life. He's not coming back. Brad has helped to ease my pain. So give me a break!"

"Mom, I'm sorry I was such a bitch, forgive me?"

"Okay, eat your eggs. I've got to get ready for work." Beverly was really steamed. Erica was contrite.

Beverly and Erica picked Helen up for mass on Easter morning. The church was crowded like it always was on holidays. Beverly was surprised to see Brad walk down the aisle. Mass hadn't started yet. "Brad, sit with us." She slid over so Brad could join them in the pew. She didn't even know that Brad was Catholic. It was nice to have him there.

They chatted a few minutes after church. Erica was polite. She shook Brad's hand. "Happy Easter, Brad, it was nice to see you this morning."

"He's such a nice man," Helen said. "I've seen him here at church a few times."

At two o'clock they headed over to the Washington's. Beverly made some crab cakes to share as an appetizer and also brought a few bottles of wine. She hoped she would be able to have a glass. She was sure she would need one. Helen brought an Easter lily.

The house was old but in good repair. Ruby probably rented it. Inside it was clean and comfortable. Ruby was very gracious. Ruby's sister, Sarah, and her husband were there with their kids. Beverly had remembered meeting Dwight's Uncle Henry at one of the basketball games. Sarah was very friendly too. Ruby's brother, Theo, was there from out of town. Ruby took Erica aside and walked with her into the kitchen. She asked Erica how she was feeling. "You look radiant, Erica. I'm glad you're starting to feel better." Dwight's sisters followed them into the kitchen. Danielle, the not so shy sister, hugged Erica. "Are you really having a baby?" she asked.

Erica smiled, "I am. You guys will be aunts!" Denise hugged Erica too. Erica was glad all that was over with. I'm sure they had a lot of questions for Ruby and Dwight, Erica thought.

Everyone chatted easily. Beverly was glad to see that Henry and Theo had beers. She knew that Ruby didn't drink. She didn't know about Sarah. "I'm going to get a glass of wine for Helen and me, would you like a glass, Sarah?"

"Sure, that would be nice. I'll have white please." *Thank God,* Beverly thought. *Erica seems to be doing okay.* Dwight almost never left her side.

Ruby had set up two tables and had bouquets of tulips on each table. She had borrowed dishes from her sister so that nobody had to eat on paper. They all sat down to dinner. Ruby said grace. Beverly held her breath because she wasn't certain if anything would be said about a new baby on the way.

Ruby prepared baked ham, sweet potatoes, collard greens, green beans, fresh fruit salad and, of course, the family favorite, macaroni and cheese. Everything was delicious.

Some of the guests went to the living room to relax before dessert was served. Beverly stayed in the kitchen to help Ruby and Sarah with the dishes. Sarah told Beverly that she knew about Erica's pregnancy, and they she and Henry would help in any way they could. "Dwight is like a son to me," she said. "I can't believe I'll be a great auntie."

Dwight was talking to his uncles when his cousin Tamika came up to Erica. "So, Dwight's the baby-daddy?" Her tone was snide, and she was looking at Erica all over when she spoke.

Erica could feel the heat in her face. She tried to be cool. "Tamika, I'm sure you figured that out."

Tamika screwed up her face. "Well, why didn't you just get rid of it?"

"Why? I love Dwight, and I don't believe in abortion. Maybe you could try and be happy for us."

"I don't think so," Tamika said. Now her look was very menacing.

Erica walked away and headed for the kitchen. Dwight saw Erica walking away from Tamika and sensed there was a problem. "Babe, is everything okay?" He saw that she had tears in her eyes. She told him what happened.

"Oh, Erica, I'm sorry. Tamika has always been one of those 'mean girls'. She gets into fights at school sometimes. I heard my Aunt Sarah say that she wanted to get her some counseling." He hugged Erica. "Babe, it will be okay."

"Dwight, I'm nervous about when we go back to school next week. Is that what we can expect?"

"I don't know, but I'm sure we can handle it. Let's get some cake now."

Sarah was quite a baker. She brought two cakes for dessert. One was carrot cake and the other an insanely decadent chocolate cake. It really was a lovely dinner and a very pleasant afternoon. Beverly chastised herself for her previous misconceptions about how black people lived in the inner city.

Beverly looked over at her daughter. She looked tired all of a sudden. Maybe it was time to call it a day. Beverly told Helen that after they finished their coffee, they should probably get going.

They said their goodbyes. Ruby and Dwight walked them out to their car.

When they got back home Beverly told Erica about possibly meeting up with Olivia and her daughter. Erica said that she would be okay with it. "Mom, did Olivia remarry?"

"She did. I've never met her new husband. He didn't come with her to Dad's funeral."

"Is the man she remarried black?"

"I don't know, Erica. Maybe Nana knows."

As it turned out, Helen did know. Helen said that Olivia's husband is white and a pediatrician. Sam had been a stockbroker. Beverly felt a little guilty that Helen knew all this about Olivia, and she did not. She wished that she had been a better friend to Olivia after Sam had died.

They made plans to meet for dinner on Wednesday night. Erica wanted to go to her favorite Italian bistro. She said that everyone loves Italian. "Erica, is the subject of you and Dwight taboo?" Beverly thought she should ask before Olivia and Robyn got to the house. They were meeting at the McIntyre's and going to the restaurant together.

"No, Mom, I don't mind talking about Dwight."

Olivia had aged well. She was a very attractive woman. She always was. Robyn was beautiful. She looked just like Sam. You couldn't tell she was bi-racial. She just looked African-American. Beverly and Olivia hugged and introduced the girls. They had a glass of wine before heading out.

"Robyn, do you want to see a picture of your mother and father in my parents' wedding album?

"It's so seventies. Wait until you see it! Come on, it's up in my room."

"Oh, look at my dad, he's got an afro!" giggled Robyn.

"Check out the moustache on MY dad," Erica said.

"Robyn, you were so young when your dad died... weren't you only about three years old?"

"Right, I don't remember that much about him, but I love looking at pictures. Thanks for sharing them with me."

"My grandmother said that our fathers grew up together in Brooklyn. They were best friends."

Erica chatted for a while with Robyn up in her room. They talked about school and looking for colleges.

Beverly and Olivia did their own catching up downstairs.

"Olivia, was it hard to start dating again after Sam died?"

"Oh God, Beverly, I was so young. I was only thirty-three. I for sure didn't want to spend the rest of my life alone. What was hard is that a lot of the men I dated didn't accept the fact that I had a three year old daughter, and she was black."

Finally, about five years after Sam died, Robyn's pediatrician retired and a new doctor joined the practice. That's when I met Steven. He wasn't Robyn's doctor, so he felt okay asking me out. He's been a wonderful father to Robyn, and she adores him. I'm very lucky."

Beverly told Robyn about her new relationship with Brad and all the guilt she was feeling. "It's hard having a relationship under the watchful eyes of a teenage daughter. I'm sure she knows we're having sex, and that's so awkward."

Olivia put a hand on Beverly's forearm. "Hang in there. If the relationship is working, you deserve to be happy."

The girls came down and they took off for the restaurant.

Beverly thought everyone seemed very relaxed. She was so glad that Olivia contacted her about getting together.

"Mom, Erica showed me a picture of her boyfriend. He's black and he's so hot!"

"Mrs. Driscoll, if you don't mind me asking, was having an interracial relationship really difficult?"

"Oh, honey, please call me Olivia. I won't pretend that it wasn't hard sometimes, but we cared for each other enough to make it work. People were just starting to come around about racial issues in the seventies, but there was still a lot of prejudice. There still is now. Some people will always be narrow-minded. My own grandmother stopped talking to be the day she found out about Sam and me. She died without ever speaking to me again."

"Oh, that's so awful. I guess most of the kids at my school were very surprised at first, but they've come around and seem to accept me and Dwight as a couple. It's much better now."

"How about you, Robyn, are the boys you date black or are they white?" Erica asked. "I'm sorry if this is too personal."

"Oh, it's okay. I don't mind you asking. I really haven't dated that much yet. I'm really into soccer, and that takes up so much of my time. The few boys that have asked me out are black, probably because I look black. I'm okay with it. I wouldn't mind going out with a white guy if I liked him, though. I try not to see people in terms of color."

Erica really liked Robyn. She was so honest. She had the most beautiful eyes. They were a dark gold. Erica couldn't help but wonder what her own child would look like. Erica was thrilled that Robyn was also interested in Syracuse. They were visiting the campus tomorrow. "That's were Dwight and I had our first date," Erica said.

Beverly wondered if Erica had told Robyn she was pregnant. She probably did not. Beverly didn't say anything to Olivia when they were speaking earlier. She felt it would be disloyal to Erica. It was Erica's news to share if she wanted to. The evening had been a big success. They vowed to keep in touch and to all get together soon. Erica and Robyn exchanged email addresses and cell phone numbers.

"Mom, I liked meeting them. They were so nice. Maybe we could all meet up again sometime."

"I really wish I had been more supportive to Olivia after Sam died. Your father called her from time to time, but I really didn't reach out."

"What do you think my baby will look like? You really couldn't tell that Robyn was bi-racial."

"I don't know honey, but I'm sure you're baby will be beautiful. You and Dwight are very good looking. Genetics are very unpredictable, but this baby has very good genes."

Chapter 26

I can't believe I'm already fifteen weeks pregnant, Erica thought, as soon as she turned off her alarm the following Monday morning. She looked at her silhouette in the bathroom mirror while drying off after her shower. *I have no idea what to wear.* She got out the belly band that she bought on an online maternity clothing site. *At least I will be able to breathe in my regular jeans if I use the belly band.* She decided to wear a camisole with a button down shirt. She didn't tuck in the shirt and left it buttoned most of the way down.

Dwight gave her his most winning smile when she walked into chem. She noticed that Mr. Novak was looking at her, and he also smiled. Her heart skipped a beat. Dwight must have told him.

Erica had told Christy that it was okay if she told Ben. Erica knew Christy wouldn't be able to keep it from Ben much longer. Christy caught up with Erica later in the day. "You're not going to believe this. Ben told me that Bobby Bauer said that he thought you got a boob job!"

"Are you kidding me? He's such a dick. What did Ben say?"

"I asked him," Christy said. "Ben just told him that he didn't know, but he doubted it."

"If Dwight heard Bobby talking like that, he'd kill him."

Paige caught up with Erica and Christy. Paige looked at Erica and narrowed her eyes. "What's up with you Erica?"

"Why are you asking?" Erica replied.

"Are you pregnant?"

"I am. Can you just be cool about it, Paige?"

"Oh my God, what did your mother say?"

"She's dealing with it. My mom's been very supportive, so has Dwight's mom."

"Oh, Erica, you never cease to amaze me. Congratulations, I guess."

"Thanks, Paige. I hope you mean it." Christy linked her arm into Erica's, and they walked away.

"That's probably as nice as Paige can get," Christy said. "Hey, let's head out to the mall and get you some stuff you'll be able to wear. It will be fun."

"Oh, Christy, I love you, you're such a good friend."

It didn't take long for the news to spread. Most of the kids were pretty good about it. Erica was a very popular girl and since basketball season, everyone really liked Dwight. By now they were a well-accepted couple at school.

Later in the week, Erica's English teacher asked to speak with her after class. Mrs. Wiggins was in her early sixties, close to retirement. Erica thought she was an excellent teacher. Mrs. Wiggin's comments took her by surprise. "Erica, is it true, you're pregnant?"

"Yes, ma'am, I am." Erica felt an odd mix of embarrassment, shame, defensiveness, and anger. She couldn't believe Mrs. Wiggins was confronting her like this. She vowed not to cry.

"How could you let that happen, dear?"

"Mrs. Wiggins, why are you trying to make me feel worse than I already do? Obviously I should have been more prudent." Erica knew that her English teacher appreciated words like "prudent".

"Yes, indeed," she said. "What are your plans?"

"I know it will be difficult, but I plan to finish high school and go on to college. I will be the best mother to my child that I can be."

"Hmm, well, good luck, Erica."

"Can I go now, please?" Mrs. Wiggins patted Erica's arm and Erica bolted out of the room.

Thank God it was her last class of the day. Dwight took off for work right after last period. Erica decided to just drop by Wegmans to say hi. After her confrontation with Mrs. Wiggins, she just wanted to see him, see his smile. That's all it would take to make her feel better.

He saw her and there it was... his winning smile. "Miss, may I help you?" It worked. She felt better already.

"No, thanks, I'm good.

"Well, you come back, now."

Erica decided that she needed Rice Krispies treats. Whenever she used to have a bad day when she was a little girl, her mother made Rice

224

Krispies treats. She bought the cereal and marshmallows on her way out. She made them as soon as she got home. She just polished off her third one when Beverly walked in the door.

"Did you have a bad day, honey?"

She told her mother what Mrs. Wiggins had said.

"God, she sounds like an old bat! I can't believe she said that to you. It sounds like it's time she retired."

Beverly grabbed a Rice Krispies treat for herself and poured a glass of wine.

On Thursday, Beverly had her usual appointment with Dr. Martino. He wanted to know how it was going for Erica at school now that her pregnancy wasn't a secret. "I think she's dealing with it better than I had anticipated," Beverly said. "Aside from Pam, my co-worker at the shop, and Brad, none of my friends really know yet. I just don't know how to tell them."

"As the saying goes, 'it's a small world,' they'll find out soon enough. I don't see why you need to go out of your way to tell them. You don't owe anyone an explanation. If you feel there's someone you want to tell, just go ahead and do it."

The only person who came to mind was Susan Dwyer. Beverly wanted to tell her. She didn't know what to do about telling Tom's family. Maybe Helen would take care of that.

"What about family? Do you think it's alright if my mother-in-law tells my husband's family? Everyone knows she and Erica are very close. She would know how to tell them. As for my family, I'm an only child. My parents live in Connecticut. Frankly, they haven't been very supportive to me and Erica after Tom died. I don't feel I need to share this with them."

"Beverly, there is no right or wrong way to handle this. Maybe it's okay to take the path of least resistance. Sometimes we have to give ourselves permission to do that."

"So tell me, what's going on in your relationship with Brad?"

"Oh God, I'm so conflicted. I care for him, but I'm afraid to care for him because I might lose him. I'm afraid of hurting him. I feel guilty about wanting him so much. I feel guilty about needing him so much. I feel like he does all the giving and all I do is take."

"He says he loves me. I'm not ready to tell him that I love him back. I'm just not ready."

"Beverly, let him love you. Let yourself love him back. I'm sure he knows what he's getting into."

"He stayed over the other night. It was the first time with Erica being at home. She was kind of nasty about it. I really resented it, and I was hurt. I've tried so hard to be supportive to her and Dwight."

"Give her time. She'll come around, especially if Brad is as decent a man as you say he is."

"Beverly, I'm concerned about all the stress you have. Please let go of some of that guilt. See you next week?"

Beverly nodded, "Thank you." She cried all the way home.

Dwight and Erica had plans on Friday night. Beverly wanted to make dinner for Brad. She asked if she could cook for him at his house. She didn't want another scene with Erica. Beverly perfected her own recipe for vodka pasta. She decided to make that, along with a salad, and Tiramisu for dessert. She left the shop a little early to get ready for the evening. There was an apricot silk blouse that just came in. She grabbed it on her way out to wear that night.

Erica watched her mother get dressed. "Mom, there aren't very many women out there that are your age and can wear skinny jeans. You look great in them. No skinny jeans for me." Beverly swept her hair up and put on the gold earrings that Brad had bought her for Christmas. "You look really pretty."

"Thank you, honey. So what are you and Dwight doing tonight?"

We're going to catch a movie. I think we're going to eat here first, maybe just order Chinese. I have this craving for something spicy, and the Chinese know spicy."

"You better make sure you bring Tums with you. It's funny you say you have a craving for Chinese food. When I was pregnant with Johnny, I wanted it all the time. Your father said that he was going to come out with slanted eyes. I'll be staying at Brad's tonight. Will you call me when you get in?"

226

Erica just raised her eyebrows. "Okay," she said. That suited her just fine. She and Dwight could have some alone time of their own.

Brad sat at the counter and had a martini as he watched Beverly at work in his kitchen. Beverly was impressed with how well equipped his kitchen was.

"I love having you here tonight. You're just so beautiful, and I've had a really ugly day. I lost one of my patients. I did surgery on her yesterday to remove a brain tumor. We were all relieved because it wasn't malignant, but then she had a stroke and died this morning. She was a young mother and left a husband and three little kids behind. God, I feel so horrible about it."

Beverly turned around and saw the tears in his eyes. She went over to hold him. She remembered how Tom was when he lost a patient. Tom would get so angry at himself. He wouldn't be the same for days. Brad just seemed so sad.

They had a nice quiet dinner. Brad seemed to come around a little bit and was more like his usual self. "Oh, honey, this tiramisu is incredible. It makes me want to take you to Italy. Will you go with me sometime?"

"Oh, definitely," Beverly said.

Brad's bedroom was so masculine, but Beverly loved it. She could tell that his housekeeper just put fresh sheets on his bed. Brad undressed her slowly and unpinned her hair. He laid her gently on the bed. His tenderness tonight overwhelmed her. He was lost in kissing her breasts then stopped suddenly. He touched an area on her left breast lightly, and then touched the same area again on her right breast. He took her hand and had her touch the place that he was focused on.

"Beverly, have you ever felt this before? It feels like there's a lump there. When is the last time you got a mammogram?"

Things got very serious all of a sudden. "I was supposed to do it in September, and then Tom died, and I guess I forgot to reschedule the appointment. I'm sure it's probably okay."

"Beverly, don't take that chance. You've got to get it checked out."

"Now you're scaring me Brad. I just can't deal with another thing in my life right now."

"Beverly, maybe it's okay. It's probably okay, but I love you, and I've got to make sure you take care of it. I just found you. I can't let anything happen to you."

"I just can't bear having it checked out at the breast clinic at the cancer center. It would just be another poor Beverly moment. I know so many people there."

"But you know Jake Goldstein is one of the best."

"I know. I just wish I could go someplace else. Brad, now I'm really afraid. Will you just hold me a minute and make love to me?"

He did and held her in his arms. *Could this be really happening?* She knew that Brad was right. She needed to get it checked out.

"Brad, I have no family history of breast cancer."

"That doesn't matter. Most women diagnosed don't. Don't get ahead of yourself. The first step is to just find out what it is. I know someone at Columbia Pres. He's very well-respected in his field. Let me give him a call. We'll fly to New York for the day and you can get it worked up there."

"Oh, Brad, you would do that for me? You'll come with me?"

"Beverly, I love you, I would do anything for you."

She was finally realizing the extent of Brad's feelings for her. Beverly didn't sleep much that night. She had too much on her mind. *What if I do have breast cancer? How I will I ever deal with it on top of everything going on with Erica? What if I die?*

Then she thought about dying. *At least I'll be with Tom again. I'll see Johnny. I've missed my little boy so much. At least I would be at peace.* She finally drifted off to sleep.

Brad was still asleep when she woke up. She slipped out of bed. She looked in his closet to see what she could slip on. He had bought her a robe and it hung in the closet for her. It was a beautiful floral print made out of a very soft cotton fabric. It was covered with blue hydrangeas. *Oh God*, she thought, *sometimes his love overwhelms me.* In the bathroom, there was a new toothbrush still in the package.

I am just too damned tired to go to the shop today, she thought. She called Pam.

"It will be fine, Bev, Julie's coming in at one o'clock. Give yourself a break and get some rest today."

She made coffee and rummaged through Brad's refrigerator to see what she could make for breakfast. It had just dawned on her that Erica never checked in with her last night. She gave her daughter a call. "Honey, I'm sorry to wake you, but you were supposed to call when you got in last night. Is everything okay?"

"I'm fine, Mom. I was just so tired. I'm sorry I forgot to call."

"What are you doing today?"

"I'm probably going to the library to work on my history paper."

"I'm not going into the shop today. I'll see you later. Call me on my cell if you need me."

"Okay, I love you, Mom."

Brad walked into the kitchen just as she was hanging up. He walked over to her and kissed her. "Will you spend the day with me?"

How could she say 'no'? "I can't believe you bought me this lovely robe."

"I'm just hoping you'll stay here more often. Now, what are you making me for breakfast?"

"Is an omelet okay?"

She made cheese omelets and toast. Brad got the newspaper and they had their second cup of coffee in bed. They made love. Brad had a Jacuzzi tub. They took a bath. She felt so relaxed in his arms. She felt like everything would be okay.

Beverly kissed him. "I could get used to this, you know."

"It's such a beautiful day. Let's take a walk," Brad suggested. He followed Beverly to her house so that she could change. Erica wasn't there. They probably walked for almost two hours. "Let me take you to lunch." Brad took her to a very charming café that she had never been to, or had even known about. They shared a bottle of wine over lunch. So far he hadn't mentioned the lump in her breast today, but she knew they had to talk about it.

"I have to be in Chicago to speak at that conference on Thursday. I'm not in the OR on Wednesday. I purposely didn't schedule any patients so that I could finish preparing for the conference. Maybe I

229

could call my oncologist friend, Ted Nixon, and he could see you on Wednesday. We could fly out for the day."

"Okay, Wednesday works for me. I hate to put you through so much trouble."

"It's okay. I trust Ted. I know he'll help me out. I operated on his wife when she had a brain aneurysm. He's good and I only want the best for you. I can understand why you want your privacy and wouldn't want to see Jake Goldstein."

"Do you think I should tell Erica?" Beverly asked.

"I think you should be honest with your daughter. Come on then, it's settled. Let's enjoy the rest of the afternoon."

Brad needed new shoes. He asked Beverly to go shopping with him. He had very good taste. He ended up buying a very expensive pair of Gucci Italian loafers. Brad cared about his wardrobe way more than Tom did. After shopping he dropped Beverly off back home. Beverly leaned over and kissed him. "Thank you for today," she said.

"Pleasure's all mine, pretty lady."

Brad called her on Monday. His friend would see her on Wednesday. She told Erica that night at dinner. "Oh Mom, no, it's got to be okay! Why do you have to go all the way to New York? Doesn't Rachael's father treat women with breast cancer? I know he took care of Christy's aunt."

Beverly explained why she didn't want to seek treatment at the cancer center. Erica seemed to understand.

"Mom, are you scared?"

"I'm a little anxious about it honey, but I know I've got to get it checked out. It might be nothing. We just have to have faith, that in the end everything will work out."

Erica turned to the last page in her notebook. "Faith is taking the first step when you don't see the whole staircase."

"That's very poignant, honey. Where is that quote from?"

"Martin Luther King Jr. said it. Dwight has it pinned up on his wall. He says that it helps him face tough times. I thought about it a lot when I first found out I was pregnant and was really scared."

230

Erica told Dwight later that night. Dwight told Ruby, and she called Beverly the next day.

"I know you want to keep this confidential, and I won't say anything to anyone. I just wanted to let you know that my prayers are with you. Don't worry about Erica. She can come here after school and have dinner with us. I'll make sure she gets home safely."

"That's so kind of you, Ruby. I know Erica's worried. I have faith that it will be okay."

"I feel the same way. You take care tomorrow, Beverly, I'll be thinking about you."

Beverly was starting to think of Ruby as a good friend. It was very thoughtful of her to call.

Brad picked her up for her up at 4:45AM for their 6AM flight to NYC.

"How are you feeling about this?" he asked.

"I'm a little anxious, but I just have a gut feeling that it will be okay. I'm so glad you're with me. I can't thank you enough for making these arrangements."

"You're welcome." He held her hand on the entire flight.

Beverly was familiar with the University of Rochester Medical Center. It was interesting to see another major medical center. Brad seemed to know so many people there.

First she had a mammogram, and then was taken to ultrasound. She met Dr. Nixon. He seemed like a very nice man. He looked at the image on the screen. Brad stood at her side. "Beverly, this has the characteristics of a fibroadenoma, which is a benign tumor of the breast. Of course I can't say for sure that's what is without a biopsy."

He went on to explain to her that these tumors were more common in women under thirty-five, but could present at any age. He asked her if she was still was still getting regular periods and about what she used for contraception.

"When will you do the biopsy?" Beverly asked. She was jiggling her leg under the sheet, like Erica, something she did when she was nervous.

"I can do it now, and rush the pathology, so that you will probably know the results by Friday afternoon. A fine needle biopsy is a fairly simple procedure." He explained what he planned to do in detail. "Now I'm going to step out for a few minutes, and Alice will get set up for the biopsy and get you prepared."

Brad looked at Beverly and smiled. "I'm encouraged," he said.

It was over quickly. "That really wasn't so bad," Beverly said. "But I'm glad it's over."

Dr. Nixon assured Beverly that he would call her as soon as he got the pathology report. He and Brad chatted while she went to get dressed.

"I feel a little better about this," Beverly sighed.

"I'm encouraged," Brad said again. "Let's not get ahead of ourselves. We've just got to keep tight until pathology's back."

Beverly wondered what he meant by "keep tight." Brad held her hand as they made their way through the lobby. They had just enough time to get lunch before getting back to the airport.

As they were walking out, an obviously pregnant woman in blue scrubs approached Brad. She was cute, brunette, with a trendy little short haircut... very perky. She was probably in her mid thirties.

"Maureen, hello, I guess congratulations are in order."

It was obviously Brad's ex. He was playing it typical Brad fashion... very cool.

"It's good to see you Brad. I see you've also moved on."

"Yes, Maureen this is Beverly. Beverly, this is my ex-wife." The two women shook hands.

"Well, Maureen, we have a plane to catch. Good luck with the baby."

"Oh God, I can't believe we ran into her. I hope it wasn't too awkward for you." Brad said. "It's hard for me to believe I ever loved her."

"I have to admit, that's not how I pictured your ex-wife."

They got into Rochester before ten o'clock. Brad dropped her off. "Brad, I can't tell you how grateful I am for arranging this and coming with me today." She held his face in her hands and kissed him.

232

"You're welcome. I love you Beverly. I'll always be here for you. Let me know as soon as you hear from Ted." He held her and they kissed again. "Goodnight."

Erica was anxious to hear about her mother's day. They talked for awhile and went to bed. They were both exhausted.

Beverly decided to go into work on Thursday. She knew it would help make the waiting a little easier. Pam knew what was going on and was being very supportive. She didn't want to miss her appointment with Dr. Martino, because she always felt better talking to him.

She got the call from Dr. Nixon late on Friday afternoon. "Beverly, Ted Nixon here, I have good news for you. As I suspected, the pathology confirmed that the tumor is a fibroademoma. Since you told me it isn't painful to you, I think it's safe just to leave it alone. If it's going to worry you, we can remove it. Either approach is reasonable. We should, however, do another mammogram and breast ultrasound in six months. You don't have to decide right away what you want to do, you can think about it."

"Oh, thank you. I'm very relieved. Thank you so much for seeing me so quickly. I have a lot going on in my life right now. I'll think about it, but I think I will probably opt not to have surgery at this time."

"Well, okay then. Please don't hesitate to call me with any further questions or concerns. You have my card. And Beverly, you have a good man there in Brad Williams."

"Oh, I know that. He really looks out for me. Thank you, again, Dr. Nixon."

Beverly was still at the shop. She came out from the back room and told Pam her good news. Pam hugged her. "Oh, Bev, thank God, I was so worried."

Beverly called Brad. He didn't pick up the call. He was probably with patients, so she left a message.

He called her about an hour later. "Oh, that's wonderful news. Let me take you out tonight to celebrate. You can ask Erica to join us, and Dwight too, if they want to come." Beverly really liked the idea. She told Brad that she would get back to him.

The four of them went for dinner. Beverly thought it went very well. Maybe it was because she was with Dwight, but Erica was at her best. She was very cordial to Brad. I'd better not push it. As much as I'd love to be with Brad tonight, I think I'll just go home with Erica. Brad dropped Dwight off at his house first.

Dwight was surprised that his mother was home. She had planned to go out with Michael Harvey.

"Ma, why are you home? I thought you had a date."

"I don't think I want to see him anymore."

Dwight could feel himself heating up. "What happened?"

"Apparently he's been seeing someone else. A woman approached us in the restaurant and asked who the hell I was. She said, 'Find your own man, bitch!' It was all very embarrassing. I really don't need that kind of aggravation."

"That's right, Mom, you don't. You deserve better. I never really liked that guy anyway."

"You know son, I don't really have time for a man in my life right now, and that's okay."

"But you deserve to be happy, too. You're young. You're ten years younger than Erica's mother. She found someone. That guy Dr. Williams is really good to her."

"Baby, you're so sweet to be concerned, but I'm okay. If it happens... it happens. It just won't be happening with Michael Harvey. I know my life is just going to get so much easier when I'm finished with school. I'm just going to stay focused on that. In just a little more than a year, I'll be a registered nurse."

"I'm proud of you Mom." Dwight kissed his mother and went on up to bed.

Chapter 27

Erica thought things at school were going pretty well. It had been two weeks since the news got out, and everything seemed to be calming down. She couldn't believe how good she was feeling. She was really able to concentrate more on her school work. Next week was huge! It was her eighteen week anatomic ultrasound. She and Dwight would know whether they were having a boy or a girl. She noticed that her mother had starting buying a few things for the baby. Beverly had put a big wicker basket in Erica's room and put baby things in there as she bought them. Erica and Beverly talked about the baby's room. The McIntyres had a four bedroom house. Johnny's room hadn't been touched since the day he died. They were trying to decide whether the nursery should be the guest room or Johnny's old room. It was a hard decision.

Beverly had a board meeting for the cancer center that week. She called Susan Dwyer and told her she would pick her up. Beverly wanted to tell Susan about Erica's pregnancy.

"Oh, honey, I already know. Rebecca has pretty much put out the word."

"I meant to tell you sooner, Susan, but things have been a little crazy."

"I know that you have a lot on your plate. So tell me, how's she's doing?"

Beverly filled her in. "She's having an ultrasound next week and we'll find out what she's having. I'm starting to get excited. I won't deny that Erica's pregnancy was very hard for me to accept. It's not just that she's a teenager, but that the baby's father is of another race. I have to say Dwight is a great kid, though. I know these two kids really love each other."

"So tell me, what's going on with you and Brad?" Beverly filled Susan in on the Brad and Beverly story.

"That was so sweet of him to take you to New York for the breast biopsy. That's way above and beyond what most boyfriends would do.

You must have been so scared. Oh, honey, I'm so relieved for you that everything turned out okay. Why didn't you just see Jake Goldstein?"

"I just didn't want Rebecca to know. I wanted my privacy, I guess."

"Beverly, Jake is very principled. He probably wouldn't have said anything to her."

"Probably not, but I just know too many people here. It would have been just another 'poor Beverly' moment."

"Rebecca has enough on her own plate right now. They had to hospitalize Rachael to get her eating disorder under control," Susan informed her.

"Oh, I'm so sorry to hear that," Beverly said. "Erica said that she was concerned about her, but never said anything about her being in the hospital."

"I think it just recently happened. In fact I'm not sure we'll see her today."

Rebecca did end up coming, and she asked Susan and Beverly to have lunch with her after the meeting. Beverly just wanted to have lunch with her friend Susan, but she knew that she would have to face Rebecca sooner or later. Rebecca could probably use some friends right now.

Rebecca seemed to be on her best behavior. For a while she was actually pleasant. Then she did ask about Erica. "So tell me, Beverly, how's Erica doing? Is her pregnancy going well?"

Beverly took a breath. "She's doing well."

"You must be mortified." Rebecca said, not on her best behavior anymore.

"I'm just trying to make the best of a difficult situation. It will be wonderful having a brand new baby to love."

"You always manage to land on your feet, Beverly."

There was a long period of awkward silence, as the three women ate their lunch. Beverly didn't want to stoop to Rebecca's level. She decided not to say anything about Rachael.

Rebecca wasn't going to let up. "Seeing a lot of Brad Williams, aren't you?"

"I am. He's single and I'm single. Brad's a very nice man. We enjoy each other's company. He's been very supportive."

"Supportive? That's an interesting choice of words." Rebecca's comments were so snide.

Beverly refused to react or to respond.

Why does this woman hate me so much? Beverly wondered.

Susan knew it was time to go. She asked for the check, and she and Beverly left.

"I admire you, Bev, there's so much you could have said that you didn't. She was really goading you."

"I can't let her get to me." Beverly dropped Susan off. She was glad to be home. Erica wouldn't be home for a few hours. It was a beautiful day. She decided to take a walk along the canal.

She noticed that the daffodils were just starting to bloom in her yard. *I can't believe that it is mid-April already. Tom has been gone seven months already. Last year at this time we were in Paris. April in Paris was beautiful. That was such a wonderful trip.* She remembered the quaint little hotel on the left bank where they stayed. She could still picture the brass bed with the beautiful lace linens. In the morning, a waiter brought a tray with coffee in a sterling silver pot, warm French bread, fresh fruit, and delicious pastries. It was kind of a second honeymoon. She was starting to forget already how it felt to be with Tom. *Oh God, have I rushed into this relationship with Brad too quickly?* Then her thoughts turned a little dark. She remembered what Rebecca said about Tom and some young resident at the hospital. That still bothered her. *Is it possible that he took me on that trip because he was feeling a little guilty?*

Beverly was deep in thought when Erica walked in from school. She asked Erica if she knew about Rachael's hospitalization.

"No, I didn't hear that. I not surprised though, she has gotten so thin, and I know her boyfriend broke up with her. Rachael's such a sweet girl, but she's got a problem. She needs some help. You know how her mom is. I can't imagine Rachael could ever live up to her expectations."

"Did Rachael say anything about you being pregnant?"

"She just said that she noticed I had gained some weight. Mom, look at me, it's hard not to notice. But I've got to tell you something! I think I felt the baby move! I felt like little flutters, like a butterfly. Do you think that's what it was?"

"If I remember correctly, that is what it feels like."

"My book says it's called 'quickening'. I can't wait for Dwight to feel it. Are you coming with us to my ultrasound next week?"

"I'd love to, if I'm invited."

"Of course you are, Mom. I think Ms. Washington is going to try to come too."

"Honey, I had an idea. I was hoping that you'd let me paint a mural on one of the walls of the baby's room."

"Oh, Mom, I love that idea. We've got to figure out what color to paint the rest of the walls. I guess we will know next week."

Erica had her doctor's appointment and ultrasound the following Wednesday after school.

Dwight and Erica drove to her doctor's appointment together in her car after school. Ruby and Beverly were meeting them there. Erica asked if she and Dwight could be alone for the first few minutes of the ultrasound, and then maybe their mothers could join them a little later. Dr. Anderson said that they were the last appointment of the day, and she would be glad to accommodate their request. Dwight held Erica's hand as the sonographer spread warm gel over her abdomen. Dr. Anderson stood by to watch. "Oh, look," she said, "the baby is in just the right position to determine its gender. Do you want to know?"

"Yes, we're dying to know!" Erica said.

"It's a girl!"

Dwight smiled. "Is that our little Martina?" He leaned over and kissed Erica.

"Martina it is," Erica replied, beaming. There were tears in her eyes. Dr. Anderson also was teary-eyed. She was very touched by the tenderness they shared, and they were only teens.

"Can I get your mothers for the rest of the ultrasound?"

Beverly and Ruby came in. "You two have a granddaughter. Meet Martina," Erica said.

238

"Oh, thank you, sweet Jesus!" Ruby exclaimed as she hugged Beverly. Dr. Anderson went on to identify the different parts of the baby's anatomy as they appeared on the screen.

"And here's the baby's heart."

"Oh my God, does it look normal?" Erica gasped. She and Beverly were so worried about the baby having a normal heart.

Dr. Anderson took the transducer from the sonographer and showed everyone the different parts of the fetal heart herself.

"Your baby's heart rate today is one hundred fifty four beats per minute, which is right on target." They were able to listen. "These are the four chambers of the heart." She went on to explain the outflow tracts. "Everything appears to be normal and we've got some very good images."

She got a nice profile image of the baby and printed a picture. Martina had Erica's little turned up nose. She took another cute picture of the baby's foot.

It had been a great appointment. "Ruby, can you get your girls? Can we all go out and get some dinner together to celebrate?" Beverly asked.

"Oh, Mom, can we get Chinese?"

Beverly laughed. "Ruby does your family like Chinese food?"

"We love it! Thank you. That sounds like a wonderful idea." They agreed to all meet at the restaurant at six o'clock.

Everyone was having such a good time at dinner, and everyone was hungry. Beverly ordered a second order of eggrolls for the table. Erica showed the twins the ultrasound pictures. They were very curious. "What will her name be?" asked Danielle.

"I hope that it will be Ashley," said Denise.

"Why Ashley?" asked Ruby.

"There's a pretty white girl in my school named Ashley, and I like that name. I think the baby's going to look just like Erica, and she's a pretty white girl."

Ruby sighed and looked over at Beverly. No one knew what to say. Dwight broke the silence. "Erica and I have decided that her name will be Martina."

"I love it," Beverly said.

"I like it too," agreed Ruby. "How did you decide on Martina?" Ruby thought it probably had something to do with Martin Luther King.

"It's a beautiful name," said Erica. "If it was a boy, it was going to be Thomas after my dad, but Dwight got to choose if it was a girl. He really admires Martin Luther King, and he thought of 'Martina'. We both wanted it."

They held up their glasses. "Well, here's to Martina then," Ruby said.

What a good day. Beverly couldn't wait to call Brad that night and share her news.

It was still fairly early. "Can you come over for awhile and have a drink?" Brad asked.

Erica was on the phone with Christy. Beverly handed her a note. "Meeting Brad for a drink."

Brad opened a bottle of her favorite Merlot. They talked for a while. "Does it matter to you that you're dating somebody's grandmother?"

He set down her wine glass and pulled her on top of him. "Well, Granny, show me what you've got."

Beverly was breathless. "Oh God, Brad, that was good!"

"Grandmother, or not, that was pretty hot. He poured her another glass of wine. Let's take it into the bedroom." They did.

Beverly had two glasses of wine at dinner and another three at Brad's. She really didn't think she should drive home. "Just stay," Brad said.

"What about Erica?" Beverly said.

"Just call her and tell her the truth," he said.

By now it was eleven o'clock. Beverly called her daughter. "Hi, honey. I was so happy about everything today, that Brad and I opened a bottle of wine to celebrate. I really think I shouldn't drive. Do you mind if I stay here tonight at Brad's?"

"That's very responsible of you, Mother." She knew Erica was trying to sound disapproving, but she also knew she was doing it in jest. Erica laughed. "No worries, Mom, I'll see you tomorrow. Will you just call me at six tomorrow morning to make sure I'm up for school?"

"Okay, honey, I love you. Good night."

"Now that wasn't so bad was it?" Brad said. He was delighted Beverly was staying. Usually Beverly slept very soundly at Brad's but not that night. Maybe it was the wine, or maybe the spicy Chinese food, but she had a very restless sleep. She had a horrible dream. She hadn't dreamt about Johnny in a very long time, but in her dream she could hear him crying.

"Mommy, Mommy, I need you." Now she heard Erica, "Mom where are you? Johnny's having trouble breathing." She could hear her children calling her, but she was in her car and couldn't find her way home. She tried to call Tom from the car. Beverly could sense that she was crying out in her sleep. "Tom! Tom!" She woke up and her heart was pounding. Brad held her.

"Beverly, you were crying out for Tom. You were having a bad dream."

Beverly felt awful about crying out for her husband, when she was in her lover's bed. She had to explain to him about the dream. What she didn't say is that she knew the dream was all about guilt. Brad just said, "Beverly, it's okay, I love you. I know your life is very complicated right now." Again, Beverly just couldn't tell Brad that she loved him back.

Brad set an alarm for six o'clock. He woke up Beverly so that she could make sure Erica was up for school. He had to get to the hospital. He kissed Beverly. "Go back to sleep for awhile. Just lock the door when you leave."

Beverly fell back to sleep for a few hours. When she woke up she started feeling guilty again. She was also a little hung over. She was happy she had her regular appointment with Dr. Martino today.

Erica couldn't wait to show her ultrasound pictures to Christy. They were standing at Erica's locker when she took out her pictures. "Oh my God, she's going to be so cute!" Christy said. "She's got your nose."

Paige came over and wanted to see the pictures, too. "Oh Erica, how sweet, you're having a girl. Do you know what you'll name her?" Paige was actually being very nice, but Erica wasn't ready to share the baby's name yet.

Soon another one of Erica's friends, Savanna, came over to see the pictures. "Do you feel her move yet?" she asked.

"I do now, all the time. I didn't know that's what it was at first."

Erica took Savanna's hand and put it on her belly. "Can you feel her? She's moving now."

Savanna's eyes widened. "Oh, that's awesome!" Christy and Paige wanted a turn too.

Bobby Bauer walked up and put his hands on Erica's belly. "Hey, I want to feel your baby bump."

Erica pushed him. "Bobby, go away!" She saw Dwight coming down the hall. Dwight grabbed Bobby by the front of his shirt and pushed him up against the lockers. "Don't ever touch her again mother-fucker." He wasn't really loud when he said it, but everybody heard it anyway.

Bobby backed off. "Sorry, man, no harm intended." By now quite a few kids were watching.

Mr. D'Angelo came out of the art room. "Is there a problem here?"

"No, Mr. D'Angelo," Erica said. "Everything's fine." She was very embarrassed. Dwight walked her to math class.

"Babe, I'm sorry that happened. I just couldn't stand that he had his hands on you."

"I guess it's probably my fault. I shouldn't have been having show and tell in the hall."

There was a lot of buzz about the incident all day. Erica wanted to go and visit Helen after school. She knew Helen would love to see the ultrasound pictures.

Helen was thrilled. Erica told her grandmother what happened at school.

"I don't know why, but now people think that it's okay to go up to a woman and touch her pregnant belly. I saw it happen just the other day at the post office. That would have never happened back when I had my children."

"I know, Nana. I see it happen, too. I told my girlfriends it was okay, but Bobby didn't even ask. I can't believe how mad Dwight got. He rarely loses his temper."

242

"Well, I think that boy had it coming," Helen said. "Try to forget about it, honey. I want to show you something. I started crocheting this blanket for the baby. I decided just to do it with white yarn until I knew what you were having. You can always use it for the baby's christening."

"Wow, Nana, it's going to be beautiful."

"Well, now that I know I'll have a great grand-daughter, I'll have to make another one in pink. Martina is a beautiful name. Tell me how you chose it."

Erica chatted with Helen for quite a while. By the time she left, Erica felt better about what happened at school.

Meanwhile, Beverly needed to share with Dr. Martino. She told him about the ups and downs of her previous day. Beverly told him about the joy she felt when watching Erica's ultrasound and how she wanted to share it with Brad. Then she told him how guilty she felt about drinking too much wine and staying the night at Brad's. And, the bad dream, she told him all about it.

"Beverly, you obviously care for Brad and wanted to share with him your happiness. People have sex when they're happy. That's okay. So you had a little too much wine, so what? I think you behaved responsibly and called you're daughter to tell her you couldn't drive home."

"I could have taken a cab, or Brad would have taken me home if I had asked him. I shouldn't have had that last glass of wine. And the real truth is that I was enjoying the sex too much."

"Oh, Beverly, you've got to ease up a little on yourself. You have been under a lot of stress. It's okay that you let loose for the night. There was no harm done."

"As for the dream, our sub-conscious has a way of selecting random events and putting them together to make a new story. You were feeling guilt, so your dream was all about guilt."

"You were probably thinking of your son and his heart defect when they were looking at the fetal heart on the ultrasound. You were in your car, probably because you were feeling guilt over not being sober enough to drive home. Then there was more guilt when you couldn't get home to your children when they needed you. Tom was most likely in your dream, because you feel disloyal to him for enjoying sex with Brad so much."

"I know," Beverly said. "I'm a mess. I probably need a priest more than a shrink."

"I don't know how to respond to that," Dr. Martino said. "You're a good woman, Beverly, cut yourself a break."

"I wish I could. Thank you Dr. Martino, I'll see you next week."

Oh my God, Beverly thought, *I can't believe I told him all of that. It did help to talk about it though. I think mostly I feel guilty about my relationship with Brad, but he makes me happy, and I don't want to give him up.*

Chapter 28

Erica and Dwight got back their SAT scores. Dwight was pleased with his scores, but Erica was not. Dwight scored a 1750 and Erica scored 1680. "Babe, don't you remember how crummy you felt that day? You can take them again in the fall, after you have the baby.

"I can't believe you got a 650 in math," Erica pouted. "I only managed a 510. That's awful."

Dwight held her. "You've got great grades and a lot of extra activities. Everyone loves you. You'll have great references. Remember they're looking for a well-rounded student."

Erica put her hands on her belly and laughed. "Well-rounded, I am."

"That you are. You're beautiful. Remember, I've got to worry about a scholarship. I might take them again, too, so I can get those numbers up."

"It's hard to think about next year and the year after that. I just can't imagine how things will work out," Erica said.

"Remember, we've got to take it one step at a time. We can't see the whole staircase yet. For now we just have to get through this semester, which is only a month and a half away. We can spend a lot of time together this summer. When the summer is over, there's only another month until Martina comes."

As soon as Dwight said "Martina", Erica felt her kick. It made everything feel so real.

"Oh, Dwight, my senior year of high school is going to be crazy. I'll miss most of the fall semester."

"Babe, we'll have lots of help. We'll make it work. Everyone will help. I've got to find an internship this summer. Do you think you'll volunteer on the pediatrics unit again?"

"I'd like to because I really loved it. I want to keep busy, because I think it will make the time go faster. I'm sure they will be a little shocked that I'm pregnant."

"I'm planning on putting in as many hours at Wegmans as I can. I really need the money. I want to be able to get some things for Martina."

Erica was relieved, because in reality, they didn't have to worry about getting things for the baby. She knew that her mother would make sure Martina had the best of everything. But she also knew that Dwight had his pride. He would want to provide for his daughter. Dwight's right, she thought, I can't look so far ahead. The junior prom was in two weeks. Erica wondered if it was a good idea for them to go.

"Dwight, do you think we should go to the prom?"

"It's up to you, Babe. If you feel up to going, I think we should go."

"It will be a challenge to find a dress, but I think it would be fun to go. I would hate to miss it."

"Get a dress then." He bent down and talked to Erica's belly. "Martina, my little princess, do you want to go to the prom?" The baby always responded to Dwight's voice. Erica felt her roll over.

That Saturday Beverly left the shop at noon. She and Erica were going to lunch and to the mall to look for a prom dress. Beverly was glad Erica was going to the prom. She wanted her to have as normal a high school experience as possible, even though she was pregnant.

They found THE dress. It was perfect. It was a soft pink knit, halter-style dress. It had soft folds that crossed over the bust. Erica looked radiant in it. Beverly cried when she saw her. She didn't know if they were tears of joy, because Erica looked so beautiful, or if they were tears of regret, because her seventeen year old daughter was going to the prom pregnant. She took a deep breath. "That's the dress," Beverly said. "Now let's go get some shoes."

"Mom, do you think Martina looks pretty in pink?"

"Oh, honey, she does. Do you know what color you want to paint her room?"

"Pink is so predictable. Definitely not a pastel pink, but I think something darker, like a raspberry color."

"I like that idea. The wall with the mural can be white, and I can bring the raspberry back in, like in some flowers or little birds, or something. Do you want the furniture to be white?"

"I think so. We're at the mall. Can we go look at some cribs, so we can get some ideas?"

"Sure, honey, that would be fun."

Beverly and Erica went shoe shopping, and then went to a children's store and looked at baby furniture. Beverly felt good. It had been a really fun afternoon. That night Erica was going to the movies with Dwight. Beverly and Brad were having dinner with the Dwyer's. Beverly decided to be right up front with her daughter. "Honey, I'm planning on staying at Brad's tonight after we have dinner with the Dwyer's."

"Mom, you've been spending so much time with him. Are you in love with him?"

"I don't know, but I do really care for him. I don't feel so sad or alone when I'm with him. He makes me feel secure. I think you know how much I loved your father. Brad just fills that painful empty void that I felt after Dad died. It's probably similar to how Dwight makes you feel. It's complicated because I still love and miss your father so much."

"Mom, it's okay. I'm glad he makes you happy. I am so tired. I'm going to take a nap before I meet Dwight."

Beverly filled her tub and took a long bath. She felt very relaxed. She was looking forward to her evening with Brad. She wore her favorite little black dress with the pink pearl chocker that Brad gave her for her birthday. Beverly bought a new pair of black heels when Erica bought her shoes for the prom. They had four inch heels. Brad was very tall, so she felt comfortable wearing them. Tom was shorter. Sometimes when she wore heels, she was a little taller than her husband. Tom never cared.

Erica was still asleep when Brad came to pick her up. "Hi, sexy lady," he said. "You look beautiful tonight." He kissed her and noticed she packed an overnight bag. "You're staying tonight?"

"If it's okay," she said.

"You know you're welcome in my bed anytime."

They had a great time with the Dwyer's. Everything was out in the open now, so Beverly was free to talk about Erica's pregnancy. It had been a really nice evening. She slept very soundly with Brad that night.

Erica had been too tired to go to the movies. Dwight came over, and they had pizza and watched a movie on TV. Afterwards, they made love. It was nice to have some alone time with Dwight, knowing her mother wouldn't be showing up. Dwight was always nervous making love to her, now that she was pregnant.

Dwight had borrowed his mother's car. As much as he wanted to, he didn't think it was a good idea to stay all night. He knew that his mother wouldn't approve. She actually had a date that night. She was going out with a male nurse that she met at the hospital. His name was Mario. He was black, of course. Dwight knew his mother only dated black men. Dwight met him when he came to pick her up. He seemed like a good guy. His sisters were staying the night at Aunt Sarah's.

He kissed Erica one last time. "Babe, it's after midnight. I better get going. You need your rest."

The following weekend was going to be so busy. There was the prom, and Sunday was Mother's Day. Erica and Dwight wanted to do something nice for their mothers, since they had been so supportive to them about the pregnancy. They knew everything could be so much worse. They also wanted to include Helen in their plans.

They decided that they were going to make brunch. Erica talked to Helen. She said that she would be happy to let them have the brunch at her house. Erica and Dwight planned to do all the cooking. They planned it for eleven o'clock Sunday morning. Erica knew she would be tired after the prom, but she really wanted to do this. The twins were included too. They were so cute. Erica put them in charge of making the invitations for Beverly, Ruby, and Helen.

Erica kept the menu simple. She decided on fresh fruit salad, sausage, pecan pancakes, and scrambled eggs. She put together a shopping list so that Dwight could get everything at Wegmans after his shift on Saturday afternoon. Erica and Christy were going to get their hair and nails done for the prom. She and Dwight were going to the prom with Christy and Ben. They were going out to dinner before the prom.

"Mom, Dr. Williams did the nicest thing. He called here the other night and asked me for Dwight's number. He didn't say why he wanted it. He called Dwight and said that he wanted to make a dinner reservation for us and another couple for before the prom. He said it would be his treat. Do you believe that?"

Beverly smiled. "That was nice. He knows how hard Dwight works and that money is tight for him. Brad never had kids of his own. I'm sure he got a lot of pleasure out of doing that for you and Dwight." Beverly knew that if Tom was alive, he would have done the same thing.

Beverly was planning on making dinner for her and Brad, so that he could see the kids before they left for the prom. Erica and Dwight made such a handsome couple. Ruby stopped over to see the kids too. Beverly and Ruby just looked at each other and smiled. It was a bittersweet moment. There were lots of pictures taken. Ruby was with a date. They were going out themselves. Ruby's date's name was Mario. Brad knew him from the hospital. He said that Mario was a nurse and worked in the operating room. He had scrubbed in on some of Brad's cases. Brad said that he was smart, and he seemed like a nice guy.

Beverly looked over at Brad as they were having dinner. She thought of all the kind things that he had done for her. I do love him, she admitted to herself. I wish I could tell him. He wasn't staying the night. He was on call and needed to be at the hospital early in the morning to round on his patients.

Mr. Novak was a chaperone at the prom. "Erica you look lovely. You two make a very handsome couple."

Dwight smiled and gave him a fist bump. "Thanks, Coach."

Dwight took Erica on to the dance floor. He held her close as they were slow dancing. He could feel Martina moving. "Erica, tomorrow is your first Mother's Day." He kissed her gently behind her ear. "I love you."

Dwight took the bus to Helen's house on Sunday morning to help Erica with the brunch preparations. When Erica answered the door, he presented her with a bouquet of pink roses. "Happy Mother's Day, Babe."

"Oh, these will look beautiful on the table. Thank you so much."

He hadn't gotten her a corsage last night. She appreciated the roses so much more. She always felt a little guilty when Dwight spent money on her, because she knew he worked so hard for the little spending money he had. She tried to get past those feelings. *The situation is what it is,* she often said to herself.

The brunch was a huge success. Beverly, Ruby, and Helen were very touched. "Erica, this is your first mother's day," Helen said. She handed her granddaughter a wrapped package.

"Oh, Nana, you finished it! It's beautiful!" It was the white crocheted baby blanket. At the bottom of the box, there was a picture. It was a baby picture.

"Who is this, Nana?"

"It's your father, honey. Wasn't he just the cutest baby?"

"I'm going to get a frame for this and put it in Martina's room." Erica suddenly became very overwhelmed. She started to cry.

"Oh, honey, I didn't mean to upset you," Helen said.

"It just hit me that Martina won't have a grandfather." There was a very uncomfortable silence in the room. For sure no one was going to mention the grandfather that was in prison. Dwight went over and put his arm around Erica.

"She'll have a lot of good people in her life. She'll be blessed," Helen said.

The group broke up shortly after that. Erica was very quiet the whole rest of the day. An overwhelming sadness came over Beverly, too. She thought back to last Mother's Day, which seemed forever ago. Sometimes the highs and lows were just too much to bear.

Chapter 29

The weather was getting warmer. It had been a beautiful spring. Memorial Day was right around the corner. Erica and Dwight took long walks on the canal and in the village whenever they could. Dr. Anderson had told Erica the exercise was good for her, and it would help to keep her weight under control. Erica felt enormous, even though she was only twenty-two weeks. Her mother said that it was because she was petite, and she had nowhere to go but out. School was winding down. Pretty soon there would be finals.

Beverly continued to spend a lot of time with Brad. They started playing golf on the weekends. She was finally able to let go of some of her guilt. Tom's colleagues wanted to hold a golf tournament in his memory. It would be in June. The money raised would be donated to a research fund for pediatric brain tumors. Tom was very devoted to research in that area. Brad was on the committee. Sometimes Beverly couldn't help thinking that Brad just stepped into Tom's shoes, and she was his by default. But, aside from them both being neurosurgeons, they were both really different.

"Honey, I've been thinking. I think it's time we packed up Johnny's room. I think it's a perfect room for Martina. It's a quieter room, and it gets more sun. Remember, before it was Johnny's room, it was your room. It has always been the nursery."

"Okay, Mom, if you think so."

"I picked up some color sample cards at the paint store. If I'm going to do the mural, we had better get started. I think I'm going to redecorate my bedroom too. When the painters are here, they can paint both rooms."

"Why are you changing your room? It seems like you just redecorated it."

"Sometimes it just makes me feel so sad. It was our room... your father's and mine. Now it's my room. I just want it to be different. I'm going to get new bedroom furniture."

Beverly thought it would be better for her and Brad if she made some changes. She knew her daughter wasn't dumb. She had probably already figured it out.

"Mom, I really like this one, 'Raspberry Sorbet'. Don't you think it would be pretty with white baby furniture?"

"Oh, I like that one too. I can't wait to get started. It will be so much fun decorating the nursery."

"Mom, do you have any plans for Memorial weekend?"

"I haven't thought that much about it. Did you have something in mind?"

"Christy invited me to her cottage for the weekend. She's having a big barbeque there on Saturday and invited a lot of kids from school. Do you care if I go?"

"Would you be gone the whole weekend?"

"Well I was planning on staying over Saturday night and Sunday night, if that's okay. I just feel like it's going to be my last chance to hang out with my friends like a normal high school kid for awhile. You know, before I'm really big pregnant and the baby comes."

"I think that it is fine, honey, if you're up to it."

"I really feel great. Dwight has to work most of the weekend, but he's going on Saturday. I've got to find a bathing suit. Christy said that she would help me find one."

Beverly did think that it would be okay. Karen Logan, Christy's mother was an OB nurse. She knew that Karen would keep an eye on Erica, and that she would keep the party under control. Beverly thought she would give Karen a call. She hadn't really talked to her since the news about Erica's pregnancy came out.

"Hi, Beverly, I'm so glad you called. I so admire how you're handling things with Erica. I'm sure it's been a challenge. Erica looks great, though, and the few times that I've met Dwight, I have to say that I really liked him."

"Oh God, Karen, sometimes I think we will never get through this, but I have to admit, I'm starting to get a little excited about having a new baby in the house."

"With adolescent pregnancies, good support from the girl's mother makes all the difference. Believe me, I know. It will be okay, Bev. These stories can have a happy ending. You know I'll help in any way I can.

Bill and I are very fond of your daughter. Carrie Anderson is a good OB doc. I'm glad that's who she is seeing."

"Thanks, Karen. I really wish I had called you sooner. It just took me a long time to sort it all out in my own head. So you think it's alright for Erica to go on Memorial weekend? I know you'll keep an eye on her."

"She's so sensible, Bev. She'll be fine. Let her be a teenager. Of course I'll look out for her."

Beverly continued to chat with Karen. She wanted to send some food with Erica for the barbeque.

Good, I'm free to spend time with Brad this weekend. I heard the weather is going to be nice. Brad had told her that he was on call Friday night, but that he had the rest of the weekend free.

Beverly planned to work at the shop in the morning, and she and Brad were going to play golf Saturday afternoon. Pam was doing a great job managing things at the shop. She had hired more part time help, and Beverly was working fewer hours.

Beverly heard Dwight tell Erica that his mother's birthday was on Sunday. Beverly wanted to give her a gift. There was a blouse in the store that she thought would be perfect for Ruby. The blouse was silk and light turquoise in color. It would look great with white or black. She called to see if she could meet for breakfast on Saturday morning. They met at the Village Café.

They always had a lot to talk about. Beverly asked her about Mario.

"Oh, Mario's just fine. He's been very supportive to me in my schoolwork. He just seems so much more sincere than Michael, the last man I was seeing." What she didn't tell Beverly was how good he was in bed. "I just don't have a lot of time for men in my life. Maybe when I'm done with school, it will be better. One more year... I've just got to hang in there one more year."

"Ruby, you work so hard, you deserve to have a little pleasure in your life."

"I felt so bad when the subject of grandfathers came up on Mother's Day," Ruby said. "Sometimes I think I'll never be able to put my past mistakes behind me. When it comes to men, I'm not the best judge of character. When I look at my children, I can see Jerome, their father. I just have to be strong enough to never let him back in my life. I'm afraid of what will happen if he ever gets out of prison. He is one of those men that can be so charming, and then turns mean and ugly. When Dwight was a little boy, he would get really angry at me and beat up on me. He was very jealous and controlling. I always found a reason to blame myself, and then I would forgive him. I can never let any man do that to me again."

Beverly was crying now. "Oh, Ruby, I'm so sorry. But there are good men out there. Maybe Mario is one of them."

"One can hope," Ruby said.

Beverly went on to say, "Martina will have two grandmothers who will love her very much."

"Yes, she will."

Beverly gave Ruby her birthday gift. Ruby was very touched. "Mario is taking me to dinner tonight, now I'll have something new and pretty to wear. Thank you so much, Beverly."

Beverly couldn't stop thinking about what Ruby had told her. They really did live in two very different worlds.

Beverly and Brad played golf that afternoon. Brad had joined the same country club where she and Tom had been members. They stayed and had dinner in the club house. It was the first time that Beverly had dinner there since Tom died. Although everyone was cordial, it was odd being there with another man.

"Are you okay with this?" Brad asked. "Is it uncomfortable for you to be dining here without Tom?"

"No, Brad, it's okay." They stayed at Brad's that night. She shared with him Ruby's story. It had been on her mind.

Brad held her and stroked her hair. "That's inexcusable. I don't think she has to worry about Mario. I think he's a decent guy." He went on to tell her about being called down to the ED last week to do a consult on a patient who had been a victim of domestic violence. Her partner repeatedly banged her head against the bathtub, and she suffered an intracranial bleed. He wasn't sure this woman would ever make a full recovery.

"I'm so happy that's not my world," Beverly said.

"That kind of problem isn't unique to poor people or people of color. It happens everywhere."

Brad turned on the television. "We need to lighten things up a little." He found a light romantic comedy for them to watch. It was a classic... the movie was "Pillow Talk," with Rock Hudson and Doris Day. Brad made popcorn and opened a bottle of Merlot, and they watched it in bed. His lovemaking was very tender that night.

Erica was having a great time at Christy's. Dwight finally got there at about two o'clock. "Babe, I can't believe how good you look in that bathing suit, and you're pregnant!"

He kissed her. Bobby Bauer was at the party. Dwight wouldn't leave Erica's side if he was anywhere near her. He brought a girl. She wasn't someone from their school. Erica didn't think Bobby would be a problem today, but she did notice him checking her out in her bathing suit.

It was a really warm day. A lot of the kids went swimming in the lake. The water felt great. She and Dwight went in. They swam over to the floating dock were Ben and Christy were lying in the sun. Dwight gently lifted her up on the dock and then climbed up himself.

"This is a great party, Christy. Thanks for inviting me."

The four of them enjoyed the floating dock for awhile. "I'm starting to feel a little light-headed," Erica said.

"I think you've had enough sun," Dwight said. He jumped into the water and reached up for her. He held her in the water. "Are you feeling any better in the water, where it's cooler?"

"A little, but maybe I should go inside for a little while."

Dwight helped her get back to shore. Christy's mother saw her and looked concerned. "Honey, I want you to go lay down on the couch in the porch. Lay down on your left side. You need to have some fluids. You've probably had a little too much sun. When you're pregnant, you can't let yourself get overheated." Dwight got her a few bottles of water and sat down on the floor next to her while she rested and sipped on her water.

"Oh, Babe, you had me a little worried."

"It's okay. I'm feeling a lot better now." Mrs. Logan came out with a blood pressure cuff.

"Well, you look better," she said. "But let's make sure. Your blood pressure is normal. Honey, is your baby moving?"

Erica put her hands on her belly. "She's okay, Mrs. Logan. I can feel her moving."

"I want to see you with that water bottle, okay? You should probably stay out of the sun."

"Dwight, who made that tray of whoopie pies that you brought?" Mrs. Logan asked.

"Oh, that would be my mom. She's a great baker."

"I had to try one. Tell your mom thanks. They're delicious!"

Everyone seemed to be enjoying the party. The kids were respectful of the ban on alcohol. A lot of Christy's parent's friends were there. Erica thought that the food was amazing.

"Wait until you try Mr. Logan's barbecued chicken."

"Babe, I can't believe how much you can eat! I brought your Tums. I'm sure you're going to need them."

Erica was glad to see Rachael at the party. She was just recently released from the hospital and came back to school. She was still very thin, but Erica thought she looked better. Erica saw her pushing some food around on her plate. She was so surprised to see her.

"Hi, Rach, it's really good to see you." Erica gave her a hug. "I love your suit."

"Thanks. You look great Erica. Is everything going okay for you and the baby?"

"It is. Thanks for asking." Erica chatted with Rachael and a few other girls for awhile. They all had lots of questions about her pregnancy. She was getting used to it and really didn't mind anymore.

The party started to break up once the fireworks were over. Erica could feel Martina moving like crazy during the fireworks. She reached out and put Dwight's hand on her belly.

"Wow!" he exclaimed. "I love feeling my baby girl when she's playing."

256

Dwight left a little after eleven o'clock. Erica gave her mother a call. "Mom, I had the best time today!"

"I hope you didn't over do it, honey."

"Mrs. Logan took good care of me." She didn't tell her mother about her getting light-headed.

Erica loved spending the weekend with the Logans. Christy had an older sister, who was back from college for the summer, and also a younger brother. The Logans treated her like family. It was nice being part of a family. She really liked Christy's father. He was so nice and had a great sense of humor. Even though she was pregnant, she didn't feel awkward around Christy's family. *I almost feel normal. I haven't felt that way in a very long time,* she thought. On Monday morning, Memorial Day, Beverly and Brad drove out to the lake to pick up Erica. Brad really hit it off with Bill Logan. They made plans to meet up for golf soon.

Beverly chatted with Karen in the kitchen. "Bev, Brad seems like a really nice guy. Do you see a future with him?"

"I don't know, Karen. It just seems so soon."

"How has Erica been about it?"

"Most of the time she's okay. But then she has her moments when she's resentful of my relationship with Brad. I guess we've come to an understanding that I need Brad in my life, just as she needs Dwight in her life. Does that make sense?"

"I think it does."

"Bev, can Christy and I have a baby shower for Erica? I was thinking maybe in early August."

"Oh, that sounds wonderful. I love the idea!" Beverly gave Karen a hug.

They all said their goodbyes, and Beverly, Brad, and Erica took off. They stopped at a restaurant on the lake for lunch on the way home. Erica saw how Brad looked at her mother. She knew he was very much in love with her. What she didn't know was if her mother was in love with him.

Chapter 30

Erica couldn't believe there were only three weeks left before school got out. She wondered if the summer would go by quickly. She had already contacted the volunteer office at the hospital. They said that they were thrilled she was planning to come back to work on the pediatric unit. They wanted her to work on a special program that prepared kids for surgery. It involved puppets. She didn't think her mother would need her too much at the shop. Actually her mother wasn't spending as much time at the shop. Pam seemed to have everything under control.

Dwight was going to try and work as much as he could at Wegmans. Mr. Novak recruited him to help at a basketball camp for inner city boys that were in elementary school. Dr. Williams landed him this great internship for the neurosurgery department. He would be doing data entry for a research study. She knew that Dr. Williams really liked Dwight. It was thoughtful of him to arrange the internship for him. Erica had to admit Dr. Williams was pretty nice. Sometimes she thought he tried a little too hard.

"Mom, I don't think Dwight is going to have any time for me this summer. He's got so much going on."

"Honey, of course he'll have time for you. He loves you. You're going to be busy yourself."

"The only thing I have planned is volunteering at the hospital."

"Honey, you're pregnant. Your job is to take care of yourself and the baby. Besides, we have a lot to do to get ready for Martina. Maybe you and I can take a short vacation, just the two of us. Once the baby comes, your life is going to change in a big way. Rest and relax and enjoy the summer."

"Well, first I've got to get through finals. It's so hard to study. Everyone has spring fever, and I've got so much on my mind. Is it okay if Dwight comes over tonight to study?"

"That's fine. Why don't you ask him if he wants to come a little early and have dinner with us? Brad's coming over when he gets through at the hospital. I think I'll grill some salmon."

"Okay, Mom, that sounds nice."

When Dwight got there Erica took him upstairs to show him where the baby's room would be. Johnny's stuff still hadn't been packed away. Dwight looked around the room and looked at a picture of Johnny and Erica's dad that was framed on the dresser. "Oh, Babe, I can't believe you've lost both your little brother and your Dad, too. Just by looking at your brother's things, I can tell he was a cool little dude. Are you okay with Martina taking his room?"

"Well, my Mom said that it's always been the nursery. It was my room too, when I was a baby. When I think of it like that, it's okay."

Dwight started thinking. *I can't believe my baby girl will be sleeping here at this house. I wish that Erica and I could be together with our baby girl. I just don't see how that would work, not yet anyway, when we're still in high school. My mom still needs me at home. I'm just going to have to spend as much time with Erica and the baby as I can.* He thought about his own father. He could hardly remember him ever sleeping at the same house where he and his mother were. Just thinking about his father caused him hurt and pain.

"Babe, it's hard to imagine how our lives will be after Martina is born. We just have to have faith that everything will work out somehow."

"I know, I can't imagine it either, but I think about it all the time."

Everyone talked easily over dinner. Dr. Williams was telling Dwight a little bit about the research study that he would be involved in. When Erica looked at Dwight she couldn't help but be proud. He was smart, he was good-looking, and just a really nice guy. She just knew Dwight had a bright future.

Then Erica thought about herself. Would she ever get her life back on track?

Dwight must have sensed that she was feeling a little down and left out. "Erica we better hit the books. Please excuse us. Thanks, Mrs. McIntyre. That was a great meal." Erica and Dwight went up to her room to study.

It stayed light for so long and it was a beautiful evening. Beverly and Brad sat on the deck and opened another bottle of wine. Beverly couldn't help but reminisce that she and Tom would often relax with a bottle of wine on the deck. They loved to watch the sunset. Beverly wrapped her arms around Brad. That was really nice of you to arrange the internship for Dwight.

"He's an impressive young man," Brad said. "Did I tell you who was in our foursome for the golf tournament?"

"No. Who are you playing with?"

"Besides me, it will be Peter Dwyer, Jake Goldstein, and Bill Logan. I asked Bill when I met him at the lake Memorial weekend. I really liked him."

"Oh, he is a nice guy. I'm glad you asked him."

"Will you be okay having dinner with their wives? I know that you aren't that fond of Jake's wife."

"I can handle Rebecca. I've had to sit with her at many other functions."

"Beverly, you know they'll want you to say a few words after dinner."

"I know. Peter already asked me. I think it will be okay." Beverly thought about being with Brad at the golf tournament.

She had that feeling again that she was his by default. Brad had just fallen into her life so easily. Beverly wasn't sure how she felt about that. *Was I desperate? Was I so sad and lonely that I let the first man that showed any interest become part of my life?*

Brad could see she was deep in thought. "Are you okay?"

She had tears in her eyes. "I was just having a moment."

It was almost like he could read her mind. "Beverly, I know it hasn't been long since you lost Tom. I know your feelings for me probably aren't as deep as mine are for you. I can accept that. I'm sure that it's probably a little awkward how I've slipped into your social circle. I sense that you're uncomfortable with our relationship sometimes."

"Brad, it's still such a confusing time for me. Please be patient with me."

"I can be patient." He kissed her. "Thank you for dinner. I've got to get going. I've got some work I need to catch up on."

Brad thought about his relationship with Beverly as he drove home. He loved her, but he realized that not once had she ever said that she loved him. *I'm probably moving too fast*, he thought. *Maybe I should give her some space.* He decided that he was going to find someone to take his place in the foursome at the golf tournament. He would go out of town that weekend and visit his sister. His sister was going through a rough time. Her husband had just left her. She had been very supportive to him when he was going through his own divorce, so he felt he should reach out to her. The more he thought about it, the more he thought it was a good idea. In the end it would probably be easier for Beverly, and he wouldn't have to endure the lurking ghost of Tom McIntyre.

Beverly sensed that Brad had left a little abruptly. She felt a little odd about it. She decided that maybe she was over thinking it. She poured herself another glass of wine and tried to distract herself with her email. After Dwight came in to say goodnight, she went up to bed. Beverly didn't sleep well that night.

Brad called Peter and told him that he wouldn't be able to play in the tournament. He said it was a family matter, and he needed to leave town. Brad said that he couldn't go this coming weekend because he was on call, so it had to be the following weekend. He didn't tell Peter the real reason he decided not to play. He called Bill Logan with the same excuse. Bill was going to ask his brother to play. Brad told him the tournament fees had already been taken care of for both him and his brother.

Beverly hadn't heard from Brad all week. She knew he was on call this weekend. She tried calling him when she got to the shop on Saturday morning. He said that he could meet her at the Village Café for lunch. As she left to meet him, an uneasy feeling came over her.

He smiled as she sat down. After they placed their orders, he said, "Beverly, we need to have a conversation. I sense that maybe our relationship is moving a little too quickly for you." Beverly felt her heart skip a beat. "I've decided to have someone play for me in the tournament next weekend. I think that being together at the tournament would be awkward for both of us. It would be a good opportunity to visit my sister. I've felt a little guilty that I haven't reached out to Maggie since her husband left her."

Beverly didn't know what to say.

Brad went on, "I'm thinking maybe we should take a little break. I know how I feel about you, but I'm not so sure that you feel the same way, and I don't want to push you."

Beverly was shocked. She could feel the heat in her face. "Are you breaking up with me?"

"No, I didn't say that. I just feel we need a break. I think you need time to sort out your feelings. If we're sleeping together and spending all of our free time together, I'm not sure you can do that. Beverly, I don't want to be a friend with benefits. I feel more deeply than that."

"But you said that you could be patient with me," Beverly said. She was trying so hard not to cry.

"I'm not breaking things off with you. I'm just giving you some space."

"Okay, but you'll call me when you get back to town after next weekend?"

"Beverly, you call me when you're ready." He paid the check and walked her back to the shop. He kissed her on the cheek. "I love you, Beverly." That was it. He walked away.

She felt stung. She couldn't decide if she was a little angry or just hurt. Then she felt guilty that she had used Brad for security and sex. She had no one to blame but herself. Pam could see how upset she was when she got back to the shop. Beverly told her what happened.

"Maybe it's not a bad idea. It doesn't sound like he's really going anywhere other than away for the weekend. He did fall into your life fairly soon after Tom died. Give yourself time, honey. You've been through so much in the past year. It will give you more time to spend with Erica before the baby comes."

"You're right. I do want to spend more time with Erica this summer."

Beverly and Erica went to mass with Helen on Sunday morning. Erica and her mother packed up things in Johnny's room that afternoon. It was a task that they had been putting off. "Oh Mom, I can't believe we're doing this after all these years. Once this room is Martina's and your room is redecorated, it will seem like Johnny and Dad never lived here."

"Oh, that's not true. We'll never really forget. We can get this picture of Johnny and Dad enlarged and frame it for the wall in the hall. Some things just have to be put away, but we will do it gradually."

Erica picked up her brother's teddy bear that he called Bob. Her brother slept with Bob every night. Whenever he went to a doctor's appointment or was admitted to the hospital, Bob was always with him. Erica remembered seeing her brother's little arm wrapped around Bob as he was lying in the casket. She also remembered the funeral director asking her mother if she wanted her son buried with his teddy bear. She had said "No," that was all she had left of him, and she wanted to keep the bear. Erica could still remember feeling horribly upset. She said, "But Mommy, you know Johnny can never fall asleep without Bob!"

She remembered her mother saying that Johnny was already sleeping and wouldn't be waking up. She was so upset and confused. She ran to her father for consolation.

Erica looked over at her mother. She was probably deep in the same memory. "Mom, can we keep Johnny's teddy bear for Martina?"

"Of course we can, honey. I think Martina's Uncle Johnny would like that."

"Oh God, Mom, our life is such a mess!"

"One step at a time, honey, it's a long staircase."

They finished packing up the room. It took most of the afternoon. It was an exhausting experience. The room was ready for the painters on Monday. Helen called and invited them for dinner. They were happy to accept. Beverly brought a bottle of her favorite chardonnay. She felt it had been a very trying weekend.

It was Thursday. Beverly hadn't heard from Brad all week. She was glad she was seeing Dr. Martino today. She told him everything.

"Beverly, I think that it's a good idea. You've always said that you were conflicted about your feelings for him."

264

"I know, but he's been such a good friend. I feel like he rescued me. He makes me feel so safe. I miss him."

"Beverly, let's back up. You used the word 'friend'. Is that what you feel for him?"

"Well, kind of, but I've enjoyed the sex, too."

"How do you mean that he makes you feel safe?"

"I don't know, he just does, like I felt safe with Tom."

"Beverly, it sounds like you're afraid of being alone."

"Maybe I am."

"He sounds like a very kind and sincere guy. From what you tell me, he feels more than friendship for you. He doesn't sound like the type of man that just wants to bed you."

"I guess I feel like I've used him a little, and I feel really guilty about it."

"I think his wanting to give you some space to sort out your feelings is actually a really good idea. It's very considerate."

"He really grounds me. I miss him already. He was the only thing in my life that I could count on unconditionally."

"Beverly, it's obvious he doesn't just want to be a friend with benefits. Take advantage of this time. You owe it to yourself. In all fairness, I think you owe it to him."

Beverly didn't feel any better after her session with Dr. Martino. He kind of confirmed what she had been feeling guilty about. She had been stringing Brad along. *He deserves better than that. I need to figure this out.*

When Beverly got home she went upstairs to check on the progress the painters had made. The job was supposed to be completed today. She went into her freshly painted bedroom. It didn't feel like her and Tom's room anymore. That made her a little sad. Her new bedroom furniture would be delivered tomorrow. Martina's room was beautiful. She loved the raspberry color that Erica chose. She couldn't wait to get started on the mural. *Painting always relaxes me,* Beverly thought. *I always do my best thinking when I'm relaxed.*

Beverly was also worried about Erica. She seemed very down lately. She knew it was because school would soon be over, and she probably wouldn't see as much of Dwight.

Beverly heard her come in from school. She came into the freshly painted nursery and just sat on the floor and cried.

"Honey, you don't like it?"

"Mom, that's not it. I can't believe this is all happening! It's starting to feel all so real. School's almost over. I love school and I won't be going back in September. I don't see how I'll ever be able to take care of a baby and finish my education. You know how much I want to be a doctor. How will Dwight and I be good parents? We won't even be together a lot of the time. I love Dwight and I love Martina, but I just want my old life back. I miss Dad so much. I can't even imagine what he would think about all of this. I feel like I've let everybody down...myself most of all."

Beverly sat down on the floor and held her daughter. "Honey, we'll get through this. I hate seeing you so unglued. I think you're really overtired from all the studying you've been doing. You've been up late every night this week. Come on let's get you something to drink and you can lay down for a while before dinner."

Beverly could feel a big headache coming on. She took the maximum dose of Ibuprofen and poured herself a glass of wine. She would make Erica's favorite pasta salad for dinner. She decided to run to the dairy and get some ice cream for dessert. Beverly was determined to get through the golf tournament this weekend and then focus on supporting Erica through final exams.

Chapter 31

Dwight was worried about Erica. She was so stressed out about finals. He didn't think it was good for her or the baby. She seemed a little down. Dwight was supposed to work all weekend. He decided to see if someone at work could take his hours this weekend. There was an older guy, Vince, who started working at Wegmans after he retired, because he lost a good chunk of his pension on a bad investment. He always wanted to pick up extra hours. He would explain to his boss that he had to study for finals. Dwight thought he needed to spend the time with Erica. It all worked out. Mr. Smith gave his permission, and Vince was happy to take his hours.

Beverly decided to ask Erica if she and Dwight wanted to come to the dinner following the golf tournament. She didn't think it would be a problem adding them to their table, since Brad wasn't coming. It would just be one extra place setting.

Erica and Dwight studied all day at the library. They thought they would be less distracted there. Although Beverly wasn't playing, she was at the club all day helping with the event. She came home late in the afternoon to shower and change for the dinner. Erica was trying to figure out what she should wear. She had a good-sized belly for twenty-five weeks. "Mom, I really don't have anything to wear!"

Beverly looked through her closet. "It doesn't have to be a dress, honey. How about these black Capri pants and this white blouse?" The blouse was soft and feminine. "You can wear your hair up and I'll lend you those gold earrings that Brad gave me. You'll look fine."

Erica tried to put on a pair of heels. "Mom, I can't even get my feet into these." Her feet did look a little swollen.

"Just put on a pretty pair of sandals."

"Mom, you look great." Beverly was wearing a powder blue silk, sheath dress and a big silver necklace. "Are you bummed that Dr. Williams isn't here? Where is he anyway?"

"He had a family situation. He needed to see his sister this weekend. I guess they're pretty close. Her husband just left her. Honey, Brad and I are taking a little break."

Erica was shocked. "Mom, was that your idea? Is that what you want?"

"No, it was his idea. I don't know what I want." Beverly was glad that Dwight was downstairs at the door. She really didn't want to discuss the Brad situation with her daughter. She thought that Dwight looked so handsome. He had on khaki pants, a navy blue blazer, a button down shirt, and tie.

Beverly was happily surprised that Rebecca Goldstein wasn't there. Apparently she had a family emergency of her own. Everyone was very welcoming to Dwight and Erica. It really didn't seem at all awkward. The golf tournament was a big success. The money raised today, along with the money donated in Tom's memory after his death, netted a significant sum. Besides Peter Dwyer, the father of a little boy who was recovering from brain tumor surgery spoke. There was a slide show showing pictures of various children touched by brain cancer. It was very moving. Beverly was the last up to the podium. She was able to deliver her remarks without breaking down. For that she was grateful. When she got back to her seat, Erica got up and hugged her mother. She had tears, but was in control. "Mom, I'm so proud of you."

After they got home, Beverly stayed up for awhile and had another glass of wine. She thought about how much she missed her husband. Tom was the love of her life. Then she thought about Brad. She wondered if she could ever love Brad enough. Beverly missed him, too, but at least she knew she could have him back. Tom was never coming back.

Erica had her first final on Monday, it was the test she dreaded most…math. By the time she handed in her test she had a wicked headache. She met up with Dwight in the hall. "Erica, you don't look so good. Are you feeling okay?"

"I just have a headache. I'll be okay."

"I want you to go to the nurse," Dwight said.

"I'm really okay."

"Do it for me, Babe."

Dwight walked her to the nurse's office. The nurse had her sit down and took her blood pressure. It was 140/94.

"Honey, that's a little high. Do you know what your blood pressure usually runs?" asked Mrs. Pearson.

"I think 120 over something," replied Erica.

"I want you to lie down on the cot, on your left side. Here, start sipping on this water. I'll take it again after about fifteen minutes." Dwight pulled up a chair and sat down next to her.

"Babe, you've been really pushing it."

Nancy Pearson looked over at the young couple. *They are so sweet together. I hope that, someday, they will be able to someday get their lives back on track.*

She took Erica's blood pressure again. "Well that's a little better. It's 130/88. I really think that you should check in with your OB this afternoon. Do you have an exam this afternoon?"

"No. My next final is tomorrow."

"I'll take her to the doctor," Dwight said. "I'm done for the day too."

By the time she got to Dr. Anderson's office, she was feeling better. Her headache was gone. Her blood pressure was lower, now 126/ 82. Dwight filled Dr. Anderson in on the blood pressure readings at school.

She listened to the baby's heart beat, and looked at Erica's feet. "Your feet are a little swollen, but not too bad. Just as a precaution, I'm going to have you get some blood work done. My concern is preeclampsia, or you might have heard it called toxemia. It's when you develop problems with your blood pressure in pregnancy. It can affect your kidneys and other organs too. We have to monitor this, because if it gets out of control, it can affect the baby. We'll check your urine sample for protein. Adolescents can be more prone to this condition. It could be your blood pressure is up because of the stress of your exams. Your headache could also be from stress, or maybe you weren't hydrated enough."

"I did forget to bring my water bottle in for the exam. My headache started getting better as soon as the nurse made me start drinking water."

"Try and put your feet up this afternoon and rest a little. If you're feeling okay tomorrow, and all your labs come back normal, you can go

269

to school. Can you have the nurse take your blood pressure again at lunchtime? Give her my card. She can call me. I'll call you with the results of your blood work. It should be back by early evening."

Beverly was sitting in the waiting room when Dwight and Erica walked out. "Erica, why didn't you call me?"

"Mom, we had it handled. I'm fine. How did you know I was here anyway?"

"Mrs. Pearson called me. She was worried about you. I really wish you had called me. What did Dr. Anderson say?"

Erica filled her mother in on everything that the doctor had told her.

"Why don't you two go back to the house and I'll make you some lunch. Erica, I want you to rest for a few hours and then you can get back to studying. What do you have tomorrow?"

"I have my English final in the morning and Spanish in the afternoon. I'm not too worried about either of them."

Dwight kissed Erica and took off after lunch. He had to go into work for a few hours. Dr. Anderson called early in the evening. All the lab work was normal. Beverly was still worried.

Erica felt much better the following day. It was raining, so it wasn't so hot. She checked in with Mrs. Pearson at lunchtime. Her blood pressure was 120/80. "You look much better honey," Mrs. Pearson said. "Just remember to stay hydrated. Can I share something with you, Erica?"

"Sure."

"My best friend became pregnant when she was sixteen. I always liked her parents, but they were awful to her when she told them about her pregnancy. Her boyfriend denied that he was the father of her baby. Her parents sent her away to live with an aunt in another state. She had a beautiful baby boy. Her aunt got her back into school, and she eventually went to college. She met someone in college. They got married, and she had two more children. She's a very successful journalist. Erica, your story can have a happy ending. You are so fortunate that Dwight has been so involved in your pregnancy, and that your mother has been so supportive."

"Thanks for sharing that with me, Mr. Pearson. Some days I'm just so overwhelmed, and I can't even imagine what my future will be."

Mrs. Pearson gave her a hug and sent her off to lunch.

Beverly was keeping close tabs on her daughter. She missed Brad. She still couldn't believe that he hadn't called her. Beverly went into the shop in the mornings and worked on sketching the mural in the afternoons. She wanted to be home when Erica got in from school. Ruby called her. Dwight had told her about Erica's blood pressure.

"Oh, Beverly, that concerns me. I had preeclampsia when I was pregnant with Dwight. They had to induce my labor when I was just thirty-two weeks. I'm so thankful that Dwight did okay."

"All her blood work was okay, Ruby. Dr. Anderson is watching her carefully. I think once finals are over, it will be better for Erica. So tell me, how are you? How are things with Mario?"

"Well, my finals were over in May, so my life is a little easier right now. I don't have any classes until the fall. Juggling work and school is always tough. Yes, I'm still seeing Mario. He's a good guy. He seems very genuine." Ruby felt their relationship was more than sex. What she didn't tell Beverly is that she had a pregnancy scare of her own. She was so busy with work and school that she missed a few birth control pills in May. Her period was a little late in coming. She was so worried that she took a pregnancy test. Thank God she got her period the next day. She couldn't believe she was that careless.

Ruby asked her about Brad. Beverly told her they were "taking a break."

Ruby was surprised. She wondered what happened.

"Things were getting serious far too quickly," Beverly sighed. "I just need time."

"I can understand that," Ruby said. "I hope things work out for you two, if that's what you want. I really like him. It was really kind of him to arrange that internship for Dwight."

"Ruby, you remember my husband. It's just hard moving on after you've had a man like Tom. I hope it works for me and Brad too. It's just so soon."

Beverly and Ruby set up a date to meet for lunch on Ruby's day off.

Erica's last final was on Thursday. It was chemistry. She felt pretty good about chemistry. Mr. Novak was so sweet. He set up a small portable fan right by her desk and told her that he had brought a few extra bottles of water if she needed them. "I can get a monitor for you, Erica, if you need a bathroom break." Dwight just looked at her and smiled. *Mr. Novak knows just what a pregnant woman needs*, she thought. Then she wondered if he had any kids.

Erica handed in her test shortly after Dwight. He was waiting for her in the hall. "Babe, what did you think?"

"It wasn't so bad. I think I might have done well," she beamed. "Wasn't Mr. Novak sweet?"

"He told me that his wife is pregnant with their first baby. She's due sometime next month. Everybody on the team is chipping in to get him a gift card."

"Oh, that's so nice! I'm starved. Let's get some lunch."

Mrs. Pearson stopped her in the hall. Can I check your blood pressure today, Erica?"

Erica thought it was so nice that Mrs. Pearson was so concerned. She and Dwight followed her to the nurse's office. "Perfect, your blood pressure is 120/78. I like that." She smiled. "You two have a great summer. She wrote down something on an index card and handed it to Erica. This is my contact information: cell phone, home phone, and email. Call me if you need anything, okay?"

Erica hugged her. "Thank you so much, Mrs. Pearson. You have a good summer too."

Erica sighed. "I probably won't even see her until after I have the baby."

They went to the Village Café for lunch. Erica ordered a turkey club sandwich. Dwight reached over and grabbed her chips.

"Hey, what are you doing?"

"Babe, you don't need all that extra salt or grease."

"Okay, be that way. I'm going to get pie."

"Well, okay, me too…I guess we should celebrate." They both ordered banana cream.

"Oh God," Erica said. "Now I'm so full! We better walk a little."

272

They stopped in at the shop to say hello to Beverly and Pam. They chatted for a while. Pam told them that Kyle and Mark were getting married. Mark wanted kids. They were going to try to have a baby with a surrogate.

Erica couldn't help but wonder whose sperm they would use. Dwight just stood there with his mouth open.

"Good for them," said Erica. "I hope it works out. They seem so happy together."

Erica knew her mother had her regular appointment with her therapist at four o'clock.

She and Dwight went back to the McIntyre's. She showed him the progress on the baby's room and took him to her bedroom to make love. Dwight made love to her very slowly and tenderly. "Erica, I love you so much. You're so beautiful."

"I love you, too, Dwight. Our story has to have a happy ending."

"Babe, I'll do everything I can to make that happen."

She rested in his arms. Dwight was surprised when she rolled over and wanted him again.

Afterwards, they went down to the kitchen to get something to drink. Dwight kissed her. "Babe, I really should get going."

"Dwight, when do you start your internship with Dr. Williams?"

"Monday," he answered.

"Don't mention my mother to him," she said. "She and Dr. Williams are 'taking a break,' whatever that means."

"I'm surprised," Dwight said. "I thought your mom was really into him. It's pretty obvious how he feels about her."

"Well I think that it's kind of good. It all seemed just too soon."

"Yeah, maybe you're right."

Brad was the topic of conversation during Beverly's appointment with Dr. Martino. Beverly told him how surprised she was that Brad hadn't called.

"I recall you telling me that he was going to wait to hear from you. I take it you haven't contacted him either."

"No, I haven't, but I really miss him. Here's some big news, another man asked me out."

"Was it someone you know?"

"I ran into the cop that gave Erica a ticket last December. I can't believe he remembered me, though he did give me his card. His name is Sean Malloy. It was at Wegmans in the produce aisle. He asked how Erica and I were doing and said that he would really like to take me out to dinner."

"Well, what did you say?"

"He really took me by surprise. I didn't know what to say, so he told me to think about it and asked for my number. He said that he would call."

"I think you should go. Maybe if you went out with someone else, it would help you decide if you would rather date other men, or just have an exclusive relationship with Brad. This man isn't in your social circle. It would be good for you."

"I don't know. I'll think about it. Right now I'm more concerned about my daughter. Now that school is out, and her life is less structured, she's getting more anxious about the pregnancy and her future as a new mother still in high school. She turns eighteen in July."

"Perhaps you should take advantage of the summer to spend some time with your daughter so that you can understand her concerns, reassure her, and help her prepare for motherhood."

"How can I reassure her, when I can't even reassure myself that everything will work out and be okay?"

"I guess you can only give her support and let her know that you're in this together. I believe you are already doing this. In reality you don't know how everything will turn out. That's the challenge we all face. You just have to find the faith and courage to move forward."

"Erica and Dwight have told me about a quote from Martin Luther King. It goes something like this: 'Faith is taking the first step even when you don't see the whole staircase.' I guess that is so true."

Dr. Martino looked very thoughtful, trying to digest those words. "Have faith, Beverly."

Chapter 32

Beverly got a call from Karen Logan. She invited her and Erica to Cape May, New Jersey for the first week in July. Karen's parents had a beach house there. The garage had been converted into a guest house, and Beverly and Erica could stay there. Karen said that both she and Christy would love having them there. "You two deserve a vacation. The beach there is beautiful. It's so relaxing. Bill is going on a fishing trip with his brother and some of his buddies, so he won't be there. Please say 'yes.'"

Beverly thought it was very tempting. She could spend time with Erica and use the time to think about things with Brad. Erica would love being with Christy, but she wasn't sure if she would want to be away from Dwight.

"Oh, Karen, that sounds wonderful. Let me run it by Erica, and I'll get back to you tomorrow. Thank you so much for thinking of us."

Beverly talked to Erica that night. "Oh, Mom, I would really like to go, but I feel bad about leaving Dwight. We wouldn't be able to spend the Fourth together."

"Honey, it's just a week. You could use a vacation. Dwight will be busy with work and his internship. You'll have the whole rest of the summer together. You should go when you're at a point in your pregnancy when you're still able to travel. Didn't you tell me you don't have to start your volunteer project until the following week? You, Dwight, and Martina will have many holidays in the future to spend together."

"I'll talk to him, Mom."

Erica talked to Dwight that night. "I think you should go, Babe, but you know I'll miss you." I'm going to work the holiday for the extra pay. Pee-wee basketball camp starts July 6th. I'll be helping Coach with that in the mornings and working on Dr. Williams' research study for a few hours every afternoon. It's only a week. We'll have the whole rest of the summer. You'll be home before your birthday."

"I'll just miss you," Erica said.

"You just take care of yourself and our baby girl. You have a doctor's appointment before you go, don't you?"

"Yeah, I have one on Thursday. Can you go with me?"

"Of course I'll go."

Erica called Christy. The girls were very excited about hanging out together at the beach for an entire week.

As promised, Beverly got a call from Sean Malloy that night. She really was not eager to go out with him. She decided to give it a chance, because Dr. Martino said it might help her to figure out how she felt about Brad. He wanted to take her to a very casual seafood restaurant on the lake. She said, "Yes."

Erica was shocked. "MOM, I can't believe you're going out with somebody else"

"Honey, I told you that Brad and I are taking a break. I'm not sure I want to continue with such a serious relationship. Maybe if I go out with someone else, it will help me to figure out what I want."

"But I thought you were in love with Dr. Williams." During the past year, Erica discovered that her mother was a much different woman than she thought she was.

"I don't know if I am. It's a very confusing time for me. Your father still holds a big place in my heart."

"I'm sorry, Mom. You do what you've got to do. It's not up to me to judge you. Besides, he seemed like a nice guy, even though he did give me the ticket."

Sean picked her up in his Jeep. He wore jeans, cowboy boots, and a button down shirt with the sleeves rolled up. Beverly wasn't sure what to wear. She decided on Capri pants and a silk tank top. She had her hair pinned up with the earrings that Brad gave to her. Beverly wondered if maybe she was over dressed.

They sat at the bar and waited for their table. Sean ordered a beer that he drank from the bottle. Beverly asked for a gin and tonic. It wasn't the type of place that you could order a good chardonnay.

It turned out that Sean was a widower. He had lost his wife to breast cancer a few years ago. He had a ten year old son. Beverly thought he might be a little younger than she was. She thought he was cute. He had boyish good looks and was very charming. They talked easily during dinner. He was really very nice, but she just wasn't attracted to him. Besides both being single parents, they didn't have much in common.

He walked her to the door. She shook his hand. "Thank you, Sean, it was a nice evening."

"Can I call you again?"

"Sure, okay, thanks again." Beverly was relieved he didn't try to kiss her. She didn't know why she said that he could call. She had no intentions of going out with him again. She felt like kind of a snob. *At least I tried,* she thought. *I wish I could give him Pam's number, but Pam's probably too old for him. I might be too old for him.*

Erica was very curious about how her mother's date had gone. After Beverly told Erica that she just wasn't interested in him, Erica said, "Mom, for the record, I think Dr. Williams is perfect for you." Beverly was astonished by her daughter's comment. She really didn't think Erica was in favor of her relationship with Brad.

Erica and Dwight went to Erica's doctor's appointment the following week. Dr. Anderson measured her belly and listened to the baby's heart beat. She smiled. "I think everything looks great. The baby's heart rate is normal, she seems to be the appropriate size, your blood pressure is good, and there is no protein in your urine. You have gained a bit of weight... six pounds since last visit."

"Oh my God, did I really?"

"She can really eat," Dwight said.

"Well, the baby really grew a lot in the last month," the doctor said. "Just try to watch the fat, salt, and sugar. You are due for your gestational diabetes test. She explained that Erica would have to drink a very sugary drink and then have her blood drawn an hour later. "You two should also think about signing up for childbirth classes." She handed them the brochure.

Erica asked Dr. Anderson about her trip to the beach. "I think that it will be fine," she said. She asked about how long the car ride was.

"It's about six or seven hours," Erica answered.

"Pregnant women can be a little more prone to the formation of blood clots. Usually they start in the legs. Make sure you stop every two hours so that you can walk around and stretch your legs. Stay well-hydrated. Drink water and lots of it. Don't stay out in the sun too long. You are better off under the beach umbrella." Then she said, "Hey, have a good time."

Erica wanted to get ice cream after the appointment. "What about the diabetes test?" Dwight asked.

"I'll do it tomorrow."

"Let's get frozen yogurt instead of ice cream. We can try the new place that opened up in the village. You've got to watch your weight, Babe."

Erica gave him a playful shove. "So, you think I'm fat!"

"I just don't want you to complain when you can't see your feet."

"Okay, yogurt it is, and then we'll go for a long walk."

Dwight kissed her. "It's a deal."

Beverly had to stop in at the Cancer Center to turn in some checks that she received after the golf tournament. She ran into Brad in the main lobby. She wasn't ready to face him yet.

He looked into her eyes. "Hello, Beverly. I've missed you."

"Brad, I've missed you too. You were so right. I've needed time to think. I also needed more time with Erica." She told him about their trip to Cape May. "Brad I'll call you when I get back into town so that we can talk. I promise."

"I'll be looking forward to it. Have a great trip."

It was such an intense moment. She had an odd feeling that someone was watching. She could feel Tom's presence in that lobby. She wondered if those feelings would ever stop. The experience really unglued her. She felt her phone vibrate in her purse. She didn't pick up in time, and the call went to voice mail. It was Sean Malloy asking when he could take her out again. *Oh my God,* she said to herself. *I'm so glad I'm getting out of town.*

Dr. Martino was on vacation, so she didn't have an appointment with him today. She stopped in the shop to chat with Pam and to see if she needed anything before she and Erica left on Friday.

Pam was very excited about news of her own. Kyle and Mark had found a surrogate. They were using her egg and her womb, so the procedure had more chance of success and would be less costly. Mark still had to take a second mortgage out on the bakery to pay for everything. "I'm happy for them, but also worried," Pam said. "What will happen if she fails to give full custody of the baby? Mark says they have a good lawyer who has made these arrangements before."

Pam and Beverly went on to talk about the irony of their lives. Beverly's daughter was having an unintended pregnancy at the age of seventeen. Pam's son, who was at an appropriate age to start a family, had to go about it in a very unconventional way.

Bev told Pam about running into Brad at the hospital. "So what are you going to do, honey?"

"I'm going to do a lot of thinking next week. I won't deny how much I have missed him."

Beverly and Erica started packing after dinner. Erica and Christy had gone shopping earlier in the week, and Erica had bought some summer maternity clothes. She showed all her new purchases to her mother. "Mom, I feel like such a cow!"

"I guess you better it used to it. You're only going to get bigger. I really like what you bought. What did Dr. Anderson say about your weight gain?"

"Not too much. I guess I'm used to being more active. I got my blood drawn for the diabetes test this morning. I hope I passed."

"I'm sure you probably did. You can make it a point to get more exercise on vacation. I'm sure it will feel great to get into the water."

"Mom, I'll miss Dwight so much while I'm gone."

"I know you will. We need this vacation. I'm sure we'll have a great time."

Erica called Dwight before she went to bed. She was hoping he would have been able to stop over, but his mother was working and he had to stay with the twins.

"Babe, you take care of Martina. Take care of yourself. I'll call you every night."

"I love you, Dwight."

"I love you too. Be safe."

Erica slept very soundly. Beverly did not. She had a horrible dream. She was wandering the halls of the hospital, totally naked, and couldn't find her way. She ended up in the lobby where she saw Tom and Brad talking. They were both wearing their scrubs. They just looked her, but said nothing. Someone at the information desk called security. Sean Malloy was the security guard. He wrapped her up in a blanket and carried her away. Beverly woke up crying. It was already five o'clock. She got up and made herself coffee. They had planned to be on the road by six-thirty.

Chapter 33

Erica loved Cape May. She thought that it was such a cute town with all the old Victorian houses. The beach was about three blocks from where they were staying, and the beach was awesome. Erica loved hanging out with Christy. She adored Mrs. Logan. Besides them, it was just Christy's little brother and a friend he brought along to keep him company. Christy's older sister stayed home to work. It was really very relaxing. Erica loved sitting in the wicker rockers on the front porch. It was great people watching. Every now and then she would hear the clip, clopping, and a horse-drawn carriage would pass by giving tourists a ride around the historic town.

There was a shopping area in the center of town with some great stores. She saw a comforter in one of the children's shops that would be perfect for Martina's crib, and there were adorable baby clothes. She kept looking for just the right present to bring back for Dwight.

As promised, Dwight called Erica every night. He told her about the Fourth of July barbecue he went to with Marcus. Dwight said that it was good spending time with Marcus again. He told her that another friend of his, Andre, was also there. He was concerned that Marcus was hanging out with Andre so much. Andre had been in trouble from time to time. His brother was dealing drugs. Dwight and Marcus suspected that Andre delivered drugs for his brother when he needed some extra cash. Dwight said that Marcus only saw the good in people. Marcus said that Andre and his brother did what they did for their family who had no money. Andre's mother was a bad diabetic confined to a wheel chair. His father had been in prison for years. There were seven kids in the family.

Erica listened to Dwight in naïve disbelief. She just knew Dwight's life. She had no idea what life was for other poor inner city people in Rochester. It frightened her that Dwight had friends like that. It was hard to even think about.

He also told Erica how much he liked working on the research study with Dr. Williams. "Babe, he's such a good guy. He even let me meet some of the patients enrolled in the study. I hope your mom patches things up with him. I think he's perfect for her."

"I don't know about that," Erica said. "Tell me about pee wee basketball camp."

"It's a lot of fun. Hey, Coach Novak's wife had her baby. She had a little girl, and they named her Monica Marie Novak. He is so proud. Her picture is so sweet. My mom made cupcakes with pink frosting, and I brought them to basketball camp."

Erica loved hearing about Mr. Novak's baby. Then Dwight said, "Babe, I can't wait to meet Martina." Hearing him say that just made her cry. "Don't cry, Babe. Everything's going to be okay. I love you."

Erica ended the call and brought a glass of ice tea out to the porch. It was just before dark. Tomorrow would be her last day here. She sat there and watched the sun set, deep in thought. She felt melancholy all of a sudden.

Was everything going to be okay? Erica couldn't help but wonder and worry. She missed Dwight, but this vacation in Cape May was like an oasis. Soon she would be home and back to face the stormy reality of her life. *What will senior year in high school be like? Will I even finish high school on time? Forget cheerleading. I doubt that that will happen for me. I can't image my old body ever coming back.* Erica didn't think the baby was going to affect Dwight's life as much as it was hers. His life hadn't changed yet. Sometimes she felt a little resentful about that, and then she would feel guilty for those feelings. She sometimes wished that Martina had never happened. She loved Dwight, but she should have waited for sex, or at least been a lot smarter about it. Martina delivered a big kick to her ribs. *How could I ever wish that Martina had never happened?*

Christy came out on the porch. "Are you okay?"

"I just want my old life back. I just want to go back to last July when my Dad was alive, and we were all happy, and I wasn't pregnant. My life has changed so much this year."

Christy sat down and looked at her friend. It was hard to know what to say to her. "You would have met Dwight anyway. You two share something special. Martina is going to bring a lot of joy to everyone's lives. Just wait and see. Your mom will get you through this. For sure you'll finish school on time. I'm counting on being at graduation with you. Maybe you'll just have to go to college in Rochester. I'm sure the University of Rochester has a great pre-med program. A friend of my sister is in pre-med at St. John Fisher.

Erica sighed, "Dwight will have his pick of schools. He will for sure get a basketball scholarship, and he has the minority thing going for him. Any school would want an African-American honor student with his athletic ability. He has his heart set on Syracuse."

"Syracuse isn't so far away. Come on, let's take a walk. We can look in a few shops and maybe get ice cream." *Probably shouldn't have ice cream*, Erica thought, but she was sick of worrying about her diet. Christy and Erica walked the promenade that was once the boardwalk before the hurricane destroyed it. The sound of the surf was very soothing. It was a beautiful night with a balmy breeze. Tomorrow would be a great beach day.

Beverly and Karen took their daughters' place on the porch after the girls left for their walk. Karen brought out a bottle of chardonnay in a bucket of ice. Beverly found it very easy to talk to Karen. She confided in her about Brad, telling her that she was supposed to figure out where their relationship was going. Still, she didn't know. She was just not ready to get married again. She wasn't even ready to just live together.

"If you don't know, then you don't know," Karen said. "Just be honest with him. What was wrong with your relationship the way it was?"

"I was happy the way we were. He wants more. I have very strong feelings for him. Maybe I do love him. I'm just not ready to commit to more. I can't handle anymore changes in my life just now. Right now my energy is focused on Erica and the baby. I guess if Brad wants me he'll just have to wait."

"Do you think he just needs reassurance? Have you told him that you love him?"

"No. I guess I do love him, as much as I could love any man after Tom. I know that since we've been apart, I really miss him."

"If you love him, tell him. Maybe that's all he needs to hear. Be honest with him. He seems like a reasonable guy. If he loves you as much as he says he does, he'll wait for you. You haven't even been together a year."

Their last vacation day was wonderful. It wasn't so humid. There were a few puffy clouds here and there, and a light breeze blew off the water. Everyone went in for a swim. Erica didn't go out too far, because she was weary of a wave knocking her down. Still, she enjoyed the water.

They had their last dinner at a seafood restaurant, known for their local lobster, scallops, shrimp, and flounder. It had been a great day. When they got back to the house, Erica and Beverly started their packing, so that they could get an early start on the road the next morning. By ten o'clock, Erica said that she was exhausted and went to bed. Dwight still hadn't called. When Erica tried to call him it went right to voice mail.

Beverly settled into bed with her book. She saw that she had a voice mail message from Brad. "Beverly, call me as soon as you can. It's urgent that I speak to you." An unmistakable feeling of doom came over her.

It was just after eleven o'clock. Beverly mustered up her courage and made the call.

"Hi, Brad. Is everything okay?"

"Beverly, I have some awful news. I got a page from one of my residents to come down to the ER. They brought in Dwight. He had been shot in the chest. The bullet hit his thoracic aorta, and he was bleeding profusely." Brad's voice cracked. "He didn't make it."

Beverly was trembling. "Oh my God, Brad! Have you seen Ruby yet?"

"I did. She came to the ER to see him. Her sister and brother-in-law were with her. She was inconsolable. Brad's voice was cracking again. What a tragedy. He was a great kid with a bright future. I've enjoyed working with him on the study."

"Do the police have any idea why he was shot?"

"Dwight was alone when it happened. They think that it was probably a case of mistaken identity."

"Erica and I are coming home tomorrow. Oh God, Brad, I don't know how to tell her. She's already sleeping. I think I'll wait until morning. She will need one last good night of rest before the days ahead."

"Beverly, will you be alright to drive all that way? I could come to get you."

"I think I'll be okay."

"Beverly, I'll be there for you and Erica when you get back. I love you."

"I love you, too, Brad." She put her trembling fingers over her mouth. *There, I've said it,* she thought.

She ended the call.

Chapter 34

Beverly could see that there were lights on downstairs at the main house. She thought Karen was still awake. She checked on Erica, who was sleeping soundly, and then walked over to talk to Karen. Both she and Christy were in the living room watching TV.

Karen took one look at Beverly and knew something was very wrong. "What is it Bev?"

"It's so awful. You're not going to believe this, but Dwight was shot tonight. He's dead."

Christy immediately burst in to tears, and her mother held her. Beverly told them all the information that she had, which really wasn't much. They all agreed it was best to wait until morning to tell Erica.

"Mom, I'm going to drive back home with them." Christy said. "Erica will need me. Mrs. McIntyre and I can take turns driving."

"That's a good idea, honey. I'll let the boys have one last day and come back on Sunday."

Christy was so upset. Beverly couldn't even imagine how Erica was going to handle the news.

It was now well after midnight. Beverly knew Ruby would be up. She felt like she should call her.

Ruby's sister, Sarah, answered Ruby's phone. Ruby had been given a sedative, and she was lying down. "I'll tell her you called, and that you and Erica will be home tomorrow."

"Oh, Sarah, I'm so sorry."

Beverly got very little sleep. She didn't know how she would tell Erica. As soon as she saw morning light through her window she got dressed and went to Erica's room. She sat down on the edge of her bed.

Erica woke up and looked at her mother. "Honey, I have some horrible news to tell you."

"What, Mom, is it Nana?"

"No, Erica, it's Dwight. He was shot last night. Honey, he didn't make it."

"MOM, NO, that can't be true!"

"Brad called me late last night. They paged him to the ER when they brought him in. The police aren't certain why it happened."

Erica was now crying hysterically. Beverly just held her. "Let me help you finish your packing, and you can get dressed. I want you to try and eat something before we get on the road. Christy is going to drive back with us."

Karen had put out some fresh fruit, bagels, and yogurt for them. She handed Beverly a cup of coffee. Erica and Christy just held each other and cried. After they calmed down a little, Christy encouraged Erica to have something to eat. "You've got to be strong, for Martina," she said.

"Honey, you've got to at least have something to drink," Karen said. She packed a cooler for the road, thinking that maybe they would have something later.

They all said their goodbyes and were off for the long ride home. The morning sun didn't last long. Soon the clouds rolled in and the rain started.

Christy and Erica sat in the back. The news had gotten out. They were both on their phones.

They stopped twice on the way home. Beverly remembered that Erica was supposed to get up, stretch her legs, and walk around a little. She was so worried about her. Beverly couldn't even imagine how difficult the next few days ahead would be.

"Enough," Erica said, and she turned off her phone. She rested her head against the car window and closed her eyes. Christy silenced her phone, too. Erica thought about Dwight. She couldn't help thinking about what he said about Marcus and Andre. She thought back to the last time he kissed her. It was after her last doctor's appointment. Then she tried to remember the last time they made love. It had been awhile. Then she remembered it was the last day of school. Erica took a big sip from her water bottle. She felt Martina roll over. *My baby will never know her father.*

Erica was so worried about facing Ruby and the twins. She was weeping quietly. Christy reached over and just held her friend's hand. *Oh God, what a nightmare,* Christy thought. She never knew anyone who died so young and didn't know what to expect. Bobby had told her about the memorial already set up on the Washington's front porch. He said that there were basketballs, jerseys, flowers, pictures, and candles. Bobby said that he and the team met Coach Novak at the school. They brought in grief counselors.

Beverly dropped Christy off at her house. "Thank you so much, honey, for driving back with us. I'm sure we'll see you later."

She brought her daughter home. Helen had heard and was waiting for them at the house. Beverly was grateful to see her mother-in-law there. She knew how to comfort Erica in a way that no one else did.

Erica wanted to take a shower and change before heading over to the Washington's house. She and her mother both hit the shower. Helen had made some chicken salad. She made Erica sit down and eat a little and made her drink a large glass of herbal ice tea. "Thanks, Nana, that was good. I guess I was hungry."

The door bell rang. It was Brad. He held Beverly for a moment and went into the kitchen. He hugged Erica. "I'm so sorry, Erica, this is such a tragedy."

Brad drove them all over to the Washington's. There were so many people there. Ruby seemed in control. She saw Erica and hugged her. "Oh, baby, I'm so sorry." That's all she said. Then she hugged Beverly. They just looked at each other. They knew there was nothing to say. After everyone had time to get their emotions in check, Sarah told Beverly about the arrangements that had been made. There would be calling hours on Sunday and Monday. The funeral would be on Tuesday. They needed time for her parents to come up from Atlanta.

Beverly noticed a man who never left Ruby's side. She suspected that it was Ruby's new boyfriend, Mario. Brad said that he knew him, and he was indeed Mario. Beverly was glad to see that Erica was sitting down. She was with Helen and the twins.

Brad was talking to Henry, Dwight's uncle. Henry said that the police were still not certain what happened, and they did not have a suspect in custody. No witnesses had come forward. Apparently Dwight had been shooting hoops with his friends at a neighborhood park before it happened. He had left before the other boys and started walking home. A fight had broken out at the park shortly after Dwight left. Apparently Dwight's friends weren't involved in the fight. They left, too, but in another direction. Dwight was shot by someone driving by in a car about two blocks north of the park. The police thought it was a case of mistaken identity, and Dwight wasn't the intended target. Henry said, "Sadly, my nephew was just in the wrong place at the wrong time."

Brad agreed, "God, what a tragedy."

"Thank you for giving my nephew the opportunity to work with you. I know how much it meant to him."

"It was a pleasure to see a young man so motivated. It was hard for me to believe that he was only a high school student. It saddens me that his bright future was destroyed." The two men shook hands. Similar sentiments could be heard throughout the room.

Beverly overheard a conversation Ruby was having with her minister. "Ruby, do you want Jerome to attend his son's funeral?"

"I don't know, Reverend. Dwight really wasn't interested in having any kind of relationship with his father, but I don't feel right denying Jerome the chance for a final goodbye. I'm worried about what the girls will think. They have never met their daddy. They don't even know he is in prison."

"Do you want me to contact the prison chaplain at Attica? This is not the first time this situation has come up. I'll just need a copy of Dwight's birth certificate and the obituary notice to fax to the prison. The Superintendant makes the final decision."

"I guess it's only right to give Jerome the chance to mourn his son's passing. It's probably the Christian thing to do. Call the chaplain, but Reverend, I don't want him near the girls."

"Okay, Ruby, we'll work it out."

Beverly looked over at Ruby, admiring her strength. *I'll be bonded to her forever. We will share a grandchild.* She went over to her. "Ruby, what can I do?"

"Everyone is helping me and taking care of things. Please, just take care of Erica and our precious grandchild."

Erica seemed to be handling herself pretty well, Helen at her side. Marcus walked over to Erica, and she got up to give him a hug. "I'm so sorry, Erica," he said. "I know how much he loved you."

"Thanks, Marcus." Erica had heard that Marcus was one of the last people who saw Dwight before he died.

290

Then Dwight's cousin, Tamika, approached. Usually the mean girl, she was really very nice. "I'm sorry, Erica, but you will always have a part of Dwight, you have his baby. We'll always be family."

"You're right, Tamika, I'll want my daughter to know her father's family." Sarah was a little nervous about what Tamika might say to Erica, so she walked over too. "Erica, honey, can I get you anything?"

"Maybe just some more water, thank you."

After a few hours, Beverly thought that it was time to get Erica home. Just as they were about to leave, Coach Novak walked in with Ruby. She was clearly very touched that he came. He spotted Erica and walked over to her. Erica stood up and hugged him. Seeing Mr. Novak really stirred up her emotions. Now she was really crying. He didn't say anything. He just let Erica sob on his shoulder. After Erica calmed down, Ruby introduced him to some of the others there.

Helen put her arm around Erica. "Oh, Nana, I'm never going to get through this."

Brad and Beverly walked over, and Beverly said, "Come on, honey, I think you've had enough. Brad's going to take us home now.

It was already early evening. They dropped Helen off. Beverly asked Brad to stay for awhile.

She made Erica a grilled cheese sandwich and encouraged her to eat something before she went to bed. She knew that Erica hadn't eaten any of the food that was set out at the Washington's. Erica took her sandwich and some iced tea and went up to her room. "Mom, I need to be alone for a while."

Beverly kissed her daughter. "Honey, I'm here if you need me."

Beverly took out the rest of the chicken salad and some cheese and crackers. She found some apples in the refrigerator and sliced them up. She put everything on a platter and opened a bottle of wine. She wanted Brad to stay for awhile. She knew that he was grieving, too.

"Brad, I'm so glad you called me last night with the news. I can't thank you enough."

"I knew you had to know as soon as possible. Beverly, I still love you, and I've really missed you."

She looked deeply into his dark brown eyes. "I love you, too, Brad. I'm just not ready to make decisions about the future. You are the only man in my life. I'm not interested in seeing anyone else. Since we've been apart, I've realized that. I don't want to lose you. Can I just get Erica through this pregnancy?"

Beverly had tears in her eyes. She sat on Brad's lap and put her arms around him. She kissed him. "Brad, I do love you." Beverly, for the first time, knew that she meant it.

She and Brad ate and they talked. She was so relieved he was there. It was well into the evening. Brad got up said that he should get going. "It's going to be a rough couple of days. We should both get some rest."

"Wait, Brad." Beverly led him into the den and closed the French doors. She kissed him, unbuttoning his shirt and pulling on his belt buckle. They made love on the big, well-worn, soft leather couch. She couldn't believe she was thinking about sex at a time like this, but she just needed to feel Brad's love and security. She needed to feel warm again.

Brad smiled and stroked her cheek. Beverly had tears in her eyes. He kissed her. "I'm glad you've come back to me. I'll call you in the morning. I've cleared my scheduled until after the funeral. I love you. I'll be here for you, and I'll be here for Erica."

Beverly felt so much better after Brad left. She felt a little more hopeful that this whole mess would somehow work out.

Brad had left a copy of the morning paper for her. Dwight's shooting was on the first page. The article made it very clear that Dwight wasn't the intended victim. It was the thirty-first homicide in the city of Rochester this year. It was hard to look at his picture. Beverly was glad that they mentioned Dwight was an honor student involved in the urban-suburban program, and that he was a star basketball player. *Oh God*, she thought, *how can Erica see this?*

Beverly looked in on her daughter before going to bed. She was happy to see her sleeping soundly.

Chapter 35

Beverly wanted to make sure she was up before Erica. She wanted to get the morning paper to read Dwight's obituary and to see if there was any more news about the shooting. She anxiously flipped through the paper and spotted the obituary.

Washington, Dwight, age 18, suddenly July 10, the victim of a random act of violence. He is survived by his mother, Ruby Washington; father, Jerome Taylor; sisters, Danielle and Denise; beloved aunt and uncle, Sarah and Henry Barnes and their children. Also survived by grandparents, Reverend and Mrs. Tobias Washington; and uncle, Theodore Washington, all of Atlanta, Georgia. Dwight leaves behind his girlfriend, Erica McIntyre, and soon to be born infant daughter, Martina. He was an honor student at Lyndon B.Johnson High School and star basketball player. Calling hours at the Newcastle Funeral Home, 1206 Lake Ave, Sunday 2PM to 5PM, and Monday 5PM to 8PM. Funeral Tuesday 10 AM, Grace Baptist Church. Internment, Holy Sepulchre Cemetery.

Beverly was surprised to see Erica mentioned, although she really didn't know the etiquette for this situation. There it was for everyone to see, Erica was a deceased teenager's pregnant girlfriend. Then she thought about Ruby. She remembered her devastating grief after losing her own son. She knew that Johnny had a very serious heart condition and may not have a normal life expectancy. She was somewhat prepared that she might sometime lose him. Dwight's death was so sudden, and senseless, and random. She felt a chill when she thought about it. She hoped that she could find a way to be supportive to Ruby.

Beverly went up to check on Erica. "Honey, come downstairs. I want you to try and eat some breakfast. I'll make anything you want. I made some blueberry muffins. I had to do something to keep busy."

"Oh, Mom, I really don't feel like eating anything."

"Honey, you have to eat. You know that it's important for you to eat, for Martina."

Erica ate a yogurt and a blueberry muffin. She looked at all the messages on her phone. She really didn't feel like talking to anybody. Christy can over to see how she was doing. She told her how all the kids at school were reacting to Dwight's death. She said that everybody was in total shock and disbelief. Kids were asking about her and how she was doing. Erica and Christy read the article about the shooting and the obituary.

"Oh my God," Erica sobbed, "somehow reading this makes it seem all more real. I'm glad they mentioned me and Martina." Erica's crying escalated. Christy and Beverly tried to comfort her. She finally calmed down a little. Beverly poured her some water. "I want you to drink this." Beverly was so worried about how this stress would affect the baby. Christy took Erica upstairs to pick out an outfit for calling hours.

Beverly had some things on her "To Do" list. She called Pam and told her she wouldn't be in all of next week. Next she called the florist and had a floral arrangement sent over to the funeral home. She couldn't help but remember the first time Dwight had come for dinner. He had brought the bouquet of pink roses, and then he had given Erica pink roses for Mother's Day. She ordered three dozen pink roses. The card would read, "With all our love and sympathy; Erica, Beverly, and Helen McIntyre. She requested no baby's breath and no gaudy bow. The flowers should be in a crystal glass vase.

She wanted to reach out to Ruby. Beverly took a deep breath and made the call. Sarah answered Ruby's phone. When she knew it was Beverly, she went to get Ruby.

"Ruby, what can I do? I'm willing to do anything to help. I know how awful the next few days will be for you. I've been there. I'm not sure you know this, but I lost a son too. My heart goes out to you."

"I know, thank you Beverly. I guess I'm doing okay. I'll get through it. I'm worried about Erica and the baby. Please just watch over her. Mario and my family and friends from the church are all helping me take care of everything else. Come to the funeral home about a half an hour early this afternoon. I want Erica to have some time alone with Dwight before everyone else starts coming. I know he would want that. It is an open casket. My son's face is still handsome and perfect." After Ruby said that last sentence her voice broke. "I'll see you soon, Beverly. Thank you for calling."

Brad came over to take them all to the calling hours. They stopped on the way to pick up Helen. As they walked in the door of the funeral home, the moment seemed surreal to Beverly. It was the second time this year she had to endure the sad, tedious hours at a wake. The funeral home was clearly one that was most frequented by African-Americans. She was on the arm of another man, and her teenage daughter was in her seventh month of pregnancy. It was hard to accept how much their lives had changed. The look of fear, sadness, and apprehension that she saw on Erica's face broke her heart. "It will be okay, honey."

Erica walked in and went over to hug Ruby and the twins. Ruby said the same thing to her. "It will be okay, honey." The funeral director led Erica into the viewing room. She made it clear that she wanted to go in by herself.

Erica knelt before Dwight's casket and just looked at him. *He doesn't really look any different.* He was wearing the shirt and tie that she gave him for his birthday. *He still looks handsome and gentle even in death. How can someone whose life ended so violently look so peaceful?* There was a basketball in the casket and a book, "The Autobiography of Martin Luther King, Jr.", by Clayborne Carson. *It's so hard to believe that I've known him only ten months, and knowing him has changed my life forever. He came into my life so unexpectedly and has gone so quickly. Now all I have left of him is Martina. Will we be okay?* Erica leaned in and kissed him. As soon as she did so, it became very real. His lips were cool and still. He was truly dead.

She walked out of the room and ran into her mother's arms. "Oh, Mom, this is so awful!"

Beverly and Ruby did what they could to comfort her and calm her down. Soon a long line of people coming to pay their respects formed. Erica insisted on standing right up by the casket with Dwight's immediate family. Beverly was so concerned for her. She was relieved to see that Dr.

Anderson had stopped in. After Dr. Anderson hugged Erica, she cautioned her that it was important to not stand in one spot for too long. She needed to walk around a little and keep drinking water. "People will understand if you take a break, Erica." She sought out Beverly and told her that it would be a good idea for her to bring Erica in for a quick check-up tomorrow.

Beverly couldn't believe how many people were there. The line went out the door to the entrance of the funeral home, it continued out onto the sidewalk. It was difficult to see all the kids lost in their grief. Some of them were black, but many were white. She observed that African-American people were highly emotional. Outside there was a camera crew from the local news station. Dwight's shooting prompted stories about inner-city violence, Rochester's high homicide rate, and the need for stricter gun control. It was all so much to take in, and this was just the first day.

After calling hours they all went over Henry and Sarah's house to eat. It was quieter over there because it was just family, no news media or any other people just stopping by. They all needed a break. Beverly had hoped to just take Erica home, but Erica felt it was right to be with Dwight's family. Beverly didn't want to leave her there alone. Ruby took Beverly's hand and said, "You stay and have supper with us, too. This baby makes us all family."

There was an incredible spread of food there. Ruby's family arrived from Atlanta. Her father, Reverend Tobias Washington, was a very intense man. Beverly was so nervous for her daughter when she saw that the reverend had approached her, but it was okay. He shook her hand and said, "Hello, Erica, I'm sorry for your loss. I understand my grandson really loved you. God bless you and that precious child that you carry."

Beverly looked at Brad and said, "Could this possibly get any more dramatic?" There was absolutely no alcohol there. "God, I could really use a drink."

After they stayed a reasonable amount of time, Beverly urged Erica to leave for home. Erica went right up to her room as soon as they got home. She gave in to her fatigue and went right to bed. Brad stayed and had a drink with Beverly.

The next morning, Beverly took Erica to see her doctor. "Your blood pressure is slightly elevated, but there is no protein in your urine. Is the baby active?"

"Yes, she's very active. I've been noticing that my belly tenses up sometimes and gets rock hard."

Dr. Anderson frowned and put her hand on Erica's abdomen. "How often is that happening?"

"I don't know, several times a day. It happened a lot yesterday."

"I want to put you on the fetal monitor to see how much uterine activity you have."

She led Erica into another room, and one of the nurses applied the monitor with two wide elastic bands. Erica watched as her baby's heart rate traced on the monitor screen. There was line on the bottom of the monitor strip that was mostly flat, then Erica had that feeling that her belly was tensing up. A little mound traced on monitor strip. Then Martina kicked and her heart rate really jumped up.

"Wow, why did her heart speed up like that?" Erica asked.

"That's good. That's what her heart is supposed to do. It tells us that she is getting the right amounts of oxygen. This little mound is a contraction. At your gestational age, it is normal to have occasional contractions. The baby's heart reacted normally to the contraction. Everything looks okay. When you feel those contractions, you need to increase your water intake. If you feel more than four contractions in an hour, I want you to call me. Call me if you are leaking any fluid or have any bleeding or spotting."

Beverly could sense that Erica was trying not to cry. "Okay, but this is so awful for me."

Dr. Anderson took her hand. "I know it is, but I'm amazed how you are handling everything. You're only seventeen and you are pregnant with your first baby. That's stressful enough, and now you lost your baby's father someone you were very much in love with. Honey, my heart goes out to you." Now, Dr. Anderson was fighting back tears. The nurse took the monitor off and wiped the gel off Erica's belly. Dr. Anderson gave Erica a hug. "Will you come back to see me on Thursday?"

"I will."

Beverly liked Carrie Anderson very much. She was very good with Erica.

Erica said that she had nothing appropriate to wear to the funeral. She wanted her mother to take her shopping to buy a new dress. "Okay, let's stop and get a light lunch first. Just a few stores okay? You have a long night ahead of you."

Erica was satisfied with the dress that they found. It was a sleeveless black crepe with a very modest neckline. The dress draped beautifully over all her curves. "Honey, these black sandals will be perfect. I don't think that it's a good idea to wear heels."

"Okay, Mom."

Beverly made Erica go up to her room and rest for the remainder of the day. Beverly went to the salon to get a manicure-pedicure. She sensed everyone's uneasiness. People at the salon, who were normally very chatty, didn't know what to say. Rebecca Goldstein was there getting her hair colored. She couldn't have been kinder. Her daughter, Rachael, was with her. "How's Erica doing, Mrs. McIntyre?" she asked.

"I guess as well as can be expected. Thank you for asking, honey."

"Dwight was such a nice guy. All the kids really liked him."

It was very hot. When Beverly got home she poured a glass of chardonnay and curled up on the couch in the den. It was very cool in there. She was hoping she could relax and take a quick nap.

They got to calling hours about a half an hour early so that Erica could have a few minutes alone with Dwight. Brad was coming later and would stop by to bring Helen. As soon as they walked in, they encountered some unexpected drama. Ruby walked out of the viewing room with a man in shackles, accompanied by two armed guards. The man was obviously Dwight's father. Tears were streaming down his cheeks. Ruby hugged him, and he was led away to a side entrance where a car was waiting to take him back to prison.

"Oh my God, that's Dwight's father," Erica said. She had her hand over her mouth.

Not as many people came to calling hours the second day, so it didn't seem as grueling.

"Mom, I'm so glad we have only one more day of this. How did we ever get through all this when Dad died?"

"Oh, honey, I don't know. It seems like it was just yesterday."

Chapter 36

Martina's kicking woke her up. *I can't believe I'm going to Dwight's funeral today. I feel like I'm on that staircase that Dwight always talks about, but now I've fallen off, and I have to start on the first step all over again. I can't see my future without him, and I can't see what my life will be like being a single mother still in high school. I guess I just have to have faith. I've got to get through today.* She knew her mother was already up downstairs. She could smell coffee brewing.

"Mom, I slept so poorly. I've been drinking so much water that I had to get up twice during the night to pee, and then would have a hard time falling back asleep. just want today to be over. Erica ate a bowl of granola with milk and had a cup of herbal tea. She went upstairs to shower and get dressed. She looked in the mirror. *Thank God that I got some sun in Cape May, or else I would really look like shit. Who am I now, anyway?*

Brad took them all to the funeral home. She was glad that her mother was back together with Dr. Williams. Erica thought her mother seemed a little more balanced when they were together.

Erica went in with the family one last time before the casket was closed. They all headed for the church shortly thereafter. Erica had never been in a Baptist church. Erica, Beverly, Helen and Brad sat in the next pew behind the family. The church was filled to beyond capacity. It was standing room only. There were kids and teachers from school, people from the hospital, from Wegmans, and firemen who worked with Dwight's uncle. The news media was stationed across the street from the church.

Reverend James and Dwight's grandfather, Reverend Washington, co-presided over the funeral service. There was a lot of preaching about the senseless act of violence that took Dwight's life. It got a little fire and brimstone. It was said that we, as Christians, needed to forgive whoever did this, but the murderer or murderers had to answer to a higher power for their sin. It would be the Lord, who would decide their fate. "Today, we have to celebrate the life of our beloved son and brother, Dwight, a child of the light." Dwight's Uncle Henry gave a eulogy, as did Mr. Novak, and Mr. Smith, Dwight's boss at Wegmans. Mr. Smith told the story about Dwight and Gary, the boy with Down's syndrome. It was very moving. Emotions were very high. A gospel choir sang. Their music was very charismatic.

Erica wept through the entire service. Beverly did her best to comfort her. Erica filed out of church behind the casket with Ruby and her family. She joined her mother, Brad, and Helen for the ride to the cemetery. Beverly noticed that Sean Malloy was one of the policemen assigned to control traffic for the funeral procession. He walked over to say hello. Beverly didn't feel she needed to introduce him. It was an uncomfortable moment. She only said, "Dwight Washington was my daughter's boyfriend."

He said, "I'm very sorry," then walked away to do his job.

After the grave side service everyone went back to the church hall. Wegmans catered the luncheon. Beverly thought it was very generous. They really went all out, and the food was delicious. Beverly has solicited charitable donations from Wegmans in the past. She knew that they were called upon a lot, and requests were not always granted. She thought that this was an awesome act of kindness. It had been a very long day, and it was already getting to be late afternoon.

Beverly and Brad said their goodbyes to Ruby and her family, and they left. They took Helen home. Erica wanted to spend some time with her friends. They were all gathering over at Christy's house. Brad convinced her that it was okay, that the kids probably needed to be together. Karen was back from Cape May, and she knew that Karen would look out for Erica. Beverly went over to Brad's. She kicked off her shoes. Brad made them a drink and they just relaxed, talking over the very overwhelming events of the day. Beverly couldn't help but think that last week at this time she had been lying on the beach. Erica called her to ask if she could spend the night at the Logan's. "Mom, Mrs. Logan took my blood pressure and I'm fine. Please let me stay." Beverly reluctantly gave her permission.

Brad looked at her. "Will you stay here tonight?"

"Oh, Brad, yes." He made love to her very tenderly, and she slept peacefully in his arms all night. She was safe.

Brad had to go to the hospital in the morning. He didn't want to wake Beverly. She was sleeping so soundly. He left her a note with his page number. "Get some rest. Page me if you need me. I love you, Brad."

When Beverly finally woke up, she just didn't want to get out of bed, but she knew there was just so much she should be doing. She should call Erica. She should reach out to Ruby. She really just wanted to hide out at Brad's all day.

She called Erica, but she didn't pick up. She called Karen Logan. She said the girls were still sleeping, but all things considered, she thought Erica was doing okay. Karen said that she wasn't working today, and Erica was welcome to stay as long as she wanted. Karen echoed what Brad said. She thought the girls needed to be together. They found comfort in each other.

Beverly called Ruby. "Ruby, I just called to see how you were doing. I thought Dwight's service was beautiful."

"Thanks for calling, Beverly. I guess I'm okay. My family is here with me. How is Erica?"

"Oh, I guess as well as can be expected. She wanted to stay at her best girlfriend's house last night. Ruby, those two kids really loved each other. She's heart-broken. It's so sad their love story ended so tragically. But about you... losing a child is the worst kind of hurt. Ruby, you will reach out to me if I can help you in any way?"

"I will. There is a support group at my church. There are others who have lost loved ones through violent acts. I am hoping my faith will see me through this. I think of that beautiful baby girl we have on the way. That helps me, too."

Beverly had a huge lump in her throat. She was so in awe of Ruby's strength that she couldn't speak. She remembered being so overwhelmed by John's death that she wouldn't talk to anyone on the phone for days, and she wouldn't let Tom leave her side.

Beverly took a sip of water. "Okay, Ruby, I won't keep you. Erica and I will be in touch. Bye for now, take care."

After she ended the call, Beverly started thinking. She knew there was a lot of crime and violence in the inner-city. Now it had touched her

301

world. *How did that happen? How did I get to this point in my life?* It was all too much. She didn't think she had the strength to cope with another crisis. She wondered why God was challenging her again. *This is a loving God that would let something like this happen?*

It was apparent that Ruby found strength in her faith in God and support from her church. When something bad happened, Beverly's first response was to turn away from God. After John died, she didn't go to mass for months, despite Tom's urging. It was finally Erica that got her back to the church. She said, "Mommy, come to church with us. God loves you, he wants to help you."

Beverly knew that people thought that she was a strong and confident woman. She knew that the real Beverly could be very weak. Sometimes she drank too much. She was a tortoise that retreated to her shell for safety. Beverly thought she had handled Tom's death a lot better than she did her son's. Maybe she was becoming stronger. She vowed to be strong for Erica. She had to help get her daughter through the days ahead.

Chapter 37

Erica's eighteenth birthday was July twenty-fourth. She would be starting her thirtieth week of her pregnancy. Beverly wanted to make it a good day for her daughter, but she didn't know how that would be possible only two weeks after losing Dwight. Beverly knew she had to help Erica see that there would be life after Dwight. There was Martina. She devoted all her energies into her plan for Erica's birthday. She wasn't far from finishing the mural in the nursery. If she painted every day, she could probably finish it in time. She would have the white baby furniture that she and Erica liked at the mall delivered. Erica had bought a baby quilt that she liked in Cape May. She would have to shop for a rug, a lamp, and come curtains. She enlisted Helen's help. Helen took the quilt, found a coordinating fabric, and was making the curtains. It was a good plan, because it kept her busy, and the painting was relaxing.

The first week after Dwight's death, Erica wouldn't do much of anything. She spent time with Helen or visited with Christy. They were both able to reach her in a way that Beverly couldn't. Erica would call Dwight's phone to listen to his voice mail greeting. She was devastated when it was cut off. Erica thought that it was probably an extra expense Ruby couldn't afford. She tried her father's phone. Apparently that had also been disconnected. She couldn't believe her mother would do that. "Mom, you cut off Dad's phone?"

"It was time, honey. Dr. Martino encouraged me to try and let go of a few things."

Beverly tried to get her daughter to open up and talk about her grief. She didn't get too far. Beverly noticed she seemed to get some comfort from playing Tom's old James Taylor albums.

"Honey, what's with the James Taylor music?"

"Dwight and I loved listening to Dad's old records. Dwight especially liked James Taylor. His favorite songs were 'You've Got a Friend' and also, 'How Sweet It Is'." They were kind of our songs."

"Oh, honey, that's precious," Beverly said. She was definitely Tom's daughter.

Beverly asked her if she still had plans to volunteer at the hospital.

"I don't know, Mom. The program that they want me to do with the puppets is just too much right now. I just don't have the energy for it."

"Maybe they have something else you could do. I sure they would understand. Why don't you call them?"

"I'll think about it."

"Dr. Martino has an associate that works a lot with teens. Would you consider seeing someone to talk about everything? I'm so worried about you, honey. You have so much to deal with. Therapy has really helped me deal with your father's death. Maybe you should consider it."

Erica's response was clipped. "Absolutely not, that's not for me."

Beverly didn't want to push.

Erica finally called the volunteer office at the hospital. They asked her to come in and read to the kids who were confined to their beds. Everyone was glad to see Erica come back. Before leaving the hospital, Erica would stop at the nursery and look at the babies. She couldn't believe that in just a few months she would have a baby of her own. One of the pediatric nurses saw Erica looking through the nursery window. She suggested that maybe they could use Erica to help feed and hold some of the babies. Once some of the premature babies were off the ventilator and stable, they still had to stay in the hospital to put on weight. It was arranged and Erica started the next day. She loved it, so she divided her time between feeding babies and reading to the younger kids.

She was with a little boy, Cody, who was recovering from open heart surgery. He reminded her of her little brother. Cody wanted her to read him his new dinosaur book. There was an inscription on the first page. It said: "Happy 4th Birthday, Cody. We love you, Grandma and Papa." Then she thought about her own birthday on Friday. She definitely wasn't looking forward to it. *Mom hasn't even mentioned it. I'm sure she didn't forget, but I'm really not up for much of anything.*

Erica loved visiting with Cody, but it was bittersweet. Johnny was four when he died, the same age as Cody. Cody had five brothers and sisters. He was somewhere in the middle. His mother just had another baby and wasn't able to visit him that often. He spent a lot of time alone. Every time Erica left to go, he would ask if she would be back tomorrow. *Oh my God,* she thought, *how can I let this little guy down?* She wondered how his family could just leave him alone at the hospital after such serious surgery.

Erica ran into Ruby Thursday afternoon as she was leaving the hospital. Ruby hugged her. "How are you, honey?" She put her hand on Erica's belly, how's Martina?"

"Oh, we're fine, Ms. Washington."

"Erica, we've been through too much together for you to call me Ms. Washington. You just call me Ruby. I've been praying for you. When you feel up to it, the girls would love to see you. They ask for you all the time."

"Okay, Ruby, for sure I'll catch up with them. Right now I'm just trying to get through each day. It has helped me a lot coming here to the hospital." She told Ruby about her work in the nursery.

"Oh, I'm so proud of you. That will be good practice for you. Well, you take care, now. I love you, Erica."

Erica felt a burst of tears coming on. When Ruby told her that she loved her, it made her feel so close to Dwight. Martina, Ruby, and the twins would always be her connection to Dwight.

Beverly had noticed that Erica hadn't taken much interest in coming into the baby's room. She thought it probably made her a little sad and overwhelmed about what was lying ahead of her. Beverly worked on the nursery when Erica wasn't home or after Erica went to bed. She wanted to keep it as much of a surprise as she could. She finished the mural on Wednesday. Beverly was very pleased with her work. It looked like a scene out of the movie "Bambi". She painted a tree with a little bird sitting in its branches, some wispy clouds, a rainbow, flowers of different colors, and even a little bunny. It was very whimsical. The furniture was delivered the next morning. Brad came over late on Thursday night and assembled the crib.

Brad kissed her. "You are amazing! I can't believe you've pulled this off. This room is beautiful."

Beverly talked him into staying the night, though it really didn't take too much persuasion. He left very early the next morning for the hospital. She didn't think that Erica had even known that he had been there.

Beverly was having coffee and checking her email when Erica came down the morning of her birthday. She hugged her daughter and wished her a happy birthday. "What are your plans today?"

"I'm probably just going to the hospital. I really not up for much of anything else."

"Honey, I was hoping you would let me invite a few people over for dinner. It is your eighteenth birthday."

Erica sighed, "Who do you have in mind?"

"Well, Nana, of course, Christy and her mother, and I thought Ruby and the girls. Would that be okay?"

"It sounds like a lot of trouble, Mom."

"Oh, honey, I want to do something. I have to confess, I have already talked to all of them about it, but told them it was pending your approval. Please say yes."

"Okay, thanks, Mom. That sounds nice."

"Do you mind if Brad comes?"

"Sure, it's okay. He's been so good to everyone."

"What can I get you for breakfast?"

"I feel enormous, maybe just poached eggs and a glass of orange juice."

Erica told Beverly all about her work at the hospital. She told her about Cody.

"Oh, honey, that has to be so hard for you."

"I'm kind of worried about him. Yesterday he was running a low-grade fever. I hope he's okay."

"Oh, I hope so too, honey. Would it be okay if I gave you your presents this morning?"

"Okay, but I've got to get going pretty soon."

First, Beverly presented her with a little wrapped box. It was a pair of rose gold hoop earrings.

"Oh, Mom, these are gorgeous, I love them!"

"Okay, come upstairs to see your birthday surprise." Beverly opened the door to the nursery.

"Ta-da! I hope you like it."

"It's incredible! You must have been working so hard on it. I love the mural."

"I had a little help. Nana made the curtains and Brad put the crib together."

Then the waterworks started. Erica was crying... and then Beverly.

"This means so much to me, Mom. I just wish Dwight was here to see it."

Beverly showed her the little stepping stool that she painted in white with pink lettering.

On the bottom step it read, "Faith is taking the first step."

"Dwight's quote from Martin Luther King, Jr., I can't believe you remembered." Erica hugged her mother. "Mom, I love you." Beverly thought it might be the first good day they had since Dwight died. Dr. Martino's pep talk the day before had helped her. She was determined to make it a pleasant day for her daughter.

Beverly got busy with her food preparation. She made the herb marinade for the chicken and the mini crab cakes she planned to serve for the appetizer. She would go to the farm market for corn and fruit for a salad. Helen was making Erica's favorite potato salad, and Ruby insisted on bringing the cake. It was Dwight's favorite chocolate cake. "I think we can all use some chocolate," she said. Beverly was so happy she was able to come. Ruby took the day off. Beverly couldn't believe she went back to work so soon after her son died.

It was a beautiful day. They could have the party out on the patio. Beverly planned to check on things at the shop and touch base with Pam. The rest of the afternoon she planned on going to the salon. She needed some pampering.

Erica was so worried when she walked into Cody's room. He wasn't any better. She could see that his IV was back in, and he was on antibiotics. He also had nasal prongs and was getting oxygen. His mother was there. It was the first time that Erica had ever seen her.

"You must be Erica. Cody has told me about you. He said that you are his special friend, and you've been reading to him every day. I can't thank you enough. It's so hard to get here to the hospital during the day, what with my other kids being home on summer vacation and a newborn to breastfeed. Cody is so brave to stay here by himself. My husband and I take turns coming in the evening."

"I'm sure you do your best," Erica said. "I love spending time with Cody." Erica stopped on the way to the hospital and bought him a new book. "Cody, you spend some time with your Mommy, and I promise I will be back in a little while."

Erica went to feed babies for a few hours, and then went to the cafeteria for lunch. She spent the rest of the afternoon with Cody. His fever spiked in the afternoon. One of the nurses told her that he had the fever because his lungs were congested. They tried to get him to take deep breaths, hold a little pillow against his chest and cough. Erica was really good at getting Cody to cooperate. Erica promised Cody she would visit tomorrow.

Erica thought about the evening ahead of her as she was driving home from the hospital. *I'm so not up for this, but Mom has tried so hard. Maybe it will be okay. It's just too hard not to feel so sad. I'm only eighteen and I've already lost my little brother, my father, and my baby's father, who was my first love. I'm soon to be just a sad statistic. I'll be a single teen mother, still in high school. Oh God, what's happened to me? How did my life end up like this? I wish I could go back to a year ago.* She started thinking about her seventeenth birthday when she had gone to Martha's Vineyard with her parents. They wanted to show her where they spent their honeymoon. They stopped in Rhode Island on the way home to see Brown University. It had been an awesome trip.

I've really got stop feeling so sorry for myself, it's giving me a massive headache.

Erica took some Tylenol and drank a large glass of water as soon as she got home. She took a shower and was starting to feel a little better. She put on a sundress and swept her hair up in a ponytail. She thought the rose gold hoop earrings looked really pretty with her hair. Her mother had great taste. Then she remembered how much Dwight loved her hair. He always had told her how much he loved to smell it and run his fingers through it. She couldn't even imagine what Martina's hair would be like. She went to look at the nursery again before going downstairs. She vowed to try her best to be pleasant and enjoy her birthday dinner.

Brad was already there. Her mother was giving him instructions on how he was supposed to grill the chicken. When Brad saw Erica he wished her a happy birthday and told her that she looked really nice. He hugged her, really taking Erica by surprise. He hadn't done that before, but it was okay. Erica realized he was genuine and just a really nice guy. He had been so supportive. She knew how much Dwight had respected him. He loved her mother, and she thought he was here to stay. Her mom was falling in love with him. If her mom had to have another man in her life, she was glad that it was Brad.

Erica enjoyed the party much more than she had anticipated. It was nice to see Ruby and the twins. They gave her the most precious gifts. They gave her two beautifully framed pictures of Dwight. One was a recent picture that Erica had never seen. It captured his smile perfectly. The other was a picture of Dwight as a little boy. Ruby also gave her one of Dwight's favorite books about Martin Luther King, Jr. Erica was so touched. She opened the book and discovered that the book had belonged to Dwight. He had written his name in it. His signature was very unique. She thought they were very thoughtful gifts. Almost everyone there shed a tear. It was truly a bittersweet moment.

Everyone wanted to see the nursery after the cake was finished. Erica was glad when everyone left. She was exhausted, both physically and emotionally. She kissed her mother goodnight. "Thanks, Mom, for everything." The day wasn't as bad as she had dreaded, however it wasn't how she had envisioned spending her eighteenth birthday just a month ago, and nothing like a year ago.

Ruby couldn't get Erica off her mind. She was glad that she and the girls had been invited to the party, but it was really a sad night. Erica not only carried the weight of her pregnancy, but she looked like she carried of weight of the world on her shoulders.

Ruby couldn't help but remember herself at eighteen, carrying Dwight. She had been scared, but she wasn't sad. She and Jerome were together, and he had made her promises about being a good father. It was before he became abusive and got into any real trouble. Ruby knew how much Erica had loved her son. This was going to be so difficult for her. She knew that money wasn't something this could fix. She had to admit that the nursery was absolutely beautiful, but it is going to take more than a pretty room to make it right for this baby. Dwight never had his own room until he was five years old. The only new thing that she had for him was a crib that her parents bought. Jerome was only a visiting daddy. She remembered being happy, though, and she loved being a mother. Ruby had a troubling thought. *Once a little time passes, and the shock and pain of Dwight's death eases, will I have much of a relationship with Erica and her mother? I wonder how much they will let me be a part of Martina's life.*

It had been two weeks, and the police hadn't gotten any further in their investigation. Ruby couldn't help but think that if it was a white boy that had been shot, the police would probably have been much more aggressive in solving the crime. She also knew that most crime in the inner city was black on black.

Jerome had been writing her from prison. He had been doing a lot of soul-searching. He expressed remorse for his abuse to her and his neglect for his children. He said that he was attending religious services at the prison and was having regular sessions with the prison chaplain. Jerome said that he had accepted Jesus Christ as his savior. Ruby wanted to believe that it was true. She knew she could forgive Jerome, but she could never let him back into her life, or into the lives of the girls. She and Mario were becoming very serious. Mario had a twelve year old son. He had full custody of him. She had hopes that one day she and Mario and their children could become a family. She thought that she was in love with him. He was a wonderful man. She felt that he could be trusted. Ruby couldn't imagine how she would have gotten through the last few weeks without Mario to lean on.

Chapter 38

Beverly could not stop worrying about her daughter. It seemed like the only thing that kept Erica going was her work at the hospital. Her little buddy, Cody, was still there. Erica said that she couldn't let him down and that she needed to get him though this hospitalization. Helen was still a big comfort to her. Erica spent a lot of time over at Helen's. Beverly was grateful that Erica had Helen, but she couldn't help but be a little jealous of their relationship. Dr. Martino suggested that maybe it was because Helen was her link to her father. He said that it was also common for children to confide in a grandparent in a way that they couldn't with a parent. It could feel safer.

Oh God, I wish Tom was here to see us through this mess, Beverly thought. *But I have Brad now. I just don't know what my future with Brad will be. I can't imagine how this will all work out. It's already August, and Erica will be thirty-two weeks pregnant tomorrow. I wish she wouldn't push herself so hard. I think that she is spending too much time at the hospital.*

Beverly took her to her doctor's appointment.

"So tell me, Erica, how are you feeling? You look a bit uncomfortable," Dr. Anderson said. Beverly could see the wrinkle in her brow and could tell she was a little concerned.

"I'm okay. I just feel so big and clumsy. I've been feeling more of those contractions lately and more pressure down below. I get tired so easily."

"Are you having any spotting or leaking of fluid?"

"No," Erica replied.

"Is the baby active?"

Erica laughed, "I feel like she is playing basketball in my belly. She's going to be athletic, just like her father."

"Your blood pressure and urine checked out okay. Teens are at a little higher risk for preterm labor. Just to be on the safe side, I'm going to have you take your bottoms off so that I can do a vaginal exam. I'll come back in a minute."

Dr. Anderson put lubricant on her glove. "This might be a little uncomfortable."

"Oh my God, you're not kidding!" Erica said, a little too loudly.

"Okay, we're done. Your cervix is long, thick, and closed. That's a good thing. So what you're feeling is just normal third trimester stuff. Maybe, though, you should take it easy. Your mom said that you are putting in a lot of hours at the hospital. Could you cut back a little?"

"Oh, they said that I can work as much or as little as I want. I'll work a little less, but I just really love what I'm doing there." Erica told Dr. Anderson about her volunteer work. She told her about Cody.

"What are you doing about childbirth classes?"

"I've decided not to take them," Erica said. Her eyes filled with tears. "I just can't do that without Dwight."

"Well, that's okay, honey. I understand. We have some DVD's you can review. Call if you have more than five contractions in an hour, are leaking any fluid, or have and bloody discharge, okay? Now you take care, and I'll see you in two weeks."

"Erica, I could go with you to childbirth classes," Beverly offered on the way out.

"No, Mom. I would feel so self-conscious. I'm sure that I would be the youngest person there, and everyone else would be with their baby's father. I just can't do it. Mrs. Logan told me she would teach me everything I needed to know, and she could be there with me when I am in labor."

Beverly felt stung. She had envisioned that she would be the one coaching Erica through her labor. "It's your call," she said tersely.

Erica could tell that she had maybe hurt her mother's feelings.

"I just thought Mrs. Logan, because she's an OB nurse, but of course, you can be there too, if you want."

"I just want to do whatever is best for you," Beverly said.

"Mom, you don't have to act so wounded. The delivery is just hard for me to think about. I am really scared."

"I understand, honey. Let's change the subject. Let me take you someplace nice for lunch."

"Thanks, but I just want to grab a sandwich at home and head over to the hospital to check on Cody."

"Okay."

Beverly couldn't help but feel a little left out. It was Karen that was throwing the baby shower for her daughter, and it was Karen she wanted to be her labor coach. It was Helen that she went to for solace.

Since her appointment with Dr. Martino wasn't until later that week, she did the next best thing to seek reassurance. She called Brad.

"Brad, are you on call tonight or do you have any plans?"

"No, I'm not on call, what's up?"

"I just need to get away from this mess with Erica. I just need you."

"You know I'm always here for you, Beverly."

"Can I cook you dinner tonight... your place?"

"That sounds great. I can probably be home by six."

Beverly wanted to make Brad something nice. She decided on lamb chops with rosemary, haricot verts, and French potato salad. She knew where she could buy lavender gelato for dessert. *I like it,* she said to herself. *It's very French and very romantic. I need to be loved tonight.* She couldn't help but remember a similar meal she had with Tom in a little Paris bistro.

Brad found her cooking in his kitchen when he got home. He walked up behind her and kissed her on the back of her neck. Behind his back was a bouquet of blue hydrangeas. "Something smells really good."

Beverly turned and put her arms around his neck. She kissed him very passionately. He presented her with the flowers.

"Oh, how could you have known how much I love hydrangeas? And blue is the perfect color for how I'm feeling."

"Well, we'll just have to fix that tonight. I'm just going to take a quick shower and change."

It looked like it might rain, so Beverly set the table inside. She found a candle for the table and put the flowers in a vase. She had a martini made for Brad.

"So tell me what's on your mind."

Beverly tried to explain to Brad about the hurt she had been nursing all day. It was about how Erica seemed to be reaching out to Karen or Helen, rather than her own mother.

"I don't know, Beverly. It seems that you've done everything possible to support your daughter through this. I can't give you parenting advice, because I'm not a parent, but I do know that teenagers can be unpredictable and moody. I know the same could be said for pregnant women. She's grieving. When people are grieving they can't figure out who or what they want. Dwight's not here. That's who she really wants. This all sounds like the perfect storm to me. I'm just sorry it is you that has to weather this storm."

Ironically, just as Brad talked about a storm, a humble of thunder could be heard. That made them both smile.

"You're probably right," Beverly said. "I just wish Tom were around to help me handle this."

Oh God, not Tom again, thought Brad. At some level it seemed like he was always there. Brad didn't want to say the wrong thing, so he said nothing. He got Beverly another glass of wine.

"Hang in there, my love, I'm here for you."

Neither one of them said much during dinner. They were at a point in their relationship when silence wasn't uncomfortable. "Beverly, this was a fabulous dinner. Thank you."

"Cooking is always a good distraction for me, and it's something I feel like I can control."

The thunderstorm moved through fairly quickly and the rain stopped. Brad suggested that they go for a walk. They walked for quite a while until dark. Brad helped Beverly clean up the kitchen and they went straight for the bedroom. After they made love, Beverly said, "Wait, Brad, I have a special treat for you."

"Better than this?" he teased.

"Oh, it's really good." Beverly put on a robe and went to the kitchen. She dished up the lavender gelato. She brought it in and fed him the first spoonful.

"Oh, baby, this is good. Can you stay tonight?"

"I was planning on it. Erica had planned on dinner with Helen. I told her I was having dinner with you, and would probably be staying the night. I'll call her to let her know."

"Hi, honey, is everything okay? I just wanted to let you know I'm staying at Brad's tonight."

"That's okay, Mom. I'm planning at staying at Nana's tonight. We're watching a movie. Tell Dr. Williams I said hello."

When Erica got off the phone, she told Helen about her mother spending the night at Brad's. "What do you think about that, Nana?"

"I think your mother deserves to have a life of her own. Dr. Williams seems very good for her. He seems like a very nice man. Besides, I love when you stay here. I get a little lonely myself sometimes."

Beverly woke up the next morning feeling much better. She got a call from Karen Logan. Karen wanted to discuss the plans for the shower. The invitations had already gone out and it was less than two weeks away.

"Karen, thank you so much for everything you are doing for Erica."

"Oh, you are so welcome. I think of Erica as almost a daughter, or maybe a niece. Bev, I want you to understand that I know this from experience, pregnant teenagers sometimes reach out to others and not so much to their own mothers. I think that it's probably because they feel that they have disappointed their mothers, and they need to handle the problem independently."

"I've been worried about that. Erica has distanced herself from me a little lately. I guess your explanation makes sense."

"Oh, Bev, when my sister was pregnant in high school, she and my mother had a very tumultuous relationship. My poor mother could never say or do the right thing. They became close again after the baby was born."

"Can you meet for lunch, Bev? We can talk more than."

By the end of the week, Beverly was feeling much better about everything, thanks to Karen, Brad, and Dr. Martino. Erica seemed a little better too. Cody was stable, and he no longer had a fever. They were talking about discharging him sometime next week. Erica said that once Cody went home, she would cut back her hours a little.

On the following Thursday, Erica got to Cody's room and found him very excited. "The doctors said that I can go home today! My Daddy is coming after work to pick me up!"

Erica hugged him. "Oh, Cody, I'm so happy for you!" Erica was glad that she had one last day to spend with him. She read to him and played Candy Land most of the afternoon. They even went down to the snack bar and got ice cream cones.

Right before Erica was ready to leave, Cody told her that he had a surprise for her. He got it out of the drawer of his bedside stand. It was a book wrapped in Sesame Street wrapping paper. She read the card first. Cody's mother thanked her for all the attention she had given to her son. She wished Erica all the best with her baby. She said that the book, "Good Night Moon", was Cody's favorite. Erica opened the book. She could tell that it was brand new, but Cody had written his name in it...kind of an inscription. She knew at just four years old, that was probably all he could write. Erica thought it was precious.

"You can read this book to your baby," he said. "I always liked that story." He gave Erica a hug. Cody's father came, and the nurse came in to give him discharge instructions. Erica saw her opportunity to slip out quietly. She had tears in her eyes as she walked out to her car. *That little guy reminds me so much of Johnny,* she thought.

Chapter 39

There was only two weeks left in the month of August. Erica couldn't believe that the summer was almost over. Yet since Dwight's death, the summer seemed to kind of drag on. Today was her baby shower. She knew that she should be excited about it, but she was not. She could only admit this to herself: she was not excited at all to have this baby. She just wanted her old life back. Then she hated herself for thinking that way. She dreaded facing all her girlfriends from school. She hadn't seen most of them since Dwight's funeral. They would be excited about senior year, back-to-school shopping, and football season. She was just a big cow with an uncertain future. *I can't do this. I've got to get it together.*

"Erica called Christy. "OMG, I can't believe I'm going to a baby shower today, and the shower is for ME! You've got to come over and help me figure out what I'm going to wear." Christy to the rescue... she was always great at bringing her friend around. "Wear these white Capri pants and this blouse. Lavender is a good color for you. Why don't you put on some makeup?"

"I haven't put on makeup since Dwight died. I'm really trying so hard, but I'm so depressed."

Christy hugged her and started Erica's makeup. "It's just going to take time. Everyone is really excited about this shower. We've been planning forever. You've got to try and enjoy it."

"I know, and I really do appreciate it, but it's just so hard."

"Everyone loves you. It will be okay."

As soon as Erica got to the Logan's she knew that a lot of effort and planning had gone into this party. She couldn't let everyone down. She was really going to try her best to be her former self.

Mrs. Logan went all out. The decorations were beautiful. She had rented tables and chairs and had them set up in the living room and out on the patio. All the tables had white linen tablecloths with pink napkins and bouquets of pink roses. The shower had a pink elephant theme. The cake was adorable! Beverly insisted on getting the cake. Mark, Kyle's partner who owns the bakery, had made it. The cake was in the form of an actual elephant. There was also a platter of wrapped sugar cookies for the guests to take home. They, too, were pink elephants.

Beverly was nervous for her daughter today, but Erica seemed to be handling it well. Everyone who was invited came. Most of the guests were friends of Erica and Christy. Karen had asked Beverly, besides Helen, who she wanted to invite. Of course she wanted Pam there, as well as Susan Dwyer. Ruby and her sister, Sarah, should be there and the twins. Danielle and Denise were so excited.

After the party got rolling, Erica did seem to relax and genuinely enjoy herself. The kids were very considerate of Erica's feelings. They didn't talk much about school starting, but instead talked about what they all did over the summer. It was mostly just a lot of gossip. A lot of the girls made a point of going over to talk to Ruby. She was touched by their friendliness and kindness.

Karen had the food catered. Everything was delicious. Erica didn't know it, but Beverly and Karen created a gift registry for her. There were so many gifts. The twins brought the gifts over to Erica to open. There were a lot of "oohs" and "aahs", especially when she opened some of the little baby outfits. "Martina is going to be the best dressed baby girl ever," Erica said. Finally all the gifts were opened, and the cake and strawberry ice cream were served.

Beverly could tell Erica was getting tired. All of the guests started to leave. Dwight's family said their goodbyes, as did Helen. Karen insisted that Erica put her feet up and brought her a bottle of water. Erica and Christy looked at all the gifts again. Karen and Beverly opened a bottle of wine and went out to the patio.

"I can't thank you enough, Karen, the shower was lovely. Erica got so much great stuff for the baby. I know she was a little nervous about seeing everyone today, but I think she had a good time. She has seemed so depressed. I wish that I could talk her into seeing a therapist, but she wants nothing to do with it. I can't even image how she will be when school starts back up, and then there is the anniversary of Tom's death."

"Oh God, Bev, that's going to be tough."

"I just don't know how to make it any easier for her. It's all such a big hot mess."

"It has to be an incredible strain on you, too."

"I'm okay. Brad's been wonderful, and I have a very good therapist."

"So, things are good between you and Brad?"

"They are. I'm tired of holding back and always trying to figure everything out. I'm just going to go with my feelings, and right now, I love Brad, and I need him in my life. I can't focus entirely on Erica and the baby. I have to figure out what makes me happy too."

"That makes sense," Karen said. "You can't help Erica to heal, if you don't heal yourself."

After a while, they loaded up all the gifts into Beverly's car. There were tearful hugs and goodbyes, and finally Beverly and Erica left for home. "That shower was so nice, Mom, but I'm so glad that it's over. I am so tired."

"I'll bet you are. Are you feeling okay? Are you having any contractions?"

"No, I'm good. Mom, do you think we'll ever be normal again?"

"I think we will find our new normal," Beverly answered. "Right now, I just want you to take care of yourself, Erica. It will take time, but it will be okay. I am going to do everything possible to make sure that happens."

Erica was crying now. "Mom, you've been great. There are just some things I'm going to have to figure out for myself."

"Okay, I understand, honey."

When they got home, Erica went right up to the sanctuary of her room. She didn't come down the rest of the night. Beverly decided to respect her privacy. Brad stopped over. Beverly was so happy to see him. He knew right away that she was troubled. He suggested that they go to the driving range and hit golf balls. Brad thought it was a good outlet for some pent up frustration. He was right. Afterwards, they took a walk.

"Can you stay tonight, Brad?"

"Of course I can, but I'm starved."

"Pizza?" suggested Beverly.

"That sounds good to me." Beverly made a salad and Brad opened a bottle of pinot noir.

Beverly looked in on Erica. She was sound asleep. "Do you think I should wake her, Brad? She should probably eat something and have something to drink."

"She probably needs the rest more," Brad said.

They found a movie to watch and ate on the couch in front of the TV. It wasn't long before Beverly fell asleep in Brad's arms. When the movie ended, Brad nudged her, and they went upstairs to bed. Beverly looked in on Erica. She was still asleep.

At about three in the morning, Beverly heard Erica call out to her from her room. "Mom, can you come here?"

"Brad, stay here, I'll see if she's okay."

Erica was upset. "Mom, I'm having contractions. This one woke me up." Beverly sat down on the bed and put her hand on the top of Erica's belly.

"Oh, honey, I can feel another one coming on."

"That one wasn't so bad."

"Brad's here. Would it be okay if he came in?"

"Are you serious? That would be so weird. I would rather call Dr. Anderson."

"Just let me ask him what he thinks."

Brad was lying in bed trying to think back to his OB rotation in med school. It had been a long time. Beverly filled him in on the situation.

"I would have her empty her bladder and then have her lay on her left side. Get her to start drinking water, and time her contractions. She might be a little dehydrated." In the meantime, Brad paged the OB on call at the hospital and told him the situation. He confirmed what Brad suspected. Erica was probably dehydrated.

The interventions were successful, and the contractions stopped completely within an hour. Erica fell back asleep, and Beverly crawled back into bed with Brad. She kissed him. "You are my hero."

The next morning Erica came down and joined Beverly and Brad for breakfast. She looked rested and even smiled. She said that she had plans to go to mass with Helen. She was feeling much better. *Thank God*, Beverly thought, *another crisis averted.* It was a beautiful morning. Beverly and Brad decided to play golf. Sometimes on days like this when she and Brad were doing something together, something normal, like playing golf on a beautiful day, she could almost feel like everything was okay, and she was happy.

The last days of August were very hot. Erica didn't do much of anything. She never went back to the hospital after Cody went home. She would just mope around the house and listen to the old James Taylor albums. Beverly tried to interest her in watching the childbirth DVDs, but she said that she just wasn't ready yet. Erica would perk up a little when Christy came over, but really didn't want to go anywhere. Beverly talked to Dr. Martino about it. He suggested that Beverly consult with Erica's obstetrician. He thought they she would probably have experience with depression in the setting of pregnancy and might know how best to intervene.

Dr. Anderson said that she would speak to Erica at her appointment this week. She did convince Erica to see a therapist. Still, Erica didn't seem much better. Dr. Anderson wanted to prescribe an anti-depressant, but Erica refused to take it. She did like going over to Helen's. At least it was something. She was out of the house.

Chapter 40

September

It was September 1st. Erica would be thirty-six weeks at the end of this week. Time was dragging on waiting for the baby to be born. Every September, Helen made raspberry jam. Her bushes were loaded this year. Helen convinced Erica to come over to help her make jam. Beverly was grateful Erica had something to do. She felt like she had been neglecting the shop lately. She wanted to go in and help Pam get ready for the summer clearance sale.

"Mom, Martina is up so high. She's making it hard for me to breathe."

"Hang in there, honey. The last month is really uncomfortable. Hopefully she will drop soon and you will get a little relief."

It was nice to chat with Pam. They hadn't really talked in a while. Pam told Beverly that Kyle and Mark were still negotiating the details of the arrangement with their surrogate. "I'm so hoping I'll be a grandmother soon, too."

Beverly laughed. We can navigate the waters together. "I just love the pink elephant cake that Mark made. I couldn't get over how cute it was. He's quite an accomplished pastry chef. It was absolutely delicious, too."

"Pam, I can't believe it is September already. Just a year ago we were getting ready for the summer clearance sale when Tom died. So much has happened in the last year."

"But, honey, you survived. I really admire how you've handled everything."

"Thanks, Pam. I did the best that I could."

Erica found her grandmother busy in the kitchen sorting though berries. "Hi, sweetheart, I'm so happy you decided to come over and help me. I think we'll have enough berries for two batches this year."

"Is there something I can help with when I'm sitting down? Martina is making me a little short of breath and my left leg is bothering me. It's a little swollen."

"Honey, you can sort through these berries, or if you want, you can just keep me company. Here, sit right down. She positioned another kitchen chair so that Erica could elevate her leg. "Here, we'll put this pillow under your leg. Is that comfortable for you?"

"That's fine. Maybe I'll just watch. I don't know what's wrong with me. I just feel so anxious."

"It's probably just because it's getting so close to your time to give birth. I think that's pretty normal for all new mothers. Can I get you anything? I've got some herbal ice tea in the refrigerator."

"That would be nice, Nana. It's so hot today."

They chatted while Helen worked at making her jam. She thought that Erica seemed a little calmer, but she noticed that she had a little cough.

"Erica, do you have a cold? I've noticed you've been coughing a little."

"It's probably just my allergies. They always kick up around now, when the ragweed is out."

"Your shower was lovely. You got so many nice things. I really enjoyed meeting your friends."

"Christy's mother went all out. I was glad that Dwight's mom and sisters came. This tea is so good, I think I'll get some more."

"Help yourself, honey."

Erica stood up, swayed a little, and collapsed on to the kitchen floor. Helen ran over to her and knelt down. "Erica! Erica!" She shook her gently and patted her cheek. "Are you okay?"

Helen ran to her phone and called 911. "My granddaughter is eight months pregnant, and she just collapsed to the floor. I can't get her to respond." The operator asked for her name and address and said that they were dispatching a mobile critical care unit there immediately.

"Helen, you stay on the line with us. Can you put the phone on speaker?" Her hands were shaking, but she did as instructed.

"Kneel down next to your granddaughter. Now take your two fingers and feel along the side of her neck and see if you can feel a pulse."

"Oh, no... I don't think I can feel one, but I'm not sure."

"Have you ever seen anyone doing chest compressions?"

"Only on television," Helen said. She was very frightened but was trying not to panic.

"You are doing a good job staying calm, Helen. I want you to put one hand over the other and place them over her chest. Now press nice and deep with the palms of your hands. You have to push fairly hard. I'll count with you as you do the compressions. One and two and three and four and..."

"Now you have to breathe for her. Take one hand and put it on her forehead and tilt her head back. Pinch her nose together and put your mouth over hers. Give her two big breaths."

"Okay, now, quick, go back to the compressions." Helen's front door was unlocked and she could hear the EMT's coming in. *Thank you, God,* she prayed.

"Good job, Ma'am." One of the men took over the compressions, while the other man ripped open Erica's shirt and stuck to pads to her chest which were hooked up to a box that talked to him. The box told him to deliver a shock, which he did. Then it told him to continue compressions. They squeezed a bag attached to a mask and oxygen instead of breathing into her mouth. An IV was put in. Helen couldn't believe how fast everything was happening.

"We better transport NOW!" the one man said to his partner. They quickly put Erica on to the stretcher and got her into the ambulance. "Ma'am, can you ride up front with me? I need to ask you some questions." Helen grabbed her purse and locked the front door on the way out.

The man in the back continued to work on Erica. The man driving said, "My name is Kevin. How old is your granddaughter? When is her due date? Was she having any problems with her pregnancy?"

Helen answered all the questions. "Now tell me how she was just before she collapsed."

"She said that she was a little short of breath and that she felt anxious. Oh, and she complained that her one leg was swollen and bothered her."

The man in back called out, "Kevin, still no pulse! Kevin called into the emergency room at the hospital and talked to a doctor there. He relayed the information that Helen had given him. Then he said that he suspected a PE.

"I really need to call Erica's mother, but I left without my cell phone. Her father, my son, is dead." Helen was feeling overwhelmed now and was crying a little.

"It's okay. We're almost at the hospital. They will take care of your granddaughter and call her mother. You are a very brave lady, Helen, you handled everything perfectly."

They pulled up to the ambulance bay and Kevin jumped out. "Okay, Dan, let's get her in there." Helen just followed them in. Dan jumped right up on the gurney and continued the compressions. She couldn't believe her beautiful Erica and her baby were fighting for their lives. Erica looked so pale.

The woman at the desk asked Helen for a lot of information about Erica: Full name, date of birth, next of kin, allergies, medications, her due date, her obstetrician.

She knew everything, but couldn't remember the name of Erica's doctor.

They let her use the phone to call Beverly. She tried Beverly on her cell phone and it went to voice mail. "Beverly, this is Helen, please come to the hospital right away. Erica collapsed, and they brought her to the emergency room by ambulance. They are working on her right now. I can't tell you anything else yet."

One of the doctors came out of the cubicle where they were working on Erica and asked if she was Erica's guardian. "No, I'm her grandmother. I've called her mother, but I wasn't able to reach her."

"Well Ma'am, I'm sorry we haven't been able to get her heart beating again, but we think that if we do a C-section right away, we may be able to save the baby. We still have a fetal heart beat. We can't wait for her mother. Can you please give us verbal consent to do the C-section? Another doctor will come and explain everything to you, and then you can sign the consent. But we have to do this NOW."

Helen was trembling. "Yes, do it, if you think it's the right thing to do." The doctor ran off to be with Erica as they transported her to surgery. Then Helen realized that Erica was probably dead. The doctor never actually said that, but Helen thought it was so. *I hope this is what Beverly would have wanted,* she fretted. I think Erica would want to save her baby. Helen reached in her purse for her rosary beads. She started her prayers.

Beverly walked into the emergency room and spotted Helen right away. She was frantic. "Helen, tell me, what's going on?"

"Another doctor is coming out to talk to me. There he is now. This is Erica's mother."

The doctor brought Beverly and Helen into a small room off the waiting area to talk.

"I am very sorry to tell you that all of our attempts at resuscitation have failed, and Erica has died. We suspect that she had a large pulmonary embolism, which is a blood clot to her lungs. Now because the fetal heart can beat on its own, as long as there is blood flow and oxygen across the placenta, we believe we can possibly save her baby. We are doing a c-section now. We were able to get your daughter here very quickly and keep compressions going. There is a chance for this baby."

"Beverly, I consented to the c-section. I didn't know what to do." Helen had signed the form that she verbally consented to the surgery.

"Ma'am, if it wasn't for you calling 911 right away and starting compressions, this wouldn't all be possible." Beverly looked at Helen and hugged her. "Thank you, Helen, it's okay, I know you did your best. You must have been so frightened."

Now they waited. Beverly had paged Brad. He came immediately and waited with them. He was holding Beverly who was crying quietly. "Brad, I can't believe all this."

It wasn't long before one of the doctors came out to give them a report. "The baby has been delivered, and they are working to stabilize her. She's a fighter. Her initial Apgar score was only three, but after five minutes, it was a seven. She is doing very well. It was so fortunate that she was thirty-five weeks gestation, and that your daughter was young and healthy. As for your daughter, I'm so sorry for your loss. We are fairly certain that she probably developed a blood clot in her leg that traveled to her lungs. Her left leg was swollen."

"Beverly, she said that she was short of breath, and that she was very anxious. She was coughing a little, too," Helen said.

"I knew she said that she was short of breath, but I thought it was because the baby was still so high," said Beverly. "She never said anything to me about her leg, and I didn't know about the cough. I feel like I missed something."

"Mrs. McIntyre, the clot probably grew in size fairly quickly. Signs of pulmonary embolism can be easily mistaken for normal symptoms in pregnancy. There is no one to blame for this. Unfortunately, it is one of the leading causes of maternal death. Pregnant women are susceptible to the formation of blood clots. It is possible that Erica had a condition that made her even more prone to clotting. We will send a sample of blood off to the lab."

Beverly felt numb. This was all so much to take in. She wondered if someone should call Ruby. Brad said that he would find out which unit she worked on, and would go up to get her. "Brad, not now. Stay here with me."

"We are just getting Erica cleaned up now, and we will take you to see her. You can see your new granddaughter too."

Brad spoke to one of the nurses who tracked Ruby down and asked her to come to the OB unit. When Ruby came in, she only knew that her granddaughter had been born. She took one look at Beverly and Helen and knew something was wrong. "What is it? Did something happen to the baby?"

Brad was the first to answer. "Ruby, they are working to stabilize the baby, but we lost Erica. She had a blood clot travel to her lungs and she had a cardiac arrest. They weren't able to bring her back."

Now Ruby was crying. "Oh my God, I can't believe this, I'm so sorry...both of our two beautiful children gone. Just eighteen years old... Lord, I just don't understand it." The two women embraced and just cried.

Beverly and Helen were permitted to go in and see Erica before they brought her body to the morgue. Helen held her hand and kissed her. She made the sign of the cross on her forehead. She left Beverly alone to say good bye to her daughter. Beverly looked at Erica, her beautiful vivacious girl, now so still. After Tom died, Erica was her reason for living. She was just beginning to think that they would be okay. She thought that with her help, Erica could be a mother to Martina, and still finish school and follow her dream of becoming a doctor. Now this... there was clearly no future for Erica.

Beverly was then swept up by feelings of anger. She was angry at Tom for leaving her alone to raise their daughter, only seventeen years old. She was angry at Erica for having sex with Dwight, and she was angry for Dwight for getting her pregnant. If she hadn't been pregnant, she wouldn't have gotten this blood clot and died. Most of all she was angry at God, who let this all happen. She sat there, deep in thought, immobilized, until Brad came in, put his arm around her and led her away.

Brad didn't know how to comfort her, so he just held her. They all went over to a waiting area in the neonatal intensive care unit. Helen sat alone, saying her rosary. Ruby had found Mario and was sitting with him. Beverly sat enveloped in the protective arms of Brad. The neonatologist, Dr. Kim, came in to introduce herself. "We have the baby stabilized now, and she is doing well." Dr. Kim's voice broke when she said, "We have all been marveling at her will to survive."

Ruby was the first to speak. "Her name is Martina. My grandbaby's name is Martina." Beverly said nothing.

"Her grandparents can come into the nursery to see her now."

Beverly reluctantly broke away from Brad and followed Dr. Kim and Ruby into the nursery. They had to wear a mask and put on a gown. They were instructed to wash their hands thoroughly.

Ruby was teary-eyed and put a hand up to her mouth. "Oh, sweet Jesus, she's beautiful."

Beverly looked at the baby and felt nothing. She watched the baby sleeping peacefully. *If it wasn't for this baby Erica would still be alive. She doesn't even look like Erica.* Beverly just wanted to leave.

She went back to the solace of Brad's arms and wept quietly. *What is wrong with me? I feel no joy over the birth of my first grandchild.*

"Brad, I want to leave now."

"Should I take you home?"

"No, can we go to your house? I just can't be at my house now. My house is so full of Erica and Martina. When people find out what has happened, and I am sure they will, they will want to stop over. I just can't handle that now."

Helen stayed at the hospital with Ruby to keep vigil over the baby. Ruby suggested that Helen call the family and maybe one of Beverly's friends to tell them what had happened. Helen made her phone calls. She decided to call Karen Logan. Helen knew that Karen and her daughter would want to know.

Brad didn't know how to comfort Beverly. He made her a drink and sat with her out on the deck. He just waited until she was ready to talk.

"Brad, I can't do this. I can't possibly endure another funeral, and I hate myself for saying so, but I don't want to be responsible for this baby. Brad, I feel nothing for her."

"Beverly, you're in shock. You need time to absorb all this. You look exhausted. I'm sure things will seem different after you've gotten some rest. I love you. I'm here for you. I'll help you to figure it all out."

Beverly just looked at him though her red and puffy eyes. Someone had to help her figure this out.

By now it was early in the evening. Brad had ordered Chinese food to be delivered. At least Beverly had stopped crying. He got her to eat something.

"I guess I was hungry," she said. They sat in silence for awhile longer, as the sun went down. Brad bought her a bottle of water and some Motrin. *I want you to drink this before you go to bed. With all the crying you've been doing, I don't want you to wake up with a headache.*

"Thank you, Brad, let's just go to bed now. I'll have so much to do tomorrow."

330

Chapter 41

Beverly woke up the next morning feeling a little more like her former self. Brad took her to the funeral home to make arrangements. She decided on a private funeral for immediate family and close friends only. Immediate family was Helen. She didn't want to deal with her parents and the rest of the McIntyre clan. She would allow Ruby and her girls to come, as well as Christy and Karen Logan. As for everyone else, there would be a memorial service in a few weeks. They could pay their respects and honor Erica then. She met with Father McMahon and made arrangements at the cemetery. Erica would be buried in a plot next to her brother. The funeral would be tomorrow.

Beverly told Brad that she was okay. She urged him to go look in on his patients or do whatever it was he was supposed to be doing that day. They rode over to the hospital together. Beverly decided to go up to the nursery to check in on Martina. Beverly looked at the baby and was overwhelmed by her innocence. It wasn't fair to blame her for all of this. How could she not want this baby? At 45 years old, how could she be a single parent to a newborn? How could she start all over? She would be 63 when Martina graduated from high school. Martina was a beautiful baby, but she clearly was African American. Maybe Martina would be better off being raised by Ruby. She would grow up in a family and have sisters. Ruby was so much younger. She was only 36. Ruby was such a good mother, and such a strong woman. Martina would be lucky to have Ruby for her mother. She tried to decide what Erica would want for her daughter.

Beverly saw Dr. Kim, who told her that Martina was doing well. She was still having some episodes of apnea and bradycardia, which they would have to continue to monitor. She was having some difficulty with feeding, so for now, she had a feeding tube. Dr. Kim asked if Beverly wanted to speak with the social worker. Beverly was taken aback. *Social worker...why would she need a social worker?* Beverly politely answered, "No".

Beverly saw that Ruby was there. Ruby was talking to one of the nurses. Beverly asked her if she wanted to get a cup of coffee.

Beverly told Ruby about the funeral arrangements. Then they talked about Martina. "Ruby, I don't think I would be the best mother for her. You are young, Ruby, and if you took Martina, she would be part of a family. Wouldn't it be better if you took Martina?"

Ruby was shocked. "I just assumed that you would want to raise Martina. Why, she is all you have left. You are a very loving person, Beverly. You could be a wonderful mother to her. You have the resources to provide her with a life I could never give her. Dr. Williams loves you. He will be there for you. Helen will be there for you, and I will always want to be a part of her life. Loving and caring for a new baby may help you to go on and survive this tragedy.

"Ruby, I just don't see that I'm the best choice. Frankly, I just don't think I can do it."

"Beverly, you know where I live. I don't even own my own house, and I can barely provide for my twins. I'm struggling to finish school. But, if you don't think that you can mother this child, of course I'll take her. She will be loved. I have a lot of that to give. I can make it work out somehow. Maybe you should give yourself time. This doesn't have to be decided today. I'm sure she won't be discharged from the hospital for a while. You can think about what is best for you. If you haven't worked it out by the time she's ready to come home. I can take her then or forever."

Beverly didn't think she could be a mother again. There was too much to lose.

EPILOGUE

September, one year later

Martina sat on Ruby's lap and blew out the single candle on her birthday cake. She clapped her little hands along with everyone else at the party after they finished singing "Happy Birthday." She was an adorable baby. Ruby had braided her hair with multicolored beads. Beverly couldn't believe she had the patience to do so, and that she could get Martina to hold still for so long. She said that she did it while Martina was taking her nap. When Beverly looked into the baby's eyes, she saw Erica. Martina was a beautiful genetic masterpiece. She had soft coffee-colored skin and vibrant green eyes. She also had Erica's little turned up nose. Beverly didn't think it was possible, but she had grown to love this child every bit as much as Johnny and Erica.

Beverly looked around at everyone there today celebrating this happy occasion. Mario was there with Ruby and the twins. Mario's son, Anthony was also with them. Ruby and Mario had gotten married. Ruby looked so happy. She had finished school and had passed her nursing boards. She was working as an RN now. Helen of course was there, doting over her first great-grandchild. Godmother Christy was there, along with her parents, Karen and Bill. Peter and Susan Dwyer were there, as was Pam. Pam had a grandchild of her own. Kyle and Mark were there with their new baby girl, Lucy. She was only eight weeks old. Mark had insisted on making Martina's birthday cake. It was an amazing and adorable Minnie Mouse. Martina was enchanted by the cake.

Brad looked over at Beverly and smiled. Beverly's misfortune had become his happily ever after. Brad had convinced Beverly that he had always wanted to be a father, and this could be his chance. He would love this little girl like it was his own daughter. After three weeks in the hospital, Martina ended up coming home with Beverly and Brad. They were married at Christmastime in Paris. Susan and Peter Dwyer joined them and served as their attendants. After they were married, Brad and Beverly Williams bought a new house and officially adopted

Martina. A couple who about to have their first baby bought the McIntyre house. They were thrilled that her baby daughter would have such a beautiful nursery.

It turned out that Erica had a genetic factor that caused her blood to clot more easily. Coupled with pregnancy, it really put her at risk. It was called Factor V Leiden. It wasn't a problem that they routinely tested for, unless there was a strong family history of blood clots or prior problems with pregnancy loss. It was then that Beverly had remembered that her father had once had a blood clot in his leg and had to be put on blood thinners. The doctor reassured Beverly that it wasn't until the early 1990s that this condition was identified, and her father probably had never been tested for it.

Dwight's murder had never been solved, but Ruby found a network of support from other women who had lost family members to random acts of violence. A candlelight ceremony was held in one of the city parks that following summer to remember these victims. It was very moving. Ruby became a community activist involved in finding solutions to help curb inner-city violence.

Martina spent a lot of time over at Ruby and Mario's home. Together, Ruby and Mario were able to afford a house in a much better neighborhood in the suburbs. They took Martina while Beverly and Brad were on their honeymoon. They were planning on having a baby of their own.

Martina Dee Williams was a very lucky little girl. When she was old enough to understand, she would be told her real story. It was truly a love story.

Made in the USA
Middletown, DE
25 February 2015